# Dido

# Belle

Kim Blake

# DEDICATION

To my son Jason and my family. With a special thank you to my twin
sister Fay for her input and her patience with the tedious
job of proof reading


To Charlotte Martin for giving me the inspiration

# CHAPTER 1

Kenwood House was well suited to its present occupant William Murray, the first Earl of Mansfield and Lord Chief Justice of England. For it presided in the village of Hampstead, surrounded by one hundred and twelve acres of the most admiring park and woodland in the environ, with a breath-taking prospect of London (rumoured to be the very words of the King whilst on a visit to Kenwood); and thus with this royal approval it could claim the distinction of being one of England's finest eighteenth century estates. Not to mention it provided easy access to Westminster and the Inns of Court, a distant of only four miles. Presently, in the year of 1760, Lord Mansfield could contemplate the rewards of his labour with great satisfaction and self-gratification at having elevated his lineage even further, as his new peerage added considerably to both the respective family lines, which any marriage alliance *ought* to. While still an ambitious lawyer with an eye to rising through the ranks of the judiciary, William Murray had for some time recognized the importance of marrying well. And in choosing Lady Elizabeth Finch, a daughter of an established aristocratic family, had much to do with Mr Murray's career ambitions than with any sentimentality of an ardent lover. Although Mr Murray considered Lady Elizabeth to be somewhat plain, her manners were pleasing and the suitability of the match, particularly where breeding and family connections were concerned was highly favourable. Lady Elizabeth, though not adverse to the gentleman's charms, was somewhat alarmed by his lively wit. But her fears were swiftly assailed when an offer of marriage was duly made and soon after accepted. And though some of her relations questioned the inferiority of the match, Lady Elizabeth was resolute in her decision and could not be shifted from it. Heavens knew when such a proposal would come along again! Lady Elizabeth concluded. She had to concede that in her youthful years she had been extravagant in her refusals of prospective suitors, confident of soon being happily settled. But as the years passed, and opportunities dwindled, she could no longer afford to be so particular. If she were a man she could be at her leisure to choose where she pleased, and be free from the constraints of maternity and beauty. Or risk the prospect of being associated with the ghastly appellation of *old maid* or worst still *spinster*, which only wealth and class could save from the humiliation of such a pitiful status.

Their marital union proved equally successful for both parties, and nothing could be wanting except an heir to seal the matrimonial triumph. But the problem of producing an heir was soon to become a grievous pastime for Lord and Lady Mansfield. Having married at the late age of four and thirty years, Lady Mansfield possessed none of the optimism of youth, and duly fretted constantly over her inability to conceive. As the years passed and all hope had begun to diminish, Lady Mansfield's fretfulness gave way to fits of nervous anxieties, which over the years eventually gave way to bitterness of spirit. For her childless state grieved Lady Mansfield far more than it did her husband. This was not because Lady Mansfield had acquired a more fervent yearning for children than her husband, but being a woman she knew that *she* would be held responsible for their infertility. Thus Lord Mansfield's sympathetic utterances did little to relieve Lady Mansfield's anxieties but instead produced much irritation as it only served to support the general assumption that in the matter of infertility the woman was entirely to blame. Lady Mansfield had many a year to lament on the wretchedness of her domestic position, as the subject of children became a source of great pain long after the ability to conceive had passed.

Lord Mansfield's decision to take charge of the upbringing of his two nieces, Marjory and Ann Murray, offered, if not an ideal situation, at least an agreeable alternative. As the years passed and both nieces were grown and removed from Kenwood, Lord and Lady Mansfield was left once again to reflect and to reconcile themselves to what might have been. Thus they continued until the untimely death of Henrietta Frederica, the wife of David Murray, a nephew of Lord Mansfield. This tragic event provided the couple with another opportunity of experiencing the joys and woes of parental guardianship. Elizabeth Murray being only an infant at her mother's death and too young to be raised by her father, was given into the care of her great uncle, Lord Mansfield. As providence would have it, as one great niece arrived at Kenwood, Lord and Lady Mansfield found themselves in the possession of another, a Dido Elizabeth Belle. Dido's father, Captain John Lindsay, also a nephew of Lord Mansfield, had for many years been blessed with a successful naval career. As captain of the *Trent* stationed in the Caribbean, Captain Lindsay received commendation for bravery in the capturing of a Spanish ship during the Seven Years War. It was aboard this vessel that Captain Lindsay found an African slave, Maria Belle, whom he kept with him throughout the duration of his stay in the West Indies. The result of their affair was the child, Dido Belle.

Talk of Captain Lindsay's affairs proved a source of avid speculation and an amusing pastime at many a dinner party. It was widely repeated and greatly exaggerated for the benefit of the listeners that Captain Lindsay was often in attendance with female natives at drunken orgies. But a far more sensible rumour had also began to circulate of Captain Lindsay being associated with a young West Indian creole, who had seduced him with her large fortune. Naturally the young woman's actions had offended the sensibilities of every decent lady but not for the reason of propriety alone. The offence went far deeper, as there were far too few desirable young gentlemen of Captain Lindsay breeding and status, for one to be taken out of circulation by such an inferior sort, while there remained ample respectable young ladies awaiting such an attachment. The feeling of condemnation against the unfortunate young woman was particularly expressive. It was everywhere agreed, how dreadful it was that such a gentleman of Captain Lindsay's statute could so easily be doped by someone so obviously beneath him. When the truth was soon discovered that the young woman in question was an unworthy slave, the news produced the expected outpouring of indignation and abhorrence that such a scandal could have taken place; though it was commonly known to many of its protestors, who wilfully refused to accept that such liaisons had existed for some time and continued to occur far too often. It was everywhere declared that Captain Lindsay's dashing good looks and his reputation with the ladies was to blame for his wayward lifestyle. Everyone agreed and supposed it to be so from the very beginning and concluded that it was therefore simply a matter of time before some such infidelity would come to light. Amid the overwhelming condemnation was also a sense of relief among the young ladies that Captain Lindsay was very much available and given the opportunity would be welcomed into any respectable family.

"A weak man is the ruin of a good woman. That is, any decent woman of breeding and consequence." Lady Mansfield almost declared out aloud but stopped herself short in fear of offending her husband. Her feelings were decided. If Lady Mansfield could have her way, Captain John Lindsay would be excluded from decent society! But she knew that her feelings alone could not dictate the matter as the family's reputation must take precedence.

"What a scandal!" Lady Mansfield repeated to herself until she was soon overcome by her morbid preoccupation and an increasing apprehension for her family's good name. Her husband's quiet and indifferent manner aggravated her. How could he be so calm at a time like this? But she resisted showing her true feelings on the matter for as long as she could; which was less than half an hour before she could no longer prevail against the urge to speak and began by saying how they would be all ruined with such a scandal hanging over their heads. Lord Mansfield gave her the same indifferent look before sighing impatiently at the regularity of her complaints.

"Enough madam. What is done cannot be undone. Let us weather the storm as best as we can." Lord Mansfield replied wearily, knowing that his words would neither comfort nor alleviate his wife's anxieties. Ever since the dreadful scandal had reached them, Lady Mansfield had been incapable of normal activity. She could not sit for more than an hour without lamenting of their present predicament until finally her head would hurt and she would be forced to withdraw to her room. Though Lord Mansfield did not doubt the feasibility of her argument he had no patience for her anxious outbursts as they were wearing on his own calm temperament, which had been severely tested during the past few days. He was well aware of the possible detriment that such a scandal could have on his professional position but having received a letter from the Prime Minister assuring him of his continued service, he had only one cause of action and that was to minimise the damage as quickly as possible. He had written in haste to his nephew a lengthy letter with the severest remonstrations against his immoral conduct and the grievous consequence of such an action on the family's reputation. Lord Mansfield's letter to his nephew had produced the expected outpouring of remorse and had uncovered the extent of the matter, the presence of an unfortunate offspring. The mother was said to be of ill health and close to death. Nothing was known of her relations having been sold into slavery many years hitherto. Several correspondences followed with the lengthy and heated discussions on Captain Lindsay's care of duty toward the child. It was eventually agreed that the best cause of action was for the child to be given into the guardianship of Lord Mansfield in order to restore, at least, some respectability in the dreadful business. In fact, the decision taken by Lord Mansfield was done with little consultation with his wife. Consequently, on the arrival of the said child there was a momentary disturbance at Kenwood, as Lady Mansfield, unable to understand the presence of Captain Lindsay's bastard child in their home, pleaded day and night with her husband to return the child to the West Indies.   But to no avail would her complaints be heard by him, until with sulky silence Lady Mansfield continued for several days, refusing to acknowledge even the presence of the child until one day after hearing from a relative Lady Carrington that Lord Mansfield's charitable undertaking was well spoken of,  she grudgingly conceded to her husband's will.   But not without taking to her 'charitable duty' with an air of a martyr condemned to death.

Captain Lindsay's brief stay in England and his subsequent return to sea served beneficial in that *he* was spared the trouble of listening to the continuous gossip, though he cared little for its censure or for its awkwardness. There was no such relief for his relations, who had to endure months of unpleasantness, of which, invariably such scandals convey.  Lady Mansfield insisted that they should rise above such vulgar society who had nothing better to do but gossip about other people's business. At which she had to be told by her husband that other people's business was the sole purpose of gossiping!  Lady Mansfield chose to ignore her husband's comment and continue to insist that they stay indoors until the nasty business had blown over. Fortunately for all, when the dust was settled, little harm was done to either the family social standing or to Captain Lindsay's reputation; he continued as he always did; a successful naval officer with an eye for the ladies and a desirable catch for any single young lady of a respectable family.

# CHAPTER 2

Dido contemplated her reflection for the first time with a look of abhorrence until she could no longer bear to look at her own countenance. She turns from the mirror, her mind filled with morbid recollection of discovering her true identity. How her heart ached at the memory. The wound was so deep that Dido was certain not even time would be sufficient to heal it. How naïve she had been! As a child Dido believed her parents to be Lord and Lady Mansfield and for many years she lived in blissful ignorance of her birth, having no concept of the differences of race and status that existed between herself and her relations. Dido felt content in the knowledge that she was treated affectionately by all, with the exception of Lady Mansfield's constant corrections, which she chose to ignore as she was particularly spoilt by Lord Mansfield. She had nothing more to wish for, save the desire of being the continued favourite of her *father* as she thought him to be. And thus her world remained until the age of seven when the innocence of her secure world was shattered on a day that she quarrelled with her cousin Elizabeth over the possession of a doll.

"It's mine! Father gave it to me!" Dido cried, stubbornly holding on to the doll that threatened to be broken in two by their tug of war.

"No it is not! It belongs to me. Just like you. You're my slave!" Elizabeth shouted back, still tugging the doll to her body.

"I'm not your slave. I'm no one's slave!" Dido cried, though she had no idea what a slave was. But it sounded wicked. She knew she could not possibly be one!

"I shall tell father!" Dido said threateningly, her temper stirred by Elizabeth's hateful words.

"He is not your father so stop calling him that." Elizabeth answered spitefully. Dido flinched and unconsciously began to loosen her grip on the doll, as in that moment all thoughts of it was forgotten. Elizabeth's words had shocked her, though she knew that Elizabeth was prone to such falsehood, and her words should have given her little cause for alarm, but the revelation was too painful to her even in jest that she had the unexpected displeasure of being deeply affected by it.

"Lizzy, what do you mean?" she asked, hastily wiping away her tears, for she felt ashamed at her show of weakness. Elizabeth on seeing Dido's tears could not help but feel a momentary satisfaction at witnessing the reaction of her cousin. But her pleasure was soon overcome by a feeling of uneasiness, on realising, rather too late, her mistake at revealing Dido's secret. Elizabeth knew that her imprudence was sure to provoke the displeasure of Lord Mansfield. She had not spoken of her knowledge of Dido's birth to anyone, for fear of such a reprimand. Though she had been desirous of revealing Dido's secret to her, and had, on several occasion to bite her tongue, it was proving to be too burdensome a task for one with such a temperament as hers, who spoke as soon as a thought came into her head. Alas, Elizabeth reasoned within herself that it was not her fault, she was only a child, and it was silly for her guardians to expect her to keep such a secret! Elizabeth concluded, completely disregarding the fact that no such secret was entrusted to her, for she had procured the news of Dido's birth through her usual pastime of eavesdropping.

"You are old enough to know the truth," she said defensively unwilling to express any sympathy.

"You are lying!" Dido shouted her temper aroused.

"You can find out for yourself. Why don't you ask *father*?" Elizabeth said defiantly though her expression changed to one of apprehension as Dido turned and ran hastily in the direction of the study, ignoring all of Elizabeth's calls for her to return. Dido was in such a state of agitation that for once she forgot to knock before entering, as was the custom. Instead she pushed the door open and ran towards Lord Mansfield. Dido's entrance caused Lord Mansfield to look up with irritation at the unannounced interruption but on seeing her tearful disposition his countenance softened to one of concern as he slowly stood up and removed his spectacles.

"I'm sorry Sir. I was unable to stop her." Miss Willows, the governess, said apologetically before casting her steely eyes in Dido's direction.

"Leave us." Lord Mansfield replied curtly before turning to Dido.

"What is it Dido?" his voice softened.

"Are you my father?" Dido asked boldly without understanding the seriousness of her question, simply expecting Elizabeth's lie to be instantly refuted.

Lord Mansfield looked thoughtful for a moment his face etched with regret.

"No child, I am not your father." He replied quietly, knowing that his words would cause her pain. Lord Mansfield had hoped to delay this matter until Dido was much older, even though Lady Mansfield had disagreed with his decision. But he had been adamant on this point, wanting to spare the unfortunate child the cruel knowledge of her slave heritage and the prejudice that inevitably came with it. He feared that there would be time enough for that when she became of age. Dido, who had not imagined Elizabeth's words to be true, became wholly distressed and began to weep uncontrollably.

"Come now stop your tears." Lord Mansfield attempted to comfort her as he took her by the hand and sat her down.

"At present you are far too young to understand the complexities of your birth. But when you are older I will tell you about your parents." He continued in this manner of speech but Dido heard little of his words, as she could only feel the unbearable anguish of losing a loved one. She had no desire to know her natural father, for his existence was now denying her of the only father she had known and loved.

"Will you send me away?" Dido asked tearfully, her heart suddenly paralysed by fear at the prospect of also losing her home.

"Of course not child. This is your home and I am still your legal guardian and your great uncle." Lord Mansfield said in his efforts to ease her distress. Dido had no idea what a guardian meant but she felt some relief in knowing that they were still related. It gave her the courage to stop crying, although it would be many years before she could cease to think of this time without pain.

"Run along now Dido and let this old man finish his work. We will talk some more later." He promised as he proceeded to walk her to the door.

"What is a slave?" Dido asked, just then remembering the name that Elizabeth had called her. If Elizabeth had been correct about Lord Mansfield not being her father, could she also be telling the truth about her being a slave? Lord Mansfield's countenance changed to one of anger of which Dido had never seen before.

"Lizzy said that I was her slave." She stuttered, for the first time fearful of her guardian's displeasure. Dido now supposed a slave to be a terrible thing to produce such a violent response at the mere mention of its name. Why would Elizabeth think her evil? Lord Mansfield opened the door and called for Miss Willows to fetch Elizabeth to the study. At which a nervous but defiant Elizabeth was promptly deposited at the study door. Immediately, Dido pitied Elizabeth the prospect of facing Lord Mansfield's wrath, but reproached herself against succumbing to any feelings of sympathy as she felt certain that Elizabeth was deserving of any punishment that her impudence would receive.

"Miss Willows, please take Dido to her room." Lord Mansfield commanded before closing the study door.

Elizabeth did not speak to Dido for the rest of the day. Instead she expressed her displeasure with resentful glares and sudden outbursts of tears, of which only an extremely sympathetic Lady Mansfield had the attention and patience to deal with. Dido refused to feel any remorse for her actions, knowing them to be free from any reproach, though Lady Mansfield would have her to believe otherwise.

"Dido, how could you tell such tales?" Lady Mansfield exclaimed, entirely taken in by Elizabeth's tantrums, certain that her husband had overreacted in his correction of the child. And believing herself to be perfectly correct in her opinion on this matter, Lady Mansfield had no reservations in raising the subject when alone with her husband that same evening. She began with much feeling, as if the offense had been charged against herself.

"Was it absolutely necessary? Elizabeth was beside herself with grief."

"And so she should!" Lord Mansfield replied unrepentant at his correction of the girl. At first he had been surprised at Elizabeth's defiant manner at being questioned. But her boldness soon gave way to tearful pleadings on realising that he would not tolerate her tantrums.

"Both girls have been left in my care. I cannot have an incident like this reoccurring in this house again. Dido should not be treated any differently." He stated soberly, before sighing heavily.

"Indeed, the slave trade is an evil benefactor of this country, to our shame." Lord Mansfield added philosophically to himself, thinking at that moment of Dido's future. While in contrast, Lady Mansfield felt positive that her husband's over protectiveness of the girl was the cause of the problem. Had he in all fairness treated the girls the same? Though there was no question of his affection for Elizabeth, it was with increasing exasperation that Lady Mansfield witnessed his partiality towards Dido.

"Sir, I do believe you spoil the girl. She is already becoming too wild, it's impossible to discipline her." Lady Mansfield stated decidedly, at which her husband shrugged his shoulders with irritation at his wife's continued nagging of his care of Dido. Lady Mansfield recalled an incident last week where she could not have been more astonished at her husband's response.

"Dido, be a dear and get Elizabeth her shawl. It's rather chilly in here this evening." Lady Mansfield said immediately after hearing Elizabeth's sneezes.

"Madam, we have servants enough to do that!" Lord Mansfield said sharply, halting Dido with his words.

Lady Mansfield was taken aback for a few seconds while an awkward silence prevailed, in which Dido could only feel pleasure at Lord Mansfield's defence of her.

"Yes, of course." Lady Mansfield replied civilly, while attempting to conceal her own displeasure.

"Perhaps Dido would not mind ringing for the maid." She added unable to keep the hint of sarcasm out of her voice.

On the matter of Dido's upbringing they were often in disagreement of which Lady Mansfield could be relied upon to argue her point to the bitter end. And though Lady Mansfield detested all kinds of disagreement, she was often the instigator of them. Her weakness being the tendency of saying exactly what she thought, without little regard for the listener, and as a result could not prevent herself from constantly offending. Her husband's care of Dido was a constant concern to her and with good reason. Had matters been different, and illegitimacy and colour not an issue, Lady Mansfield would have nothing to be anxious for. But as it was, Dido, being an illegitimate black child of a slave, could not be on an equal footing with her cousin Elizabeth, regardless of the aristocratic connections on her father's side. To disregard the status quo, Lady Mansfield concluded, would be to the detriment of civilised society. Yet Lady Mansfield could not confess, even to herself, that she had developed a dislike towards Dido, which was vented in her constant reprimands at the girl's manner and dress and instead, did what was natural to most people in her situation and appropriated the blame to her nemesis. Seeking an ally to pour out her grievances to, Lady Mansfield took more frequently to writing to her sister, Lady Charlotte. Being at liberty to express her complaints freely, and even to exaggerate them, Lady Mansfield wrote in this manner,

> Oh dear sister, how I lament of my situation, as I am completely alone in my endeavours to discipline the girl in the correct manner. Lord M is completely oblivious to the dangers of his actions and does not listen to a word I say! If left alone he would have the girl run the whole house! I'm sure he would think nothing of putting her needs before my own! Dear sister, I suffer miserably! The girl is already headstrong, and does not listen to anyone but Lord M! I am sure that nothing but ill will come of his attention towards her, it will bring confusion in the poor girl's mind of her position in life!

Mark my words, dear sister, I am absolutely sure that some such disaster is ahead...

# CHAPTER 3

The revelation of her true identity produced upon Dido's cheerful disposition a spirit of gloominess that was unfamiliar to her. Each morning she would wake up with her usual exhilaration at the prospect of a new day before remembering all that had befallen her and would immediately become solemn and tearful, wishing that she had never been born. In her moments of reverie she wondered how strange that she had wholly dismissed the paleness of their skin in comparison with her own! She had been blind to any such distinction! She had always supposed that Elizabeth superior and bossy attitude, and the predisposition of always wanting to have her own way in everything was due to her being a year older in age. But Dido now wondered if this was ever the case at all! Only now she recalled, an earlier occasion when she had innocently called Lord Mansfield *father* at the dinner table and her appellation was met with stunned silence and Lady Mansfield becoming rather agitated and soon after asked for both Elizabeth and herself to be removed from the dinner table. Dido had remembered feeling perplexed by the strangeness of their reaction but had not thought anything more of it until Lord Mansfield spoke to her the following morning and had instructed her on the propriety of addressing him as *sir*. Dido understood little of its meaning and thought only to please him.

Though Dido had for some time become aware of Lady Mansfield's partiality towards Elizabeth, she had thought it only fair as her uncle's marked affection for her had caused her to pity Elizabeth for her inferior position in his regard. Dido was sure that she could not give sufficient pleasure to Lady Mansfield, aside from what invisibility or death could allow and therefore had given up every attempts of succeeding. At every opportunity her aunt would find fault in everything she did, whether in her manner, speech or dress, and would often exclaim with great exasperation,

"Do not talk so wildly child!"

"You must be the most ill-dressed young lady I have ever seen!"

And on another occasion,

"Dido, do not slouch so. Stand up straight, it's so unflattering."

Dido contritely listened to every daily reprimand with increasing indifference. But in light of the revelation of her parents, Dido could at last declare that her aunt's disapproval of her was undoubtedly due to her colour and inferior birth. There could be no other explanation! Though it gave her no comfort, at least now, Dido understood the reason for Lady Mansfield's obvious dislike of her, seeing that she was no more than a slave. Dido's judgment of Lady Mansfield may not have been so severe had she known that her aunt's dislike was formed from her resentment of her husband's partiality towards Dido. But as it was, Dido's ignorance produced in her a prejudice towards her aunt that made her affection for her uncle all the more fervent.

For days Dido remained in this state of solemn detachment, observing her relation's every gesture, impression and speech as a way of marking any peculiarity in their treatment towards her. The weeks and months passed, and still Dido continued with a fretful disposition, fearing rejection, until realising, perhaps far later than she ought, that there was little in the way of change in her family's treatment of her. Elizabeth continued to tease and annoy her; Lord Mansfield to spoil her and Lady Mansfield to correct her, all to Dido's great relief! Thus, the reserve manner in which she had continued for many months was soon replaced once again by her natural cheerfulness. It was with renewed vigour that Dido said her prayers vowing that she would do all in her power to please her guardians, even Lady Mansfield, in the hope that her life would remain as normal. But normalcy could never be reclaimed. A change had already occurred within her that Dido refused to reveal or acknowledge to herself or to anyone, not even Elizabeth. The reality of her birth could not be concealed. Dido was now a daughter of a slave; a slave by inheritance. The word pierced her heart, though as a child she had not fully understood the enormity of its meaning. Nevertheless, it tormented her solitary thoughts and caused her moments of great inner suffering. She detested looking at herself and avoided the mirror at every opportunity. But Dido's woeful preoccupations would be given a new direction through an unexpected ally in her governess Miss Jane Willows.

Miss Willows had arrived at Kenwood two years previously when Lady Mansfield felt it necessary for proper instructions to be given to the girls. Both Dido and Elizabeth had contrived to play the usual tricks and games, not out of any grand scheme of getting rid of their new governess, but merely as an opportunity of having a more amusing pastime. When Miss Willows made it quite clear that she would not tolerate any such insubordination, Elizabeth, having pulled several tantrums, had failed in her attempts to sway her aunt in dismissing the new governess. But for once Lady Mansfield had not given in to Elizabeth's tantrums as she had received it from the most trusted authority that Miss Willows had come highly recommended. There was little resistance from the girls, who took to disliking Miss Willows for no good reason. Dido's dislike of Miss Willow was formed merely on the premise that she often kept them from their play. Thus Dido felt a degree of self-satisfaction at being able to outwit her governess, as her daydreaming provided an opportunity of escaping the boredom of her lessons. While Miss Willows read aloud from a book on English grammar, Dido could be free to run through the arbour into the garden; to play by the lake or find an undiscovered place in which to play hide and seek with Elizabeth. Sometimes her reverie was disturbed by the call of Miss Willows' voice or the rap of the ruler on the desk but on rare occasions her stolen moments went uninterrupted.

One late afternoon, when Dido and Elizabeth had completed their lesson, Miss Willows called for Dido to stay behind. At first Dido thought that Miss Willows had intended to discipline her on her lack of attention in the lesson, and so awaited her correction with an air of expected remorse.

"I have something that you may be interested in seeing." Miss Willows said instead, holding in her hand a large book. Dido looked at it curiously but made no effort to take it.

"It is a book on slavery." Miss Willows continued, placing the book on the table. Dido's countenance changes to one of displeasure, as she began to be overcome with shame that she could scarcely speak.

"Do you not want to know about your own people?" Miss Willows asked, surprised by Dido's look of aversion.

"Dido, there is nothing to be ashamed ..."

"I hate you!" Dido shouted heatedly, before running hastily from the room, leaving Miss Willows alone to contemplate with astonishment the reason for her unexpected reaction.

For many days Dido continued in silent indignation, resisting every attempt of Miss Willows to approach the subject of slave or slavery. Dido could only feel mortified by the mention of the word. And though she felt pricked by the impudence towards Miss Willows, Dido could not find it in her heart to express regret at her behaviour, as Miss Willows' words had offended her too deeply to overcome her impropriety.

"There is something wrong. You are not your usual self, child." Lord Mansfield said, knowing what truly troubled her, having been informed by Miss Willows of the incident and her concerns for Dido's education.

"I am well, Sir." Dido lied, looking away as she spoke, feeling guilty for hiding the truth from him.

"You can tell me child, what is it?" Lord Mansfield urged, but to no avail. Dido could not be compelled to divulge her secret anguish, not even to her uncle.

"It is a dreadful matter when a person is taken from their home and family and sold like an article of clothing."

"Who sir?" Dido asked curiously, fearing that such a thing could happen to her.

"Someone like your mother who was sold into slavery, taken away from her family and loved ones, to a strange country." Lord Mansfield added looking closely at Dido, who looked startled at the thought.

"Aren't such people worthy of our sympathy and protection rather than our aversion?"

"Why would anyone sell another human being?" Dido asked, unable to believe that such a thing could be done. Lord Mansfield sighed,

"That is a question that I have been asking myself for many years."

Her conversation with her uncle had aroused within Dido sentiments of great remorse until she became overcome with shame at her former feelings. How wretched! Dido thought. She had no idea that a person could be forced to be a slave against their own will and had naively believed that her mother's colour was the sole reason for her slave status. For the first time she felt an overwhelming compassion towards her mother, whose existence had previously, only produced within her feelings of abhorrence. She had considered her mother unworthy of any pity or just feelings. How cruel were her thoughts! Her poor mother stolen from her family and sold against her own will, while her parents were left to weep for a child lost to them. Dido's senses were suddenly alive with great curiosity. She began to wonder what kind of woman her mother was and what had become of her? How did she meet her father? Did he have any affection for her, a slave? Her mind filled with questions that she possessed no answers to, a preoccupation that could only yield frustration and dissatisfaction. Nevertheless, her inquisitive mind wished to know more.

"I would very much like to see that book on slavery." Dido said to Miss Willows, though she could not bring herself to apologise, she hoped that in asking for the book it would express an attitude of penitence. Miss Willows appeared surprised but pleased at Dido's change of heart.

"Yes, of course." She replied graciously

Miss Willows, ordinarily a sober and reticent woman answered Dido's many questions on slavery with great interest and much patience.

"Are all slaves black?" Dido asked incredulously, as she observed the painting of black ghoulish faces that stared back at her.

"No, it depends on where the enslaved people are captured. The slaves we see today are taken from Africa and Asia. But in different times, for example, during the Roman Empire, there were both black and white slaves."

Some of the paintings were so hideous and frightful, that Dido felt fearful of continuing, but she found herself compelled to read and look at all she could.   Miss Willows was pleased at Dido's interest and was willing to spend time after lessons showing her various books on the subject. During these readings Dido's sentiments were wholly affected, that for days she could not sleep without fear of being stolen. Yet she endeavoured to learn all she could, and soon became knowledgeable of the horrors of slave life.  Her new found knowledge caused her to look upon her privileged position with far more gratitude, in spite of its painful moments. It helped to alleviate if not all, at least, some of her own pride and produced in her a more devotional love towards her guardians.  When Dido discovered that Miss Willows had connections with one of the increasing numbers of women's anti-slavery societies, she could not help but feel a growing esteem towards her governess, a sentiment that previously she would have deemed impossible!

The following morning Miss Willows came bustling into Dido's room with a newspaper clipping of the case of Somerset, a runaway slave, recaptured by his owner in London and imprisoned on a vessel set to sail for the Caribbean.  As Dido read the article she was unable to contain her distress for the plight of the unfortunate fellow.

"Do you know who is to be the judge in this case, Dido?" Miss Willows asked with much more animation than Dido had ever known her to display.

"Lord Mansfield!" she answered eagerly with immense satisfaction before Dido had an opportunity to respond.  Dido was both amazed and pleased to hear that her uncle was involved in the case, as the very thought of anyone being held in bondage against their own will, produced in her a feeling of great agitation. Surely her uncle would not permit such an evil act to continue! Dido could not think of anything else but of gaining the opportunity of questioning her uncle on the subject. Having discovered that her uncle had not yet returned home, she waited impatiently, expecting his return at every moment. While they were seated at dinner Dido's constant fidgeting and looking towards the door soon caught the attention of her aunt and an immediate reprimand followed. Lord Mansfield arrival gave Dido much more pleasure than usual. She had hoped to speak with her uncle alone but being used to having her own way, especially where the gentleman was concerned, she could not contain her excitement any longer.

"I do not think that anyone has the right to own another person. Do you not agree Sir?" Dido asked boldly, willing to incur the censure that was sure to come from her aunt. Her question was met with silence before Lady Mansfield, recovering from the shock of Dido's impudence, exclaimed,

"Hold your tongue girl. Do not speak of such things at the dinner table!"

"But do you not agree Sir?" Dido insisted ignoring Lady Mansfield's look of displeasure.

"Dido!" Lady Mansfield cried again exasperated by the lack of decorum of her ward, whose behaviour only confirmed her worst fears.

"I am of the opinion that all men should be free." Lord Mansfield replied, giving Dido a wink. His good-humour only served to increase Lady Mansfield's irritation as she began to complain of Dido's lack of discipline.

"I am glad." Dido smiled happily at Lord Mansfield, confident that Somerset would be freed.

# CHAPTER 4

It was not until Dido was fifteen that Elizabeth announced, with much excitement, that she had discovered the identity of Dido's father. The news had come as a shock to Dido and for a moment she was uncertain of whether to believe Elizabeth's boast. But her eagerness to obtain the news gave way to pleading with her cousin for almost half the morning but with little success of receiving any satisfaction, as Elizabeth's pleasure appeared to be heightened by her knowledge of obtaining news that she alone possessed. At lengths, Dido, being filled with vexation, decided it useless to continue while Elizabeth was in such a mood. "Selfish girl!" Dido cried, unable to suppress her temper. But she had no desire to give her cousin the satisfaction of seeing her distress. Dido decided instead to feign indifference, hoping that this change of tactic would gain her the desired news that her pleadings had failed to accomplish. By the end of the evening, Dido had kept earnestly to her objective and had not broached the subject again, even though there was ample opportunity to do so, when she sat alone with Elizabeth after dinner. Instead Dido gave greater concentration to her reading than was necessary, only looking up once when Elizabeth gave a violent yawn. Elizabeth having expected her cousin to continue in her pleadings, had not anticipated Dido's indifferent manner and was rather put out when Dido could not be prevailed upon to speak even one word! Elizabeth soon became bored with keeping such exciting news to herself and conceded that she had tortured her cousin sufficiently enough to reveal her secret.

"I have decided that I can no longer keep you in suspense!" Elizabeth declared suddenly, at which Dido could only shrug her shoulders with irritation at her words.

"His name is Admiral John Lindsay," she said smugly, watching Dido closely to see what her reaction would be.

Dido did not know how to feel, for she had rejected any existence of her father since discovering her identity. But she could not deny that there was a curiosity to know what manner of man he was; though his character was doomed in her eyes, having abandoned her these past fifteen years and without any acknowledgement.

"How do you know this?" Dido asked quietly, not sure if Elizabeth was playing again with her.

"I overheard Lady Mansfield talk of it to Miss Haversham. It's quite true, you know. Aren't you not diverted by my news?" Elizabeth asked gleefully. Dido would have liked to have declared that she felt nothing at all at hearing the name of a complete stranger. But her pretence would have been ineffectual as she could not help but be deeply affected by the news. She felt an instant vexation at her desire of wanting to know more. Her curiosity overcame every aversion, as now that she knew her father's name, Dido found she could not resist the compulsion of finding out all that she could about him. She read of his naval career and discovered that he was married. Is that why he had made no attempts to make her acquaintance? Dido wondered. But then decided to spare herself the grief of pondering on such a question. The answer was obvious even to her. Her eyes were now open to perceive the prejudice of both the new servants and visitors. At first, this revelation disturbed Dido greatly that she cried bitterly for days at the cruel injustice of her fate. Then she realised that this would have certainly been so from the very beginning, but her childish innocence had spared her years of pain. For months Dido dreaded seeing any visitors for fear that they would be offended by her colour! It took all her will power to prevent a feeling of self-aversion to her own colour, knowing as she did that it was the cause of her pain. She was desirous of not feeling so ashamed of herself! But Dido could not deny that she felt it acutely and was constantly in danger of succumbing to overwhelming feelings of revulsion against her race. How she wrestled against feelings of shame toward her blackness! Had she not acquired knowledge of her race through the aid of Miss Willows, Dido was sure that she would have been carried away by these dishonourable feelings. Yes, she despised the 'inferior' status that was forced upon her race! And was determined to prevail against those prejudices, refusing to harbour any feelings of inferiority as regards to herself. Especially when she soon discovered that those who looked down upon her with their superior ways were far inferior in mind and moral feelings that their opinions were not worth caring about!

Dido could not disguise her surprise on being called into the drawing room by her uncle to find seated before her the same gentleman, who had possessed all her waking preoccupation for many weeks. Now that she was being formally introduced to Admiral Lindsay, Dido found herself suddenly overcome with shyness. She observed that his face was distinguished and very handsome, his dark hair neatly combed back.  Dido did not expect to feel the sudden wave of regret of what might have been if circumstances had been different.

"I'm charmed." Admiral Lindsay said graciously, looking at Dido with a great deal of interest.

Dido hoped she had not given anything away as she struggled to control her countenance.

"Dido is growing into a handsome young woman and already accomplished for one so young.  She sings and plays exquisitely." Lord Mansfield boasted to Dido's embarrassment.  Not that she felt that his praise was unduly given but rather because she presumed that his boast could hardly be of any interest to the listener.

"How old is she now?" he asked directing his question to his uncle, to Dido's irritation.

 "Do you not know?" Dido almost asked, immediately recognizing that Admiral Lindsay could not possibly know her age, even if he were her father and had been intimate with her these past fifteen years!

Dido caught Admiral Lindsay's gaze often upon her. She wondered if he saw any resemblance of her mother in her.  Or perhaps he was attempting to see if there was any resemblance between them? She felt the awkwardness of his gaze.  Perhaps he was disappointed in what he saw? Dido thought, then immediately rebuked herself.  Surely it should be *she* who should be disappointed in him!  Her uncle was asking Admiral Lindsay how long he was to stay in London. His response became hesitant.

"I'm not sure. I have a few weeks leave after which I am not sure where I will be." He replied distractedly and for the first time Dido considered the possibility of Admiral Lindsay being just as nervous as herself.  There seemed to be an air of expectancy in his voice, which caused Dido to wonder at the reason for it. But she was soon distracted from pondering on this thought by the arrival of Lady Mansfield and Elizabeth.  Lady Mansfield's countenance appeared flustered by the awkwardness of the meeting, looking to her husband for direction as to how to act.

"Admiral Lindsay how is Mrs Lindsay?" Lady Mansfield asked though having little interest of being acquainted on the wellbeing his wife, as her inquiry was asked primarily out of the necessity of having something to say in order to conceal her uneasiness. Time meant nothing to Lady Mansfield. She hated scandals and infidelity of any kind and was a severe judge of their offenders.  It was merely out of duty to her husband that Lady Mansfield was forced to receive Admiral Lindsay's address and to accept Dido's presence in their home.  She had been appalled by her husband's decision to take guardianship of Admiral Lindsay's child, as she was certain that they would one day regret the decision. And having taken this premonition to heart, Lady Mansfield lived in a state of expectancy of some future misfortune occurring from Dido's presence in their home. Her uneasiness was rewarded whenever a disagreement arose between herself and her husband on Dido's upbringing. But being a dutiful wife Lady Mansfield had little choice but to accept her husband's say on the matter, and put aside her own complaints. This, Lady Mansfield did very badly, as she was, more often than not, repeatedly voicing her complaints to her husband when he cared to listen, and taking out her frustration by scolding the girls when her protests went unheard. Presently, Lady Mansfield observed Captain Lindsay as he stood before his daughter looking somewhat ill at ease. "And rightly so! What a dreadful scandal!" Lady Mansfield thought to herself. To think that Admiral Lindsay would insist on seeing his daughter after all this time was incomprehensible to Lady Mansfield. She conceived the very idea to be a careless gesture on his part, though she would grudgingly concede that, as yet, Dido's presence had caused no harm to the family's social standing.

Admiral Lindsay stayed for dinner and entertained his family with the tales of his adventures at sea, that even Lady Mansfield was able to forget her uneasiness, at least for the remainder of the evening. Dido thought him to be an excellent storyteller and extremely amusing and his tales certainly enlivened their usual dreary dinner table conversations. But then remembering herself, Dido became reserved, feeling a sense of guilt at having succumbed to his charms. Had he not abandoned her at birth and had made no effort to contact her until now? Surely she had a right to feel, at the very least, indignation? Dido observed Admiral Lindsay steadily, as she attempted to conjure up feelings of resentment, as he sat charming them all with his merry tales. She wondered how he would respond to her asking him to retell the tale of her mother. Luckily for Admiral Lindsay, Dido did not have the courage to do so or the heart to act so maliciously. As the evening continued Dido discovered as she attempted to determine the extent of her sentiments towards her *father*, that she felt nothing more than regret. After dinner, Dido expecting to be called upon to play, did so with a keen determination to please, and with the intention of showing her *father* that Lord Mansfield's boast of her accomplishments were well placed. Admiral Lindsay bestowed upon Dido's performance, sincere and generous praises, so much so that Dido could not help but be pleased by them. Thus, Admiral Lindsay left, with great satisfaction that the evening had went very well, while Dido was left to feel disappointed at her own conduct, having to confess to herself that she had been too easily flattered by Admiral Lindsay's praises than she ought.

How could she know then that it would be the first and last time that she would see her father? The news of Admiral Lindsay's death, a few years later, brought a period of mourning to the household at Kenwood. Dido was finally informed by Lord Mansfield that Admiral Lindsay was indeed her father. She was shown a copy of her father's obituary in a London newspaper, which gave mention of her. Dido remembered their brief meeting and felt regret that she had been denied the privilege of being acknowledged by him while he was alive. She could not help but wonder at the hypocrisy of her father's public acknowledgement at death but while living, he had kept secret, what was already widely known among his circle. Though Dido had, for some time, understood why she had been given into the care of her uncle so many years ago, as what would a young man of means do with a black child? She had no regrets concerning her childhood, as she could not think of a better home than her beloved Kenwood. Her affection for her uncle had only increased over the years. She remembered now her childhood wish for Lord and Lady Mansfield to be her parents. With all her heart, she wished it still, as she would not have to suffer the pain of being inferior to her own relations!

"He has left you a good sum of money in his will." Her uncle continued, "And now that you are of an age, I will do my best to tell you all I know of your mother."

Dido remained silent incapable of telling him that she had no wish to know any such revelation. After all, what good would it do to know the identity of her unfortunate mother? She must be forgot.

"Do you not want to know anything about your mother?" Lord Mansfield asked, though he had little information to satisfy her, he felt it necessary to disclose what he knew.

"No, sir." Dido was forced to answer to her uncle's enquiry.

"Are you sure?" he cried astounded by her negation but did not continue on seeing her anxious expression.

"Ok, Dido. Perhaps now is not a good time." He said with some disappointment.

Dido hated to disappoint him but how could he know of her suffering? The woman who had been lost to her at birth would remain lost forever. What choice was there? Her mother being a black slave, was not worthy of being mentioned in decent society. She had become a ghastly phantom, haunting both Dido's present and future position, bringing nothing but shame to her entire existence. By the age of fifteen Dido had come to despise all thoughts of her mother and her slave heritage, wishing only to be the same as everyone else. Yet, how could she despise her own self? Her pride could not consent to such unjust feelings! Her suffering was grave indeed! Having received all the privilege of an aristocratic upbringing and had obtained the social manners and graces of a lady of the highest nobility, Dido discovered that her acceptance or rejection was dependent entirely on the whim of those within her social circle and even by the most inferior of creatures. It was mortifying to her dignity that she was often treated as an object of curiosity or an outcast, pitied or ridiculed and looked down upon! To think that she should be offending the sensibilities of such people, who considered themselves so superior, was at times too exasperating for Dido to bear! But yet she was forced to hold her tongue more than she ought, for fear of displeasing her guardians. Instead Dido had to be content with re-enacting scenes where she was free to express herself as she chose to the shock and displeasure of her guests. And though it proved an amusing pastime, it did little to alleviate the pain and humiliation she felt at being so unjustly slighted. It was with these daily battles that Dido struggled to prevail against the tide of prejudice. And with this resolution Dido decided for the sake of her own self-preservation, dignity and sanity, never to be influenced by the opinions of others.

# CHAPTER 5

Five months before Elizabeth's eighteenth birthday, all that preoccupied the inhabitants of Kenwood was the lively preparations for Elizabeth's coming out ball. There was not a word or action taken that did not relate to the organising of the ball. Dido's initial excitement soon turned to envy, and as the months continued, she had acquired a resentful and impatient spirit towards Elizabeth's continual outbursts of blissful exhilaration and eager anticipation at the forthcoming event.

"Oh I cannot wait for everyone to see me in my beautiful new dress!" She cried with delight. Dido could have borne it if it had not been previously spoken of, at least a dozen times! There was not an hour that went by that the ball or something relating to the ball was not enquired of or discussed in great detail.

"There shall be so many young gentlemen there I am sure to see someone I like." Elizabeth declared ecstatically that Dido could scarcely keep from rolling her eyes with irritation. How different it was for her. She could not dream of having such fuss being made over her, as there would be no coming out ball for *her*! Oh how she wished that she were not a black daughter of a slave! Dido cried selfish tears, feeling the full injustice of her race. It was in this state of misery that Dido continued for many days, while the excitement of the preparations continued as if indifferent to her sufferings. Lord Mansfield observed her gloomy manner and attempted to cheer her, guessing that her sadness was due to Elizabeth's ball, but not even his words could comfort her. A few weeks before the ball, Lady Mansfield announced that Dido would not be able to attend, which added deeply to her sufferings. Though she had become exasperated by all the continuous fuss being made over the arrangements and had greatly disapproved of Elizabeth's excessive behaviour, Dido had concealed within herself an eager anticipation of the event. The thought of not being able to attend had not entered her head. How could she be so naïve! Of course, Lady Mansfield's constant fear of offending certain important personage, as there were to be a few members of the royal family in attendance, could be the only reason for her insisting on Dido's absence. If only such consideration could have been given to her! Dido thought resentfully. But Lord Mansfield put an end to the matter by insisting on Dido's presence.

"Anyway, I'm sure Dido is the reason why so many people will be attending." He said wryly before winking at Dido, who felt mortified at his words. The thought of being gawked at made her feel very ill at ease. She hoped her uncle was merely teasing them.

"Oh, Uncle William that's just ridiculous!" Elizabeth exclaimed feeling displeased at the thought of Dido receiving more attention than herself. After all, it was her coming out ball and she had hoped to be the centre of attention. Lady Mansfield tried to reassure Elizabeth that the idea was indeed ridiculous, as well as calming her own irritation at her husband's words.

"Sir, I'm sure what you say is not true." Dido said sensing Elizabeth's distress as well as Lady Mansfield's, who always talked more hurriedly when she was trying to control her temper or avoid any unpleasantness.

"You shall see for yourselves." Lord Mansfield replied unperturbed by the disturbance his comment had caused. Dido knew it was useless to argue with him when he spoke with what she called his judicial voice. But Lady Mansfield continued for at least ten minutes attempting to dissuade her husband of his decision but to no avail. When her husband left the room it was Dido who was left to feel the full force of her disappointment.

"How can he think such a thing? Lord Mansfield does not understand the delicacies of these matters. Or he would not talk so carelessly."

"Surely Dido you must see the necessity of not giving offence? It is not for myself that I am thinking of. It is for your own welfare. And think of poor Elizabeth, after all it is her first ball. Do you not want it to go well?" Lady Mansfield coaxed in her attempt to persuade Dido of the benefit of her absence.

"You must dissuade Lord Mansfield at once of any desire of wishing to attend the ball." Lady Mansfield continued relentlessly, oblivious of the affect that her words were having on Dido, as her only concern being the family's reputation and standing before their royal guests.

Dido sat stunned, feeling the pain produced by the full meaning of Lady Mansfield's words and the misery she felt gave her no power to speak but merely a desire of quitting the present company.

"Does it really matter whether Dido attends?"

"Do not talk so foolishly girl! Of course it matters." Lady Mansfield cried indignantly, and began once again to explain the importance of the evening.

Elizabeth tiring of her aunt's complaints came to her cousin's aid by changing the subject.

"Dear Aunt, when shall I see my dress?" Elizabeth asked excitedly, at which Lady Mansfield answered again a question that had been so often asked, since the announcement of the ball. Elizabeth's distraction worked as Lady Mansfield instead began to worry about the possibility of the dress not arriving on time as the ball was less than two weeks away. This then gave rise to fears about the preparation for the dining hall and food, until all other thoughts were forgotten and the housekeeper was called to repeat the menu and reassure Lady Mansfield that all the preparations were in order. Dido was grateful, at least, for Elizabeth's timely diversion and reproached herself for her insensitive behaviour over the past few weeks towards her cousin, who was entitled as was any young lady in her position, to be overly excited at the prospect of their first ball. The revelation may have come rather too late but Dido vowed to take greater pains in future to listen to every repetitive chatter and squeals of delight, in a calm and genteel manner.

The day of the ball finally arrived with lively expectation by the entire Kenwood household, now that the long wait was at an end. Lady Mansfield had failed in all her attempts to dissuade Lord Mansfield from allowing Dido to attend the ball. Though Dido had in her despair consented to inform Lord Mansfield of her wish not to attend, he had merely looked at her in such a way to make it plain that he had seen through his wife's scheme and he would not relent. Instead, Lady Mansfield had the added worry of acquiring a gown for Dido, which could not be done without great distress at the shortness of time, as a seamstress had to be called in to tailor a dress for the occasion. The servants were busily working from the early hours of the morning, thoughtless of their gruelling tasks, worked with excitement at receiving their first royal guests. Lord Mansfield busied himself in his study until reminded of the lateness of the hour by Lady Mansfield, who was aghast at her husband's total indifference to the importance of the ball. But Lady Mansfield, too preoccupied with instructing the housekeeper with the final preparations and making sure that everything was completed to perfection, had little time to fuss over Lord Mansfield. Elizabeth, overcome with excitement and gaiety, took twice as long to get ready, as she could not be prevailed upon to keep still for more than a few minutes. Similarly, Dido could hardly contain her own emotions while dressing, but for entirely different reasons. She had become so filled with immense apprehension at remembering her uncle's words that she now wished that Lady Mansfield had prevailed in her argument. As the guests began to arrive Dido delayed in her room as Sarah made the last touches to her hair.

"Oh Miss you look lovely." She said smiling, as she looked with satisfaction at Dido's reflection in the mirror. At any other time, Dido would have appreciated Sarah's compliment had she not felt so completely overwhelmed by the occasion and the importance of her appearance that she now surveyed her reflection with a very critical eye, until she could see nothing but flaws! It took Dido all the courage she possessed to leave the safety of her room. When she did, she was immediately greeted by the sound of faint humming of music and voices. But her courage waivered and could take her no further than the top of the stairs, where she peered down wide-eyed at the spectacular sight before her. The hall was crowded with ladies with gowns, of silk and muslin, colours of green, lemons, pinks, blues and creams complimented by the brightly ornate jewels of their diamonds, emeralds and sapphires. While men in the black and white moved like chequered boards between the dashes of vibrant colours. Dido fled back to her room afraid of being seen. The thought of facing so many people filled her momentarily with dread. She had not anticipated feeling such distress, that she felt utterly ashamed of her timidity. Dido could only conclude that making her first appearance in society at just seventeen, was proving to be an overwhelming experience. A knock on the door caused her heart to jump. What was wrong with her? When had she become so cowardly?

"Miss Dido, Lord Mansfield is waiting for you to join him in the hall." Sarah said giving Dido a concerned look,

"Is there anything wrong Miss?" she asked, when Dido did not move.

"No!" Dido replied hastily.

"Thank you Sarah. Please tell Lord Mansfield that I will be down directly." Dido answered firmly, attempting to appear calm as she forced herself to smile.

"Yes miss." Sarah replied before quitting the room.

"I am a gentleman's daughter." Dido told herself repeatedly, in hope of gaining the boldness that she so craved. Oh, how vexing it was to feel so timid when one needed to be bold! Dido thought exasperated by her own cowardice. Was she now to be ashamed of her own self? Surely not! Dido felt her spirit revile against such a sensation, giving her strength to fight against all feelings of intimidation, and at last finding the courage, she had until then lacked, left the confines of her room.

The hall was crowded with people and at first Dido had difficulty finding Lord and Lady Mansfield amid the crowd, until finally catching a glimpse of them standing near the entrance of the hall with a beaming Elizabeth standing beside them as they greeted their guests. Dido carefully made her way through the crowd, deliberately ignoring the open stares and whispers as she went. Lord Mansfield took her hand as she approached and gave Dido an affectionate smile and instantly she felt at ease.

"What did I tell you, eh?" He whispered with amused satisfaction.

Dido wished that she could be as amused at his words as he was. Her heart was fluttering too much to be anything but self-conscious of her appearance. Inevitably it had to be so, as there was everything to be conscious of, from her dress, her hair, to her countenance and colour!

"Duchess of Devonshire may I introduce you to my ward Miss Dido Elizabeth Belle." Lord Mansfield announced.

"How charming she is." The Duchess of Devonshire remarked looking intently at Dido.

Dido curtsied and smiled pleasantly. She was determined to show herself equal to every person in the room! There were endless introductions to lords and ladies, royalties and dignitaries, that Dido was sure that she would forget half of their names before the end of the evening.

"How lovely, you look my dear!" Miss Haversham cried loudly drawing the attention of many a disapproving looks, of which the lady was oblivious to.

"There are many a young gentlemen here tonight. No doubt there are some that have caught your eye." She continued winking crudely, oblivious to Dido's mortified look. Though Dido considered Miss Haversham to be a very talkative but good-natured woman, she found it difficult to feign any interest in her constant talk on her favourite subject of beaus and marriage.

"I am not interested in finding a beau." Dido replied and immediately realised her mistake in responding at all.

"Not interested? Come now Dido, you are of an age to be married you know." She remarked dismissively, finding it incredulous that Dido did not have any interest in finding a husband. To her mind, all young ladies were attracted to the idea of falling in love.

"Lady Mansfield, do you not think that Dido is of an age to be married?" she asked, continuing to talk of the advantages of marriage, before Lady Mansfield could respond.

"Both Dido and Elizabeth should no doubt draw attention of many a beaus tonight." She added, to the displeasure of Lady Mansfield, who deliberately did not respond but instead turned back to continue her conversation with Lady Carrington, as if not hearing Mrs Haversham's words. Though Lady Mansfield considered Miss Haversham's society to be all very well and good in intimate circles, she found that the lady's manners among dignitaries to be somewhat lacking in propriety. As for Miss Haversham, she chatted on caring little if anyone listened or not. Before long she caught the attention of a young officer who was passing by.

"Ah, Captain Alwyne! You are just the kind of gentleman that will make a suitable beau!" Miss Haversham cried with delight.

To Dido's mortification the officer stopped and bowed gallantly looking unashamed but rather amused by Miss Haversham's remark.

"Captain Alwyne, at your service" He said, smiling amiably. Dido had to concede that his face and appearance was both handsome and agreeable.

"Let me introduce you to Miss Dido Elizabeth Belle, ward of Lord Mansfield." Miss Haversham stated feeling rather pleased with herself for ceasing the opportunity of bringing the two young people together.

Dido curtsied but dare not lift her eyes to his face, suddenly overcome with shyness.

"Charmed," He replied, bowing this time less ostentatiously.

"How do you like the ball Miss Dido?" Captain Alwyne asked in an easy manner.

"This is my first one. I'm not sure if I care for them." Dido replied truthfully with a nervous smile.

Captain Alwyne laughed openly.

"I do not care for them much myself. You soon discover that after a while you tend to meet the same set of people, which can be a frightful bore." He remarked with an air of serious displeasure.

"Present company not included of course." He smiled, and Dido thought that his handsome face was made more pleasant by it. She could not help but smile at his unassuming manner in which he put her completely at ease so that she became quite unaware that they were drawing some attention from more than a few people in the room.

"Who is the gentleman speaking with Dido?" Elizabeth asked to no one in particular.

Lady Mansfield looked in the direction of her niece's glance but could not satisfy the request, as she herself was totally unacquainted with the gentleman in question.

"Ah, that is Captain Alwyne, a very eligible young man. His father is Lord Alwyne." Lady Carrington answered, a little alarmed at seeing the young gentleman behaving so attentive to the black girl. Like most mothers with daughters of marriageable age Lady Carrington had taken upon herself the odious task of being acquainted with as many eligible gentlemen from distinguished families as possible, for the sole purpose of finding her daughters suitable husbands.

"I hear he is quite a favourite with the young ladies." Lady Carrington added, with some concern. She had heard his name linked with one young lady or another through the course of the year, without forming an attachment with either. She felt it quite disturbing that the young man should be playing with the affections of vulnerable young women. But her daughters were her only concern and the purpose of them being both well settled was of paramount importance. Alas, Lady Carrington resolved that a wayward young man was better than no man at all! For this reason alone Lady Carrington insisted on extending dinner invitations to Captain Alwyne at every possible opportunity.

Elizabeth listened with interest, while her eyes continue to roam the room for amiable young men. She was happy to declare that she had seen many that had taken her fancy during the course of the evening, and Captain Alwyne had been one of them. She was quite at a loss as to which one to choose, if any choice had to be made. Although Elizabeth would have readily chosen the first gentleman who would show her the slightest interest! When no introduction was forthcoming, she found herself looking enviously over at Dido with much ill humour. It was unfair that on the night of her coming out ball Dido should be receiving more attention than herself! Elizabeth would have remained in this state of vexation had not James Hector appeared before her and asked if she would give him the honour of accepting the next dance. All Elizabeth's former feelings of displeasure were immediately replaced with the joy of receiving a gentleman's attention and her previous anticipation and excitement returned to bring a smile of delight to her features.

"See that gentleman standing with the lady with the enormous diamond necklace?" Captain Alwyne whispered to Dido, who followed his eyes to meet the face of a tall middle-aged gentleman, who was talking rather loudly to an elegantly dressed woman, whose diamond necklace flashed as she moved.

"He has a terrible weakness for cards but always tries to beg off his debts." Captain Alwyne revealed mischievously.

"You are trying to shock me with your stories." Dido remarked with amusement, feeling quite at ease in the gentleman's society.

"No. My purpose was only to impress you with my extensive knowledge of many of the people in this room." He answered pretending to be offended by her impression of him.

Dido did not know how to answer his response without feeling self-conscious. Her emotions had turned from playful to awkwardness in an instant. She had not been used to receiving any such attention from a gentleman, let alone a gentleman as amiable as Captain Alwyne. Her embarrassment did not go amiss. Dido willed herself to say something, anything that could be deemed as intelligible. But nothing could be thought of. Oh how she loathed her shyness!

"Miss Dido would you do me the honour of the next dance?" Captain Alwyne asked graciously.

Dido was surprised by his request but could not help being pleasantly affected by his attention.

"I would be honoured sir," she answered shyly, finally finding her voice as well as a strong desire to flee from the room.

Captain Alwyne returned to escort Dido to the dance set. Dido was conscious of all eyes upon them. There was a sudden hush around the whole room, as curious faces turned with sly glances towards them, while others stared openly in their direction. Then the music and voices mingled together again so suddenly so as to make Dido wonder if she had imagined the brief lull.

"You have caused quite a stir. I'm sure I have not been an object of such attention as I've been tonight." Captain Alwyne remarked amused at the whole evening. He had heard stories of Lord Mansfield's black ward but had not expected to find her quite so charming. He was pleasantly surprised by her elegant and attractive manner and had found her innocent nature rather becoming. Dido felt horrified that he should find such attention amusing. She was unaccustomed to attention of any kind with the exception of playing the pianoforte to guests after dinner. For Dido this attention could only mean one thing, the distinction of birth and status. As a child she remembered feeling hurt and rejected as a social outcast within her own home. She knew that Lord Mansfield did all he could to protect her, as she grew old enough to be able to understand the social norms and what was considered acceptable within refined society. Dido endeavoured to understand if only to please her uncle, though she could never call him such in public, but her heart had to suffer the pain of the constant reminder of her inferior position. For Dido to find herself the centre of attention was something that was totally foreign to her. Perhaps, if she were of a different disposition she would have fancied herself to be most fortunate of women. But unfortunately for Dido she found no pleasure in being an object of curiosity.

"Do not look so alarmed. People may begin to think that I am saying something I shouldn't?" Captain Alwyne warned mischievously

"Oh, I've made you blush." He laughed, drawing more attention to them then her look of alarm may have attracted.

"I think it is my own thoughts that have made me blush." Dido said openly, then remembering herself, became embarrassed at the thought of his taking her words completely the wrong way.

"Why, Miss Dido, you are very honest but I would prefer it if your blushes were of my own doing." Captain Alwyne confessed.

"Now you are teasing me I think." Dido replied unable to stop herself from smiling.

Captain Alwyne laughed freely and at that moment he was completely taken in by her charms.


"Oh Miss Dido, I think that you have won yourself a beau!" Miss Haversham cried excitedly, giving Dido a vulgar wink that made her feel grateful that Captain Alwyne was already out of earshot. Unfortunately, Miss Haversham's words were not lost on Lady Mansfield and her party standing directly behind them. Dido could not help but notice the look of alarm on Lady Mansfield countenance as she glanced towards her. Her look hid none of its disapproval and Dido felt an instant indignation at its implication. She had not acted inappropriately to warrant such reproach, at least nothing to feel that any impropriety was done on her part, nor for that matter on the part of Captain Alwyne.

"Do you not agree Lord Mansfield?" Miss Haversham asked quite delighted at her own small part in introducing the couple. She always prided herself on being a good matchmaker of the young, though she never had any success with her previous predicted matches but she had never supposed this to be any fault of her own. Miss Haversham had for many years frowned on the increasing capriciousness of young ladies in their choice of a suitor and she had put this down to having too much choices. She simply could not understand it. In her opinion, the pastime of setting one's heart on a suitor was often delayed by choices which was liable to risk the opportunity of having no suitor at all! Presently,

Miss Haversham was certain that in Captain Alwyne she could not have found a better match for Dido. But then she had thought and said as much about her niece Olivia Mortimer and Edward Hunsford but nothing came of that match. And again with Lady Carrington's daughter Ann Carrington and Henry Balfour not to mention the numerous others failed predictions too soon forgotten by her.

"No, I do not." Lord Mansfield replied sharply unconcerned by the incredulous look that Miss Haversham gave him.

"Surely not, Lord Mansfield! I can assure you Miss Dido is of a good age to marry..." Miss Haversham began to say again, not being one to give up on any subject, particularly the subject of marriage.

"We shall not talk of marriage here, madam." Lord Mansfield interrupted, giving Miss Haversham no opportunity to argue.

"Excuse us." He nodded politely before giving his arm to Dido.

"Well!" Miss Haversham's voice could be heard saying to anyone who cared to listen.

"I was right. Everyone came to have a look at you. Poor Elizabeth, I'm afraid you have stolen her limelight." Lord Mansfield said rather amused.

"I hope it wasn't too taxing for you?"

"No. But I'm glad it is almost over." Dido answered but in truth she had enjoyed herself far more than she had expected. She could not deny that she had been pleased by the attentions of Captain Alwyne.

"So, you did not enjoy the company of a certain young gentleman?" Lord Mansfield teased, as if reading her mind. Dido blushed as she felt that her uncle had found her out.

"I didn't disappoint you?" Dido asked quickly changing the subject, as she desired to hide her embarrassment.

"You could never do that child." He reassured her with a smile, touching her cheek affectionately.

Dido smiled, pleased to hear his commendation. Nothing pleased her more than to give him pleasure. She knew she could not love anyone more than she loved her uncle, who she knew, had only her best welfare at heart.

# CHAPTER 6

"You seem to be quite a favourite at the ball last night." Elizabeth remarked with a mischievous air at the breakfast table.

"Miss Haversham was in raptures over your success!" She continued teasingly as she awaited Dido's response.

"I'm sure you are mistaken." Dido answered, knowing Elizabeth well enough not to take her teasing to heart.

"I noticed that Captain Alwyne was quite taken with you." Elizabeth persisted, not satisfied with Dido's answer. Dido attempted to feign indifference at the mention of the gentlemen's name.

"If only by one dance a gentleman could be said to being *taken with me* then you have had much more success than I." Dido replied astutely before smiling sweetly at Elizabeth.

Lord Mansfield laughed aloud looking up from a letter he had been perusing.

"Well said Dido! Now Elizabeth what do you have to say on that score?" Lord Mansfield asked looking amused.

"Uncle William, Dido knows that I'm only teasing her." Elizabeth replied expressively.

"Do not tease her so William. I heard the Prince Regent comment on how beautiful she looked." Lady Mansfield stated with an air of satisfaction at this royal distinction.

"Yes, I also heard him say that both of our wards were hidden gems." Lord Mansfield added.

"I myself have nothing to complain of, since I had my fair share of admirers!" Elizabeth smiled sweetly

"James Hector is such an amiable gentleman, is he not?" Elizabeth stated categorically, expecting only a chorus of consensus to her statement.

"He is a charming young man and so affable." Lady Mansfield added and the two ladies continued to talk of the gentleman's dress, manner and speech.

"Sir, who was the young man you were speaking to for such a lengthy time?" Dido addressed her uncle, again trying to turn the subject from a certain gentleman.

"Ah yes. Someone I think you should all meet." He replied mysteriously. Dido had not expected such a response.

"Who?"

"Which gentleman?"

The ladies all said at once.

"Mr Granville Sharp" Lord Mansfield answered after a momentary pause, as if to further increase the suspense. But all the ladies were still in the dark as to the gentleman in question. Dido felt the name sounded familiar but could not recollect where she had heard the name spoken of. Both Lady Mansfield and Elizabeth looked curiously having no clue of whom it could be. They all looked to Lord Mansfield to provide them with more details of the gentlemen's credentials.

"Who is he?" Elizabeth asked curiously but her interest in the said person evaporated with the arrival of fresh fruits.

"Is the gentleman single?" Lady Mansfield enquired, as she saw no other reason for his name being mentioned.

"All I will say is that he is very active in the abolitionist cause. I have invited Mr Sharp to dine with us tomorrow evening. Perhaps this will be a good opportunity as any for you all to be acquainted with him." Lord Mansfield announced deliberately ignoring his wife's surprised look.

"Tomorrow? Good heavens how are we to prepare with such short notice." Lady Mansfield exclaimed in dismay at the inconvenience at arranging dinner with so little warning.

"There is no need to make a fuss." Lord Mansfield said, failing to see the reason for his wife's alarm. They enjoyed a veritable feast every evening and this would serve sufficiently for any guest.

Lady Mansfield looked at her husband incredulously. Men had little notion of the importance of observing the formalities that came with arranging dinner parties. Lady Mansfield could not help but be concerned as a family of their social standing could ill afford to entertain guests of importance, great or small, without some show of ostentation. It was a matter of status. Lady Mansfield believed that once a guest went away talking of the delights of the meal it was a sure commendation to be spoken of at other dinner tables. With this in mind, Lady Mansfield called for the housekeeper without delay, still weary of the limited time she had to prepare. If the lady had known that Mr Sharp would be totally uninterested in the sumptuous meal that would be laid before him and that her efforts were in vain, it would not have made the slightest difference to the energy that was put into the arrangement of it.

Dido could not hide her pleasure at the opportunity of being acquainted with Mr Sharp. Not often was a dinner invitation extended to her when important guests were present. She had learnt to reconcile herself to this exclusion, painful though it was. But it had not always been so. She remembered the first occurrence when she had just turned fifteen, there was much talk of important guests arriving for dinner and Elizabeth had expressed her delight at being able to attend now she was considered a young lady sensible enough to dine with distinguished guests. Dido had shown her enthusiasm at the prospect of joining the guests and had said as much at tea. Lady Mansfield looked at her in astonishment as if she had said something entirely out of term.

"Dido you will not be dining with us. But of course you will be able to join us after dinner."

"Why am I not permitted to dine?" Dido asked quietly, ignorant of the answer that her aunt was reluctant to give.

"We are having very important guests tomorrow. You know that we think highly of you but we must consider our guests. There are people who would object to your society. You understand don't you Dido? We do not want to offend anyone—"

"There is no need to explain, madam. I understand you perfectly." Dido replied hurt by the bluntness of her aunt's words. Had her colour deemed her so unworthy of sitting down with important guests that she had to be slighted by her own family? So affected were her feeling that she refused to join the family and their guests after dinner pleading a headache. Dido's excuse was not far from the truth as she had spent the greater part of the evening crying in her room. The following morning she was unrepentant as Lord Mansfield, having called Dido into the library, tried in vain to ascertain the true reason for her absence. Dido sat rigidly, her hand tightly clasped and her eyes downcast as Lord Mansfield stood attempting to make out her temperament. The library or the Great Room as it was sometimes referred to because of its grandness, boasted elaborately painted ceilings and walls, styled elegantly in ancient Roman art. Along the north wall tall ornate mirrors hung from ceiling to floor, giving the room an appearance of being larger than it actually was, as well as harvesting the light coming from the windows directly opposite, with a beautiful prospect of the south side of the grounds and of London. Directly above the grand fireplace hung a large portrait of Lord Mansfield wearing his official robes of office. Dido had once thought the library to be her uncle's favourite room as a child but she learnt later that although Lord Mansfield used the room extensively for visitors on business and for private guests, he had found the room too ostentatious to be comfortable.

"It impresses the guests and shows me in a most befitting light don't you think." He had teased with a wink.

"We missed your company after dinner." Lord Mansfield spoke presently, eyeing at Dido closely. Dido did not respond the hurt and resentment still too acute to give voice to.

"Why do you not answer me child!" His voice became inpatient. How could she? What could she say that would not cause pain to them both? Dido was not indifferent to the feelings of others. Quite the contrary, her whole existence seemed to depend on pleasing others, even strangers who cared little for her feelings. That she had no choice in the matter made it all the more unjust! Was she to despise her own self, her ancestry for the acceptability of society?

"There are many practices that may seem unfair and even cruel. I am not asking you to accept them but only to tolerate them for the sake of your family." Lord Mansfield said resignedly as he felt regret that it should be so. Dido looked up at him on hearing his words. It was the first time he had referred to her as a member of the family, and she felt an instant gratitude at his attempt to comfort her. His words diminished all her former feelings of resentment, of which Dido hastened to express and to relieve her uncle of any pain by reassuring him that she would perform her duty to her family when the occasion arose. This she was willing to do without complaint now that she was aware of her uncle's feelings that her exclusion was not a sign of rejection by her family but a social custom. Thereafter, Dido was able to join her family and their guests in a dignified manner and soon discovered that on many instances she was more desirous of being excluded than included in their party! The talk of the weather, fashion, food and social gossip did not appeal to her as she found it just as tedious as being indoors on a rainy day! During these evenings Dido's patience was severely tested, no more so than when a distant relative of Lady Mansfield, Lady Reynolds and her children visited Kenwood.

"I think it extremely generous of Lord Mansfield to take this young lady under his care. It is absolutely amazing how well she speaks." Lady Reynolds stated expressively, eyeing Dido curiously as she spoke.

How generous indeed! How generous of Lord and Lady Mansfield to put up with your trying company! Dido thought as she attempted to control her temper. Lady Reynolds had not stopped talking since she sat down. Her thin but attractive frame moved with every gesture of self-importance. Dido kept her composure as the lady continued to talk of her, as if she were nothing more than a child or a servant.

"Dido, why do you not play for us?" Lady Mansfield suggested knowing that Dido's accomplishment on the pianoforte was much praised and their guests had become accustomed to hearing her play and sing. Dido on the other hand saw her performances as an opportunity to show herself equal to anyone. She worked hard at practising her skill like a critical taskmaster, so much so that Elizabeth often teased her for being too fastidious.

"Dido, you play delightfully. Why do you continue to be so hard on yourself?" Elizabeth asked unable to understand Dido's exasperation at the slightest mistakes.

"Oh Lizzy, how can you understand." Dido sighed impatiently. Elizabeth had little interest in doing anything well. That she was able to do them sufficiently was satisfactory enough for her. She found it difficult to concentrate on anything for too long and therefore cared less for the exercise of it.

"People look at me and see some curiosity to be accepted or rejected at a whim. All I have is my accomplishments." Dido cried fervently

"Oh nonsense you have your good looks." Elizabeth answered affectionately. Dido could not help but smile at Elizabeth's good humour.

"Anyway, we are to be painted soon it would not do for you to be pouting as you are." Elizabeth warned, dismissing Dido's concerns. Dido had to confess that she did not know how Elizabeth could be so carefree about everything. She could not be so, even if she desired to be!

"Then you'll not only have your accomplishments but also a portrait to admire and show off your fine looks." Elizabeth teased to Dido's displeasure.

# CHAPTER 7

Dido had not expected Mr Sharp to be such a slender man with such plain features. He appeared to be somewhat preoccupied, as he sat at the dinner table looking rather astonished at the meal set before him. So ill at ease was he that Dido concluded that he would have been far more comfortable at an inn with an offering of boiled stew.   Dido observed that he seemed to watch the courses with some impatience, as if dinner was in the way of far more urgent matters.  Lady Mansfield would have been mortified if Mr Sharp had not attempted to compliment her on the taste of the veal or on the sweetness of the fruits, and therefore had not been completely inattentive to the great effort that had been made for his benefit.   Dido noticed that Mr Sharp appeared more attentive whenever she spoke.  His eyes seemed observant of her every speech, movement and gesture.

"What exactly do you do Mr Sharp?" Lady Mansfield asked, making a concerted effort to appear interested in her guest, who she thought to be a rather plain and ill-dressed gentleman.

"I am a civil servant, madam." Mr Sharp replied, "Although my work is often overtaken with the abolitionist cause."

"A very worthy cause, Sir." Dido remarked approvingly, looking at Mr Sharp with feeling.

"Surely there are not so many slaves in England?" Elizabeth asked earnestly.

"Too many I fear." Mr Sharp replied

"I read about the Zong massacre.  Is it true that over a hundred slaves were killed?" Dido asked, keen to obtain first-hand knowledge of what she had previously read in a national newspaper.

"Dido please let us not talk of such things over dinner." Lady Mansfield interrupted before Mr Sharp could response.

"Madam, you are quite right. Dido, you will have ample opportunity to drill Mr Sharp after dinner." Lord Mansfield agreed.

"I will be happy to answer any questions." Mr Sharp said pleasantly.

After dinner, when the party retired to the Great Room, Mr Sharp was as good as his word.  His manner became animated as he spoke of the cruelty of slavery, seeming more comfortable in his oration than he ever appeared at the dinner table.  Dido listened fascinated by every word and annotation.  Could it be true that after all these years ex slaves were still being treated appallingly and even recaptured and forced back into slavery?

"It is an appalling practice. We are planning to get support from the House of Commons and the House of Lords to put an end to this heinous trade." Mr Sharp stated confidently as he continued to talk of the activities being planned.

"The slave trade is an evil business but it is also a very profitable one. You will find it hard to gain allies in government." Lord Mansfield remarked certain of the opposition that would undoubtedly be raised.

"Maybe so, but try we must." Mr Sharp replied adamantly.

"How delightful the sky looks tonight." Lady Mansfield sighed, looking towards the windows.

"Do you not think that young gentlemen in parliament are more like an unruly mob?" Elizabeth asked, wishing that there could be talk of a livelier nature.

Mr Sharp laughed at the accuracy of Elizabeth's comment, which would have received avid agreement in some quarters.

"Edward says that Members of Parliament are paid a pittance for the work that they do." Elizabeth added remembering a conversation she had with Edward York, a friend of a distant relative, who would have been a handsome catch had he not been as unattractive as he was boring.

If only Lady Mansfield and Elizabeth would stop interrupting, Dido thought as Mr Sharp attempted to answer Elizabeth's question.

"Mr Sharp, do you think that the abolition of slavery will be achieved? " Dido asked ignoring the speculative glances from both Ladies.

"My answer would have of course be yes, but it is not a case of will but when, Miss Dido." Mr Sharp answered assertively.

"Do you think it could be this century?" Dido inquired pressing Mr Sharp for an answer.

"Well anything is possible, if we look at the recent event in America and the achievement of independence, then I feel there is definitely an air of change." Mr Sharp replied optimistically.

"It is questionable whether the change is a good one." Lord Mansfield answered solemnly

"How could it not be a question of good for man to fight for his freedom?" Mr Sharp returned passionately unable to restrain his emotion.

"Surely a man's freedom is worth fighting for?" Dido said defensively siding for once against her uncle.

"I do not refer here to slavery but the system of change itself. One cannot guarantee that change will be beneficial."

"This is too depressing a subject, gentlemen. Let us speak of more cheerful things." Lady Mansfield interrupted before Mr Sharp could reply to Lord Mansfield's philosophical statement. Dido, for one was very happy to listen to a conversation that did not include hats, dresses, beaus or the weather.

"Yes, Mr Sharp, what did you think of my ball?" Elizabeth said excitedly, now that she was able to talk on a subject that was of great interest to her. Mr Sharp conceded generously to the ladies' plea and answered eloquently. But his eloquence did not do justice enough to please Elizabeth who was aghast at his lack of attention to names, faces and fashionable attire.

"How did you come to be involved in the Zong case Mr Sharp?" Dido asked keenly now that she had an opportunity of gaining Mr Sharp's attention while Elizabeth and Lady Mansfield were preoccupied with their favourite topic of the ball.

"That was easy. A gentleman of colour Mr Equaino a free man and an abolitionist, made me acquainted with the facts. You should meet him. He is quite a speaker." Mr Sharp replied eagerly, willing to make the acquaintance if the lady so wished.

Dido could not hide her astonishment at the mention of a free black abolitionist. How much she was ignorant of! Dido thought.

"Are there many free black men here in England?" she asked keenly

"There are a few but not many I fear. But Lord Mansfield's ruling has made it easier for free black men to escape recapture in this country." He answered before he was interrupted from saying anything further by Elizabeth's question.

"Do you think Mr Sharp that the view from the terrace is delightful?" Elizabeth asked, attempting to alleviate her own boredom. Her interruption was most untimely Dido thought.

"Yes, indeed." Mr Sharp replied with much feeling.

"Perhaps we could take a walk as we have such a breath-taking view of London from here." Lady Mansfield added boastfully, knowing that the view was one of the highlights of Kenwood.

"It is true Mr Sharp. One cannot come to Kenwood without seeing it." Dido said wryly as she ignored Lady Mansfield's stern look.

"I would be happy to see such an amazing sight." Mr Sharp answered agreeably.

With this consent the whole party quit the library to take a walk along the terrace. Any further opportunity of talking privately with Mr Sharp proved impossible. Lady Mansfield and Elizabeth seemed both revived in their efforts to ensure that Mr Sharp was acquainted with every viewpoint of Kenwood and London. Dido did not mind, as the evening had been a very pleasant one. Even after years of enjoying this beautiful prospect her pleasure of it had not diminished. It was impossible to be in anything but in good spirits on an evening like this Dido thought as she walked beside her uncle.

When Mr Sharp said goodnight and took his leave of the ladies, Elizabeth gave a gasp of relief as soon as the door was closed.
"Oh, what a positive bore! I'm sure I don't know who is worse, he or Edward!" Elizabeth exclaimed with much deliberation.
"My dear, Mr Sharp is an intellectual who is more concerned with politics than women."
"Did you not see his manner of dress? What he needs is a good wife." Lady Mansfield continued, genuinely concerned for the young man's future.
"I'm sure Mr Sharp will have no problem in finding a good wife. If indeed he is in need of a wife" Dido replied appalled at their abuse of Mr Sharp who was completely undeserving of it.
"If I had known in advance that Lord Mansfield would be inviting someone like Mr Sharp I would have made sure to invite livelier company. Miss Haversham would have been a gem to have with us tonight." Lady Mansfield added and then proceeded to list the names of those who would have made their party more agreeable. Dido could not have been more in disagreement with Elizabeth and Lady Mansfield. She had enjoyed the evening immensely and felt that Mr Sharp had proved himself to be pleasant and interesting gentleman.

# CHAPTER 8

"Oh Dido, I am completely distracted I could not possibly sleep tonight." Elizabeth cried with a passion, unconcerned at disturbing Dido at her leisure. Her unsuppressed exhilaration was brought on by a weekend invitation to London from Margaret Ashley and her mother Lady Ashley, who had just that moment departed from Kenwood after dining with Lord and Lady Mansfield.

"There are sure to be dinners and parties to go to. I have it on good confidence that James Hector will be there." Elizabeth cried with delight at the prospect of meeting Mr Hector again as he was a very good friend of the Ashley's. Six months had passed since the ball but Elizabeth had not ceased to talk of James Hector. Dido had to listen on more than one occasion as Elizabeth attempted to describe every inch of Mr Hector's person until she could not bear to hear the gentleman's name mentioned. She made every effort to show as much interest on the subject but Dido found she could no longer oblige sufficiently to give Elizabeth satisfaction. Now, as Elizabeth stood before her once again talking fervently of Mr Hector's appearance, manner, dress and speech Dido could not stop herself from feeling a moment of apprehension at Elizabeth's infatuated manner, especially while in Mr Hector's company. Good heavens if this was love Dido decided that she could happily live without it! Elizabeth had contrived with every form of persuasion to convince Lady Mansfield to invite Mr Hector to dinner. And had succeeded within the course of the day. On that evening Dido was present to observe Mr Hector carefully and found him to be overly pompous and boastful. But what was far more alarming was her cousin's manner in Mr Hector's society, which caused Dido some concern. If Elizabeth was not smiling widely, she was giggling in a childish manner so as to make Dido conclude that she was in danger of becoming a complete simpleton! Poor Elizabeth! It appeared to Dido that she had greatly over estimated James Hector's partiality towards her. Dido was sure that on the night of the ball when Mr Hector had asked Elizabeth to dance that *she* had considered it to be a declaration of love! Dido was fearful for Elizabeth that her attachment to Mr Hector would not be reciprocated. The following day after the dinner party, Lady Mansfield expressed her concerns when speaking to her niece, cautioning her on her feelings towards Mr Hector. In vain did

Lady Mansfield chastise and discourage her niece's flirtatious conduct, but her words did little to change Elizabeth's sentiments.

"I think you should at least let me get some sleep." Dido said, not able to stop herself from smiling as Elizabeth's face became crestfallen as a disappointed child.

"Dido, how can you be so unfeeling!" She scolded playfully pretending to be hurt at Dido's insensitivity.

"One day you will be as happy as I am." She warned, looking at Dido and laughing at her look of disgust.

"I am happy now." Dido replied sincerely

"Oh but when you fall in love you will think differently." Elizabeth declared, speaking as someone with many years' experience of being in love and not as one of just six months!

"I think I can wait." Dido said not wanting to confide to Elizabeth that she had no intention of falling in love or of getting married.

"You won't miss me too much while I'm away?" Elizabeth teased.

"You know I will." Dido answered quietly, as Elizabeth had been the only friend she had known. Throughout her childhood they had quarrelled as sisters and between them had existed moments of jealousy and rivalry. But as they had grown into adulthood Dido found that she could depend on their friendship in spite of the growing differences that threatened to draw them apart. Dido did not blame Elizabeth in the least for thinking herself to be superior after all it was expected of her. But Dido knew that there would always be an attachment between them. It was this attachment that made her ignore Elizabeth's faults, her selfishness and inconsistencies. Elizabeth smiled and touched Dido's arm with some amount of sympathy mistakenly thinking Dido to be devastated at being excluded from the trip to London. Dido did not attempt to dissuade her, as it would have been useless to do so.

"I'll bring you something nice from London to cheer you up when I get back." Elizabeth said trying to console her. Though Dido did not doubt the sincerity of Elizabeth's declaration, she did not expect to receive anything. This was not due to lack of feeling on her cousin's part, but more to do with her selfish tendency to forget all others especially while she was having so much fun. Dido bade her cousin goodnight, smiling to herself as Elizabeth left her room still sighing and declaring how she could not possibly sleep.

"James Hector is a complete bore. It is lucky for him that he has wealth and connections to secure him any match he chooses." concluded

Elizabeth at the breakfast table the morning after her return from London. Dido glanced at Elizabeth in complete shock at hearing this revelation. Could she be speaking of the same gentleman? Elizabeth's weekend at the Ashley's had not turned out as well as she had expected. It was vexing that she should have spent so little time alone with James Hector than she had in all their previous encounters. Elizabeth had hoped for a more intimate setting but instead found that they were constantly crowded by people she hardly knew. Mr Hector hardly spoke a word to her in the whole weekend that they were in each other's company that Elizabeth sulkily declared that she would think no more of him. A task Elizabeth found to be impossible. How vexed she was at having such an uneventful weekend! She only hoped that her chances were not lost. Elizabeth was sure that things would have been more agreeable had she had the opportunity of gaining Mr Hector's attention.

"Do not be absurd Elizabeth. Choosing a husband on the criteria of him being nothing but a bore is utter foolishness." Lady Mansfield declared in astonishment in response to her niece's statement. She could not help but feel despair at the ideas of young ladies nowadays, as she believed them to be too whimsical in their views.

"Imagine if we all choose our beaus on this premise. Many of us will still be old maids!" Lady Mansfield cried aghast at the thought.

"James Hector is a gentleman from a very prominent family. Mark my words there will be many a ladies after him, including your cousin Margaret." Lady Mansfield stated astutely.

Elizabeth laughed at the very idea, as she could not imagine Mr Hector and Margaret together.

"Dear Madam, Margaret has no interest in James Hector." Elizabeth replied confidently. As far as she knew Margaret had not shown Mr Hector any such attention in that way. She was openly playful with him and it is true that Elizabeth did think her quite wayward at times in his society but she had always accounted this for their having grown up together.

"And why not?" Lady Mansfield was asking credulously.

"Do not be deceived. Lady Ashley has spoken to me of her wishes for Margaret to settle down with someone like Mr Hector." She warned. But her words were not able to convince her niece.

"I'm sure that my aunt is wrong." Elizabeth said defensively after Lady Mansfield had left the room.

"And I'm sure that your aunt is only trying to help Elizabeth." Dido said attempting to appease Elizabeth's indignation.

"Do you no longer find Mr Hector agreeable?" Dido asked attempting to ascertain her cousin's feelings for Mr Hector.

"Of course I do." Elizabeth replied nonchalantly and then suddenly became irritable at the remembrance of Mr Hector's indifferent manner towards her in London.

"But you said just a moment ago that he was a complete bore." Dido said in astonishment.

"Oh, that is nothing. Let's just say that he is not as charming as I first thought him now that I am better acquainted with him."

"And anyway she was not there. James Hector doted over me for the entire weekend." Elizabeth said smugly, her pride not permitting her to give up the pretence. Dido hoped for her sake that she was right. Elizabeth had a tendency to see circumstances and events in an entirely different light than they actually were. She had always been that way as long as Dido could remember. She was forever getting into trouble simply because she showed a wilful propensity in thinking herself right about a person or a circumstance which usually turned out to be the reverse. There was the time when Elizabeth had boasted to Dido that Lord and Lady Mansfield would have no objection to her going to Bath with friends but the following day she was proved wrong when they refused to grant their permission. Her response was credulous "how strange!" she had cried unable to understand the reason for their refusal. At the ball Elizabeth had talked of James Hector showing her such great attention. But according to Miss Haversham's account James Hector had not shown her any more attention than he had given to any other girl that he had danced with.

"Has Mr Hector arranged to call?" Dido asked in order to find out the degree of his attachment.

"No. Not as yet." Elizabeth answered hesitantly

"But I am positive that he will."

"Oh Dido if only you could have been there. We had such a delightful time!" Elizabeth exclaimed with excitement. Which was partly true, once she was able to get over the disappointment of Mr Hector neglect of her.

"We dined. We went to the theatre in the evening. Oh, there were such people to admire! And the following evening we went to a party at Lady Bancroft. Mr Elliot Bancroft was so agreeable." Elizabeth cried with delight.

"Elliot Bancroft?" Dido asked curiously. She could not imagine Elizabeth getting excited on meeting Lord Bancroft.

"Yes, Lord and Lady Bancroft's son." She answered, at least here she could boast of some attention. Mr Bancroft, although rather a dull young man, could not be compared with the charming manners and dashing good looks of Mr Hector, was at least attentive and rather flattered by her presence.

"Oh, London is such a marvellous place, so full of diversions." Elizabeth continued excitedly

"I do not know what I shall do here at Kenwood. Aunt and Uncle hardly have anyone to dine except complete bores."

"Oh to be married and to leave this place!" She cried longingly to Dido's amazement. To think that Elizabeth saw her home as a kind of prison astonished her. For Dido Kenwood was a haven from the uncertainties of life. The contemplation of such an act of marriage produced much disturbance to her spirit. She had no desire to leave Kenwood. It was impossible for Dido to have Elizabeth's confidence and fearlessness to desire a life outside of Kenwood. Elizabeth was free while she was bound by her inheritance. It threatened the stability of her whole existence. She would be no more than an outcast to be belittled, censored, patronised and despised. At least at Kenwood she was safe. Dido had no reason to leave its shelter. For Dido, marriage was unthinkable!

# CHAPTER 9

Within a month of Elizabeth's return from London, the occupants of Kenwood were acquainted with the news of the engagement of Margaret Ashley and James Hector.    Lady Mansfield's prediction had proved correct.  But before the lady could take any triumph in her premonition, a commotion broke out as Elizabeth, on hearing the news, fainted, thereby giving her relations moments of anxiety.  After she had momentarily recovered, there followed an onset of incessant tears that resulted in her having to be sent to bed for the rest of the day.  Elizabeth's outburst lasted only one day, which Dido conceded was a vast improvement on previous occasions, as she was known to cry for days on end.    Dido hoped that this was a sign of the frivolity of Elizabeth's affection for Mr Hector. The following day witnessed a more surprising change as the tearful and emotional Elizabeth was replaced by a solemn and dignified one.  For Lady Mansfield, the sudden change was cause for concern.

"I am seriously worried about Elizabeth." She announced fretfully to her husband after the invalid had retired to her room.

"I did warn her that something like this could happen." She continued, sighing at the recollection of it.

"She is young. It is a common occurrence for young ladies to be wounded in love." Lord Mansfield replied, providing no consolation to his wife's concerns.

"I hope she does not become too melancholy as to spoil her chances with other young men." Lady Mansfield added anxiously

"Nonsense." Her husband replied dismissively.

"I agree Sir. I do not think that Elizabeth's attachment to Mr Hector was a serious one.   When she returned from London she talked very favourably of another young gentleman that she had become acquainted with." Dido said, hoping to reassure Lady Mansfield.

In truth, Dido felt that Elizabeth's attachment to Mr Hector was rather too whimsical to be considered anything of substance.  To say that she had been slighted in love would be doing Mr Hector a disservice.  Dido too would have had cause for complaint if this was the case, as poor Mr Hector had paid her some attention by asking, "How she liked living at Kenwood?"  At such an enquiry Dido could only endeavour to answer him as civilly as she could.  It did him much injury in her eyes as his question, if it had been asked in awkwardness or of want of something to say, could be forgiven. But Mr Hector had in his possession neither awkwardness or of embarrassment. His question would have been better suited if it had been addressed to a visitor or a governess but not to one who have lived in a family home from infancy. His ignorance vexed her. But in her position Dido learnt that it was best to develop a sense of humour, as she would be always in a state of vexation at the folly of others. Did she think Mr Hector a suitable match for her cousin? Of course not! Elizabeth could be selfish, head strong and showing little regard for others, as her only concern being her own contentment, but for all her faults she was not unfeeling. Elizabeth was of a disposition that her generosity could be just as fervent as her selfishness.

"I hope you are right." Lady Mansfield replied with little satisfaction.

"Perhaps what she needs is a little diversion." Dido offered.

She knew that Lady Mansfield's fears were unwarranted where Elizabeth's ability to quickly recover from moments of distress, were concerned. Being her close companion for many years had made Dido intimate with Elizabeth's disposition. Unfortunately for Lady Mansfield, the passing years had not given her any such knowledge. She continued to be taken in by Elizabeth's bouts of tantrums.

"What an excellent idea. Perhaps we could organise a dinner party and invite a few young people along. That will cheer her and take her mind off this dreadful business." Lady Mansfield suggested, feeling much better about her plans to get Elizabeth back on the road to recovery. Dido would have interjected and said that this was not what she had in mind, if she had not perceived that Lady Mansfield was quite taken by her little scheme. She would have suggested a change of environment, a trip to some unacquainted place. Dido had quite fancied a trip to the coast. But perhaps in this case, Lady Mansfield was a better judge of Elizabeth's temperament than Dido in predicting that Elizabeth would much prefer a dinner party with friends than a trip to the seaside.

Lady Mansfield set to work with vigour, organising the arrangement for the dinner party aided by an enthusiastic Elizabeth, who had swiftly recovered upon hearing the news. The task of going out to visit all the intended guests, with invitation card in hand, took up the preoccupation of both ladies for several days. Once the invitations were given out then the fuss of preparing the menu took up the remainder of the week. Lady Mansfield's diversion had paid off as Elizabeth could talk of nothing else but the forthcoming event and the pleasure of seeing Mr

Bancroft again. Dido feared the worst as she thought it too soon for Elizabeth to be excited about anyone.

"He was so charmed by our invitation that he talked of nothing else while we stayed there the whole hour." Elizabeth beamed with delight. Dido remained quiet not wanting to give encouragement to her enthusiasm. But she could not help but wonder how charmed or enthusiastic Mr Bancroft really was. Dido looked to Lady Mansfield who did not contradict her niece's words.

"Mr Bancroft is a charming young man with excellent manners." She said as if not expecting to find him so.

Dido almost asked, in jest, if an invitation had been given to Margaret Ashley and Mr Hector, but thought it too early for such a subject to be even contemplated. But she was proved wrong.

"There is, of course, the matter of Margaret. One cannot leave her out of such an invitation without slighting her." Lady Mansfield said, revealing her concern once Elizabeth had left the room. Dido considered it strange that the diversion, which Lady Mansfield had so carefully planned to take Elizabeth's mind off Margaret Ashley and Mr Hector's engagement, should now throw her headlong into it!

"How does Elizabeth take this news?" Dido asked, surprised to hear Lady Mansfield had indeed extended an invitation to the undeserving couple.

"Oh, Elizabeth has assured me she is perfectly calm and does not care if they are there or not. " Lady Mansfield answered but sighed heavily. Dido perceived from Lady Mansfield's expression that she was not completely at ease with Elizabeth's assurances. Knowing Lady Mansfield's disposition as she did, Dido feared that her aunt would become overly anxious at the prospect of facing any unpleasantness. But Dido also knew that her aunt's idea of unpleasantness could range from the serious to the absurd. This could include not having the right sort of meat on the dinner table to the infidelity of a gentleman, or even worse a lady. Lady Mansfield could not abide scenes of any nature without abhorrence.

"But I have my doubts. She is used to getting her own way. I do hope she does not make a scene." Lady Mansfield continued, having second thoughts about the dinner party that was now only a few days away.

"Madam, please do not make yourself uneasy. I think you should give Elizabeth credit for knowing her own feelings. She has too much pride to let Miss Ashley or Mr Hector see that she had been injured by their alliance, if indeed she has been." Dido reassured her.

"I hope that you are right." Lady Mansfield replied unable to shake off her uneasiness. Dido was left to feel that nothing she could say would relieve her aunt's anxiety on this matter.

On the evening of the dinner party Dido had prepared to catch up on her reading in the quiet comfort of her room. She was therefore taken aback on seeing Elizabeth, dressed for the evening in a fetching pale yellow evening gown entering into her room hurriedly, and eyeing her in astonishment.

"Are you not ready?" she asked staring at Dido's attire.

"Goodness the guests are soon to arrive."

It was Dido's turn to look astonished, as she had not considered the possibility of being invited.

"I did not know that I was expected to dine." Dido replied calmly, feeling no desire to attend.

"But you must, I need you there!" Elizabeth cried moving to Dido's dresser to call for the maid. Dido could not think of any reason why she would be needed except as a useful diversion.

"I shall have a friendly face to give me courage!" Elizabeth declared warmly leaving Dido feeling guilty for thinking ill of her cousin's intentions.

"Of course I will come." Dido said, putting aside her own feelings for Elizabeth's sake. She dressed hastily not wanting to be late, brushing aside Sarah insistence of re-doing her hair, so that she was able to stand beside Elizabeth before the first guest arrived. Dido was not acquainted with many of the guests with the exception of Margaret Ashley, James Hector and a young lady whose name had escaped her. At the dinner table Dido was able to observe the guests more closely. She took particular interest in Mr Bancroft who was seated to the right of Elizabeth but she found herself to be at a disadvantage, as she could not see him as she was seated to the left of Elizabeth. His manner seemed more reserved than James Hector, who at present was expressing the honour of the invitation to Lady Mansfield, which could be heard by the entire table. Dido noticed that Elizabeth deliberately kept her eyes from looking to Mr Hector but instead concentrated on speaking quietly to Mr Bancroft. Dido was seated between Lord Mansfield and Elizabeth but she paid close attention to the other end of the table where Margaret Ashley and James Hector sat. Directly across from Dido was Lady Mansfield's nephew George Finch-Hatton. Dido thought it odd that he should be among the guests, as he was considerably older gentleman, and unacquainted with Elizabeth. He said little, except to Lord Mansfield but whenever Dido glanced at him she found him staring thoughtfully in Elizabeth's direction. Though the young lady, Miss Banks, seated beside him, attempted to gain his attention by talking of the delights of the meal, she could only force from Mr Finch-Hatton a monosyllable response. Dido could see that the conversation at the other end of the table was much livelier. Margaret Ashley was talking of her wedding arrangements with much animation and for a moment Dido felt for Elizabeth, who could not help but hear what was being said. Surely Lady Mansfield must now be questioning her own judgement at extending an invitation to Margaret Ashley and James Hector, Dido thought. Thankfully, Elizabeth was rather preoccupied and was smiling at something that Mr Bancroft had said.

"Elizabeth is a keen painter, you know." Lord Mansfield said to Mr Finch-Hatton. Dido looked at her uncle in astonishment, as she could hardly believe her uncle's description of Elizabeth. What mischief was her uncle up to? To state that Elizabeth was keen on anything as creative as painting was an exaggeration of the extreme!
"I would be interested in seeing some of your paintings, Lady Elizabeth." Mr Finch-Hatton said civilly. Dido looked at him with surprise, as his show of interest seemed rather odd, as she supposed him incapable of being interested by anything. But Mr Finch-Hatton observed Lady Elizabeth not as a lover contemplating his future wife but as a man keenly aware of the mutual advantages of their match. When he had approached Lady Mansfield regarding his possible choice in Lady Elizabeth, he had been delighted to discover that Lady Mansfield was of the same mind regarding the favourability of the match and had desired it for some time. She warned him of the trifling affection Lady Elizabeth had toward a certain young man but due to their brief acquaintance it had not given rise to anything of substance. Mr Finch-Hatton could be satisfied by what he witnessed tonight that there was no risk to his plans where Mr Bancroft was concerned. Although she gave attention to the young man for much of the night her manner was not that of a woman in love. She was young and very impressionable and with his guidance and instruction their marriage would become a successful alliance. His only reservation was the family's attachment, in particular, Lady Elizabeth, to the black girl. In time, Mr Finch-Hatton hoped the proper etiquette would be restored and the attachment removed.

"My uncle is too kind in his praise. I hardly paint as I should!" Elizabeth replied somewhat taken aback by her uncle's praise.

"On the contrary I am well aware of your accomplishments." Lord Mansfield declared mockingly. At which Elizabeth laughed, unperturbed by her uncle's humour. Dido looked to Lord Mansfield with a lively interest, desirous of knowing the meaning for his teasing. Although Lord Mansfield was use to teasing Elizabeth on her lack of application to her art, he rarely complimented her on her talent. That he should do so now in the presence of Mr Finch-Hatton must, without doubt, place Elizabeth in a favourable light before the gentleman. Dido was curious to know her uncle's motive for doing so. But she could not dwell on the subject for long as her attention was once again taken by Margaret Ashley's cry of excitement at the other end of the table.

"Mama has promised me faithfully that we should be married at St Paul's," the lady boasted proudly. Dido hid her annoyance at Miss Ashley's constant talk of her wedding arrangements, deciding that the young lady could do with a good dose of modesty! She had hoped that Lady Mansfield would have had more success at discouraging Miss Ashley's outbursts for Elizabeth's sake. But she could not have known that Lady Mansfield, had, with increasing anxiety, listened to the excited chatter of Miss Ashley, while hoping that their utterances would not be heard at the other end of the table. Her attempts to show as little interest in the subject as possible did little to discourage the young lady. As Miss Ashley was determined to talk of nothing else but her forthcoming felicity and could not be deterred from the subject for long. Equally, Lady Mansfield's attempts to change the subject had failed on several occasions. Miss Ashley seemed determined to overwhelm everyone with her merriment, leaving Lady Mansfield to fear that her invitation had been ill judged. There was no way of avoiding the awkwardness that would come from her gaiety, which Lady Mansfield knew would be unpleasant for her niece. And though she ought to have felt gratitude to the young man who was taking up much of Elizabeth's attention, even this gave her cause for concern. Lady Mansfield had hoped that the evening would bring an opportunity for Elizabeth to become acquainted with her nephew George Finch-Hatton. Her intentions were simple enough. She had, for many years now, been secretly desirous of a match between her great niece and her nephew but had kept silent on the matter until Elizabeth was of a marriageable age. The favourability of the match could not be overlooked. The Winchilsea earldom on her father's side was a very important family seat. To join the two families again would be to both their advantages. The only concern for Lady Mansfield was Elizabeth's childish attachments for young men like James Hector and now Mr Bancroft. But she had not dissuaded Elizabeth's invitation to Mr Bancroft simply because she did not want to arouse any suspicion. When Lady Mansfield had first discussed the suitability of the match with her husband she was astounded to find that he was not in favour of it, as he thought Elizabeth too young and immature in her disposition to be suited to Mr Finch-Hatton, though he knew little of the gentleman's character. Lord Mansfield had been acquainted with Mr Finch-Hatton only briefly and found him to be a rather studious and haughty gentleman. But Lady Mansfield, being more familiar with his character had assured her husband of the respectability of his manners and the high regard in which he is held by those of his acquaintance. It was with great pains that Lady Mansfield continued to stress upon her husband the advantages of the union to both the respective families. Giving the matter his serious consideration, Lord Mansfield wasted little time in arranging private discussions with George Finch-Hatton, which showed the gentleman in the most favourable light. There was no doubt that Elizabeth would indeed benefit from the marriage and perhaps Mr Finch-Hatton's influence would go far in maturing her disposition. Lord Mansfield had to concede that all his wife's arguments were valid and once the benefits to Elizabeth could be seen, all resistance was removed. It was soon after agreed that Mr Finch-Hatton should be invited to the dinner party as a way of introduction, as well as providing Mr Finch-Hatton with the opportunity of observing Elizabeth before Lord and Lady Mansfield could arrange to speak to Elizabeth regarding the gentleman's proposal. Presently, Lord Mansfield found it quite amusing that their plan had gone awry, as the young gentleman had taken up all Elizabeth's attention, making it impossible for an acquaintance to be made with Mr Finch-Hatton within the course of the evening. However, Lord Mansfield observed that Mr Finch-Hatton's features did not show any signs of displeasure at being ignored by the lady. With the exception of his asking how long Elizabeth had known the young man at which Lord Mansfield had informed him that they had only been recently acquainted. Mr Finch-Hatton nodded throughout but said little, which left Lord Mansfield to wonder if he had not been right in his earlier assumption that the gentleman was far too serious to interest anyone as frivolous as Elizabeth.

Dido took her usual position at the pianoforte after dinner, preparing to perform for their guests, confident of the praise that would come from her performance. Her confidence was not a product of conceit, as Dido did not have a trace of vanity in her character. Rather her confidence came from her belief in her abilities and her power to please. She took little value in the praises of her audience, as she learnt from past experiences that there were some that were insincere in their salutations and others, she was sure, were often given either grudgingly or far too excessively in an effort to conceal feelings of envy. Dido had come to discern the varying compliments she received, which at first had caused her much vexation at not being duly appreciated. But time is a great healer and Dido was determined not to be so easily affected again. As she had learnt that appreciation came from those who were lovers of music rather than those who were lovers of fashion. Therefore Dido had acquired an indifferent attitude towards her audience and this helped her to find amusement in discerning their reactions. This little pastime calmed her nervousness, which she was obliged to feel from the anticipation of every performance. Thus, Dido was not surprised to find Margaret Ashley to be the most vocal among her admirers but she knew her exclamations came from her desire to sound more pleased that she actually was.

"How delightful! I'm sure I should have Dido play and sing at my wedding." She cried warmly. Her words proved too much for Lady Mansfield, who had become tired of hearing of the lady's forthcoming nuptials, and greatly regretted the invitation. Elizabeth perceived that Margaret Ashley's boastings were intended for her benefit and therefore gave greater efforts at trying to ignore them. Even James Hector was becoming bored of the subject as he gave Miss Ashley a dubious look.

"Dido's playing is capital but she would not do for such an occasion." Mr Hector stated nonchalantly and his words were received with an awkward silence.

"What makes you think that I would permit Dido to play at your wedding? You should be lucky to have her!" Lord Mansfield replied coldly. Mr Hector attempted with much stuttering to apologise for any misunderstanding, after realising too late that his comment had offended his host; but with little success was his continued apologises received. Mr Hector was left to feel Lord Mansfield's displeasure, as well as those who, for the sake of their host, contrived to express an offence that they did not actually feel. With the exception of Mr Finch-Hatton who looked on with an air of disapprobation. He had heard that Lord Mansfield pampered his black ward but he had not thought it be so unreserved in public. At least Mr Hector had succeeded where Lady Mansfield had failed for the entire evening to accomplish. There was no more talk of wedding arrangements for the rest of the evening.

After all the guests had taken their leave and Dido was alone in her room, her door was opened quietly by Elizabeth, who she half expected to see after an evening where there was much to be talked about.

"Margaret Ashley has shown herself to be rather disagreeable." Elizabeth remarked disapprovingly as she came into the room and sat on Dido's bed.

"And Mr Hector too, I dare say." Dido added, remembering his last comment with some mirth.

"I am sure you do not regret his choice now?" Dido asked after a moment's pause.

"No, I have been more fortunate than I first supposed. Margaret Ashley is welcomed to him." Elizabeth replied forcing a smile.

"Do you not think that Mr Bancroft conducted himself in a gentleman like manner?" Elizabeth boasted with pleasure.

On this occasion Dido was able to agree with her.

"Yes. Thankfully, Mr Bancroft has none of the ostentatious display of Mr Hector. He was very attentive to you." Dido said teasing her.

Certainly Mr Bancroft was a gentleman of a quiet and studious disposition. He talked much as he listened but was very thoughtful of every word that he spoke. In this he was the complete opposite of Mr Hector. But Dido could not see that he was any more suited to Elizabeth's disposition than Mr Hector. Elizabeth seemed to be taken with him though she was not as exuberant in her praises as she had been with Mr Hector. Dido was sure that here there was no real attachment at all and that Mr Bancroft had merely served as a distraction to disguise any hurt feelings on Elizabeth's part, at the sudden engagement of Mr Hector and Margaret Ashley.

"He is completely taken with me, don't you think?" Elizabeth smiled smugly. At this Dido was thankful that she could agree wholeheartedly.

# CHAPTER 10

"Miss Haversham has requested your company this weekend in London. I've agreed that you should go. I think the change would do you good." Lord Mansfield announced after breakfast. Dido looked to her uncle in amazement. Had she heard correctly? She was to go to London to visit Miss Haversham? Lord Mansfield had always been reluctant to let her go and stay with Miss Haversham in the past, in spite of Miss Haversham's constant pleadings. Dido was taken aback and said nothing for several seconds, wondering at the reason for his change of heart.

"I am pleased to go if you can spare me." Dido said simply, as she had no reason to feel any aversion to the plan. On the contrary, Dido felt pleased for the opportunity of going to London. Though she had been on more than one occasion with her family to their London home in Bloomsbury Square, it had been sometime since they had last been. Dido had always wanted to see a play or go to the opera, which she had only heard spoken of or read about in books or newspapers. She hoped that she would have the pleasure of doing so on this visit, knowing that Miss Haversham was very keen on the theatre. Lord Mansfield gave her a look of surprise as if expecting some protest on her part. But since none was forthcoming he shrugged his shoulders.

"Well it is settled then! "He said emphatically, leaving Dido to feel as if he was disappointed with her reaction to the news. How strange! Dido thought but then after some consideration concluded that perhaps she had mistook her uncle's reaction.

Dido waited out the remaining days until her departure with an air of increasing anticipation. Miss Haversham had written to assure her with much exhilaration that she would show her all the prominent sights that Dido, by the end of the letter was in high spirits at the prospect of her trip. She did not realise how excited she was becoming until her exuberance courted Elizabeth's displeasure, who had hoped to be included in the trip to London. Failing to persuade her aunt and uncle, Elizabeth had gone into a sulk which threatened to dampen Dido's merriment. If Dido was of a spiteful disposition she could have reminded her cousin of her own excitement, not so long ago, at being invited to stay with the Ashley's, but she was sure it would have made no difference where Elizabeth's sulky deposition was concerned. There was nothing to be done but to confine her merriment until when she was alone.

When the day of her departure to London had arrived and her aunt and uncle were there to see her off, Dido was surprised to hear that Elizabeth chose to stay indoors, complaining of a terrible headache and did not wish to catch a chill. She hid her disappointment at the news but she would not let it spoil her excitement at the prospect of seeing London again.   The journey to London filled Dido with immense pleasure.  There was so much to see that she did not know where to look.  There was such a mixture of sights to behold, people, houses, crowded streets and markets, imposing structures that inspired awe, so much in contrast to the squalid and dirty buildings filled with despair. Dido watched as ladies and gentlemen strolled along fare-ways and parks.  She was totally engaged by the sights before her that she was unaware that the carriage had stopped outside the house of Miss Haversham and the carriage door was opened immediately by Miss Haversham herself, who was talking away excitedly even before the face of Miss Dido could be seen.

"You are here at last! Oh I have such treats for you!" Miss Haversham cried eagerly as she led Dido into the house.  Dido could only smile, as she had no time to answer her question before another was posed, as Miss Haversham rattled away,

"How was your journey?"

"You must be tired, how would you like a lovely cup of tea, my dear?"

"Or perhaps you would like to freshen up instead?"

Miss Haversham continued in this vain scarcely listening to Dido's response, before depositing her in a charming guest room, with the assurance that a maid would be sent to her presently.  Dido smiled to herself at the swiftness of Miss Haversham's decision-making, thankful for a moment's peace.  Though she was very fond of Miss Haversham and thought her to be a good natured woman, her continuous chatter could be rather trying even for her patience, Dido thought as she moved towards the window to peer out at the view.  Her room faced the front of the house, and she could see identical houses around the square, which looked down onto a small but pleasant green. Dido contented herself with observing the people and carriages that passed by until she was interrupted by the arrival of the maid.

Dido found Miss Haversham in the drawing room awaiting her return.

"Ah, Dido, how charming you look." She remarked smiling pleasantly "Have some tea dear."

"Thank you." Dido replied courteously, taking a seat next to Miss Haversham.

"How are Lord and Lady Mansfield? Such charming people."

Dido had scarcely finished answering this query before Miss Haversham began to talk of something else.

"I was pleasantly surprised at Lord Mansfield finally consenting to your visit. Though I don't know why he should delay so long. We should have such fun. I have planned a delightful evening for us." Miss Haversham said pleased with herself for having arranged dinner with Mrs Gray at such short notice.

"We will dine out with Mrs Gray and her family, a dear friend of mine. Let's just say it's a small party but I'm sure you will enjoy yourself as there will be several young people of your age." Miss Haversham continued without taking a breath, as Dido felt slightly alarmed at the news of having to form new acquaintances so soon after arriving in London.

"Tomorrow I shall show you the sights. Perhaps we could go to the theatre in the evening. How does that sound? We shall see if we can find you a nice young gentleman, eh?" Miss Haversham said with a short laugh.

Dido immediately felt ill at ease at the idea that Miss Haversham's intention of inviting her to London purely for the purpose of finding her a suitor. How disagreeable! All her former excitement immediately diminished and every hope of a pleasant stay in London seemed threatened by the fear of Miss Haversham succeeding in her scheme of finding her a beau. She could never consent to any such match making schemes, and attempted to make her feelings clear.

"Please, Miss Haversham, I have no interest in finding a beau." Dido said firmly but graciously.

"I'm sure when you find someone agreeable you will change your mind." Miss Haversham replied dismissively, as she was convinced that every young woman was desirous of being courted. Dido protested but to no avail. Miss Haversham could not be dissuaded, so Dido decided to remain silent and let the matter drop.

While they were seated in the carriage on the way to Mrs Gray, Miss Haversham began again where she left off on her favourite subject.

"There is a fine young gentleman, Mrs Gray's nephew, a Mr Robert Harding. A charming gentleman, I am sure you will find him very agreeable." Miss Haversham remarked and went on to give a full description of Mr Harding's person and character. Dido forced herself to smile agreeably but felt little merriment as she suspected that the whole evening to be ruined by this news. But when they entered the dining room of Mrs Gray, Dido found to her relief that although there were a few young people gathered, there was no one fitting the description of Mr Harding.

"Oh dear, your nephew is not here tonight Mrs Gray?" Miss Haversham asked as soon as the introductions were made, feeling some disappointment at the gentlemen's absence.

"No, unfortunately he had another engagement." Mrs Gray replied apologetically, sensing Miss Haversham's disappointment.

"What a pity." Miss Haversham remarked regretfully.

"So we finally have the pleasure of meeting Miss Dido. It is indeed a great pleasure." Mrs Gray said pleasantly, rather amazed by Dido's superior manner and speech. Mrs Gray acknowledged that though her skin was dark, her features were attractive and very appealing.

Dido soon discovered that the young people consisted mainly of Mrs Gray's children. There were four young ladies between the ages of eighteen and twenty-three years, a young man aged two and twenty, a Miss Ross, a friend of the eldest Miss Gray and an elderly gentleman, Mr Adams an acquaintance of Mr Gray. Dido was delighted at the outcome, and felt immediately at ease, pleased that Miss Haversham's matchmaking scheme had been put on hold for the evening. Miss Gray was very eager to converse with Dido, being the eldest and boldest of her sisters she was use to speaking for them. She acted as mediator for her sisters who were too shy to ask questions directly to their guest. Dido was left the task of answering numerous questions from the sisters, who in excited whispers passed the queries to the eldest Miss Gray.

"Do you live only at Kenwood Miss Dido?"

Have you been to London before?"

"How old are you?" Have you any brothers or sisters?"

Dido was pleased to answer their questions and did so with much patience, until Mrs Gray feeling that her daughters were taking advantage of their guest's kindness put an end to it. But not before Miss Gray was able to request that Dido play for them after dinner, as they had heard from Miss Haversham that she played exquisitely. Dido assured her that she would be delighted to play for them. At the dinner table Miss Gray was quick to take a seat beside Dido eager to continue their conversation.

"It is not often that we get such important guests here." Miss Gray said civilly

"I heard that Kenwood is a beautiful estate, is it very large?" the young lady continued

"Yes, it is very beautiful but it is not very large." Dido replied

"Is it true that the King visited Lord Mansfield?"

"Yes, it is true." Dido replied, smiling at the look of amazement on the face of Miss Gray.

"Have you received many a royal guests at Kenwood?"

"On occasion." Dido replied, and felt compelled for Miss Gray's sake to describe some of the events at which there were royal guests in attendance.

The evening passed pleasantly and at the end of it Mrs Gray and her daughters pleaded for Dido to come again.

"Lord Mansfield is so protective of her. I do not know when I will be able to have her again, I'm sure." Miss Haversham said to Mrs Gray in earnest. Dido left feeling very satisfied with her first night in London. As for Mrs Gray and her family, they were so delighted with Dido's visit that it proved a popular talking point for their future guests for many years.

The following morning Miss Haversham took Dido out in the open carriage for a sightseeing tour of London. Once again Dido found herself mesmerised by the sights of crowded streets and the variety of people that walked about. It was a pleasant spring morning and Dido although enjoying the view from the carriage was desirous of walking. She paid little attention to the stares that she received, as she was far too excited to be affected by them. Soon after, her attention was completely taken up by the sight of a black boy, no more than seven or eight, walking hurriedly behind a well-dressed lady. Dido could not help but stare openly, turning her head almost completely around to watch him until he disappeared out of sight. She did not know how to feel so disturbed were her thoughts at the sight of this poor wretched child. Was he a slave or a servant? Was he happy? What had become of his parents? These questions preoccupied her thoughts as the carriage took him further away from her. She could not help but feel a pang of sadness at the thought that she would never see him again. If Miss Haversham had spoken she had not heard her. Not that it mattered, as the lady was quite content to chatter away to herself without the interaction of others.

"Time for some tea I think." Miss Haversham suggested and had to repeat it several times before a distracted Dido was able to answer in agreement.

"We are here at last!" Miss Haversham exclaimed with some relief as the carriage stopped and the footman helped her down. Dido followed, looking curiously about as they proceeded into a large impressive building, rather crowded with people sitting down to tea. Dido hardly knew where to look so conscious was she of the open stares that she received. How ironic, she thought, that simple decorum was disregarded for the satisfaction of an eager curiosity. To Dido's relief, they were finally seated at a table. No sooner had they sat down Miss Haversham was calling to various people of her acquaintance. Some of who returned her greeting with forced politeness, while others pretended not to see or hear her at all. Miss Haversham was oblivious to any slight, much to Dido's embarrassment, she continued to call to familiar faces as and when she saw them.

"My, it is crowded in here today." She said pleased at being familiar with many of the people present.

"There are so many young men too." She added winking vulgarly, looking around her and smiling broadly. Dido thinking it best not to encourage her remained silent. To Dido's dismay, a young gentleman approached their table and bowed gallantly to Miss Haversham and then to herself.

"Ah! Mr Harding, what a pleasant surprise!" Miss Haversham exclaimed with delight.

"How naughty of you to abandon us yesterday evening" Miss Haversham scolded him, as he attempted to apologise with the reason for his absence. He spoke eloquently with good humour and pretended to be suitably chastised by Miss Haversham's words. Dido thought his appearance to be tolerable but his manner and speech were not to her liking as they were very much like those of Mr Hector's.

"Let me introduce you to Miss Dido, ward of Lord Mansfield." She announced proudly

"A pleasure Miss Dido." Mr Harding said and nodded smiling as Dido returned the greeting.

"How are you enjoying your stay in London, Miss Dido?" he enquired pleasantly.

"Very well, thank you, sir. It is rather more crowded than I expected." Dido replied civilly.

"No doubt, but there are many diversions here. And I'm sure Miss Haversham will give you the opportunity of enjoying the delights of the theatre."

"What a splendid idea!" Miss Haversham declared excitedly

"I have a box with available seats. Perhaps this evening if you are free?"

"Thank you Mr Harding we will be delighted to take you up on your offer." Miss Haversham eagerly accepted the invitation for both of them. Dido decided that the delights of seeing the opera ought to outweigh any matchmaking designs of Miss Haversham.

"Isn't it splendid luck, meeting Mr Harding here? His father is Sir Harding, and he is quite a catch being his only son, you know." Miss Haversham said beaming with satisfaction, as soon as Mr Harding had left their table. But Dido was fearful of Mr Harding still being in earshot, could hardly contain her embarrassment.

"My word, I could not have planned it better myself." She declared with a laugh.

Dido had to endure the chatter of Miss Haversham's delights on the journey back to the house, as she continued to congratulate herself on their fortuitous engagement for the evening. But Dido was able to listen with reasonable calm as the pleasure of attending the opera added much to her fortitude.

Dido's heart was beating with excited anticipation as they neared the theatre house. She could hardly listen with patience as Miss Haversham rattled on about Mr Harding's gracious invitation. Dido nodded whenever she felt she was required to, in an effort not to appear discourteous. Her only fear was that her pleasurable evening might be spoilt by the unwanted attentions of Mr Harding. But she could not dwell on this for long as her mind had already raced ahead to the crowded hall and to the opening curtains, which would signify the first act. As they entered the crowded reception hall Dido did her best to ignore the many stares that she received, thankful for the extra care that she had taken with her dress. They arrived in Mr Harding's box to find him already seated with two ladies. One of them he introduced as his sister, Miss Mary Harding, the other a friend, Miss Sylvia Curtis. Miss Harding's countenance did not change during the exchange. She merely nodded politely. Her dark hair pulled tightly into a bun made her appear rather austere than perhaps she was. Miss Curtis, on the other hand, smiled prettily, bringing a glow to her handsome features, which Dido felt that Miss Curtis was rather confident of the fact. Dido could not help but think that Miss Curtis was the sort of person who enjoyed the company of plain people, knowing that her own beauty was shown to its best advantage. In this, Miss Curtis had chosen her friend well, as in Miss Harding she had found the perfect companion to show herself off. Miss Curtis smiled often whenever Mr Harding spoke, which led Dido to conclude that perhaps there was some attachment between the two, or at least a desire of one on the lady's part. Dido was relieved to find herself seated behind the trio beside Miss Haversham. But her relief was short-lived as Miss Haversham continued to interrupt her with tedious questions throughout the first two acts of the play, until Dido could hardly give her complete attention to the enjoyment of it. If Miss Haversham was not asking questions she would be fidgeting and sighing noisily, so much so that on a few occasions Miss Harding or Miss Curtis would turn and stare disapprovingly, so as to make Dido feel rather embarrassed by her company. Dido thought that even the attentions of Mr Harding would be much preferred to this! She now realised how wholly mistaken she had been in thinking that Mr Harding had any interest in her. Except for a polite enquiry during the break as to whether she was enjoying the play, he had said little else in her direction. She was left to feel rather foolish for her earlier concerns but had never felt more relieved at being so mistaken in her judgement. Dido was grateful that during the middle of the second act that Miss Haversham quietly dosed off and she had the opportunity to enjoy the performance. Her enjoyment of the theatre was all she had anticipated, so as to make Dido decide it to be one of the highlights of her stay in London.

# CHAPTER 11

"Who was that severe looking gentleman? I am sure I have seen him before but I cannot remember where." Dido said to Elizabeth when they were alone at leisure.   Earlier that morning, Dido had seen the gentleman in attendance with Lord Mansfield when coming down from her room. His face was so familiar that Dido felt sure she should know him.   At her enquiry Elizabeth's complexion became flushed and her manner awkward for several minutes.

"Mr George Finch-Hatton." She answered demurely. Then suddenly grasping Dido's hand with great agitation, she cried unhappily,

"My aunt and uncle says that he is to be my future husband!"

Dido was startled by her cousin's sudden outburst and for a second this robbed her of all ability to speak.

"Your husband?" Dido exclaimed in disbelief, when she could find her voice.

"Are you sure? How is it possible? He is far too old for you!" Dido added not waiting for Elizabeth to reply.  So stunned was she by the news that she could scarcely comprehend poor Elizabeth's miserable state for she had so many questions but no patience in which to listen to the answering of them.

"When did Lady Mansfield inform you of this?" she asked, staring intently at Elizabeth's countenance for a hint of any possibility that this could be all a dreadful mistake.  Surely it must be!

"When you were away at Miss Haversham's in London."   Elizabeth answered trying to compose herself once again.

"But what of Mr Bancroft? Were you not fond of him?" Dido enquired, remembering how enamoured Elizabeth had been just only last week when she had continued to bore Dido with repetitive talk of Mr Bancroft's affability and amiable qualities. Dido was certain that some sort of attachment had been formed.

"Oh Dido, it is not as simple as that!" Elizabeth exclaimed irritably.

"There is the matter of family obligation. In our social standing it is paramount that we are connected with the *right* family. Granted I am not keen on the idea but George Finch-Hatton is a man of importance. The marriage is most favourable and my family will benefit from the alliance." She concluded with an air of resignation.  Dido was astonished both at hearing Elizabeth speech and manner. She could not recognise the creature before her. Where did she acquire such a calm and subdued manner? The Elizabeth who could be irrational and self-centred and quite wilful in getting her own way, had completely vanished in that moment.

"Then you have accepted?" Dido asked in amazement.

"Of course, what else am I to do? It is the wish of Lord and Lady Mansfield. How can I possibly refuse after all that they have done for me." Elizabeth replied in equal astonishment at Dido for even asking such a question.

"But you don't know him?" Dido cried forcibly unable to contain her emotions.

"That will come in time I suspect but we are not getting married tomorrow you know. I have almost a year before then." Elizabeth replied distractedly.

Dido was all astonishment. She did not know which was most astounding. The news of the Elizabeth's forthcoming engagement or her impassive acceptance of it! Perhaps Dido would not have been so aghast at Elizabeth's manner had she witnessed her initial reaction upon hearing the news. She would have been more pitiable of her cousin's position. For on hearing the news from her uncle and aunt, Elizabeth had cried violently for the whole afternoon and had pleaded with her aunt to reconsider, as she was sure to be marrying Mr Bancroft soon. It took Lord and Lady Mansfield a considerable length of time that evening to calm and convince her of the benefits of the match. Elizabeth had at least a year in which to prepare herself for the marriage, as her uncle thought her far too immature at present. Their words had produced such a positive affect that when she met George Finch-Hatton several days later Elizabeth was tolerably composed enough to receive him in a civil manner. Though she found him stiff and formal and not as agreeable in appearance as she would have desired, his distinguished air commanded respect and his manners were not displeasing. Elizabeth was hopeful that her affection would grow with time. Dido on the other hand was in a state of astonishment at the very thought of Elizabeth's marriage, which continued for days and weeks. Her mind was in a state of disturbance as she attempted to irrationalise her feelings. How dreadful to be given away like a piece of property for the mere gratification of social status and standing! Were women no more than property and marriage no more than a business agreement? How much difference was there from a position of a slave that simply class and money could justify? The more Dido thought on the matter the more inclined she was to keep to her earlier vow of never being married. She was grateful that no such demand could be made upon her. Dido was persuaded that even on the eve of the day of Elizabeth's wedding to George Finch-Hatton, she could not reconcile herself to the suitability of the match. She had on several occasions sought to bring the subject up with her uncle but feared that he would talk of finding her a husband! Feeling only pity for her cousin, Dido continued to marvel at the calmness in which Elizabeth faced her impending doom. But Dido's fears for Elizabeth were unfounded, as Elizabeth had begun to look upon her impending marriage in a more favourable light. The announcement of her engagement had produced much fuss and attention, that Elizabeth found wherever she went she was highly praised for the match, and this had done much to sway her opinion.

# CHAPTER 12

The rest of the winter at Kenwood passed uneventfully until the coming of the spring and summer. Lady Mansfield had been less than her usual self. She stayed more frequently in bed, sometimes calling for Dido or Elizabeth to read to her in the afternoons. Dido was happy to do so, but she was becoming anxious as each new day that passed brought no improvement in her aunt's condition. She spoke to Elizabeth, who also noticed the prolonged duration of her aunt's illness.

"I'm sure she will recover in time. Remember the old have not the quickness of recovery as the young." Elizabeth remarked

"Yes. I'm sure you are right." Dido replied, feeling perhaps she had been overly anxious. But Dido could not help voicing her concern to her uncle a few days later.

"We are getting old Dido. It takes longer for our bodies to recover." He answered, saying the same as Elizabeth had said, but his eyes betrayed a troubled look.

"I give you leave to call the doctor if she does not improve in a few days." He conceded in hope of appeasing her worries. His manner only added to her fears. Could it be that he was trying to hide something from her? How is it that she had not given more attention to them both? Dido chided herself severely. She decided to keep a closer eye on Lady Mansfield, as she sat beside her bed the following morning desirous of discovering her aunt's ailment.

"Are you going to read that book?" Lady Mansfield asked impatiently, interrupting Dido's thoughts. Lady Mansfield had not opened her eyes but was forced to by the absence of a response to her question.

"Are you not well girl?" Lady Mansfield asked with a hint of concern.

"I am perfectly well, madam. Would it not be more pleasant to sit in the garden? The weather is so agreeable..."

"I have no wish to be caught outdoors!"

"If you are still feeling poorly, please let me call for a doctor." Dido cried, even as she spoke she knew that her words would be met with disapproval but she could not keep silent.

"Have you gone completely mad? Stop fussing girl..." Lady Mansfield cried but could not finish as she began to cough excessively.

"Please tell me what is wrong? How can I assist?" Dido said anxiously moving towards the side table to fetch some water as Lady Mansfield gestured with her hand in the same direction. But she shook her head as

Dido came with the water, still pointing towards the dresser. Dido turned to look back at the dresser, uncertain of her aunt's request.

"In, in the drawer-" she said breathlessly in between coughs

Dido moved quickly to the dresser and opened the drawer and reached for a small medicine bottle, which could only be what her aunt was in need of. She opened it not knowing what was inside and placed it into the outstretched hand. Dido stood transfixed as she watched her aunt drink hurriedly from the bottle before lying weakly back against the pillow. The cough had not yet subsided but Dido quickly took the bottle from her aunt's hand and attempted to administer some more medicine. Lady Mansfield shook her head, her eyes tightly closed. To see her aunt like this gave Dido moments of great distress. She hurriedly called for the maid to fetch Elizabeth and to send for the doctor immediately. Unsure of what else to do, Dido sat beside her aunt, anxiously waiting, afraid to leave her alone in the event that she would have another attack. She had known all along that something was wrong but she could not possibly have guessed that her aunt was so ill. Elizabeth arrived looking anxiously at Dido.

"What is it? Is there something wrong with my aunt?" she asked, her anxiety increasing on seeing Lady Mansfield pallid face.

Dido proceeded to tell her of what had occurred, adding that she thought it best to send for her uncle who was working in London. Elizabeth agreed.

"Yes it is for the best." Elizabeth replied absently, as she went to sit beside Lady Mansfield. A messenger was sent to Lord Mansfield to notify him of his wife's worsening condition. There was nothing to do but wait for the arrival of the doctor. It was above half an hour before the coughing had stopped and Lady Mansfield's countenance appeared now serene. Dido now began to feel that perhaps she had overreacted in calling for the doctor and for her uncle. Her aunt seemed to be dozing peacefully just as the doctor arrived.

"How is she?" He said hurriedly as he neared the bed, placing his bag on the table.

"She is much recovered." Dido answered. Doctor Robertson smiled reassuringly at seeing the apprehension on the faces of both the young ladies.

"Ah, your ladyship is still with us." He said in mock relief upon feeling her pulse, at which Lady Mansfield awoke and pulled her arm away.

"What are you doing?" she asked sharply, giving the doctor an irritable look. Doctor Robertson took little notice of Lady Mansfield manner. He was too familiar with her complaints over the years that he had learnt that the best way to handle her ladyship was with humour and much patience, which sometimes irked as well as puzzled his patient.

"Your ladyship is not well?" he continued as he attempted again to check her pulse

"Don't tell me you have been listening to that foolish girl." Lady Mansfield replied in the direction of Dido but without the harshness her words meant to convey.

"It is best to check to make sure everything is as it should be. Perhaps the young ladies could leave us for a moment, while I examine your ladyship." Dr Robertson stated

"I will call you presently." The doctor reassured them both on seeing their hesitation.

Dido and Elizabeth left the room reluctantly, unable to remove the uneasiness they both felt at their aunt's condition.

"Will her ladyship be alright, miss?" one of the maids asked, as they stood in the corridor.

"Yes, of course." Dido replied hastily but feeling none of the confidence her voice attempted to express.

"Matthews said that Lord Mansfield would be on his way shortly, Miss Dido."

"Thank you." Dido replied distractedly. Once again she wished she had not sent for her uncle so quickly. Her message would no doubt bring much anxiety and would have worried him unduly! Though Dido regretted her decision, it was too late to worry at present. Dido said as much to Elizabeth,

"Oh nonsense. I'm sure Uncle William would want to be informed." Elizabeth encouraged.

"Dr Robertson how is Lady Mansfield?" Dido asked on seeing the doctor closing the door to Lady Mansfield's room.

"Is Lord Mansfield here?" he asked instead, not answering her question.

"I have sent for him but he has not yet arrived." Dido replied anxiously, waiting for Dr Robertson to say more but he appeared reluctant to speak further.

"Dr Robertson, please do not humour us. How is Lady Mansfield? Why do you not tell us? Is she so poorly?" Elizabeth cried, then suddenly broke into tears and had to be taken to her room aided by both Dido and Dr Robertson. After tending to Elizabeth Dr Robertson asked to wait to see Lord Mansfield.

"Of course doctor, please follow me." Dido said politely, but feeling rather fretful that he had failed to answer their question. Was she right in assuming that Lady Mansfield's condition was far more serious than they had first suspected? Why did he not say? Dido could not keep silent any longer.

"Lady Mansfield will be ok?" Dido asked again

"Lady Mansfield needs complete rest." He answered and said no more.

"Will you keep me in suspense? I am not a child!" Dido cried unable to contain her temper any longer for the turmoil of her feelings.

"Dido, my reason for saying little is because I do not want to worry you unduly."

"I apologise for my impudence. I speak only from my affection for Lady Mansfield." Dido spoke tearfully.

"I know child." Dr Robertson said kindly, feeling a sense of regret at the prospect of having to give bad news.

"Ah! Dr Robertson-" Lord Mansfield could be heard saying from the hall. He had hurried from the carriage not knowing what to expect. On hearing that his wife had taken ill, he had feared the worst. As he sat in the carriage, every delay to his journey caused his mind to be in a state of disturbance and impatience to be home. Now his face appeared grave and etched with worry as he stood before the physician.

"-how is she?"

"Lord Mansfield, if I may have a word with you in private?" Dr Robertson asked soberly

"Yes, of course." He answered, before leading the doctor into the library.

Dido stood motionless for several minutes, not sure how to act or to think. She walked towards the library door with thoughts of eavesdropping but felt guilty for such a contemplation. She could not be idle! So anxious was she to hear of what was being said. Rather than suffer the misery of waiting for news, Dido decided to return to her aunt. She had not taken but a few steps up the stairs when the door was suddenly opened and Dr Robertson appeared closing the door directly behind him. Dido watched him walk to the door and for a moment she thought he would leave without retrieving his hat and coat, so distracted was his manner but then, as if remembering himself, he suddenly stopped and collected them from the doorman. Dido waited until he had left before she went to the library and knocked on the door. When there was no response to her knock she took courage and entered. Lord Mansfield was sitting at the desk, holding a book in his hand. His face was drawn and tired as he sat in silent contemplation. Dido moved into the room and for a moment he did not seem to be aware of her presence. She stood silently, regretting her decision to intrude upon his privacy. Lord Mansfield looked up suddenly and on seeing her gave a weary sigh and held out his hand. It was all the assurance that Dido needed to go to him. She knelt beside him waiting for him to speak. She could no longer ask the question that she had for so long waited to hear the answer to.

"We must prepare ourselves." He said shortly, his voice losing its strength. He did not have to say anymore. Dido knew that they would soon be alone. She could feel his grief and forgetting her own she yearned only to comfort him. How old he looked and yet like a lost child he appeared helpless at the prospect of his inevitable loss. Dido could not find words of comfort but instead silent tears fell. She held tightly to his hand and they remained in this solemn position, neither able to express the sorrow that had overcome them both.

# CHAPTER 13

The loss of Lady Mansfield was grievously felt at Kenwood but each expression of grief was displayed discreetly, with the exception of the occasional outbursts by a distraught Elizabeth. Lord Mansfield continued to go about his work and leisure with much effort but would often find his thoughts drifting back to his wife and would sigh deeply and then carry on as before. Dido watched him with a heavy heart and made every effort to cheer him when she could. There were times when she felt the sadness of their loss overwhelmingly and when free from observation, alone in the privacy of her room would cry silently. Dido felt that Elizabeth took the loss of her aunt as well as could be expected. There were moments of alarm when she refused to leave her room on the morning of the funeral, and the doctor had to be called and the invalid confined to bed for the rest of the day. Then there were days when Elizabeth would become melancholy and insist on being taken to her aunt's grave, where she would weep hysterically for hours afterwards. Dido made every effort to cheer her but her fears that Elizabeth's grief would affect her health had her pleading with her cousin to exert herself to recover.

"She was like a mother to me." Elizabeth whimpered before falling back on her pillow in fits of tears.

"She loved you like a daughter." Dido said knowing this would please her.

"Oh Dido, what will I do without her!" she cried again

"Lizzy please, you must be strong. What good would it do to make yourself ill? Lady Mansfield would not have wanted it." Dido pleaded hoping to influence Elizabeth with her words.

"I know-" she agreed weakly

"Come now, everyone is anxious for your health. It would do well if you show them that they have no need for concern. " Dido encouraged as she attempted to persuade her. She knew all too well that Elizabeth was an emotional creature and was therefore accustom to giving into her feelings with much passion. Not that Dido doubted the sincerity of Elizabeth's grief, knowing how much she had loved her aunt. But she feared that Elizabeth's emotional state could lead to much injury.

"Think of your uncle. You know how much he suffers himself. It would not do for him to be worried about you as well." Dido pleaded

"Of course not, poor uncle, he misses her dearly, as I do. I will do my best to appear cheerful." Elizabeth relented, so as to cause Dido to give her a look of disbelief.

"Dear Dido, I promise."

Dido smiled gratefully at Elizabeth, thankful that her pleadings had proved beneficial.

Once Elizabeth was able to come to terms with her grief, Dido's sole concern was for Lord Mansfield. She fretted when he did not eat or if he stayed too long at his work. She hovered cautiously making sure he did not go to bed too late. Her anxious nagging often received a sharp rebuke but she could not deny her feeling of responsibility towards him.

"You are behaving like a tiresome old woman." Lord Mansfield crumbled in response to her reminder for him again to stop and eat.

"I am only looking after your welfare sir." Dido replied disregarding his complaints.

"Would you prefer I neglect you?" Dido asked purposely sounding hurt at his words. She was satisfied that her words produced the desired result, as Lord Mansfield shifted and mumbled to himself as he attempted to take a few more mouthful of the food.

"You are all I have now." Dido said earnestly unable to look at him for fear that he would see her tears.

"Hush child." He said patting her hand affectionately.

"I give you leave to bully and cajole me in any which way you choose." Lord Mansfield added good-humouredly

"Do not tease with me, sir. I am afraid you will leave me too." Dido said tearfully.

"I have no plans to go just yet. Come now you will have me cry too?"

Dido smiled incredulously at the idea of her uncle crying. In all her years she had not seen her uncle showing his grief with the exception of Lady Mansfield's death. How she yearned to embrace him but had to refrain from such a warm display of affection. An embrace from a daughter or a niece was acceptable. But not from an illegitimate black niece, all propriety must be observed. Dido could remember as a child how in her innocence she had openly shown her affection for her uncle with her embraces, unaware that her actions were being frowned upon, until one morning Lord Mansfield brought it to her attention. In truth, Lord Mansfield had seen nothing wrong with Dido's display of affection as her fondness pleased him. But though he disagreed with his wife's disapproval of Dido's open affection, Lord Mansfield had to concede that his wife's concerns could prove well-founded in the future, if Dido's affectionate nature was not soon after constrained. It pained Lord Mansfield to explain the awkwardness of Dido's displays of affection, knowing as he did that she could not possibly understand the impropriety of it.

"It is best if we do not displease anyone further. Do you understand child?" Lord Mansfield asked affectionately as Dido stared blankly at him.

"Yes sir." Dido answered obediently though she understood little of the meaning of his words. She was sure Lady Mansfield was the cause of this talk as she always rebuked her sharply whenever she had shown any affection towards her uncle. How mean of Lady Mansfield not to allow her the pleasure of embracing her dear uncle if she so wished!

"A lady must curtsey, like this." He said and attempted to demonstrate. Dido looked on rather amused as she thought her uncle looked rather funny holding out the tail of his coat like a dress.

"I know how to do it. I have seen it done many times, sir." Dido said and curtseyed accordingly.

"Good, good. Well now you are a perfect young lady." Lord Mansfield teased. Dido was so pleased by her uncle's praise that she had forgotten for a moment that she would no longer be permitted to embrace her uncle as before. It was with remembrance of her loss that the feelings of ill will towards her aunt kindled in Dido's heart. In her childish indignation she had vowed never to speak to Lady Mansfield again. The vow lasted only a few days as Dido held to her vow stoically, deliberately ignoring Lady Mansfield's words while pretending to be ignorant of them. Dido had taken great delight in seeing her aunt's increasing annoyance.

"Have you gone deaf girl?" lady Mansfield was forced to say on more than one occasion.

"The girl has gone positively wild!" She exclaimed on another occasion when Dido sat down without answering a word to her enquiry. Lord Mansfield look of concern aroused in Dido a feeling of guilt, which forced her to confess that perhaps her vow of silence was rather impractical and was likely to send her to an orphanage if she were to continue! Dido resolved instead to restrict her replies to monosyllables and civil salutations. This she did. But instead of exasperating her aunt as she had hoped, to her mortification, after a few weeks into her scheme, she discovered that she had accomplished the complete opposite when Lady Mansfield's commented on her change of behaviour.

"Finally you have learnt to hold your tongue. Perhaps there is some hope of your turning out well after all." Lady Mansfield said grudgingly.

"Elizabeth you too can learn something from Dido's conduct." Lady Mansfield added to a bewildered Elizabeth who had no idea of her conduct being anything but proper.

Dido was astounded. Until that day she could not remember ever receiving any praise from her aunt, only criticism. Perhaps it was not such a bad thing to be in her aunt's favour. Dido had never entertained the thought of deliberately displeasing her aunt until her recent scheme but she had found it almost impossible to please Lady Mansfield even when making an effort to do so! If all it took was an abstinence from speaking, Dido felt this could be easily accomplished. When it was discovered that Dido had an exceptional talent for playing the pianoforte, her worth was further increased in Lady Mansfield's esteem. And for the first time Dido could not help but be pleasantly affected by her favoured position with her aunt.

# Chapter 14

Elizabeth and George Finch-Hatton were married the following year after Lady Mansfield death. The wedding was a regal and lavish ceremony, to the delight of Elizabeth, who glowed with self-importance at the attention bestowed upon her by all the guests. Dido observed Elizabeth's countenance with bewilderment as she could not reconcile herself with the happiness that she saw there. How could her cousin be so content to be married to a man she knew so little of, and seemed so ill suited to. Surely the mere idea of being admired could not be the reason for Elizabeth glowing features? Dido pitied such shallow feelings. But Elizabeth could well afford to be content, as Dido feelings were among the minority as there were many young ladies who looked on with both envy and admiration at the happy bride.

A letter from Elizabeth arrived at Kenwood House one afternoon while Lord Mansfield and Dido sat at leisure.

"Ah! A letter from Elizabeth," Lord Mansfield said with interest, looking pleased to hear from his niece again. Several months after settling into her new home at Eastwell Park, Elizabeth had sent an invitation requesting her uncle's presence at their first dinner party. After some discussion as to whether the invitation should be accepted without Dido, it was eventually agreed that Lord Mansfield should go alone. Dido assured her uncle that she had no wish to cause any problems, as she had long become indifferent to the slight of strangers, whose opinions she cared little for. Dido suspected this deliberate *slight* was all Mr Finch-Hatton's doing. She could not imagine for a moment that her cousin would leave her out of an invitation to visit. Elizabeth had included in the letter her regret of not extending her invitation to Dido on *this* occasion adding with all raptures that she looked forward to the prospect of seeing her fairly soon. Elizabeth was true to her word.

"She appears to be under the weather at present." Lord Mansfield said with concern.

"What ails her?" Dido asked anxiously, watching Lord Mansfield closely as he perused the letter.

"She does not say what but she is asking for you to be sent to stay for a few weeks. You will go of course the change of scenery will do you some good." Lord Mansfield said not waiting for Dido's response. Although Dido was happy to be of assistance to her cousin in her time of need, she did not like the idea of being *sent* anywhere as if she was a piece of baggage. Besides, the thought of leaving her uncle alone for any length of time gave Dido some anxiety.

"I would love to go and visit Elizabeth, but I could not leave you alone." Dido said adamantly, hoping that Lord Mansfield would reconsider his decision for the present.

"No. You must go, as Elizabeth needs your companionship." Lord Mansfield replied observing her look of disappointment.

"Do not worry about me, I shall be well. Miss Jenkins will keep an eye on me while you're away." He assured her with a smile

"You must be tired of looking after an old man." He added teasingly but Dido was not in the mood for his teasing. She felt deeply disappointed that he should send her away for two whole weeks. How was she to ensure that he was being properly cared for? She hated the thought of leaving him alone. It took her several days before she could reconcile herself to the thought of going to Eastwell Park. But by the day of her departure Dido found to her surprise that she was actually feeling excited at the prospect of seeing Elizabeth again and a little curious as to see how well she was settling into her new life as Lady Finch-Hatton. Perhaps her uncle was right a visit with Elizabeth could prove beneficial for her. Since Lady Mansfield's death Dido had been wholly preoccupied with her uncle's health that she had completely neglected herself. She had missed her cousin dearly. Especially during the long winter months when Dido was often confined to the house, and with no Elizabeth to talk to and not being able to spend as much time with her uncle as she would wish, she often found herself feeling rather melancholy. Now as she felt the fresh breeze against her face and Kenwood disappearing into the distance an unexpected feeling of freedom rose within her, bringing a smile to her countenance. Dido sat back and breathed in deeply. The first part of her journey went by without notice, as Dido was struck once again by the crowded London streets. The scene changed as they moved further out of London to what Dido could only assume to be the Kent countryside. She marvelled at the picturesque landscape that greeted her, gasping with delight at the splendour of the trees, fields and hills, and the vibrant and varying shades of reds, oranges and browns of the leaves. It was a warm autumn day and Dido found much to delight in the natural beauty of Kent that accosted her senses. But the increasing darkness that was slowly descending robbed Dido of her pleasure. There was nothing left to do but sit back and attempt to get some rest. But every attempt proved fruitless, as she could not attain a comfortable position. The hours gave too much time for thought and Dido soon began to fret about her uncle and began to wish for the security of Kenwood with every increasing distance. She waited in wearisome anticipation, expecting at every moment when the carriage slowed or stopped that this would signal the end of her journey. It seemed an eternity before the carriage finally turned into the entrance of Eastwell tower, the grand entrance to Eastwell Park, and Dido was able to get out of the carriage with much relief. She could scarcely make out its features in the diminishing light but the size of the house was immense. It stood an imposing but elegant stately home. But Dido viewed it with bias eyes. Nowhere to her could be as beautiful as Kenwood but Eastwell Park was indeed breath-taking.

"Lady Finch-Hatton is expecting you Miss." The doorman said, before a maid led her to the drawing room and her presence announced. The drawing room was a spatial and ornate room with large framed paintings on every wall, and the elegant furniture of pale lemon and cream gave a much needed lightness to the room. Dido was surprised to see Elizabeth sitting at tea with a guest, a young lady of whom Dido was not acquainted with.

"Oh Dido, I am so glad that you are finally here. I hope your journey was not too tedious? I myself felt it positively dreadful when I first took the journey." Lady Finch-Hatton talked on without waiting for Dido's response.

"I begged poor George if we could move closer to Kenwood but alas, I am happily settled now."

Dido smiled at the thought of the impossibility of Mr Finch-Hatton consenting to such a request.

"Oh where are my manners. This is Miss Abigail Tudor a close neighbour of ours. You've heard me speak of dear Dido, ward of Lord Mansfield." Lady Finch Hatton announced.

"I have indeed. It is a pleasure to finally meet you Miss Dido." said Miss Tudor, her voice and smile was pleasant. She was a young lady of possibly four and twenty, and extremely slender, her long pale face seemed to give her the appearance of someone rather sickly.

Dido smiled and curtsied in response to her greeting.

"I am glad to see that you are in good health. Are you much improved?" Dido asked Lady Finch-Hatton after they were all seated.

"Do not be deceived. I am just putting a brave face on things. If you only knew the pain I have been suffering for the past few days." Lady Finch-

Hatton complained.  Dido found it difficult to imagine Elizabeth putting a brave face on in any circumstance.

"What did the physician say? What is your ailment?" Dido enquired curiously, as she could see no indication of any illness as she eyed the piece of cake that Elizabeth helped herself to with great alacrity.

"I am with child." Lady Finch-Hatton replied almost regretfully.

"But that is marvellous news! Why did you not tell your uncle of the good news in your letter?" Dido enquired with astonishment, so overwhelmed was she at hearing the news.

"I have just discovered it myself. I did not want to cause a fuss. I will tell him in good time." She answered shortly as if not wanting to continue the subject.

"This is such a joyous occasion." Dido continued in a state of both astonishment and disbelief.  The very idea of Elizabeth being a mother was incredulous to her, not that she believed Elizabeth incapable of being a good mother but it seemed inconceivable that she could consider the interests of another above her own.  Perhaps Dido was doing her an injustice.  Having a child could prove the best remedy for Elizabeth's self-centred disposition.

"I can't imagine why.  Having a child is most uncomfortable condition. I shall feel wretched being confined to the house while everyone else is enjoying themselves." Lady Finch-Hatton pouted at the thought of her confinement.

"Of course there must be some pain…"

"Oh do not talk to me of pain! I am already suffering. To think I will soon be miserable and fat is too much to bear." Lady Finch-Hatton interrupted Dido hastily not wanting to hear any more unpleasantness on the subject.

"Come now Lady Finch-Hatton do not upset yourself." Miss Tudor attempted the fruitless task of trying to comfort her, for Lady Finch-Hatton was now becoming increasingly agitated at the thought of her miserable state. Dido had not expected Elizabeth's condition to be one so natural to woman and one so inevitable for a married woman that one could not possibly think it an inconvenience! Poor Elizabeth, Dido lamented. How could a woman wholly concerned with herself think nothing but selfishly of her own body?

"Please excuse me, Miss Tudor but I'm feeling quite poorly. Dido please assist me to my room."

Dido sat with Lady Finch-Hatton above an hour and listened with forbearance to her complaints. In an attempt to change the subject Dido remarked on how agreeable she found Miss Tudor.

"Yes, quite agreeable. There is something quite refreshing about her total disregard for her own appearance. I could not do it myself as I have my reputation to think of. One must look ones best even in my condition. Anyway, I would not have the courage for it." Lady Finch-Hatton said with much seriousness.

Dido almost laughed at the absurdity of her cousin's observation as she had not observed anything amiss in Miss Tudor's dress with the exception of it being plain, but she did not think *this* should signify a lack of care or indifference. Dido did not attempt to leave the room until Elizabeth had fallen asleep, and tiptoed quietly out of the room in fear of waking her. She made her way to the guest room where her belongings had been earlier installed, her thoughts troubled by a niggling concern for Elizabeth's care, which she could not rid herself of. Perhaps her coming to Eastwell Park would not prove as beneficial, as she had first believed. The thought of spending more than two weeks away from Kenwood to nursemaid her cousin was not an appealing prospect. Dido sighed deeply and then began immediately to berate herself for her selfishness. A knock on the door interrupted her thoughts as the housekeeper came in directly.

"Excuse me Miss Dido Mr Finch-Hatton would like you to join him for dinner in half an hour." She announced.

"Yes, of course." Dido answered, unable to keep the surprise out of her voice. She had no idea that Mr Finch-Hatton was at home and assumed him to be away as Elizabeth had not mentioned her husband's whereabouts. Presently, Dido wondered whether Mr Finch-Hatton's absence was a deliberate act to avoid welcoming her to Eastwell Park.


On arriving in the dining room Dido found Mr Finch-Hatton and Miss Tudor already seated.

"Ah, Miss Dido! It is an honour to have you with us." Mr Finch-Hatton said so formally and without any sign of pleasure that Dido wondered at his sincerity.

"It is a pleasure to be here, sir." Dido replied attempting to give an impression of being duly honoured for the invitation.

"I hope you find Eastwell Park to your liking Miss Dido?" Mr Finch-Hatton asked civilly

"Indeed. I find it very impressive, the little that I have seen. I do hope to have an opportunity to get better acquainted with the house and gardens." She answered enthusiastically.

"I'm sure my wife will want the pleasure of showing you around herself." Mr Finch-Hatton continued, as he summoned the servants to serve the dinner.

"Is not Lady Finch-Hatton joining us?" Dido asked, surprised at Elizabeth's absence.

"Regrettably my wife is unwell and unable to join us." He said with weariness in his voice that could have been interpreted as displeasure at his wife's absences from the dinner table. Miss Tudor expressed the felicity that a child would bring to Eastwell Park. This remark was barely acknowledged by Mr Finch-Hatton. There was an awkward pause as Miss Tudor then repeated herself as if in hope of receiving a more satisfactory response. Dido observed with interest that there was scarcely any sign of pleasure on the part of Mr Finch-Hatton. But in her judgement Dido was much mistaken, as Mr Finch-Hatton had every feeling of joy of any expectant father but was a man of little emotion.

"An heir is always important for the family seat, the Earl of Winchilsea and Nottingham." He said proudly. Dido hid a wry smile at Mr Finch-Hatton's condescending manner. She felt that at least on this subject, Mr Finch-Hatton expressed some feeling! He continued to enlighten the ladies of the subject of his ancestry until the end of the meal.

The following morning Dido proceeded to go for a short walk after breakfast with the hope of taking a much-anticipated discovery of the gardens. She had spied it from the window of the house and was delighted by its prospect. Dido had not wondered far when she heard a distant voice calling from behind and on turning she saw a figure of one of the servants hurrying towards her. Dido could not imagine what could be the matter but she concluded it had to be of some urgency for her attention to be desired in such haste. She walked quickly to meet the servant in an attempt to gain satisfaction of the news.

"Miss Dido, her ladyship is calling for you." He announced quite out of breath

"She has taken ill."

"Ill?" Dido repeated with concern following the footman in the same hurried pace. Lady Finch-Hatton was in her room looking pale and agitated.

"Oh Dido I am suffering and in such pains." Elizabeth cried with much agitation her hand touching her stomach which caused Dido some alarm at the thought that maybe something had happened to the child.

"As the doctor been called for?" Dido asked hurrying to Elizabeth's side.

"Yes miss." the maid answered

"Where is the pain?" Dido enquired searching Elizabeth's face intently for any clue.

"Everywhere! I have such pains in my head." She complained touching her temples. Dido felt Elizabeth's forehead, although it felt warm there was no fever. Dido was relieved that there appear to be no danger to the child.

"Perhaps a cold compress will help." Dido suggested as she went over to the water jug to pour some water on a towel.

"Where is the doctor?" Lady Finch-Hatton cried impatiently

"Please try not to upset yourself." Dido attempted to calm her

"How can I calm myself when I am suffering so!" she shouted with increasing irritation. Nothing Dido could do or say would give her comfort. Even Dido was relieved to see the appearance of the doctor hurrying into the room.

"Oh Dido!" Lady Finch-Hatton moaned.

"I will need a few moments to examine Lady Finch-Hatton," the doctor announced to Dido before giving instruction to the maid.

"Yes, of course." Dido replied before leaving the room. She had not long departed from it, when Mr Finch-Hatton appeared looking rather uneasy. On seeing Dido he hurried towards her.

"How is she? The child?" he enquired hastily giving little attention to Dido's response.

"She is in some pain but I do not think it is anything serious. The doctor is with her." Dido tried to relieve his anxiety but she could see that he hardly heard her as he went directly into his wife's room. At that moment Dido was willing to concede that perhaps her first impression of Mr Finch-Hatton's regard for his wife and child may have been ill judged. His behaviour, though distracted, allowed her to see him in a more favourable light. Dido admonished herself for her error of judgement, promising to think more kindly of Mr Finch-Hatton in future.

"Both mother and child is well. Lady Finch-Hatton will need considerable rest," the doctor was assuring Mr Finch-Hatton as they exited the room. Dido could see that Mr Finch-Hatton look less grave and was pleased that the anxiety was over. Dido quickly enquired whether it was possible for her to see Elizabeth.

"She is resting. But I see no harm in you looking in on her for a brief moment." Mr Finch-Hatton answered

Dido observed that Elizabeth's face was pale but serene in sleep, now that the anxious moments had passed. Though Dido was confident that Elizabeth was in no danger, she felt it necessary that Lord Mansfield be told of her condition. But Dido could not do so without at first speaking to Mr Finch-Hatton. This was done the very next day when they were seated alone at the breakfast table.

"Yes, of course, I had wanted to tell Lord Mansfield of the news but Elizabeth wanted to wait until she was feeling better. I'm afraid we shall need to impose on your kindness until Elizabeth is much stronger."

"I could not think of leaving." Dido reassured him hastily.

"I had intended to travel to London next week on urgent business" he said after a moment's pause.

"I thought I might have to cancel but since, I am sure, it will be only for a week perhaps less…"

"If I can be of any assistance with the care of Lady Finch-Hatton, I am at your service." Dido replied reassuringly.

"Excellent. With you here, I am sure Lady Finch-Hatton will be well taken care of. That settles the matter." Mr Finch-Hatton said with much elevation, so that Dido was momentarily surprised by his sudden gaiety and had to remind herself of her earlier promise not to think ill of him. His manner toward her was far more amicable than Dido had ever encountered since their first meeting as he talked of sending an urgent letter to Lord Mansfield as soon as breakfast was concluded.

To Dido's surprise Elizabeth did not take the news of her husband's imminent trip too well. Despite Dido's efforts to calm her she became increasingly overcome with vexation with every word.

"He does not care that I am gravely ill or how can he think of going to London at a time like this?"

"Oh Lizzy, you are mistaken. You should have seen how concerned he was at your illness."

"Well I should think so!" Lady Finch-Hatton replied with ill humour.

"Oh, Dido no one knows how I suffer!" She cried continuing to lament her condition.

"You must not upset yourself, think of the child. "

"The child that is all everyone cares for!"

"You know that's not true."

"Your uncle will visit next week I'm sure." Dido said hoping the news would cheer her. She was certain within the forthcoming days that they would hear news of when to expect Lord Mansfield's arrival at Eastwell Park.

"How I dearly long to see him." Lady Finch-Hatton cried again

"Lizzy please, try not to make yourself ill." Dido pleaded anxiously

"If only I was not confined to this wretched bed!"

"The doctor says in a few weeks when you are strong again, you will be able to get out and..." Dido reminded her,

"A few weeks...!" she exclaimed in despair and then began again to grieve of her constant suffering.

Dido felt that nothing she could say would satisfy Elizabeth's disposition. Her complaints only ended when the maid came in with her meal. Then to Dido's exasperation Lady Finch-Hatton confessed herself to be too poorly to eat. Dido spent several minutes pleading with her to at least eat something. She had to be satisfied when Lady Finch-Hatton grudgingly took a few spoonful of broth then stubbornly refused to eat anymore. She left Lady Finch-Hatton's room only after she had fallen asleep, her mind still disturbed by her conduct. Why had her husband's absence affected Elizabeth so acutely? Since her confinement Mr Finch-Hatton sat with his wife once during the day when he was not about the estate on business, then again in the evening. On many of these visits, Elizabeth was often asleep, and knew not whether her husband was absent or present. Dido could only conclude that Elizabeth's emotional state was owing to the delicacy of her condition.

# CHAPTER 15

A letter did not arrive from Kenwood the following day, but instead Lord Mansfield's carriage could be seen driving into the entrance of Eastwell Park. He had left Kenwood almost immediately upon receiving the news. Lord Mansfield had not stepped from the carriage before he was inquiring anxiously of Elizabeth's health. Dido went quickly to meet him wanting to calm any anxious concerns he may have had. But she could not contain her happiness at seeing him that she kissed him energetically on the cheek, something she had not done since she was a child. Lord Mansfield, although taken aback smiled with pleasure at her affectionate greeting.

"Thankfully, they are both well, sir. But Elizabeth is still weak. The doctor says that she needs plenty of rest." Dido answered Lord Mansfield's questions as she led him upstairs to Lady Finch-Hatton's room.

"How are you Dido?" Lord Mansfield asked warmly

"I am very well sir." Dido replied cheerfully

"It is good that Elizabeth has you as her nursemaid, she is in perfectly good hands." Lord Mansfield declared decidedly.

On entering Lady Finch-Hatton's room Lord Mansfield teased "So you are with child. Should I wish you congratulations?" ignoring Elizabeth's pallid face. Lady Finch-Hatton brightened on seeing her uncle and then she began to weep as both Lord Mansfield and Dido tried to comfort her. Dido feared that there was to be a repeat of Elizabeth's hysterics of yesterday as she began to repeat to her uncle the news of her husband's planned trip to London.

"Remember, the doctor warned against too much excitement." Dido reminded her, concerned that Elizabeth would become overly upset.

"Yes. We should do as the doctor says. Now that you are expecting you must take extra care. Come now Dido, let us leave the patient to her rest." Lord Mansfield stated.

"I'm sure you would like to freshen up after your journey." Dido added knowing that her uncle must be tired after such a long journey.

"Oh, I'm so tired of sleeping." Elizabeth stated vexingly, not wanting to admit that her body was not as strong as she would like.

"Come now let me fix your pillow for you to make you more comfortable." Dido volunteered in hope of easing Elizabeth's discomfort.

"Don't make such a fuss." Lord Mansfield said to Dido before coming closer to his niece's bed.

"Elizabeth, get some rest. That's an order." He said firmly as he patted her hand affectionately.

"Yes, Uncle William." Lady Finch-Hatton answered meekly

"Good girl."

"Where is George?" Lord Mansfield asked after they had quitted the room.

"I am not sure. I was told that Mr Finch-Hatton left the house early this morning. If we had known you were coming I'm sure he would have been here to welcome you." Dido replied earnestly.

"With Elizabeth expecting and being poorly I would have thought he would stay indoors." Lord Mansfield said more to himself than as a reply to Dido's words. Once Dido had escorted her uncle to one of the guest rooms she went to speak to the housekeeper about arranging tea, before quickly checking once again on Elizabeth.


"I'm glad to see that George has upheld the maintenance of this great house." Lord Mansfield said with satisfaction as they were seated for tea.

"It is certainly a fine house. The gardens and ground are breath-taking." Dido said warmly.

"Ah, I think Dido has lost her heart to Eastwell Park." Lord Mansfield teased

"Who could not?" she answered in her own defence.

"But Kenwood will always be the most beautiful place for me." Dido finished with a smile.

"It's your childhood home that's why you are so partial to it." Lord Mansfield replied.

"Perhaps but I think I would love it still even if had not grown up there." Dido replied decidedly.

"Dido you are far too sentimental. What will you do when you are married? " Lord Mansfield asked in jest. But he had given much thought to Dido's future of late, now being desirous of seeing her well settled before his death.

"I do not think I will ever be married." Dido said rather too emphatically.

"You only say so because no one has asked you." Lord Mansfield teased making light of the subject as he felt now was not the time to discuss the seriousness of her claim. His words were so far from her heart's desires that Dido could not find the courage to reply in kind, instead choosing to ignore his words she quickly changed the subject.

"What news is there of Kenwood since I have been away these few days?" she asked forcing herself to sound cheerful. There was an awkward pause, which caused Dido to look to her uncle, sensing that there was something amiss.

"Is there anything wrong?" Dido asked uneasily.

"Of course not child. Kenwood is much the same. I'm just an old man and Mrs Haversham has spent too much time there of late and has spoken of you constantly. I am sure she is dying to have you stay with her again, as she won't have any trouble finding you a husband." Lord Mansfield answered with his usual wit.

The timely arrival of Mr Finch-Hatton saved Dido the trouble of responding.

"Lord Mansfield, Miss Dido." Mr Finch-Hatton bowed formally before taking a seat.

"I do apologise for not being here on your arrival, sir. If only I had known I would have delayed my business until later." Mr Finch-Hatton said apologetically to Lord Mansfield.

"Do not trouble yourself. As soon as I heard the news I could not wait even to write a note. I thought it best to come as quickly as I could." Lord Mansfield replied.

"I can assure you that everything is being done for her comfort. The doctor says all she needs is rest." Mr Finch-Hatton answered in his attempt to reassure Lord Mansfield.

"Dido's presence has been a great comfort to Elizabeth. I hope you are able to spare her for a little longer." Mr Finch-Hatton added humbly to Lord Mansfield.

Dido tried to control the irritation at his speaking of her as if she were a child that had no say in their adult conversation. She knew it was not intentional but it was irksome all the same.

"I hear that you are going to London on business, surely your business can be delayed for another time?" Lord Mansfield asked a little surprised at his leaving his wife in such a delicate condition.

"I assure you sir, that my business in London is of the utmost importance or I would not even consider leaving at this time." Mr Finch Hatton replied with much cordiality endeavouring to hide the annoyance he felt at any question of his sentiment towards his wife.

"Of course I understand that the business of the estate is of great importance." Lord Mansfield conceded, noting the brief look of displeasure in Mr Finch-Hatton's expression.

"Well if you must go, you must go!" Lord Mansfield added categorically.

"We will stay here in your absence. Although I myself have official business to attend to in a few days but Dido will take good care of her, I have no doubt."

"Yes of course." Dido agreed

"You are very kind." Mr Finch-Hatton replied warmly.

Mr Finch-Hatton, Dido perceived, though showing all cordiality, had not taken kindly to Lord Mansfield's words. She suspected that Mr Finch-Hatton being master of all he surveyed was not *used* to being told what to do, did well to restrain himself with all civility to suffer the censure of his relative.

"So you have fallen in love with Eastwell Park?" Lord Mansfield asked again after dinner, as they were seated in the drawing room, Mr Finch-Hatton had that moment left to sit with his wife.

"Who could not, sir? It is very charming. The park and forest are so beautiful. There is so much that I have not seen, I am sure." Dido answered warmly, certain that her words had not done justice to the grandness of the estate.

"So you have not missed Kenwood I see." Lord Mansfield teased.

"I always miss Kenwood when I am away from it." Dido replied knowing better than to take her uncle's jest seriously.

"Well the place is not the same without you." He said, smiling wearily.

Dido felt the pleasure of being missed, but observed that Lord Mansfield looked tired and wondered why she had not noticed this before.

"You are quite well sir?" Dido asked searching his face intently for any sign of his ill health.

"Yes, as well as can be expected." Lord Mansfield responded dismissively.

"You need not give me that look. You should not worry about me, child."

"And you have not been working too hard?" Dido persisted knowing that he would shrug aside any of her concerns of his over working. She suspected now that she was unable to keep an eye on him, Lord Mansfield was guilty of perusing through documents long after everyone else had retired to bed.

"Ah, but I have lost a faithful secretary. Now I have not only my own work to do but yours also." He replied good-humouredly, trying to make light of the matter.

"Sir, I think you exaggerate my loss." Dido replied, and remained silent, sensing that her uncle desired to change the subject.

Dido found the pleasure of having her uncle at Eastwell Park short lived, as the four days passed far too quickly, and Lord Mansfield could not delay any further from returning to his work. But his stay had done Elizabeth's health an enormous good. Lady Finch-Hatton was content in her uncle's company and seemed to exert herself more to recovery. Her condition was so much improved, that she pleaded to be taken out to sit in the garden one afternoon. The weather though gloomy was relatively mild for autumn. The rain held off and there were even occasional appearances of sunshine, which was frowned upon by Lady Finch-Hatton who thought it rather a nuisance that it should be always coming and going just when they was getting accustomed to its warmth. Lady Finch-Hatton's maid remained to ensure that her mistress was kept warm to avoid catching a chill. Dido thought her rather zealous in her task, as at every interval she would ask Lady Finch-Hatton whether she was warm enough, at which her mistress would be as unpredictable as the weather and requested that her shawl be put on, and then taken off in the next instance. Dido wondered at the maid's fortitude in obeying her mistress' every whim, without the slightest hint of impatience and could scarcely hide her amusement when Lord Mansfield said with much candour, which could only be tolerated from someone of mature age.

"Your devotion to your mistress would be praised indeed, if it were not such an unnecessary waste of your time!"

Its meaning was lost on Lady Finch-Hatton, who continued to speak of her growing discomfort, but Dido was pleased to see a glimmer of humour in the eyes of the maid before it was agreed that Lady Finch-Hatton should be taken back indoors.

Dido feared that her uncle's impending departure from Eastwell Park would upset Elizabeth, knowing how attached she had become to his company. But this was not what troubled Dido's thoughts at that present moment. Her concern was purely selfish. Her uncle's presence at Eastwell Park had made her all the more homesick. How she desired to be leaving with him in the next few days! There was also the question of her uncle's wellbeing, which was now a cause for concern.

The thought of staying a further week or two filled Dido with much despair. But she had given her word to Mr Finch-Hatton that she would tend to Elizabeth in his absence. Poor Elizabeth desperately needed her support and Dido could not think of leaving her, though her heart wished to be home. There was nothing more to consider or hope for, Dido concluded. She would have to cope as best as she could, while disregarding her own desires in the best interest of her dear cousin.

As was expected, the day of Lord Mansfield's departure arrived and so did the flood of Lady Finch-Hatton's tears, as she tried to prevail upon her uncle to stay a further week but without success. Lord Mansfield was adamant that he had to return to business as he had delayed as long as he could. Dido took to the task of comforting Elizabeth as well as reassuring Lord Mansfield that he should not delay any further.
"Elizabeth will be fine. She will miss you dearly."
"Promise me you'll let me know if you need me." Lord Mansfield commanded, before giving her hand an affectionate squeeze and getting into the carriage. Dido could scarcely keep the tears from her eyes as the carriage pulled away, wishing with all her heart that she could be seated beside her uncle. She returned hurriedly into the house to flee from her melancholy disposition and found Elizabeth, instead of tearful and bemoaning her uncle's absence, in a more cheerful mood. Her disposition gave Dido some hope that perhaps Elizabeth was exerting herself for the sake of the child. When her cheerful disposition continued into the following day, Dido did not know what to think. At times she had to stop herself from questioning the reason for Elizabeth's cheerfulness, for fear of not wishing to tempt fate. Perhaps the return of Mr Finch-Hatton had much to do with Elizabeth's mood. It was foolish of her to worry, Dido decided. She could only hope that Elizabeth's good spirits would continue.

# CHAPTER 16

The smell of freshly scented trees and fields after the morning rain provided Dido with an exhilarating sensation of pleasure. The rain had cleared by the afternoon and the sun was attempting to shine through persisting clouds. Dido paid little attention to the muddiness of the field and paths, as she walked energetically, her mind thus occupied. A week had passed at Eastwell Park since her uncle's visit and Dido had no idea of when she would be returning to Kenwood. Her heart was impatient to be home. Though her stay at Eastwell Park had passed far pleasantly than she could have hoped, Dido felt confined by the stately formality and longed to feel the familiar comfort and security of Kenwood. Elizabeth's condition was much improved, and Dido had attempted to hint at every opportunity the subject of returning home. On every occasion her attempts were met with tearful refusals on Elizabeth's part, who would not hear of it, until Dido became most alarmed at having caused her such distress that she was resigned to reassure her cousin that she would not leave if her services were still required. Though this promise was given in sacrifice of her own feelings, Dido could not bring herself to revert from her promise. How to be free like the wind! Dido sighed, turning her face to the brightening skies. The clouds were breaking up, and the sun, seeing its opportunity to shine, did so with all its glory. Dido stood to admire and feel the warmth of its rays. Her walk had taken her to the edge of the woods, and in that instant, Dido was seized by a sudden spirit of adventure to take a walk along one of the paths into the woods. She was drawn by the elegance of the tall hanging trees. They seem to speak to her through the rustling of the leaves, beckoning her to come in. She could not decline such an appealing invitation and walked toward its entrance, gasping with pleasure as she stepped into an ancient world that appeared untouched for hundreds of years. Dido observed in awe these great ancient trees as they stood tall, twisted boughs intertwined, like arms stretched out across the expanse of time, huge magnificent boughs, preserved and aloof observers of those who would dare to trespass. A stirring in the trees, as the birds in flight disturbed the calm, only added to the enchantment. Dido turned suddenly, startled by a swift movement behind her. Perhaps a deer or a unicorn? Dido mused to herself, as she continued her walk along the path, her previous preoccupation forgotten. She did not know how long she walked, but fearful of being

missed Dido decided to turn to walk back to the house. It was not long
before the path forked into two, and for a moment Dido was alarmed as
to which path to take, as she had no recollection of turning neither left
nor right when she had walked the path earlier. How she wished she
had been more observant! Dido thought, staring intently at each path
in hope of seeing a sign of something familiar. A choice had to be made,
as there was no time to waste. Dido resolved to take the path that led
to the right, as it seemed to her to be going in the direction of the
house, which would take her to the edge of the woods and back to the
fields. But as she continued along the path, Dido discovered that she
was going further into the woods. She stopped, looking anxiously about
herself as a sudden feeling of dread overwhelmed her, robbing her of
the power to think. "It will do no good to panic!" Dido cautioned
herself. But her reprimand had little effect in dispelling her fears. What
if she could not find her way out before dark? What if she should come
across a stranger, a thief? These gloomy thoughts threatened to
overcome every effort to remain calm. No! Surely she would be missed.
Elizabeth would be worried and alert the servants to search for her.
Yes, of course. This thought gave Dido some hope as she hurried back
along the path to where she had started in order to take the left path
instead. She quickened her paste as she glimpsed through the trees to
the darkening skies. With her thoughts so preoccupied, Dido did not
sense the stranger coming towards her until he was only a few feet
away. Had Dido given thought to the possibility of him being a labourer
from the estate, she would have saved herself the torment at beholding
his presence. But in her present state of agitation, her heart was
paralysed with fear, wildly alerted to the present danger. The stranger
walked towards her, his frame becoming larger and all the more sinister
that Dido could barely let out a scream as she stumbled back, losing her
footing she fell heavily, surrendering to unconsciousness, she
remembered nothing else.

Dido was awakened by the sharp and powerful scent of smelling salts.
She heard voices around her, before her eyes, fluttering open could
focus on the anxious face of Elizabeth.
"Thank goodness you are awake!" Lady Finch-Hatton cried anxiously.
Dido's confusion was evident as she attempted to sit up against the
protest of her cousin but soon was hindered by the pain that throbbed
at the back of her head. Then the recollection of her walk came
flooding back, giving Dido an instant feeling of relief at being back in the

house, before this sensation was quickly replaced by shame at having worried her relations so unduly. Dido observed that Mr Finch-Hatton and several servants were also gathered in the drawing room. What must he think of her? Dido wondered as she observed that Mr Finch-Hatton appeared to look rather irritated at being disturbed from more importance matters. Presently, the footman announced that the physician had arrived, which added further to Dido's discomfort.

"I am well. Please I have no need of a physician. I was more frightened than anything." Dido mumbled uneasily, feeling the pain in her head protesting against her own words. Lady Finch-Hatton would have none of it, insisting that the physician examine the patient at once. Dido was left in the care of the physician as a fretful Lady Finch-Hatton accompanied by her silent and indifferent husband quitted the room. After a full examination Dido was declared to be in good health, despite the nasty bump on the head, which was dressed and the patient ordered to bed for a few days.

As soon as Dido was suitably recovered, she had since her confinement made a resolution of apologising once again to her relations for the unfortunate incident. No sooner had she settled at the breakfast table Dido began an awkward but sincere apology, which was received by Mr Finch-Hatton with haughty silence and by Lady Finch-Hatton with the repeated fears of Dido's welfare, and then to relate once again her anxieties when Dido had not returned from her walk.

"Women have the romantic notion that the woods are a place for a leisurely stroll, but in fact it is a dangerous place for a solitary walker." Mr Finch-Hatton stated condescendingly. Dido would have protested had she not felt the truth of his words where she was concerned. Instead she remained silent, humbled by his intended chastisement.

"It was fortunate that Higgins found you when he did! Oh to think that they are thieves and such bad sorts in the woods. One cannot imagine what terrible misfortune could have occurred. Oh Dido, promise me that you will not walk there again." Lady Finch-Hatton pleaded becoming more agitated, that Dido had to reassure her again and again before she could be satisfied.

"I hope you have learnt a lesson, Miss Dido." Mr Finch-Hatton added to Dido's chagrin. She had no wish to give Mr Finch-Hatton any satisfaction in pointing out her failings, but by losing herself in the woods, she had done exactly that. Dido supposed that she could have taken his chastisement better had Mr Finch-Hatton not received so much pleasure in the administration of his reprimand.

# CHAPTER 17

"Oh how delightful to have the opportunity of being in good society again! Present company excluded of course." Lady Finch-Hatton said sweetly after reading a card that she had just removed from its envelope. Dido looked up from her book to observe her cousin opening another envelope of a similar size and colour as the first.

"Excellent!" she exclaimed, causing Dido's curiosity to be awakened by so much excitement. Her curiosity was soon relieved with the following words.

"We are having a dinner party next Friday evening." She announced to Dido's surprise

"Do you not think it too soon? I mean, you have only recently recovered your strength." Dido began to voice her concerns.

"You know that I have been perfectly well for the past few weeks now." Lady Finch-Hatton interrupted, brushing aside Dido's protest. Dido wanted to reply that she had known no such thing. For had she known, she would have requested to return to Kenwood as soon as could be arranged!

"Really Dido, I've been confined to bed for weeks and finally I am well enough to have visitors, surely you cannot deny me the pleasure."

"It is not in my power to deny you anything. I'm merely concerned for your welfare. I only fear you may make yourself unwell again by taking on too much in your condition." Dido said resignedly although she was unable to rid herself of uneasiness she felt at what was to come.

"I promise I will not. Anyway you are here to help me." Lady Finch-Hatton replied smiling sweetly.

"And I can't possibly cancel now as we have just received replies from all our guests." She replied lifting up the cards from the table as evidence of the finality of the event. Dido began to wonder why she had taken the trouble of telling her at all! She knew it was impossible to dissuade her, not that Dido supposed her opinion counted for much. It was clear to her now that this planned dinner party was the reason for Elizabeth's calm composure at her uncle's departure. No doubt Mr Finch-Hatton had thought up the scheme to keep his wife distracted so as to avoid any further upset that could threaten Lady Finch-Hatton's condition. Dido was not far from the truth. In fact Mr Finch-Hatton had consented to the idea as a way of making amends for his trip to London. Lady Finch-Hatton on hearing the news was not only excited by the forthcoming event but was determined to show her new maternal condition in the most flattering light. For Dido, the news of a dinner party produced nothing but indifference. She could not imagine what assistance she could give, as she had no experience of arranging dinner parties and had no other desire but to keep well out of the way of any such preparations. Dido was equally desirous that her presence would not be required on the evening of the dinner. Though Elizabeth had not informed her of this, Dido decided to remain silent on the subject fearing that to speak would bring an invitation that she did not wish for. As the evening of dinner party approached and nothing was said, Dido could allow herself to feel confident that her presence was not needed.

On the morning of the dinner party, Dido noticed that Lady Finch-Hatton's manner displayed signs of nervous anticipation at the proximity of the event.

"I hope the cook has remembered that the vegetables need to be completely fresh." She said, as an afterthought, then looking about herself as if expecting to find the cook standing directly behind her.

"It's a frightful bother if the food is not at the right temperature. Lady Hillingdon is quite particular and likes to make such a fuss about absolutely everything!" Lady Finch-Hatton complained.

"I'm sure everything is perfectly fine." Dido said hoping to relieve her of the unnecessary anxiety, but with little success as Elizabeth proceeded to ring for the housekeeper to check once again if everything was in order. It was useless for Dido to even attempt to dissuade her from troubling the housekeeper, who no doubt had plenty to do before the guests arrived.

"An acquaintance of yours will be joining us this evening." Elizabeth announced smiling slyly as she noted with satisfaction the effect her revelation had upon Dido, who was duly surprised by her words. Dido, having sufficiently recovered, while the housekeeper was given once again instructions regarding the temperature and the readiness of the meal, waited curiously for Elizabeth to continue, having no idea of whom she could be referring to and said as much.

"Take a guess?" she teased enjoying the suspense, her head turned rather mischievously, reminding Dido of a youthful Elizabeth.

"Mrs Haversham?" Dido played along, still unsure of whom it could be.

"No silly. Try again." Lady Finch-Hatton replied with a look of disbelief.

"Lizzy, I cannot possibly guess who it could be." Dido answered resolutely.

"I shall give you a hint. Remember my coming out ball?" she asked excitedly with an air of expectancy that Dido should surely now know to whom she was referring. Dido looked quizzically, her mind trying to recall names and faces of an occasion several years previous.

"Come, come now. You cannot surely be at lost to whom I am referring to." Elizabeth said losing all patience with Dido.

"Indeed I am." Dido declared, though she could recall the face of an officer of which she had conversed and danced one dance with. But it would be a far stretch of the imagination to consider him an acquaintance, as she never laid eyes on the gentleman again.

"Oh, you are a simpleton!" Elizabeth declared.

"I'm sure you know who I am alluding to. Captain Alwyne. Don't tell me that you do not remember *him*."

"Yes, I do recall Captain Alwyne but I think you must own that to call the gentleman an acquaintance is an exaggeration."

"An acquaintance; a friend what difference?" She waved dismissively.

"He remembers *you* very well. He asked after your wellbeing you know." Elizabeth said with more meaning than was warranted, which Dido deliberately chose to ignore.

"I have not seen Captain Alwyne since the night of the ball. No doubt he was just being polite." Dido said casually hoping that her indifferent tone would put an end to the subject and was grateful for the opportune arrival of Mr Finch-Hatton into the drawing room which brought about the desired result. As Elizabeth immediately began to question her husband on the expected arrival of the guests and then proceeded not to listen to any of her husband's responses.

"We will expect you to join us after dinner, Miss Dido" Mr Finch-Hatton said courteously. If he expected more enthusiasm at the invitation it could not be given. Dido had no intentions of indulging his vanity as he was rendering her no favours. That she was forced to be present gave her little pleasure at the prospect of spending an evening with inquisitive strangers. She was forced, however, to answer as amicably as she could.

There was a general air of expectancy amongst the guests of experiencing an enjoyable evening, as they arrived almost simultaneously. Instead of the expected ten there were nine, which put an already flustered Lady Finch-Hatton into a state of hysteria at the thought of the dinner arrangements being spoilt by the oddness of the numbers, and could spare the absentee guest no sympathy for the inopportune timing of their illness. It was decided at the last minute that the only possible solution was to include Dido in the dinner party. Dido having no opportunity of protesting was summoned to the dining room. The dinner table was lavishly laid, far more than Dido was used to at Kenwood. Elegant tall crystal glasses placed with precision, with glistening silverware laid beside white lace embroidered napkins and porcelain china dinnerware, all served to impress even the most influential of guests. Lady Finch-Hatton smiled with much satisfaction at the compliments made by both Lady Hillingdon and Miss Thorpe.

"The table is absolutely divine, one can simply eat it!" Miss Thorpe declared laughing loudly at her own joke. Miss Emily Thorpe was a single woman, aged six and twenty and in possession of a great fortune. Miss Thorpe's father was a wealthy sugar planter who had accumulated his wealth in the West Indies and shamelessly used it to buy both lands and titles. It was from this inheritance that Miss Thorpe used her wealth and influence as a way of amusement. She had developed a reputation of giving the best parties in the highest social circles. A dinner party with the name of Miss Thorpe amongst its guest list was considered highly fashionable, especially among the young. This was reason enough for the Finch-Hatton's invitation, though they both agreed that Miss Thorpe was rather lacking in social decorum. But the lady found pleasure in her power, particularly over those nobility who prided themselves on their noble ancestry but possessed little wealth to maintain such a claim; of which she had in abundance. She had no illusions about the gossip that circulated of her inferior breeding and her scandalous reputation with the opposite sex. It was widely known that Miss Thorpe's name had been linked with more than one eligible young gentleman but nothing had come of any the acquaintances. Miss Thorpe had merely toyed with the idea of marriage, as she was far too content with her present situation to exchange it for the prospect of being controlled by one man. And thus she cared little for the gossip, which she found rather amusing as it only added to her fame. Dido was quite aghast at the vulgarity of the lady's manners but this appeared to be lost on everyone, with the exception of Lady Hillingdon, who could hardly bring herself to reply to the lady's greeting. That Elizabeth should consider it acceptable to seek Miss Thorpe's society was beyond Dido's comprehension.

Besides Miss Thorpe and Lady Hillingdon, the other guests included Lady Hillingdon's husband Lord Hillingdon, a long acquaintance of Mr Finch-

Hatton and their niece Lady Louise. Miss Tudor, and her cousin, Miss Charlotte Palmer, Mr John Edwards, a clergyman, Mr Robert Cavanaugh, another acquaintance of Mr Finch-Hatton and Captain Alwyne. Dido saw that due care had been taken by Mr Finch-Hatton to ensure that she was well placed at the dinner table. She was seated between Lady Finch-Hatton and Miss Tudor and directly opposite to Captain Alwyne, all of whom were previously acquainted so as to avoid any possible indelicacy or embarrassment for the other guests, who would not have been forewarned of her society. Dido's first introduction to the party had produced the usual curious looks and some whispered exchanges. Only Miss Thorpe appeared enthralled by the meeting. At first, Dido felt grateful for her openness and attention, until the patronizing manner of Miss Thorpe's address began to cause Dido great offence. It took all of Dido's fortitude to tolerate Miss Thorpe's ignorance.

"Where have you been hiding her Lady Finch-Hatton? She is positively delightful! I have heard all about Miss Dido for years now and finally I have the opportunity of meeting her." the lady raved on, smiling at Dido like a simpleton. Dido could not imagine of whom Miss Thorpe could have heard her spoken of in *her* circle.

"I am sure you exaggerate my fame entirely." Dido replied graciously, which caused Miss Thorpe to laugh with delight.

"Oh, isn't she delightful. And she speaks so well!" Miss Thorpe cried, as if not expecting her to do so. Her response did not endear her to Dido, who could not help but be mortified by Miss Thorpe's habit of referring to her as if she were a child or a pet! Dido did not know how she appeared under the scrutinising eye of Captain Alwyne, as she struggled to control her countenance. She had not the courage to look at the gentlemen for fear of seeing amusement in his eyes. By the end of the introductions Dido decided that she much preferred the silent snobbery of Lady Hillingdon and her niece Lady Louise than the condescending outpourings of Miss Thorpe.

"Dido has lived with Lord and Lady Mansfield since infancy." Lady Finch-Hatton added, as if by way of explanation of Dido being well bred. Dido was almost tempted to remind Elizabeth that this was also her situation until recently.

"Dido sings and plays the pianoforte exquisitely." Lady Finch-Hatton boasted claiming Dido's accomplishments as if they were her own, making Dido to feel the awkwardness of being publicly praised, as her cousin continued to recall an occasion when Dido's accomplishments was distinguished by a royal guest. She knew her cousin meant well but she wished that Elizabeth would not go on so.

"Perhaps we could hear her play later?" Lady Hillingdon asked somewhat curious to discover whether the girl played as well as was boasted.

"I will be delighted to." Dido replied, before Elizabeth could answer for her. She had no desire to be talked over or to be talked at, for she had long learnt to consider herself equal to any person of whom she came into acquaintance with, though society would dictate otherwise. Her accomplishments were her only opportunity of showing her superior social upbringing, an art which Dido learnt to use greatly to her advantage.

"Miss Dido is too innocent a creature to know of the wickedness of this world." Captain Alwyne remarked good naturedly to Miss Thorpe of whom he was conversing with on a crime of passion that he had read in a national newspaper only yesterday. Dido looked up startled at hearing her name spoken so openly in a conversation that she had no participation in. She was not entirely sure of what to make of Captain Alwyne's statement, as she thought that the gentleman seemed to take more than an avid interest in drawing everyone's attention to her, which caused Dido to blush. To her shame, she had held the gentleman in some regard since their meeting at the ball. It was not just his attention to herself which had been pleasing but the way in which he made no distinction between her and any other lady at the ball. Dido could not help but admire his manners. When Elizabeth had mentioned that Captain Alwyne was going to be among the guests, Dido had foolishly felt a tremor of anticipation at the prospect of their being reacquainted. She had resisted every emotion in her art of concealment, as she attempted to sound completely indifferent to the news. Luckily for Dido, Elizabeth had not detected her inward struggle. Presently, Captain Alwyne eyed Dido smiling charmingly, Dido began to wonder at his possible motive for his statement. Miss Thorpe laughed aloud courting the attention of the whole table.

"Miss Dido has lived a very sheltered life." Miss Thorpe stated categorically, speaking as one who was intimately acquainted with Dido. "Indeed, Dido knows no other place but Kenwood, except for the occasionally visits to the country and London." Lady Finch-Hatton replied to Dido's displeasure. Dido wished that Elizabeth would not speak for her as if she was incapable of speaking for herself. Her sudden irritation gave Dido the boldness to speak.

"I do not think that because I have lived only at Kenwood that it must therefore conclude that I know nothing of the evils of this world. One does not have to experience evil to know that evil exists. Stories of evil doings can be read and heard even in the confines of Kenwood. " Dido remarked and then fell silent.

Captain Alwyne looked intrigued. Miss Thorpe amused. Lady Finch-Hatton looked fearful at the possibility of Dido's words offending any of her guests. Dido had not meant to speak so freely but she felt entitled to an opinion as any other guest in the room.

"Let's not speak of such a morbid subject." Lady Finch-Hatton said hoping to change the subject.

"Oh, I think the subject an interesting one." Miss Thorpe said, as she was having too much fun to let the subject go, as the black girl was proving to be rather more interesting than she had anticipated.

"What subject?" Miss Tudor enquired curiously.

"The subject of evil, of course. Take the subject of slavery." Miss Thorpe stated innocently.

"What might I add is so interesting about it?" Lady Hillingdon asked incredulously, not amused by Miss Thorpe's forwardness.

"I know that Lady Milton owns a slave and simply delights in the fact and she treats him perfectly well. But yet slavery is said to be an evil trade." Miss Thorpe replied slyly, knowing the subject to be a controversial one.

"Is it true?" Lady Louise asked excitedly, and then remembering herself blushed and fell silent.

"Do not be so ridiculous Louise!" Lady Hillingdon cried appalled by her niece's question.

"Upon my word, it is true. I saw him myself." Miss Thorpe declared and went on to describe the slave in much detail. Dido was uncertain how to feel. She felt that she ought to feel awkward and ashamed, certain that all present knew that she herself was born a *slave*. And yet she felt more outrage at the careless manner in which Miss Thorpe spoke of slavery.

"It is a fact. I know a dozen families who own one." Captain Alwyne replied plainly.

"Mr Finch-Hatton I implore you to ask Miss Thorpe to end this subject at once." Lady Hillingdon demanded looking to Mr Finch-Hatton to perform his duty.

"I wish not to offend anyone." Miss Thorpe laughed easily and winked in the direction of Dido who could hardly contain her aversion at the lady's crudeness.

The ladies gathered in the music room after dinner, while the men retired to the drawing room. If it were not for the continuous chatter of Miss Thorpe and Miss Tudor, the conversation would have proved rather dull, as Lady Finch-Hatton and Lady Hillingdon were preoccupied with the activities of the men in the drawing room. Dido found it difficult to appear wholly interested in their discourse, which continued in this vain.

"I am curious as to know what the gentlemen are up to in the drawing room." Lady Finch-Hatton remarked expressively, giving the impression that the gentlemen were on the other side of the world rather than on the other side of the hall.

"One often wonder why they seem so happy to be apart from us." Lady Hillingdon stated thoughtfully. Dido immediately began to muse to herself that she could think of several perfectly good reasons why they would be so inclined.

"No doubt they will be gossiping about one subject or another." Miss Thorpe interjected, feeling bored with her conversation with Miss Tudor. She too was wondering what a particular gentleman was up to.

"Men do not gossip, my dear." Lady Hillingdon stated emphatically.

"I'm afraid they do madam, but they have another name for it, politics." Miss Thorpe replied wittily. Dido smiled openly and received a disapproving look from Lady Hillingdon. On this occasion, Dido could not help but be amused at Miss Thorpe's words, and felt that the lady seem to take a delight in causing an disturbance whenever she spoke.

"Well, I do not know how we will do without them." Lady Finch-Hatton added, choosing to ignore Miss Thorpe's remark.

"If only they could say the same of us. A woman, when she is widowed is happy to mourn her husband for years, if not for the rest of her life. But a husband, on losing his wife, is likely to be re-married within a month." Miss Thorpe said gaily, at which there were several disagreeable looks from Lady Hillingdon and Miss Palmer. Dido looked somewhat amused, as was Lady Finch-Hatton, who having some experience of marital relationships and the ways of men, was inclined to agree with Miss Thorpe.

"Well I must confess to there being some truth in Miss Thorpe's statement. I know of a few recent examples." Miss Tudor said almost sheepishly

"Oh, do tell." Miss Thorpe coaxed eagerly

"What nonsense! How much longer must we listen to such talk?" Lady Hillingdon cried, appalled by the young lady's impropriety.

"How ridiculous!" Lady Hillingdon mumbled again.

"In my opinion these young ladies now a-days talk a lot of nonsense." She said aside to her host.

"I hope you do not include all of us in your censure." Miss Palmer said quickly

"Certainly not, I... "

"No. Lady Hillingdon is referring to me. She disapproves of my society" Miss Thorpe interrupted, in an amusing tone, showing neither mortification nor offence. Lady Hillingdon, in turn, displayed an awkward displeasure at the accuracy of Miss Thorpe's words.

"Perhaps Dido would like to play for us now?" Lady Finch-Hatton suggested, seizing the opportunity to put an end to the un-pleasantries. All seem to be in agreement to this end and Dido was not opposed to the idea of playing, as she thought it would be a more pleasurable diversion. Taking her place at the pianoforte, Dido realised that she had not had the opportunity of playing this splendid instrument, its polished oak veneer, appeared new and un-used. She wondered if its owners ever played it, but as soon as her fingers touched the key she found it in perfect tuning. Dido completed one rendition, which was greeted with enthusiastic applause, no one more appreciative than Miss Thorpe, who outdid everyone in her exclamations. There were requests for more singing at which Dido graciously obliged.

"Her voice is like a voice of an angel." Miss Thorpe enthused.

"Yes, it is a handsome voice." Lady Hillingdon was forced to concede.

"How delightful!" Miss Tudor commented trying to match Miss Thorpe in her praise.

The arrival of the gentlemen in the middle of Dido second performance did little to take her concentration from her task, though some of the ladies attention was immediately taken up with fussing over the seating arrangement for the gentlemen. At the end of her performance, Dido was once again called upon to sing.

"Please, Miss Dido, if you would be so kind as to start again so that we can have the pleasure of hearing you from the beginning." Captain Alwyne asked graciously. There was a chorus of agreement as everyone settled down to listen. Dido could have been overawed by such attention that was given to her but she had learnt to take these moments as an opportunity of showing herself to the best advantage. Although Dido could confess to a little boastfulness in her manner, her temperament was not conceited. She had learnt her art very well and was confident of her own ability. This confidence gave improvement to her accomplishment and her love of music. And this pleasure was displayed in her performance in both her playing and singing.

"Thank you for a somewhat interesting evening." Lady Hillingdon remarked with considerable contemplation.

"Lady Finch-Hatton, I would be more careful in my choice of guests if I were you." She announced officiously as if her words came from a divine authority. Lady Finch-Hatton looked puzzled uncertain of to whom Lady Hillingdon was referring to, and then thinking it to be Dido, felt compelled to say a word in her defence.

"Miss Dido is highly esteemed by my family," Lady Finch-Hatton began

"No, no it is not Miss Dido to whom I referring. I speak of Miss Thorpe."

"Miss Thorpe is welcomed in the best societies." Lady Finch-Hatton replied, surprised at Lady Hillingdon censure of Miss Thorpe. In truth, Lady Finch-Hatton had no regrets about her decision to include Miss Thorpe among her guests, as the lady was sure to discuss her dinner party wherever she went. Consequently, Lady Finch-Hatton was sure that the whole of London would be talking of it within the month. Her response to Lady Hillingdon was said solely with the purpose of appearing totally ignorant of any knowledge of Miss Thorpe's reputation among certain circles.

"Not in any *decent* society." Lady Hillingdon continued adamantly. Lady Finch-Hatton was wont to disagree but listened with all forbearance.

"Never mind, my dear, you are not to blame. Perhaps you will remember my words when you next consider a dinner party. Please keep an eye on dear Louise as she is so easily influenced, as young people are these days. But she entreated me to stay over and I know how good an influence you are on her." she said apprehensively as Lady Finch-Hatton attempted to reassure her that Lady Louise would be perfectly safe under her care. Armed with this assurance Lady Hillingdon was able to finally take her leave with her husband. Lady Finch-Hatton was relieved that Lady Hillingdon's complaint was made out of the earshot of Miss Thorpe and the rest of the party. As far as Lady Finch-Hatton was concerned, Lady Hillingdon words had been inconsequential, as the evening had been a great success and was sure to be talked of at many a dinner party.

Captain Alwyne, Lady Louise and Mr Cavanaugh stayed at Eastwell Park for the remainder of the weekend. Dido felt that the house appeared to take on an air of gaiety, which seemed far from the confines of the regal setting of Eastwell Park. Lady Finch-Hatton, at least, was delighted at having the extended presence of her guests. It was true that the dinner table was more enlivened for Captain Alwyne's society. Lady Louise, free from the shackles of her aunt's dominion, was far more lively and animated in Captain Alwyne's presence than she had been on the previous night of the dinner party. She was a young lady of one and twenty years, with fair hair and a perfectly oval shaped face. Her features were pleasantly attractive with a very pleasing smile, but Dido would not have known her so changed was her manners. Perhaps it was the overwhelming presence of Miss Thorpe, who had commanded so much attention that every other woman present could easily have gone unnoticed failing colour or exceptional beauty. But Dido supposed that Lady Louise's demure manner had more to do with her aunt, Lady Hillingdon, who kept her niece very much in check, though the lady had a keen interest in everything that was said but for fear of her aunt's censure did not speak.

Mr George Finch-Hatton did not show any displeasure at the scene before him. He could not pretend to be interested in the small talk on fashion, art or gossip. He seemed to be content to be a spectator, talking only to Mr Cavanaugh. Dido too had listened with keen interest to Captain Alwyne and Lady Louise's conversation on the subject of inheritance and the question of property. The conversation, which was started rather coyly on Lady Louise's part, began with her stating the unfairness of the eldest son inheriting all of his father's estate leaving little for the younger siblings. Captain Alwyne being the youngest son of Lord Alwyne was all agreement. Captain Alwyne knew all too well that his allowance and anything else allotted to him, although more than enough for a single gentleman of leisure was far from adequate to support a wife and children.

"I am no better off than a woman." He remarked amusingly expecting to hear the cries of denials, which his remark provoked.

"Captain Alwyne, how can you say such a thing?" Lady Louise cried incredulously her cheeks flushed with pleasure.

"You must own that men have far more choices than we do." Lady Finch-Hatton remarked entirely in disagreement with Captain Alwyne statement.

"I'm sure that it is true but that does not concur that my statement is false." the gentleman continued amid the protest of the ladies.

"I see you do not agree with me, Miss Dido." Captain Alwyne said mischievously, causing all attention to be drawn to Dido. Dido knew exactly what Captain Alwyne was trying to do. He had caught her out before but she would not fall a victim to his trickery. She could not imagine that he was any more interested in her views than anyone else in the room. Though on occasion she caught him looking fixedly at her but she could not think that he could possibly have any intentions towards her.

"I have no thoughts on the subject." Dido replied courteously, not wanting to be drawn in by any game Captain Alwyne may be scheming.

"Oh come now, I can tell that you think I do your fair sex an injustice." Captain Alwyne insisted, desiring to hear the lady speak. His intention was a selfish one. He had thought Miss Dido's silence too dull to gratify his sense of amusement, as he was rather bored with the childish giggles of Lady Louise.

"Please do not assume to read my mind you may be surprised to find that I may actually agree with you." Dido replied earnestly. In truth she felt that Captain Alwyne being a younger son had less security concerning his financial prospects and if being a man of extravagant means, as Dido was sure that Captain Alwyne was, would no doubt choose a wife primarily on the basis of her wealth rather than for love.

"I think Miss Dido is teasing me." Captain Alwyne laughed heartily.

"I think that it is you who is teasing me, sir." Dido replied before regretting the forwardness of her words. She immediately reproached herself for allowing her tongue to slip. How had she allowed herself to be drawn in by Captain Alwyne? Not that she felt any impropriety had been done on her part. It was only for Elizabeth sake that Dido was wary of her conduct. But she observed from the look of displeasure from Mr Finch-Hatton that she had failed where the gentleman was concerned. And directly after dinner, he made his feelings known to her.

"Your conversation at dinner has done a disservice to both myself and Lady Finch-Hatton. We have allowed you into our circle of friends because I know how much you are valued by your family. But to entertain a gentleman in such a way may cause some misunderstanding." Mr Finch-Hatton said austerely, wanting to make it perfectly clear that he would not tolerate any impropriety at Eastwell Park. Dido would have laughed at his description of what had occurred, if she had not been so injured by his insinuation. It was rather amusing that Mr Finch-Hatton should think her *entertaining* Captain Alwyne when she had spoken but a few words to the gentleman. What of Lady Louise who had talked half the evening with him? His reprimand was totally absurd. Dido listened with fortitude and passivity, which she knew was required of her. She had no particular concern for Mr Finch-Hatton's opinion or for his approbation. There was nothing in her conduct to reproach herself for. Dido realised, after only a few days of being at Eastwell Park that it was necessary to appear humbled and chastised even when one had no desire to be either. George Finch-Hatton was a dictatorial man, who could not tolerate anything but submission to his authority. Being much older than his wife, Mr Finch-Hatton had taken the role of both the husband and father figure and this seemed to compliment Elizabeth's childish nature. Though Lady Finch-Hatton had little trouble getting her own way, even she understood, like every dutiful wife, that her husband's word was final. Dido pitied her cousin's marital status. She would not be married for the world! Mr Finch-Hatton did not fail to see the indifference in Dido's eyes which provoked within him a feeling of irritation. He thought her far too outspoken being left at liberty to say what she pleased. While this was acceptable to Lord Mansfield it certainly would not be tolerated by him.

"May I remind you Miss Dido that you are here only at the benevolence of Lady Finch-Hatton."

He saw immediately that his words had the effect that he had intended. Dido squared her shoulder as she fought to contain her vexation at the meaning of his words.

"Is that all, sir?" Dido asked trying to muster all civility, before curtseying and quitting the room.

# CHAPTER 18

Dido stole an opportunity to go for her usual walk soon after breakfast, hoping to have a moment of solitude. She had discovered a delightful spot in the garden a few days earlier and was eager to return to enjoy its solitary pleasures. Dido seated herself anticipating a peaceful morning of reading, but found herself soon after unexpectedly interrupted.

"I did not expect to find you here," Captain Alwyne spoke taking Dido completely unaware. She stood up to greet him, and being rather surprised by his presence did not know how to act. She had not thought to be disturbed in this part of the garden so Dido could only assume that Captain Alwyne had seen her walking in this direction and had followed her. But recovering herself quickly she cordially accepted his invitation to sit down.

"I have only recently found this spot. I find its seclusion very inviting." Dido said pleasantly, unaware that her smile added greatly to her features and gave a pleasant shine to her eyes, which did not go unnoticed by Captain Alwyne.

"It is a pity that my stay is so short, we could have enjoyed exploring this haven together." He replied with a smile.

Dido was lost for words. She was afraid that any affirmation might give the gentleman the wrong impression. She felt the awkwardness of her silence but could not speak. Dido was sure that Captain Alwyne had not meant anything underhand in his words and yet his look and manner appeared rather strange. Dido could not make him out at all.

"You are leaving tomorrow?" Dido forced herself to enquire in an attempt to relieve her uneasiness, knowing already that all the guests were leaving Eastwell Park in the morning. Captain Alwyne remained silent as if not hearing her. The intensity of his gaze added further to her discomfort.

"Yes." He answered belatedly, and said nothing more. Dido wished for some conversation, but could not think of anything to say. Captain Alwyne, usually a lively talker, appeared to have no inclination for it. His timing was ill, Dido thought. Then Captain Alwyne moved suddenly towards her, sitting so close that Dido felt compelled to stand up. She was quite alarmed when his hand touched her arm and held her still.

"Sir?" Dido started to speak but stopped suddenly when she felt his hand touch her cheek and his lips come violently upon hers.

"Please stop!" Dido cried weakly, when she was able to escape his lips. So stunned was she by his intimacy that for a moment she had lost all power to struggle free from his grasp.

"Come now, you cannot be so naïve." Captain Alwyne asked playfully, all civility removed. Dido felt helpless at his words. Her heart was beating violently and she could hardly breathe. She fought to control herself as feelings of both shame and indignation filled her with revulsion at his abuse.

"You are mistaken. I do not know what you are referring to." Dido struggled to speak, her voice trembling.

"You are quite beautiful. You have a charm that is quite beguiling. But what is your price?" he asked, holding Dido's chin and moving her face from side to side as if inspecting her. Dido pushed his hand away, finding an opportunity to move out of his grasp.

"How dare you speak to me in this manner? I am not for sale!" Dido panted barely able to speak for the shock of his changed character.

"All slaves are for sale." Captain Alwyne replied wryly

Dido gasped, she did not think that any other insults could cause her more pain. His intention was not lost on her. Dido felt revulsion in the pit of her stomach, which left her with no strength to retaliate.

"I am not a slave." Dido whispered her voice so weak she scarcely knew if she had spoken the words. She was held helpless once again in his clutches.

"Your mother was a slave and so are you. A slave even in all its finery is still just, a slave." He spoke close to her ear.

"But I am willing to accept you as you are. I will provide for you, I assure you that you will not lack for anything." He continued, his eyes searching her face.

His words pierced her heart and scandalised her sensibilities, releasing within her all her darkest fears. Dido was numb. She had no power to defend herself, as her tears wet her cheeks. She could not look at him nor could she give thought to his pernicious words.

"You think me wicked, yet I am an honest man. I can take care of you." He said, releasing her wrist suddenly. Dido found herself in a position to escape and fled towards the house. Such was Dido's distress that she ran directly into Lady Finch-Hatton and Lady Louise who had just at that moment decided upon taking a stroll in the garden. Unable to say a word Dido hurried into the house in a state of anguish, oblivious to their cries of concern.

"Dido?" Lady Finch-Hatton called anxiously, alarmed at the tearful disposition of her cousin.

"Is she ill?" Lady Louise asked, both unable to guess the cause for her distress. A moment later they could see Captain Alwyne coming from the same path of which the lady had just fled from.

"Captain Alwyne, do you know what is wrong with Miss Dido?" Lady Finch-Hatton asked directly, her anxiety for Dido's welfare left her with little regard for the impertinence of her question.

"I cannot say madam." Captain Alwyne replied blankly before excusing himself, leaving both ladies astonished and completely at a loss as to what had taken place. Lady Finch-Hatton thinking only of Dido's distress had taken little consideration of Captain Alwyne's blunt response. Lady Louise, not believing Captain Alwyne's words for one moment, supposed that the lady's distress was no doubt due to her being slighted by the gentleman.

"Dido, goodness, what is the matter?" Lady Finch-Hatton cried violently on seeing Dido crying upon her bed. Lady Finch-Hatton had returned directly to the house, apologising to Lady Louise for postponing their walk as her concern for Dido had given her no pleasure for the exercise.

"Come now, please tell me?" She encouraged pleadingly, her alarm increasing at Dido's continued distress. Lady Finch-Hatton had not seen Dido in such a state since they were children. She was at a loss to know what could have caused such an outburst.

"Maybe I should call for the doctor?"

"No! Please it is not necessary." Dido forced herself to speak and attempted to control her tears.

"You must tell me what is wrong? Why do you suffer so?" Lady Finch-Hatton asked anxiously. Lady Finch-Hatton's manner was so distraught that Dido relented and began to account the incident with Captain Alwyne. As she spoke Lady Finch-Hatton looked at Dido in total disbelief.

"No. It's outrageous! Are you sure? Are you positive that this is what he said?" Lady Finch-Hatton asked, and continued to repeat these questions throughout Dido's revelation.

"How can this be?" Lady Finch-Hatton exclaimed. Astonished, she began to pace the room in silent contemplation. Then stopping suddenly she came back to sit beside Dido.

"The best thing to do is to stay in your room for the rest of the evening. Captain Alwyne and the other guests will be leaving tonight. There seems to be a change of plans, which is just as well considering what has just occurred. I will make your excuses." Lady Finch-Hatton stated thoughtfully

"Dido, you cannot mention this to anyone, especially not to Lord Mansfield." Lady Finch-Hatton advised. Dido gave Elizabeth a look of astonishment, as she had no intention of telling anyone of her humiliation, the thought horrified her. And yet Captain Alwyne's conduct towards her had been disgraceful. How could he be made to go uncensored?

"It will only make matters worse. What good will it do for you to disclose the incident?" Lady Finch-Hatton was saying, thinking of the unnecessary ugliness of such a revelation. Dido conceded that perhaps Elizabeth was right. What good would it do for her reputation? A gentleman was able to escape such acts of indecency without little or no consequence to their moral standing, whereas a similar hint of indiscretion was enough to put into question a lady's reputation.

"Yes, it is for the best." Lady Finch-Hatton repeated in an attempt to reassure Dido as well as herself. What a wretched business! What would her husband think on the matter? She wondered anxiously, as she was sure that he would have to be told. This was done without delay directly after dinner. Mr Finch-Hatton received the news with a certain amount of self-conceit, at having the satisfaction of hearing his prophetic words coming to pass. It was just as he had supposed. He had known that such liberality given to one of inferior birth could only end in this kind of indiscretion.

"Did I not warn the imprudent girl that her behaviour would cause such an incident to happen?" Mr Finch-Hatton stated angrily and at that moment Lady Finch-Hatton felt a pang of regret at having told him. She had always considered her cousin's manners to be nothing but exemplary and attempted to say as much to her husband but with little success would he hear her argument.

"My wife has informed me of the – err – incident with Captain Alwyne." Mr Finch-Hatton remarked calmly at the breakfast table the following morning. Dido looked accusingly at Elizabeth. She had not expected Elizabeth to disclose the incident to her husband. But even as she thought it, she knew it to be a matter of naivety on her part. Nevertheless, Dido was mortified at being spoken to in front of the servants on what was a private matter that concerned her alone.

"I am quite sure that there has been some misunderstanding. Captain Alwyne is a respectable gentleman from a fine family."

Dido sat motionless in shame and displeasure. Mr Finch-Hatton's words increasing her agitation at his callous indifference to her feelings.

"I did warn you Dido about your conduct a few days ago." He continued coldly, making Dido to gasp with shock at the implication of his words.

"I disagree, sir. My conduct was neither indecent nor improper!" Dido cried warmly

"You may not think so but look where it has led." Mr Finch-Hatton responded unpleasantly.

"I would think that would say more for Captain Alwyne's conduct than that of my own." Dido replied hurt by the cruelty of his words. Unable to listen to any further accusations, Dido stood up to excuse herself.

"Sit down at once! You are acting childishly." Mr Finch-Hatton commanded, losing his temper.

"Please Dido, sit down. It will do no good to get upset." Lady Finch-Hatton agreed, hoping to influence her cousin. Dido sat back reluctantly in her chair in silent indignation.

"At least do me the courtesy of listening." Mr Finch-Hatton stated in a patronizing tone, attempting to control his temper at Dido's impertinent manner. Dido had to hold her tongue from replying in like fashion.

"Needless to say, I think a lesson has been learnt here. This is where your imprudence has got you. I see no need to act on the matter further or to even broach the subject again." He said coldly before turning his attention to his newspaper with a dismissive air. Dido willed herself not to cry, as she had no desire to give Mr Finch-Hatton the pleasure of knowing how much his words had wounded her feelings. To suffer the abuse of a stranger was one thing but to suffer the same abuse from one's relative was far worst. How she wished she had not told Elizabeth! If she had not pressed her Dido would not have divulge her suffering to a living soul. She could not stay here a day longer in the company of those who blamed her for her own misfortune. Dido longed to be home at Kenwood, to see her uncle again.

"Can I request that the carriage be made ready tomorrow to take me back to Kenwood?" she asked, to no one in particular as she no longer felt that her request would cause any displeasure, except perhaps to Elizabeth. Her request was greeted with silence. For a moment Dido thought that she had not spoken the words aloud, until Elizabeth began to plead for her continued companionship.

"How can you think of leaving now? I cannot possibly agree to it." Lady Finch-Hatton cried selfishly as Dido's presence had been a great comfort for her.

"I have stayed here for almost six weeks now, which is longer than I had expected. You are much recovered now and I feel that I should be at home." Dido argued unwilling to give in again to her cousin's pleas.

"I think Miss Dido is quite right. I see no reason why she should not leave within the next few days." Mr Finch-Hatton said, failing to keep the impatience from his voice. He had suffered her presence in his house only for the sake of his wife. Though he had to concede that her manners were genteel, he decided that her society could only be tolerated within the confines of her family, as having her presence at the dinner table with their guests had been a regrettable mistake. Lady Finch-Hatton lamented the loss of Dido though she still remained with them for a further two days. She continued to plead tearfully for Dido to stay though she knew her efforts to be fruitless. When the day of Dido's departure arrived, Lady Finch-Hatton had intended to see her off but was ordered by her husband to remain in bed, as the weather was too cold for her to be out in. Dido had to be content with saying a brief farewell to her tearful cousin before her departure but nothing could spoil her pleasure at the prospect of returning to her uncle and Kenwood.

# CHAPTER 19

Dido could not express her feeling of utter delight on arriving home at Kenwood. Her return gave her the sensation of being too long away, so much so that every familiar sight gave her great pleasure. Lord Mansfield had welcomed her back with much fuss that she felt pleased in the knowledge that she had been missed by him. She had missed her uncle dearly and appreciated the opportunities of being in his company. Now that she was home Dido intended to keep a watchful eye on her uncle's health. She could immediately see from the tiredness of his features that he had been overworking in her absence and she scolded him for it. Lord Mansfield mumbled disagreeable at her nagging but he was pleased to have her back at Kenwood. A week had already passed and Dido had fallen back into her familiar routine. She had on her return, promised that she would reacquaint herself with all her favourite walks and had wasted little time in doing so. A smile came to Dido's lips as she walked the familiar paths of the gardens and woods and felt the rustling wind brush her face and dress. She felt the sensation to shout with delight at the pleasure of being at home again. She spent hours of each day walking about the grounds recapturing her enjoyment that her absence had denied her. Dido was desirous of immersing herself within her secure world, where evil recollection of recent events at Eastwell Park could be, at least, reflected upon with calm. Captain Alwyne's offensive conduct could now be examined with less pain. Dido decided that his manner, though it had injured her, had done more injury to his person. He had revealed himself to be a gentleman of inferior breeding. How disdainful that *he* who considered himself to be of superior birth, having failed to demonstrate any of the privilege of education and moral upbringing obtained, should condescend to look upon her as his inferior. Captain Alwyne, Dido decided, had clearly shown that it was not important to whom one was born but to how one was brought up. In this respect Dido need not be ashamed. There was nothing in her manner and conduct that would have condoned Captain Alwyne's behaviour. Dido could only feel loathing at the recollection of his address. Her only desire was to conceal the incident from her uncle and put the unpleasant experience behind her, with the hope of never seeing Captain Alwyne again.

She was back in the safe cocoon of her world, secure from the risk of offending or being offended. Here she could avoid the censure of the odious system of hierarchy that related to race and class. She was not ignorant of the fact that her cocoon had its conditions. She knew all too well her position in her family and the rules to which she was to adhere to. Dido had learnt from an early age to play her role obediently, even at the expense of her own feelings. But now they rarely had visitors as her uncle had little time or inclination for entertaining guests and Dido was glad of it. This provided all the contentment that she needed.

"Now that Elizabeth is gone, it will do well for you to have an occupation." Lord Mansfield announced a few weeks after her return.

"An occupation?" Dido repeated, curious to know what her uncle had in mind. She had considered the possibility of doing something to occupy her time besides the usual pastimes of sewing, reading, drawing and practicing on the pianoforte. The thought of getting involved with charitable work had often crossed her mind but she was helping her uncle with his correspondence more often of late that it always seemed impractical. In the past she would occasionally accompany the late Lady Mansfield to the local alms houses to distribute food and clothes for the poor. Dido found these trips both disturbing and fascinating to her senses. It provided her with a first glimpse into the lives of people far less fortunate than herself and she had at first been appalled at the horrid conditions of these houses. The buildings appeared tolerable on the exterior but once inside the state of them were far deteriorated. The walls were dull and badly faded with dim light adding to the squalid-ness of the house. The furniture was modest but in similarly bad condition. The occupants mainly elderly and children looked unkempt and hungry. Dido wondered at the care these poor creatures received and was shocked to hear the warden, Mr Edward Griffin, telling Lady Mansfield how well they fared.

"Everyone is well looked after here thanks to your kind benevolence, Lady Mansfield." Mr Griffin said graciously, smiling widely.

"What of the chimney? Has it been fixed?" Lady Mansfield asked, as if not hearing what Mr Griffin had said. She looked about herself discerningly, taking everything in with one glance.

"Not yet my ladyship," the gentleman answered apologetically bowing his head to hide his irritation as he shifted nervously from one leg to the other.

"It should have been done long ago. The winter is swiftly upon us, sir. Fix it." Lady Mansfield said sharply turning away before Mr Griffin could respond.

"Yes, yes of course Lady Mansfield." He repeated apologetically.

Dido watched this exchange with interest. Mr Griffin was a short slim man with a sly look to him. His father, Rev. Charles Griffin was the parish chaplain until his death eight years earlier, and had presided over the parish board of several of the alms houses with a great deal of attention. Expecting his son to follow him into the clergy, Rev. Griffin had found it difficult to accept the news that his son had chosen a different path. Rev. Griffin would have continued lamenting his son's fall from grace had Mr Griffin not decided to take over the running of one of the alms houses, which enabled the father to come to terms with his disappointment. Mr Griffin's real motive in taking the position was an attempt to appease his father, thus he had little love for his vocation, and so found himself fixed in a position, which he had no desire to stay, but no resilience to leave. Dido thought Mr Griffin would rather have done without the instructions of his benevolent benefactor if it had not been for her much-needed contribution. It was little wonder that his salutations appeared insincere in its generosity. Dido voiced her concerns to her aunt on the journey home.

"Can Mr Griffin be trusted? I mean, is he an honourable man? " Dido asked then felt it necessary to continue as Lady Mansfield gave her an incredulous look.

"There is something in his manner that does not appear trustworthy." Dido said trying not to sound too incriminating.

"Nonsense girl. Mr Griffin has been running the alms house for many years now. I have not seen anything untoward in his treatment of his occupants."

"I fear the people do not look so well looked..." Dido continued

"They have three good meals a day. They have a place to live which at least in that respect they are better off than most." Lady Mansfield stated with a finality that showed she did not want to hear another word on the subject. Dido did not press her any further. For the next few months, whenever Lady Mansfield went on her charitable rounds she took a reluctant Elizabeth with her. Though Elizabeth protested her aunt would have none of it. Dido supposed her aunt was slighting her for her criticism and so decided not to say another word on the subject. But for many months now Dido had thought of joining the abolitionist cause. Mr Sharp's visit had inspired her to take action. And Dido read with interest the increasing activities of anti-slavery societies around the country, many of them established by women. With much excitement she had corresponded expressing her interest for details of membership for one such society, pleased that she was able to help in some small way. Dido had thought better of telling her uncle, ignoring the momentary pang of guilt for the concealment of her secret, reasoning within herself that she was doing nothing wrong. In any case she was using her personal allowance to pay for her monthly donations, and therefore did not require his permission. But perhaps now was a good opportunity to express her interest to her uncle.

"I have often thought of the abolitionist cause" Dido began cautiously, "Meeting Mr Sharp has made me think that perhaps I could assist in-"

"I do not think it advisable to consider it as a pastime as it is a serious cause." Lord Mansfield cut in. Dido felt hurt at his questioning her sincerity and dedication to the cause.

"I am well aware of it, but surely I would think that the little I could do would be better than nothing at all."

"Dido, you do not understand the complexities of these societies"

What was there to understand? If others, who had less to gain than herself, could voice their complaint and protest, why could she not do the same? Dido wanted to say as much but kept silent, as her uncle's reaction was so unexpected.

"You have read on the subject in newspapers and magazines but believe me the reality is much different." Lord Mansfield continued to Dido's annoyance.

"Perhaps sir, if I could just speak to Mr Sharp-"

"No. That is enough, child. I want no more talk on this matter!" Lord Mansfield commanded angrily to Dido's astonishment, leaving her in no doubt of his opposition. Wherein had she erred? He, who had done much to promote the freedom of slaves, should refuse her participation in the fight for abolition? How naïve she was to think that he would support her decision.

"I have your best interest to think of." Lord Mansfield said after a moment pause, regretting his severity. Dido could not speak her temper would not allow her to. Did he really consider her to be so childlike that he had to protect her from everything? Lord Mansfield could see her displeasure and wished to change the subject.

"I was thinking of a more realistic occupation such as supervising the dairy farm and perhaps the poultry too. There is much work to be done and it will benefit from a keen eye," said Lord Mansfield good humouredly

Dido could find little enthusiasm for his suggestion. But she had never disobeyed her uncle and she could not do so now.

"If it is what you wish sir." She replied civilly as she could and said nothing else, of which Lord Mansfield had to be content with.

# CHAPTER 20

A letter arrived from Eastwell Park announcing the news of the birth of baby Louisa to Mr Finch-Hatton and Lady Finch-Hatton. Both Lord Mansfield and Dido were delighted at the news and were desirous of seeing both Elizabeth and child. A day was set for their journey to Eastwell Park, as Elizabeth was eager for a visit. As they journeyed to Eastwell Park, Dido's thoughts became increasingly overcome by the intrusive recollection of her last visit, which kept her much distracted that her uncle enquired on more than one occasion whether she was feeling unwell. Her uncle's concerns gave Dido the power to exert herself to feeling and sounding more cheerful than she actually felt.

"I wonder how Mr Finch-Hatton takes to having a girl instead of a boy?" Dido asked her uncle, as she knew how much Mr Finch-Hatton wanted an heir.

"I should not think he ought to be worried. There will be plenty of opportunity of having a boy. After all, girls aren't so bad you know." Lord Mansfield said with a smile, at which Dido laughed, although she wondered at Elizabeth's forbearance at the idea of having many more opportunities. Dido insisted on their stopping for a rest at several stages of their journey so as the break up the tediousness, as her uncle looked so frail she did not want to risk the chance of him becoming unwell. When they finally arrived at Eastwell Park Mr Finch-Hatton was present to meet them. Dido found to her surprise that his manner and appearance was very agreeable.

"Welcome Lord Mansfield, Miss Dido. Lady Finch-Hatton will be delighted to see you both." He announced with such warmth that Dido would not have known him. Perhaps fatherhood had done much to improve the severity of his manner.

"How are Elizabeth and the child?" Lord Mansfield asked with interest

"Her condition is very comfortable. Louisa is in good health. They are both resting, I'm sure you will have an opportunity to see them later. I know you will want some refreshments after your long journey."

They both agreed simultaneously and were both refreshed and entertained throughout by Mr Finch-Hatton, whose manner did not cease to amaze Dido. She looked to Lord Mansfield to see if he had noted the change and saw that he too appeared to express a look of surprise from time to time. After they had been adequately refreshed they were shown to their rooms to rest before dinner. Dido had expected to see Elizabeth before dinner but was informed, to her disappointment, by Mr Finch-Hatton that both baby and mother were resting. The custom of dinner had to be performed. As she ate, Dido could not help but feel that they were like naughty children being kept from their play. Finally the eagerly awaited meeting with mother and child arrived to the delight of Dido and Lord Mansfield. Dido was astonished on seeing Elizabeth how well she looked. Though she complained continuously of the pain she suffered, she was pleased by all the attention she was receiving. The nurse brought a sleeping baby Louisa and all attention was given to her looks and weight and healthy features.

"Is she not the most beautiful baby you have ever seen?" Lady Finch-Hatton exclaimed with the bias of a new mother. They were all in agreement, as they knew that every mother considered their child the most beautiful. Dido was pleasantly surprised by Elizabeth's display of affection towards her child that she was confident that Elizabeth had now been cured of all her selfish tendencies. The rest of the visit was spent waiting for the infant to awake, at which, the infant obliged and opened her eyes but only for a few seconds after which they were closed again. Then began a discussion upon the colour of her eyes before the visit was brought to an end by a doting Mr Finch-Hatton, who stated that his wife be provided with a much needed rest. Being satisfied with the health of both Elizabeth and Louisa, Lord Mansfield and Dido's visit was a short one. They departed with the assurance from Elizabeth of visiting Kenwood in the following months.

Five months later Lady Finch-Hatton arrived at Kenwood with Louisa and her nursemaid for a stay of several weeks. Dido was delighted as she felt that Kenwood was once again filled with laughter and happiness. There were many days spent outdoors with the fine summer weather, of which Louisa was happy to play. One afternoon Dido sat with Elizabeth and Louisa in the garden as Louisa struggled to get out of the grip of her nursemaid then presently began to cry.

"Perhaps you should take her in." Lady Finch-Hatton suggested to the nursemaid

"Yes Lady Finch-Hatton"

"Please let me take her. I think she only wants to play." Dido said, already attached to Louisa since her stay at Kenwood.

"I'm sure she is tired." Lady Finch-Hatton said unable to tolerate Louisa's crying, as it made her head hurt.

"Surely not, she has just awakened from her nap just over an hour ago." Dido stated, taking Louisa from her nursemaid, who gave her a disapproving look before turning to her mistress in the hope that she would command the child to be given back into her care. But Louisa immediately stopped crying and began to gurgle, which made her mother relent in her first decision and allow Dido to walk Louisa around the garden to show her the flowers.

"You spoil her too much." Lady Finch-Hatton declared on another occasion when Dido sat playing with Louisa. Dido had to concede that she was very fond of playing with Louisa whenever she could, as the child was of such a happy disposition and hardly ever cried unless taken from her play.

"Are you still set against marriage? I can see when you are with Louisa that you have already changed your mind as you yearn to have children of your own. I knew it would be so." Lady Finch-Hatton declared decidedly to cause Dido to protest at her cousin's words.

"No, I have not changed my mind as you would think. Though I am greatly fond of Louisa, my thoughts on marriage are as they were." Dido replied adamantly.

"You only say such things because you have not fallen in love."

"What good did love do you?" Dido said and immediately regretted her words. She had not meant to be discourteous to her cousin or to hurt her feelings but the meaning of her words were deeply felt.

"Please forgive me..."

"I know that you disapprove of my marrying Mr Finch-Hatton because I was not in love with him. Perhaps you will not be so despising of my marriage if I told you I was more than content with my situation."

"I did not mean to imply_"

"I know very well what you intended in justifying your decision. And what will your situation be after Lord Mansfield death? How will you support yourself? Will you be able to justify your decision then?" Lady Finch-Hatton said angrily, losing her temper with her cousin's ignorance. Dido was left feeling remorseful at her carelessness. Though she attempted to apologise again and again her cousin's humour was spoilt for the rest of the day.

Four weeks had passed so quickly that Dido could hardly hide her tears as she waved goodbye to Elizabeth and Louisa. Dido's attachment to Louisa had grown more deeply than she would have expected in the short time of their visit. Louisa's happy disposition had brought much joy to Kenwood that it was with a sad heart that Dido kissed her healthy rosy cheeks as Elizabeth promised to invite her to Eastwell Park soon. Dido was convinced that she would be willing to endure the unpleasantness of staying at Eastwell Park simply to see Louisa again. Perhaps Elizabeth was right. Could she possibly consider marriage for the joy of having children of her own? And for a moment Dido dreamt of the possibility, before reality and common sense prevailed. No, it could never be! To sentence a child to the heritage of slavery could never be contemplated.

# CHAPTER 21

The day that Dido dreaded since the death of Lady Mansfield had arrived very much like any other day but with such unexpected brightness that she could not have anticipated the gloom to come. The sun had cast its rays on the walls of Dido's room that she impulsively stopped her toiletry to run to the window and threw them open to appreciate the beauty of the day. Dido, laughing playfully, did not heed the look of utter astonishment from an impatient Sarah, who was eager to finish Dido's toiletry, so as to continue with the rest of her duties.

"Miss Dido you are a fine one this morning." She said tutting and shaking her head.

"Come now we must finish Miss." Sarah added sharply, but she was unable to stop herself from smiling at the display of her mistress's youthful exuberance.

Dido moved reluctantly away from the window, as the sound of Mrs Jenkins voice could be heard from downstairs.

"I wonder what is up now." Sarah asked curiously, sure that Mrs Jenkins was complaining of something and nothing.

Dido had already returned to the dresser where Sarah was just in the process of fixing her hair, when sound of the commotion below increased a pace, and Dido, unable to stay in her seat any longer, ran to the door to satisfy her curiosity. The voices grew louder as Dido hastened into the hall followed directly by Sarah.

"Is there something wrong?" Dido asked as she observed the servants gathered outside Lord Mansfield's dressing room talking anxiously amongst themselves.

"Lord Mansfield has fallen ill Miss Dido."

Dido did not wait to hear another word, before running hastily into his dressing room to find her uncle lying on the floor with Mrs Jenkins and Watkins the valet kneeling beside him. His face was pale and lifeless. Dido let out a cry and fell helplessly on the floor to the alarm of poor Mrs Jenkins. Dido could not recollect what happened next as her emotions was such that she had no control over them. In the commotion that followed Lord Mansfield had recovered consciousness and was attempting to get to his feet but with little success.

"What is all this confounded noise?" he could be heard saying.

"No my lord, you must not move." His valet went to his aid.

"Nonsense. Who says? Am I to sit here on the floor indefinitely?"

Lord Mansfield was helped to his chair. Dido, with an anxious and tearstained face, knelt beside him unable to speak.

"Will you stop gawking at me as if I'm a fish in a bowl!" Lord Mansfield growled and then closed his eyes momentarily, which caused everyone to gasp with fear.

"What is it now?" he said wearily.

"Are you in pain, sir?" Dido asked anxiously. On hearing her voice Lord Mansfield manner softened.

"Dido, get these people out of here, that's a good girl." He requested quietly.

Dido felt reluctant to leave him alone but nevertheless obeyed his instruction.

The doctor arrived and presently examined the patient. Dido stood outside with the servants anxiously awaiting the doctor's return. Even Mrs Jenkins waiting for news, forgot to order the housemaids back to work. When Dr Robertson came out he made arrangements for a bed to brought down to Lord Mansfield's dressing room as he felt it best for the duration of his illness. Taking Dido aside Dr Robertson stood for a moment in thought.

"Lord Mansfield is a sick man. He will need complete rest for some time."

"There is to be no work or visitors permitted. Dido, do you hear, even if he feels better he is not to exert himself. I know how headstrong he can be." He stated firmly.

"I will do my best doctor." Dido replied

"If anyone can keep his lordship in place, it is you."

"Sir, I think you greatly overestimated my powers of persuasion" Dido replied hesitantly, knowing all too well her uncle's disposition.

"Do your best." Dr Robertson encouraged firmly.

"He will need to take this if he feels any pain." He said holding out a bottle towards her.

"What is it?" Dido asked anxiously

"Let us just say it is a pain relief." He said gravely, placing the bottle in her hand.

"Will his health improve?"

"It is possible, with rest. He is strong for his age. At least he has that to his advantage."

"I'm sorry I cannot give you the assurance you desire." He said sadly before taking his leave promising to return in a few days. Dido returned to Lord Mansfield and found him asleep. She felt the wretchedness of her grief as she watched him sleep. Her thoughts disturbed by a darkness of another time. Could this be her uncle's final hours? Her sentiments reviled against such thoughts though she knew it could not be long before he would be lost to her. She was unable to withstand the torment of her feelings and feebly succumbed to its anguish. She wept silently in fear of disturbing her uncle, as her tears would only meet with his disapproval. Her weeping soon gave way to fervent prayers, as her mind clouded with the gloomy prospect of her uncle's death that would destroy everything that was dear to her. Kenwood was the only world she had ever known and loved. How could she survive the lost? How would she live? The thought made her tremble with apprehension. It was in this state of torment that Mrs Jenkins returned to find her.

"Come away now Miss Dido. It would do you no good to stay here. Lord Mansfield will be well taken care of." She said softly guiding Dido out of the room. Dido did not resist her command but walked quietly from the room. Mrs Jenkins showed a look of concern as she led Dido away. The girl appeared to be in a state of shock, walking lifeless as if in a trance. Without delay Mrs Jenkins called for Sarah.

"The poor girl is in a terrible state." She said aside to Sarah after they had settled Dido into bed.

"What will happen now that Lord Mansfield is ill, miss?" Sarah asked curiously

"The master is not dead girl!" She replied irritably.

"Things will continue as normal until Lord Mansfield recovers." Mrs Jenkins added more calmly, though she dare not share her fears, as she too had no idea what would become of them should Lord Mansfield pass away.

"Make sure you keep an eye on Miss Dido." She instructed before quitting the room.

"Yes, miss." Sarah answered meekly.

"What if he doesn't recover?" Sarah said to herself sighing deeply. She dearly hoped that the master recovered not only for her own sake. She was very happy at Kenwood since the start of her employment five years hence. There had been little reason for complaint, with the exceptions of a few minor confrontations with Mrs Jenkins. Sarah had kept herself to herself and got on with her work and thought herself very fortunate to be a lady's maid to Miss Dido. At first, Sarah had been overcome with fear when she had discovered from the other staff that her mistress was black. But those fears were soon dispelled when she became acquainted with her mistress. Miss Dido's manners were like any other lady, even more so, Sarah would boast. She considered Miss Dido to be such a good natured and kind-hearted mistress, who had always treated her with nothing but kindness and respect that it was impossible for Sarah to feel anything but the highest affection for her. It was this affection that caused Sarah to think with sadness on the master's illness. Everyone knew that Lord Mansfield doted on her mistress, but if he were to suddenly die, who would look out for Miss Dido's interest? Sarah could not help but feel anxious for her mistress' future.

The business of informing Lord Mansfield's relations of his illness was done in earnest the following day. No sooner had the letters been sent the visitors arrived within two days. Lady Finch-Hatton and her husband Mr Finch-Hatton arrived first but it was just above half an hour before the carriage of Miss Marjory Murray, Miss Ann Murray and their brother Mr David Murray, the 6th Viscount Stormont, could be seen pulling into the entrance. David Murray, father of Lady Finch-Hatton and nephew and heir to Lord Mansfield, was a sober man without pretension. Though like his sister Ann Murray, he wore a superior air, but this came not from a feeling of self-pride but rather from a sense of responsibility of the importance of his position. Dido felt pained at the arrival of further relations, so unaccustomed was she to such crowds. Their presence brought a rather sombre atmosphere to Kenwood, that Dido thought they would soon turn the house into a wake!

"My uncle is not dead yet, why are they all here." Dido said to herself as they all gathered in the library. She sat silent and rigid, having no desire to be present.

"Poor Uncle William looks dreadfully ill." Marjory Murray cried, suddenly becoming overcome with grief.

"I am so afraid he shall not survive for long." She continued gloomily.

"Come now Marjory, Uncle William's condition is poorly but he is not near to death. There is no need for alarm." David Murray replied as he tried to console his sister.

"But brother you must confess that it is a dreadful state to be sure." Ann Murray added decidedly

"Simply dreadful." Marjory Murray agreed, consoling herself with a generous slice of cake.

Lady Finch-Hatton had by now given into her tears and had to be consoled by her husband.

"Let us not have any more gloomy talk." Lady Finch-Hatton declared once she had recovered sufficiently enough.

"I am not one to think the worst but we cannot avoid looking ahead." Ann Murray said calmly.

"Uncle William will need looking after." She continued tactfully. There was a consensus of agreement.

"There is no question of that." Mr Murray added.

"Marjory and I will stay here to take care of Uncle William. It's the least we can do in the circumstance."

"But Dido is here. Do you really think it necessary?" Lady Finch-Hatton asked, looking to her father.

"Yes, of course she is but Uncle William will need the *best* care." Ann Murray replied, unconcerned of Dido feeling the full meaning of her words. Marjory Murray who shifted uncomfortable in her chair gave Dido a nervous smile. Dido sat silently listening to their conversation with increasing vexation, her heart beating violently as the desire to leave the room increased. Who would notice? No one had paid her the slightest attention with the exception of Elizabeth. They had all talked around her as if she were invisible and unworthy of any consideration. How she wished to be anywhere but in the present company! But she had little choice but to remain in her seat and suffer their impertinence. Dido knew exactly why they were here, no doubt out of concern for their now impending inheritance than Lord Mansfield's health. Perhaps Dido's judgement was ill founded and possibly misplaced where Marjory Murray was concerned but she was certain it was the case for Ann Murray and Mr Murray. Now that her feeling had been injured, Dido cared little for the injustice she may have inflicted upon her relations.

"Dido has always looked after Uncle William with the best of care." Lady Finch-Hatton came to Dido's defence. For this Dido felt an enormous gratitude towards her dear cousin.

"I do not doubt Dido's err _ devotion. I am merely stating that greater care is needed"

"You do understand don't you Dido?" Ann Murray asked sweetly, drawing everyone's attention for the first time to Dido's existence.

"Of course." Dido replied courteously, reproaching herself for being so compliant.

"There! You see Dido understands!" Ann exclaimed with satisfaction at Dido's response.

"It will also be beneficial for Dido too. The poor girl will not have to bear the burden of looking after Lord Mansfield alone. She looks positively ill." Ann Murray continued not able to resist the fun she was having at Dido's expense. She began to examine Dido's features intently, expressing more concern than she actually felt.

"Don't you think?" she asked with false apprehension. For the second time all eyes were turned to Dido's complexion and a discussion began as to whether it was true or not, which caused even Dido to believe in the possibility of Ann Murphy's diagnosis.

"Yes, sister, I think you are right she does look a little tired." Miss Murray agreed with much deliberation. Then followed a consensus of agreement that Dido was actually ill and had to be sent to bed at once. Dido was glad of the excuse to leave the room, though she knew that Ann Murray might have had her own motives for her removal. She had no wish to listen any longer to their talk of impending changes. However, instead of going straight to her room Dido decided to first look in on her uncle. To her surprise she found him awake peering intently at a book.

"Ah, Dido come and sit with me a moment." Lord Mansfield said, removing his glasses and putting his book aside.

Dido did not hesitate but entered and sat down at the edge of the bed.

"I see that we have been invaded." He said wryly.

Dido was forced to smile.

"What fuss and nonsense!" He grumbled irritably

"Do not excite yourself sir." Dido prevailed upon her uncle to rest.

"Stop fussing, child. I have not begun to get nearly excited!"

"Nevertheless the doctor says you must not get upset." Dido said firmly. "Can I get you anything before I retire, sir?"

"No. I have been asleep all day. What am I supposed to do for the rest of the evening?" he complained as he began to look about himself before reaching for his glasses. Dido smiled sadly. She thought he looked like a little lost boy in need of care and protection. She thought it best not to mention what had already passed in the library, as she could not bring herself to do so. No doubt Miss Ann Murray, who prided herself on knowing what was *best* for her uncle, would inform him of their plans. Dido feared that her uncle's present situation was no more secured than her own, now that they were both at the will of their relations. What would become of them now? Dido sat with her uncle in silent contemplation until hearing voices in the hall, quietly quitted the room for fear of being discovered.

# CHAPTER 22

Miss Marjory Murray and Miss Ann Murray were the unmarried nieces of Lord Mansfield; the former a spinster by choice and the latter by circumstance.  Miss Marjory Murray being the eldest sister would naturally be looked upon as having authority over the younger. But those who were well acquainted with the sisters would know this to be the reverse. While Marjory Murray was the senior in age she was not in mind. Miss Murray being of a delicate and poorly constitution since her early childhood was used to being told what to do and had grown into adulthood with neither the desire or ability to make decisions for herself without the aid of others. She shunned decision-making like the plague and cared little for anything too strenuous. Her solace was her paintings and books. She had no interest in love or courtship and was unable to understand the excitement of those who did. She grew up in this manner until her old age changing little in her disposition or tastes. She considered herself to be quite contented to live out her days as such. Ann Murray as the cleverer of the two sisters was much more inclined to take control of all matters concerning them both from running the daily needs of the household to deciding their pastimes. She had done so since their childhood after the early death of their mother and consequently as a natural progression, continued to take charge of the care of her sister.  Ann Murray was superior in manners and accomplishments, and so was inclined to think rather highly of herself. Being under the guardianship of her uncle Lord Mansfield, Ann Murray had acquired a conceited self-importance that had led her to aspire to become a great lady and mistress like her aunt, Lady Mansfield. But her hopes were dashed at the age of two and twenty, by a gentleman of birth and consequence whom after having formed an attachment of several months had disappeared without a word, leaving Ann Murray injured and humiliated by the desertion.  It was later discovered that the gentleman had formed an attachment with another young lady and was speedily engaged to the horror of Ann Murray. And though she was told by her relations that the attachment had been but a brief one and therefore could not have done much damage to herself, Ann Murray had failed to agree.  The notion of marrying beneath her ideal had caused her to disregard the attention of those who may have in time asked for her hand. But as it was Ann Murray passed the years with growing resentment at being cheated by life's injustice. Her character was such that she took no pleasure in the felicity of others. Thus she became both cynical and envious of those who had achieved what she had failed to accomplish. Though she had accepted the indignity of being an unmarried woman and had become accustomed to some of its benefits, nevertheless the idea of being a spinster, a word she detested as far too common and vulgar a word to be used for a woman of her social standing, had not diminished over the years. Ann Murray decided that the only acceptable course of action was to embrace the role of a single woman. Thus, she spoke of her single lifestyle as if it was her intended destiny all along. As to confess otherwise, would be to admit to a deficiency, which was wholly unthinkable, the inability of securing a husband. Luckily for Ann Murray, it was becoming more fashionable to be single, which made the job of convincing every one of its joys far easier than it might once have been. Both sisters on hearing of their uncle's illness had agreed unanimously that there was no question of their residing at Kenwood for the duration. In fact it was Miss Ann Murray who had made the decision and had merely informed her sister of the fact. Miss Murray happily agreed, as she was anxious for her uncle and desirous of being at Kenwood again. Now that they had arrived, Ann Murray wasted little time in casting a disparaging eye around the estate with a keen intent of making various changes.

Dido scarcely slept the night so troubled was her thoughts. The morning afforded her little relief as the house was bustling with activity brought on by the extra guests. Poor Sarah had little time to attend to Dido's dress, being required by both Marjory and Ann Murray, who demanded much of her attention. It was not that Dido was concerned at Sarah's lack of attention to herself, as she had little trouble with dressing herself. But their constant calls upon Sarah's service produced within Dido a feeling of indignation at their ill-treatment.
"How outrageous!" Dido muttered at all the fuss that was being made and the extra work that was being put upon the servants. On arriving at the breakfast table Dido found Elizabeth, Miss Murray and David Murray already seated. She was informed that besides the Miss Murrays, only Lady Finch-Hatton and her father David Murray had stayed over. Mr Finch-Hatton had left yesterday evening. Lady Finch-Hatton would stay only a few days before returning home, as she did not want to be away too long from husband and daughter.
"How are you this morning Dido? I must say you look better, my dear." Miss Murray enquired.

"I am well thank you." Dido replied courteously but Miss Murray had already continued to lament again of her uncle's illness.

"Oh these are dreadful times!" she stated with a hint of melancholy.

"Please let's not sound so gloomy Aunt Marjory. It is far too early in the day!" Lady Finch-Hatton cried with much impatience.

"I quite agree." David Murray added, looking up briefly from his papers.

"I do not think I was being gloomy." Miss Murray said defensively

"Anyway, it is too fine a day to be gloomy." She added, though little attention was paid to her remark.

"Please find out if Lord Mansfield is up?" David Murray commanded to the butler.

"Yes sir."

Dido thought better of informing Mr Murray that she had checked in on her uncle before she had come down to breakfast and he had been still asleep.

"I think it far too early for Uncle William to be up yet." Miss Murray ventured

"Nevertheless I would prefer to have our talk as soon as possible, seeing as I will have to leave at the earliest convenience." David Murray said looking at his watch.

Dido was curious to know what Mr Murray's talk with Uncle William could be about. What business could be so urgent when her uncle was so grievously ill?

"Have I missed anything?" Ann Murray asked as she took her seat at the table.

"That maid of yours is absolutely useless. It is a wonder that I am ready for breakfast and not for tea!" Ann Murray stated to Dido with great exasperation, as if some great calamity had befallen her.

"Sarah has always been very efficient." Dido said in her defence.

"Perhaps you are used to her fumbling ways." She replied condescendingly.

"I fear the servants are too spoilt here." Ann Murray continued with displeasure.

"I disagree. Lord Mansfield is not in the habit of spoiling anyone," said Dido, feeling it necessary to correct Ann Murray's unjust remark.

"I beg to differ dear Dido!" Ann Murray exclaimed

"We know that he spoils you a great deal." She added slyly.

Dido's countenance could not conceal the sting she felt at her intended insult.

"I was referring to the servants." Dido replied confused, as she attempted to mask her hurt.

"Yes of course you were my dear that is what Ann meant, I'm sure." Miss Murray said in an effort to soothe her.

Dido was inclined to doubt Ann Murray's sincerity. The full meaning of her words had not escaped anyone in the room, excepting Miss Murray, who could not think ill of anyone. Until then she had not thought that Ann Murray had harboured any ill will towards her. Since her childhood both Ann and Marjory Murray were frequent visitors to Kenwood for many years, though she knew that they had not held her in the same esteem as Lady and Lord Mansfield and Elizabeth but she could not recollect an occasion of them ever showing any dislike of her. Miss Murray especially, had shown her nothing but kindness. Perhaps now that Lord Mansfield's influence was weakening as fast as his health, it was no longer necessary to show even the slightest civility towards her. Had it come to this? To be treated like a servant by her own relations? David Murray had hardly said one word in her direction, speaking either to his sisters or his daughter, only referring to Dido indirectly and yet she had been acquainted with him since a child. Elizabeth's manners were as they had always been, talking only of herself and her daughter Louisa. Of this Dido was grateful.

"Dido you must come and see dear Louisa. She took her first steps a month ago and now she is walking about the place. You have not seen her since she was only a baby." Lady Finch-Hatton remarked, thinking their last visit to be almost a year ago.

"It has been less than a year, in fact it has been only six months." Dido replied

"Oh really? But that seem such a long time ago. Why not come back with me tomorrow. The change of scenery would do you good."

"What an excellent idea!" Ann Murray agreed immediately before Dido could object.

"I cannot possibly leave now not while uncle...Lord Mansfield is so ill." Dido said decidedly, having no desire to leave her uncle.

"A few days will do no harm. After all we are here now." Ann Murray said brushing aside Dido's objection.

"Yes, I think it is a splendid idea. The rest would do you good." Miss Murray agreed enthusiastically as she thought that Dido needed the rest.

"You see. That's settled then." Lady Finch-Hatton said with such finality expecting no further objection on the subject.

"I could not possibly go without first speaking to Lord Mansfield." Dido said as a last effort to resist the weight of consensus against her.

"Nonsense. I'm sure Lord Mansfield can spare you for a few days." Ann Murray stated putting an end to her protest.

Just then Mrs Jenkins came into the room to announce that Lord Mansfield was requesting to see Miss Dido.

Dido could have kissed Mrs Jenkins for her timely interruption. She could barely hide her satisfaction at her uncle's request.

"Please excuse me," said Dido, attempting to contain her mirth.

"Well if Uncle William is able see *her* surely he will be able to see you David." Ann Murray remarked sorely.

"Yes, inform Lord Mansfield that I wish to see him immediately." David Murray insisted.

"Yes Sir." Mrs Jenkins replied before leaving the room.

"I tell you he positively dotes on the girl." Ann Murray could be heard saying as the door closed.


"What is going on downstairs?" Lord Mansfield asked with interest.

"Why nothing sir." Dido said hesitantly, not wanting to be the one to inform him of their plans.

"Come now, my nephew and nieces are scheming behind the back of a dying man." Lord Mansfield declared bluntly not failing to notice Dido hesitant manner.

"Surely not sir?"

"Maybe so, but they are up to something. What is all the fuss about?"

"They are only concerned for your health sir." Dido said in their defence, which she had to admit to being true, though their plans were not to her liking.

"Blah!" Lord Mansfield uttered irritably

"Elizabeth has requested that I stay with her for a few days." Dido said thinking it best to change the subject.

"Tired of this sick old man already?"

No, of course not. I would prefer to stay here."

"No, no. Perhaps the change would do you some good. I have been too selfish with your time." Lord Mansfield said after some thought.

"Please do not say such a thing." Dido cried warmly

"Nevertheless it is true. Do not think that I am not grateful." He smiled

"Anyway, I am feeling much better. What I would like to do is get out of this confounded bed!"

"No, it is far too soon, sir. Dr Robertson will be here to see you later today. At least wait until his visit." Dido cautioned in her attempt to dissuade him from doing anything drastic to affect his health.

"Well I am at my leisure. I shall hear what my nephew has to say. Send him up."

Ann Murray accompanied her brother to see their uncle with the sole purpose of ensuring that the arrangement for his care would be suitably conveyed. The usual pleasantries were said before Ann Murray, not wanting to waste any time began informing her uncle of all their concern for his health.

"Uncle William, I'm sure you'll appreciate that our presence here will be of great necessity." his niece announced then began to talk of the benefits of their presence at Kenwood.

"I have no need of any further nursemaids." Lord Mansfield said brusquely.

"Sir, that is not what Ann is implying." David Murray interjected.

"Dido and the servants are here. I see no need for any further assistance."

"Dido cannot do everything. The poor girl is ill herself." Ann Murray pointed out, deliberately exaggerating Dido's condition. It proved rather effective as Lord Mansfield hesitated momentarily.

"Surely the running of the household and the estate as well as taking care of you is far too much for one girl." She continued seeing her uncle weakening at her argument. Ann Murray hoped that her uncle's fondness of the girl would work to her advantage. She soon realised that her uncle had little concern for his own health but if he were made to see that Dido's health was also at risk, then perhaps her uncle could be swayed to see reason. In truth the estate could run sufficiently enough during his illness, thus it was useless to argue the point.

"Dido is a sweet girl, she would never complain even if she had cause to."

Ann Murray felt sure now that she had succeeded in removing her uncle's objections as he remained in silent contemplation.

"After all, we only have your best interests at heart. It may be that your illness will only be for a short duration in which case Ann and Marjory's stay will only be temporary until you are back in good health." David Murray added taking his uncle's silence as a good sign. Both brother and sister had been very persuasive that Lord Mansfield could find no argument in which to resist, what he must confess to be a reasonable arrangement. Though the prospect of having two of his nieces fussing over him gave him little pleasure, he could not deny his concern for Dido's health. Perhaps he had put too much upon her shoulders. It was this thought that made him grudgingly concede to their wishes. On hearing the news, Dido could not deny her disappointment at the ease in which her uncle had conceded. If she had known that her uncle's capitulation had been wholly for her benefit, Dido would have done everything in her power to dissuade him from this decision. As it was she remained in ignorance of the fact and could not help but feel saddened that her uncle had been so easily persuaded by his niece.

Ann and Marjory Murray wasted little time in arranging for several items of belongings to be moved to Kenwood. Ann Murray having the inability to entrust any task, great or small, to the responsibility of others, decided to go back home to ensure that all the arrangements were in order and that the correct items were being conveyed. Lady Finch-Hatton left the same afternoon after taking leave of her uncle, with the assurance that Dido would follow in a few days. Dido saw no need to object to this plan now that her uncle had consented to having his nieces at Kenwood. Perhaps a trip to Eastwell Park was not such a bad idea, Dido reflected, as she missed dear Louisa and would be glad of the opportunity of seeing her again. It would give her time to get used to the changes that would inevitably take place at Kenwood. Dido was reminded of the day when she had vowed to never leave her beloved home. How difference things were then! Kenwood was no longer her beloved Kenwood. Little by little her secure world was being threatened by Lord Mansfield's impending death. To Dido, her uncle's death appeared far greater a reality than it actually was, unthinkable though this assumption was to her, it haunted her every thoughts and threatened to stifle any hope of her uncle's full recovery.

# CHAPTER 23

It was in this state of turmoil that Dido left Kenwood for Eastwell Park. She had no thought to where she was going, as her mind was far too preoccupied. The natural beauty of the landscape and prospects escaped Dido's attention. The tediousness of her worries and the length of the journey were given over to fitful sleep. Thus on her arrival at Eastwell Park, Dido found that she was not only exhausted but had acquired a headache. Lady Finch-Hatton greeted her with such raptures that it would appear to any onlooker that their meeting was one after a long absence and not of just three days.

"Oh, Dido you are just in time to see Louisa before she is settled for bed." Lady Finch-Hatton said. Dido had hoped to retire to her room at least to rest before dinner but she could not deny Elizabeth's excitement of seeing her little Louisa. The nursemaid arrived with the Louisa who on recognising Dido came immediately to her and placed her arms around her dress. Dido could not help but laugh as she knelt down to embrace her. All her tiredness disappeared on seeing Louisa dear face, who had grown so much since Dido last saw her. Louisa was rather an affectionate child and Dido was very fond of her and would play with her for hours. On which her mother would complain of her spoiling Louisa too much. While Dido attempted to tickle Louisa who squealed with enjoyment, Elizabeth appeared suddenly displeased at Louisa's attention to Dido.

"Come and give your mother a kiss." She said stretching out her hand. Louisa toddled across towards her mother but then on finding something more interesting to play with stopped to investigate and had to be called several times before her nursemaid led her gently to her mother, at which Louisa began to protest noisily. Lady Finch-Hatton held her daughter and attempted to entertain her will kisses and cooing in order to get her to laugh. Dido soon found herself cooing and smiling in the same manner. This preoccupation did not give Dido any displeasure, as Louisa was an adorable and happy child and would gratify her mother and aunt with a laugh from time to time until she became tired of the game.

"Darling, are you tired?" Elizabeth cooed. Dido hoped she did not expect a response as Louisa wriggled to get free. She presently gave her up to the nursemaid kissing Louisa on the cheek as she went. Dido could only marvel with pleasure at how much motherhood had changed Elizabeth.

"She has grown more beautiful since I last saw her." Dido said to the delight of her mother. For these are the words every mother desires to hear in reference to their child as it satisfied a natural vanity. After all, praise of the child is an indirect praise of the parent. It would be an injury to any mother if her child did not receive either praise or attention. Lady Finch-Hatton was no exception. Her vanity, having no moderation, received with great delight Dido's compliments on Louisa's beauty.

"I'm sure she is the most beautiful of creatures! To think she is soon to be a year old. My, how quickly the time goes!" she declared

"But I do not think I will have anymore. When I think of how painful it was to have her, though she is a perfect little dear." She continued, and then went on to give an account of her confinement and delivery of Louisa, though she had told Dido on numerous occasions.

"But is it not worth it?" Dido asked certain that Elizabeth had no regrets about having Louisa.

"Yes, but if only all the pain and suffering could be avoided all together," replied Lady Finch-Hatton, wondering why it was not humanly possible for women to forgo the whole unpleasant experience of childbirth.

"I am sure it is not so difficult for all mothers." Dido said which made Lady Finch-Hatton gasp in distain.

"You could not possibly know that until you have a child of your own then you would not talk so easily." Lady Finch-Hatton warned

"Perhaps it is better to adopt." Dido teased.

"Don't be ridiculous. Adoption is out of the question, unless it is one's own relation." Lady Finch-Hatton rebuked.

"I do think that women have a terrible job of it all in all." Lady Finch-Hatton bemoaned unable to cease from the feeling of revulsion at the prospect of having to go through confinement and childbirth again.

"I am sure when you become a mother one day, then you will know exactly what I mean." Lady Finch-Hatton said with satisfaction as if the only purpose for her desiring Dido becoming a mother was so that she could experience the displeasure of childbirth.

"I shall never marry, therefore I shall never have children." Dido announced

"It is not always a choice we can make for ourselves. When Uncle William dies and the new Lord Mansfield resides at Kenwood, what do you think will become of you?"

Dido remained silent, unwilling to confess that Elizabeth's words were more to the truth than her own. Yet Elizabeth's words had shocked her in their frankness. Dido had imagined the possibility of the new Lord Mansfield living at Kenwood but she could never bring herself to contemplate the likelihood her departure from the only home she had ever known.

"Your only option is marriage." Lady Finch-Hatton concluded.

"It is the only way. No doubt something will be arranged…" Lady Finch-Hatton continued oblivious of Dido's pensive state.

"I'm sorry…" Dido stood up suddenly unable to listen to any more talk of marriage.

"…I do not feel well,"

"Of course, how thoughtless of me. You must be tired from your journey." Lady Finch-Hatton moved to ring for a servant.

"You sure there is nothing I can get you? Perhaps I should call the doctor?" She said with concern on seeing Dido's complexion.

"No! Please do not trouble yourself. I am merely tired and in need of rest." Dido answered doing all in her power to reassure Elizabeth that rest was the necessary remedy. When the maid arrived to take her to her room, Dido was forced to reassure Elizabeth again that a doctor was not necessary. In the solace of her room Dido was able to consider the full meaning of Elizabeth's words. Could it be true? Could her uncle consider arranging her marriage? This thought troubled her greatly but it would do no good to brood over it in her present state of exhaustion. Dido exerted all her will power to cease from feeling melancholy. She went to the basin to wash her face, and then moving to the window, was struck by the sight of a flock of birds in the sky. She envied their freedom.

Dido found that the morning provided little relief from her anxious thoughts, as she could think of nothing else but of the prospect of an arranged marriage. Even as she played with Louisa her smiles were soon replaced by a solemn and distracted manner. She could not continue in this state of agitation, she simply had to know from Elizabeth if anything had been said or hinted at. Dido decided to raise the subject at dinner.

"Has anything been said regarding my future?" Dido asked directly. If there had it would do well to know presently. Elizabeth appeared surprised at her question but shrugged her shoulders rather casually.

"Not in any real terms." She replied indifferently

"What do you mean?" Dido asked warmly, unable to accept the thought that any such arrangement could be made without her knowledge or consent.

"Surely you must know that everyone is concerned for your welfare in the event of Uncle William's death."

"Who exactly is everyone? And why is it that I am not consulted by everyone's concerns?" she cried indignantly.

"Well, I'm sorry to have mentioned it." Lady Finch-Hatton said with some annoyance.

"Please Lizzy, do not withhold anything from me!" Dido pleaded causing Elizabeth much alarm at the violence of her manner.

"Come now Dido, do not upset yourself so. It's so unbecoming," she urged, feeling compelled to relief her cousin's distress.

"I simply heard Aunt Ann mention to my father that it was time to seriously consider plans for your marriage."

"Lord Mansfield is planning an arranged marriage for me?" Dido cried astonished. She ought to have considered it a possibility and yet she did not want to believe its reality, for she had deemed it to be impossible!

"Dido, surely you must know that marriage will be in your best interest."

"I have no wish to be married!" Dido cried heatedly

"No wish! What is it for a woman to wish for anything?" Lady Finch-Hatton answered losing all patience with her cousin. How naïve she was to think that she was in control of her own destiny, Lady Finch-Hatton thought. She blamed her uncle for spoiling Dido too much.

"What options do you have? Where will you live? How will you support yourself? Lady Finch-Hatton asked pointedly.

Dido could not reply. Elizabeth was right. The reality of this revelation caused Dido to feel the full extent of her vulnerability. It proved a difficult task to control the emotions that threatened to overwhelm her with helpless tears. How miserable was her situation! Lady Finch-Hatton manner softened when she observed her cousin's countenance.

"Believe me marriage is not such a miserable situation as you may think."

"In time you will think better of it." She encouraged

Dido doubted her words, as she had no intention of ever *thinking better* of the prospect of marriage!

# CHAPTER 24

The journey to Kenwood seemed intolerably slow to an impatient Dido, who felt the urgency of speaking to Lord Mansfield on her return. Her mind was in turmoil as a result of having Elizabeth's words for company the entire length of her journey. Dido could not have imagined that her situation could have become any more miserable. Not only was she soon destined to lose her uncle and her home but also faced the prospect of a loveless marriage! What preparation could be attained in readiness of such a gloomy future? To think that Miss Ann Murray was at this very moment persuading her uncle of the suitability of marriage, gave Dido a feeling of increasing vexation. Surely her uncle would not consent to such a proposal? The very thought of there being any possibility of his agreeing, produced within her a feeling of dread. How could she resist his authority? Oh, it was unbearable to consider such thoughts without the satisfaction of knowing the truth!

"I will go mad if I do not cease these wretched thoughts." Dido cried aloud but in vain. As every thought must return to the possibility of such a marriage. She could not escape the enormity of her situation. How she longed to be home to put an end to all her speculations!

Dido found on her return to Kenwood that changes had already begun in earnest. She had expected to see her uncle later that evening but found Miss Murray and Ann Murray at afternoon tea and was called upon to join them. Tea was far earlier than Dido was use to but she was sure that this was just one of many changes, as she soon discovered that the schedules for the dairy and poultry had been changed to allow for what Miss Ann Murray referred to as *greater productivity*. Dido found that Miss Murray and Ann Murray preferred to sit in the library after breakfast rather than in the morning room as Dido was accustomed to. Afternoon tea was taken in the drawing room while dinner was set an hour later than usual. The servant's quarters were in an uproar at the sudden changes. Mrs Jenkins complained daily out of the earshot of the Misses Murrays, while, the servants complained to her regarding the extra work they had been given. Dido listened sympathetically to Sarah's complaints but with little power to affect any change. The thought of speaking to Lord Mansfield was out of the question. He was far too ill and in any case could not be troubled with the business of running the house. Dido forced herself to pluck up the courage to speak to Ann Murray but when she attempted to raise her concerns she found that Ann Murray repelled her objections in a polite but dismissive manner.

After several days following her return from Eastwell Park, Dido had failed to find an opportunity of speaking with Lord Mansfield, having had little chance of being alone with him. She began to despair of her ever having an occasion, with Miss Murray and Ann Murray constantly fussing over their uncle. Must they always be about! Dido complained unable to control her temper. She observed grudgingly that her uncle looked much improved since she last saw him, but it gave her little pleasure to relinquish her responsibility of caring for him herself. When Lord Mansfield asked with interest for the details of her visit to Eastwell Park and of the welfare of Elizabeth and Louisa, Dido hoped that an occasion had finally arose. But Ann Murray remained seated and began to complain of her uncle's need for rest. Thankfully for Dido, Ann Murray's continuous fussing proved too much for Lord Mansfield, and provided Dido with the opportunity that she had long been desirous of.

"We must allow Uncle William to rest we do not want him to get too excited." Ann Murray announced as a way of signalling an end to their visit.

"I think I am still in soundness of mind to know if I've had too much excitement!" Lord Mansfield growled to Dido's delight.

"I am only thinking of your health, sir." Ann Murray said rather offended by her uncle's outburst.

"Let me alone with Dido. You have fussed over me quite enough for one day!" he stated adamantly

Ann Murray reluctantly gave in, seeing that her uncle could not be persuaded.

"Dido please try not to keep Uncle William too long from his rest," she said sourly before withdrawing from the room. Dido could not believe her luck of finally being alone with her uncle.

"Peace at last!" Lord Mansfield exclaimed. Dido felt she should say something in defence of Ann Murray but thought she could not do so without being false in her application, so instead remained silent.

"How are you child?" he asked looking intently at Dido.

"I should be the one asking you that, sir." Dido said warmly.

"There is a matter..." Dido began hesitantly now having the opportunity lacked the courage to speak.

"What is it? I know how much things have changed since my nieces' arrival here." Lord Mansfield began thoughtfully

"It is not that." Dido said and paused again.

"Well out with it!" Lord Mansfield encouraged with some impatience.

"I have heard that plans have been made for my future marriage." Dido asserted finally bringing herself to say the words.

Lord Mansfield sighed heavily and did not speak for a moment. His silence gave Dido a feeling of anguish, as this was not the response that she had expected.

"So it is true." Dido said quietly, stunned by the painful realisation.

"Dido, you are my responsibility. It is my wish that you be taken care of after my death, whenever that time will come."

"It would grieve me if I were to fail in this. A marriage would secure your future." He continued soberly.

Did he not know that he had sealed her doom with his words? Every hope was lost to her. How could she possibly hope to resist the prospect of marriage if the very person in whom she depended upon for protection was in consent of the scheme?

"May I be permitted to ask who it is?" she forced herself to enquire.

"Nothing has been arranged as yet, Dido. I would not have you marry where you do not choose. Don't think me so unfeeling. I would be failing in my duty towards you if I were to leave you defenceless and unprotected." Lord Mansfield said after a moment's pause. Dido sat in stunned silence. Had she the will to protest or to resist she would have done so. But the utter dismay of her situation robbed her of any strength. Her fate was sealed. Dido had never gone against the wishes of Lord Mansfield. She had always trusted in his judgement explicitly. But now that judgement was going against her own wishes. How was she to act? How could she disobey him? It would pain her to displease him but the thought of marriage to someone she did not know or love, caused all her senses to revolt. Dido had to concede that within herself that there was an even greater fear. The incident with Captain Alwyne had left her horrified at the possibility of a reoccurrence. Would her husband look upon her as a slave to be abused and ill-treated? She was not ignorant to suppose that every gentleman would possess the same vile opinion as Captain Alwyne but the thought that there *were* men of like mind was reason enough for Dido to shun any such connection.

## CHATPER 25

The winter months signalled the end of an old year and the beginning of a new at Kenwood. Lord Mansfield's health was much the same. He remained confined to his dressing room, but refused to stay in bed. He conducted from his dressing room, his reading and the writing of his correspondences to various friends and relations, with Dido's help. Miss Murray and Ann Murray's residence was now a permanent fixture at Kenwood. The household had survived the various changes and was able to continue if not in a happy state, at least in a tolerable one. The servants were now resigned to accepting the new regime, knowing that to find another position as advantageous as the one presently occupied at Kenwood would prove difficult. Therefore, contented themselves with airing their grievances to one another out of the earshot of their employers, with the exception of Dido, who they looked upon as one of their own. But this allegiance would soon be shattered by an incident that would change this harmonious relationship at Kenwood. The butler was first called in by Ann Murray and questioned on the damage of the vase discovered in the Dining room. After assuring his employer that he had cleaned and left the china intact, the maids were called in and interrogated in a similar fashion. When no one would confess to the heinous crime, Ann Murray became almost violent in her resolution to catch the miscreant. Dido had not heard about the incident until later that evening when Sarah arrived to attend to her dress.

"Nancy didn't mean any harm by it. It was an accident, Miss Dido." Sarah explained.

"Mrs Jenkins was terribly upset. But we were not letting on it was Nancy, see." She continued as she finished helping her mistress into her dress.

"I think you should tell Mrs Jenkins the truth, I'm sure she'll understand." Dido advised not wanting the problem to escalate.

"It's not Mrs Jenkins I'm worried about. It's Miss Ann who's the problem, Miss."

"Sarah, do not be ridiculous. Miss Ann is not unreasonable." Dido attempted to defend her relation.

"I'm sorry Miss Dido but she is a wicked woman." Sarah spoke plainly, before realising her mistake on seeing her mistress' countenance.

"Sarah, I beg you not to speak of Miss Ann in that manner again in my presence." Dido said soberly aghast at Sarah's forwardness.

"I beg your pardon miss." Sarah replied, looking suitably chastised by Dido's rebuke.

Sarah's words had shocked Dido. Though she was willing to admit that Ann Murray could be unpleasant, she could not, in all fairness, assent to her relation being *wicked*. Sarah was such a kind natured girl, that Dido began to wonder at the feelings of the other servants. Could this be the general consensus? Dido hoped that through her own conduct she had not been at fault in encouraging such sentiments. This thought troubled her as she attempted to recollect anything in her manner or temperament that could have given the impression of her having any ill feelings towards her relation. Though Dido disliked Miss Ann's dishonesty and could not condone her apparent pleasure in making others feel inferior, she had never considered her an enemy. Try as she might, Dido found it difficult to think of any good traits that her relation possessed, but was saved from despair when she remembered Miss Ann's love for Kenwood, and her care of her uncle. Indeed Dido could not find any fault with her own conduct and possessed complete assurance that her conscious was clear in this instance. Thus Dido sat in the drawing room totally unprepared for what was to follow. After dinner the subject of the broken china was once again raised by Ann Murray.

"How poor dear Lady Mansfield would turn in her grave at the careless destruction of her beloved home." Ann Murray remarked with total aversion. Both Miss Murray and Dido looked up from their occupation to Ann Murray, the first from her sewing and the latter from a book. Dido wondered what else had happened to cause Ann Murray to express so violently her feelings of indignation.

"The servant's disregard for valuable heirloom is absolutely intolerable," she continued unrelenting in her complaint.

"It is very unfortunate." Miss Murray added with dismay.

"I do not think it was done intentionally." Dido remarked unable to keep silent.

"Not intentional? Not intentional? My dear Dido you are so naïve." Ann Murray replied becoming peeved by Dido's comment.

"I'm sure Nancy did not intend..." Dido began then realised rather too late from the reaction of both Miss Murray and Ann Murray that she had committed a grave error.

"So it is Nancy who is responsible for the damaged vase?" Ann Murray stated with satisfaction while getting up to ring the servant's bell.

"How long have you known about this?" Ann Murray asked sternly, taking her seat once again.

"There was no secret..." Dido began but feeling the guilt of her discovery could not continue.

"And when did you intend to inform us?" Ann Murray asked cynically. Mrs Jenkins arrival into the room saved Dido from replying.

"Ah, Mrs Jenkins, were you aware of who broke the china vase?"

"No Miss Ann. As I told you, the girls refused to tell me." Mrs Jenkins replied

"I see. It appears that Dido knows who is responsible." Ann Murray stated, causing Mrs Jenkins to give Dido a curious look.

Dido found it difficult to look Mrs Jenkins directly in the eyes, as she felt too ashamed of her careless mistake.

"Please call Nancy here at once Mrs Jenkins." Ann Murray ordered.

When Nancy arrived looking anxious and guilty, Dido could only feel miserable at the prospect of witnessing what was to come.

"I will give you an opportunity to confess before I ask you again the same question I asked this morning." Ann Murray said with such quiet menace that Nancy broke down and confessed weeping uncontrollably. Her tears were lost on Ann Murray who looked on indifferently. Dido watched in horror at the poor girl's pleadings fell on death ears.

"Your services are no longer required. You have Miss Dido to thank for that. You can pack your belongings and leave in the morning." Ann Murray announced coldly, disregarding the tearful pleadings of Nancy. Dido gasped. She had not expected the poor girl to lose her job.

"Surely this is not necessary!" Dido exclaimed horrified by the scene before her.

"Please miss, I didn't mean any harm! It was an accident!" Nancy pleaded to no avail.

"Dido please remain silent this is no concern of yours." Ann Murray interjected with cold civility

"You cannot treat her so unjustly!" Dido cried in astonishment

"Mrs Jenkins please can you remove this – girl from the room." Ann Murray finished, ignoring Dido's plea.

Once the door was closed Ann Murray turned to Dido with a superior air.

"How dare you speak to me in such a manner in front of the servants?" Ann Murray seethed angrily.

"Perhaps it is *you* that is in need of being reminded of your position."

"What? Would you have me thrown out too?" Dido cried as she fled from the room, too distressed to give thought to the impropriety of her conduct.

"How disgraceful!" Ann Murray cried, finally losing her temper all together.

Dido returned to her room trembling with indignation and humiliation at Ann Murray's treatment of her. How dare she? To think how grossly she had misjudged the extent of Ann Murray's maliciousness. Her censure of Sarah now appeared rather misguided. If she had only her feelings to consider, she could have borne it sufficiently. But she felt wretched knowing that she was in some way responsible for poor Nancy's dismissal. How could she have been so negligent? Her indiscretion had cost Nancy dearly. Yet Dido knew that she could not have kept Sarah's revelation to herself. To keep silent would have been unthinkable, as she could never condone a lie. Ideally, Dido had hoped of gaining an opportunity of persuading Nancy to confess the truth then perhaps her punishment would not have been so severe. As it was Dido was left to feel only regret whenever she thought of the incident.

Immediately after Nancy's departure Dido detected a change in some of the servants' behaviour towards her. She supposed that it was inevitable that they would see her conduct as an act of betrayal. But she had not expected to be subjected to hostile silence and suspicious looks from many of the servants as they went about their duties, of which Dido chose to ignore, though it gave her great pain. She had always felt content in the knowledge that her relationship with the servants had always been a harmonious one. But this unanimity had been broken by the unfortunate incident. She could understand their resentment towards her, though their behaviour at times was bordering on insolence. Ought she to tolerate their impropriety? And yet Dido's fear of any of the servants losing their livelihood was reason enough to remain silent. At least she could be grateful for Sarah's loyalty.

"It's not your fault Miss Dido. If anything it's mine for letting slip in the first place." Sarah said thoughtfully, though she had been greatly saddened by Nancy's dismissal.

"Don't you mind them, Miss. If I was you Miss, I'd get rid of the lot of them for their insolence." Sarah added clicking her fingers dismissively.

Dido would have thought Sarah's remark rather amusing if it had not been so ridiculous. She had no jurisdiction to dismiss anyone! If anything, Dido thought that she was just as likely to be dismissed as any of the servants! Ann Murray had made it apparent with every gesture and words of the inferiority of her position. Her manner had deeply wounded Dido's feelings, knowing now that she was considered by her own relation merely a servant in her own home.

"I hope Dido that you will kindly respect the decisions made in future. After all it is solely for the purpose of keeping order at Kenwood." Ann Murray declared at the breakfast table a few days after the incident. Dido was expecting a reprimand of some kind but nothing was said until then.
"I am not the cruel creature you think me." She continued when Dido made no response.
"You think me unjust in my treatment of that servant. But I disagree entirely."
Dido had to listen again to her reasons for dismissing Nancy.
"Ann did what she thought was best." Miss Murray added siding with her sister, though she thought her judgement to be rather harsh where the servant was concerned.
"Really Marjory there is no need to defend my actions." Ann Murray reproached her sister.
"Indeed, there is no need to justify yourself to me. I may not agree with your actions but I would like to apologise if my conduct was inappropriate." Dido forced herself to say to the surprise of Ann Murray.
"I'm so glad that we are not completely out of your favour." She replied sardonically.
"Well that settles it! I'm so glad that this nasty business is finished with." Miss Murray exclaimed, thankful now that the unfortunate business could finally be forgotten. She detested disagreements of any kind as they always made her feel uncomfortable. Dido glanced at Miss Murray and smiled. She could not help but be amazed at the immense differences between the sisters. One was of a simple and good-natured disposition without any guile, while the other was conceited and vindictive with a cruel tongue. Is it possible that one of them could have been exchanged at birth? Dido wondered amusingly.

Dido chose not to confide in her uncle on the matter of Nancy's dismissal. The thought of worrying him unduly hindered her, though his health was much improved of late. Dido observed, as he sat dictating his letters to her that she had not seen her uncle look so well in weeks. When the weather was pleasant enough he would spend up to an hour in the Orangery, tending to his plants and flowers, while Dido listened as he talked of the variety of flora. Particularly at these moments, Dido could believe that her uncle could recover to full health again, and that his nieces would return home and everything would be as it was before. If Dido allowed her imagination liberty to hope, it was purely to relive much happier times and to drive away the dreadful months of present suffering. But she knew she could not give into such indulgence for long. Reality could be a cruel master demanding every hour of each day. Lord Mansfield's illness was such that for every good day there were equally bad days. As a result her thoughts fluctuated between morbidity and optimism and back again in a moment at the varying condition of her uncle's illness. It grieved Dido to know that far worse was yet to come, that she could not bring herself to think on it.

"You have changed child. You always look so troubled." Lord Mansfield observed one afternoon. Her uncle's words cause her some alarm. Had she become so transparent?

"I can assure you sir, I am well." Dido replied not wanting to reveal her inward suffering.

"You would tell me if anything was wrong?" Lord Mansfield asked with concern.

"Yes, certainly sir. Please do not worry about me." She answered brightly, trying to withhold the misery that was threatening to engulf her, and at the same time feeling the temptation to express her despair. But she knew she could not risk burdening her uncle with her pain. No, she could not find it in her heart to worry him.

"I'm not ready to leave just yet." Lord Mansfield said encouragingly, knowing that much of her melancholy was due to his ill health.

"I'm glad to hear it sir." Dido smiled for the first time in weeks.

"Ah, that's better. That's my Dido!" He exclaimed with a wink.

Dido laughed softly. Could she dare hope? When alone with her uncle, Dido could feel as she used to. She could forget her present woes and pretend, at least for a brief moment, that everything was as it had always been. And yet, deep in her heart, Dido wondered if they could ever be again.

"Uncle William is rather concerned about your health." Ann Murray announced to Dido soon after her return from her afternoon walk. Dido felt disappointed that her uncle should find it necessary to voice his concerns to his niece.

"Did you say anything to him this morning to cause him to feel so?" she asked suspiciously

"No, nothing." Dido replied in earnest.

"I don't have to remind you that Uncle William's illness is of such a delicate nature that any upset could be detrimental."

Dido could hardly control her temper at the supposition. Was there no end to this woman's insults?

"I am quite aware of my un– of Lord's Mansfield's health. I assure you I would not do anything to jeopardise it." Dido replied with as much civility as she could command.

"I am glad to hear it. After all you must know how protective Lord Mansfield is of you. Perhaps Dido you could try to be more cheerful, at least while you are in his presence." Ann Murray added wryly before leaving Dido alone in a state of desperately trying to control her emotions.

# CHAPTER 26

The spring months gave way to warmer summer days and summer turned grudgingly to autumn. The household of Kenwood settled into a routine under the close scrutiny of Ann Murray. Dido applied herself to finding places of retreat from her relations. In the summer she at least had the good weather as an excuse to take advantage of every opportunity for long solitary walks or just sitting in a secluded childhood haunt discovered many years ago. Dido loved walking down to the lake from the south terrace of the house. The prospect was so breath-taking that one could not tire of its view. During the summer, the rhododendrons where in full bloom, pinks, reds, lilacs and whites, and the richness of the green leaves of the elms, oak and chestnut trees added to the vibrancy that was exhilarating. But in the autumn the trees outshone the flowers with splendid red, yellow and russet leaves. Even now, Dido could not decide, despite the advantage of many years of occupancy, whether she preferred the wild natural charm of the woods or the cultivated beauty of the gardens. As the autumn set in and the weather became more severe, Dido had continued to persist in her walks until finally forced to stay indoors by the elements. But at least Dido could be content with sitting in the Orangery during the cold and rainy afternoons. The pianoforte served as another form of escape for Dido. She could tolerate almost anything while practicing, even Ann Murray's watchful eye and patronising words. But even this had its limitations, as no amount of playing could remove the gloomy prospect of her future. Dido found it difficult, not so much in hiding from her relations, but in finding excuses for spending so much of her pastime alone, without being discourteous. However, she was required by Ann Murray to be present at breakfast, tea and dinner, as well as when they were at leisure. On these occasions Dido sat in silence saying as little as possible and talked only when required. Some days the conversation between the sisters offered some amusement, not so much in its content as in its execution. The sisters would begin in this manner.

"Uncle William is much improved these past few days that perhaps a change of scenery would be rather beneficial." Ann Murray ventured

"Is it wise to change rooms since he is so improved at present?" Miss Murray asked in alarm

"Not rooms dear. I was only thinking of Uncle William spending some time outdoors."

"Oh yes, of course. I'm sure that will be a splendid idea. But do you think it will rain?" she continued, looking out at the dark clouds that filled the sky.

"If it rains then it would be awfully dreadful for Uncle William, we don't want him catching a cold." Miss Murray continued with concern.

"If it should rain today then we will have to postpone for another day." Ann Murray insisted,

"What a pity I was so looking forward to it. I'm sure Uncle William would have enjoyed the fresh air." Miss Murray remarked with an air of disappointment.

"There is still an opportunity that the weather may be fine this afternoon dear." Ann Murray stated with some emphasis, though this was entirely lost on Miss Murray.

"Yes, but all the same it shall be a pity."

Ann Murray knew it was useless to continue and quickly changed the subject.

"It appears that a mutual friend is coming to Kenwood." Ann Murray announced mysteriously.

"Pray tell, who?" Miss Murray exclaimed eagerly.

"Mr Arden. He will be accompanied by a Captain Davinier."

"Mr Arden? I do not recollect the name." Miss Murray declared with some confusion. She had a terrible memory for both names and faces, and was often in the habit of confusing acquaintances of many years.

"Yes you do dear. The husband of the late Mrs Amelia Arden whose company we had the pleasure of for several years before her death. Don't you remember her husband a very respectable gentlemen." Ann Murray explained

"Ah yes, of course. Now I remember, yes, Mr Arden, such a charming man!" she exclaimed half-heartedly as she vaguely recollected the gentleman.

"What on earth would they be coming here for?" she asked with such bewilderment as to make her sister turn and look at her in astonishment. Dido observed that Ann Murray seemed to be lost for words.

"It is merely a social visit." Ann Murray replied briskly which seem to satisfy her sister's curiosity. But her response did the contrary for Dido, as she sensed that something was not quite right, and although she was not quite sure what it was, she had a peculiar feeling all the same. Nothing had been said recently with regards to a future husband, that Dido had hoped that the subject was at an end. Though she hated to think the worst but she had learnt not to underestimate the guiles of Ann Murray. Could this captain be her intended suitor? The idea of Miss Ann secretly scheming away filled her with apprehension but also made her desirous of finding out all she could.

Lord Mansfield illness took a turn for the worst and for a few days Dido was not able to think of anything else. Nothing was mentioned about the guests and their impending visit so that Dido had entirely forgotten the whole conversation between Miss Murray and Ann Murray until a week later when Ann Murray announced that Mr Arden and Captain Davinier were expected in the next few days. Dido's emotions were all a flutter and she did not know how to act as she awaited the visitors with an agitated curiosity, having failed to gain any intelligence of Mr Arden, though she attempted to extract from her uncle any clues as to the purpose of their visit.

"I have only a vague recollection of meeting Mr Arden on two occasions but that was many years since. I know my nieces are well acquainted with the gentleman. It would do them some good to be reacquainted again." Lord Mansfield replied to Dido's question.

"What of his companion Captain Devier? I forget his name." Dido probed

"Captain Davinier's father, Charles Davinier, worked for me as a steward before his death, many years ago now." He replied plainly.

"I do not recollect him." Dido said thoughtfully

"Well you could not have been more than five years when he died." Lord Mansfield replied.

"Did Captain Davinier live here at Kenwood?" Dido asked eagerly.

"What are all these questions?" Lord Mansfield asked curiously, at which Dido coloured guiltily

"Well if my memory serves, yes but it would not have been for long." Lord Mansfield concluded.

Dido was all astonishment. Could it be possible? Surely now there could be no question of Captain Davinier being her intended suitor.

The day of the visit finally arrived. Ann Murray made much fuss over the dinner preparations for the guests, so as to make Dido suppose, that they were expecting royalty. Dido thought Ann Murray's excessive attentions for such an old acquaintance scarcely remembered by Miss Murray, was rather misplaced. Her curiosity of the gentlemen had increased upon hearing of their arrival but she deliberately stayed in her room, occupying herself with reading a book, which she failed miserably at, as she could not concentrate on one line, before she was summoned to dinner. She was introduced to Mr Robert Arden and Captain John Davinier as Lord Mansfield's ward, as was customary. Mr Arden's appearance and manner was exactly what Dido had expected. He was a gentleman of mature age in his sixties but in good health. He had rather a short and round stature, a jovial red face, with the largest whiskers Dido had ever seen. He talked freely and with much gaiety. So much in contrast with his companion Captain Davinier, a young gentleman, who looked rather grave, though his appearance was not displeasing. He stood tall and handsomely dressed in his regimentals, but Dido thought that perhaps the shortness of Mr Arden's height caused Captain Davinier to appear taller than he actually was. Dido found herself almost mesmerised by the immaculate shine of Captain Davinier's coat buttons, as she listened with interest as he described his service with the British East India Company and his time spent in India. Having spent more than six years there, Captain Davinier had been rather glad of the opportunity of returning to England. Dido observed that he spoke well and even appeared rather animated when he talked of his adventures.

"India sounds such an exciting place!" Miss Murray exclaimed eagerly

"It has its beauty." Mr Arden remarked

"Have you been to India too Mr Arden?" Ann Murray asked purely in order to make conversation, as she had recalled his late wife speak of his time in India frequently in the past.

"Oh yes, but that was many years ago as a young government official." Mr Arden answered proudly.

"It also has its dangers too. The heat is unbearable and many die from malaria and other diseases. The savages are hard to control. There are often outbreaks of rebellion, fighting and even war. If you can survive all that then there is always a chance of being eaten by a tiger." Captain Davinier declared drolly. Dido could not help but feel insulted by his reference to the Indians. Did he think them apart from humanity? What made one man a savage and another a human being? Dido considered Captain Davinier to be very much lacking in moral principle.

"Yes, that is true." Mr Arden agreed.

"It was far worst in my day. I was just glad I didn't have to do any of the fighting!" he laughed loudly

"But I always had a great fascination with the place."

"Captain Davinier, will you be returning to India in the future?" Ann Murray inquired with interest.

"No. My service in India is completed." Captain Davinier replied and then was silent.

"And how do you find England now? Is it much different than the England you left?" Miss Murray asked curiously.

"Yes indeed. I am delighted to be back. It was strange at first, as one is so use to the climate abroad and the occupation that one does not know what to do to occupy the time. But it is pleasant to be back in civilised society again."

"Are the Indians so uncivilised Captain Davinier?" Dido asked, before realising that she had spoken the question aloud. She did not regret it, though this was followed by an awkward pause and a disapproving look from Ann Murray.

"I'm sure Captain Davinier meant nothing more than that the natives are less civilised." Ann Murray replied hastily in an attempt to repair any offence.

"You must own that our civilisation is far superior to that of India." Captain Davinier stated un-phased by Dido's question.

"What of the poor of England? Are they more or less civilised than the Indians?" Dido inquired, unable to help herself.

"Dido! Please do not carry on so!" Ann Murray cried sharply before softening her tone on recollecting her guests

"What will Captain Davinier think of us if you continue to interrogate him in such a way?" She said forcing herself to laugh gaily to hide her irritation at Dido's impertinence.

"I see that I will have to watch what I say." Captain Davinier said good-naturedly, so as to cause Dido to wonder at why he had not been offended by her words.

After dinner Dido was called upon to play the pianoforte. Both Mr Arden and Captain Davinier were liberal in their praises and Miss Murray and Ann Murray gave their commendations to the performer, after which Dido was requested to play again. Soon after, the guests were taken to see Lord Mansfield before their departure. Dido was surprised at this meeting and said as much to Miss Murray when they were alone.

"I was not aware that Lord Mansfield was well enough to receive our guests." Dido said unassumingly.

"Yes, it was arranged earlier before they arrived." Miss Murray answered calmly as if it was common knowledge to all.

"It was?" Dido asked in astonishment then remembering herself, attempted to recover her composure.

"Oh yes, I was there when Uncle William expressed an interest in seeing the guests when Ann told him of their intended visit." She added quite innocently.

Dido said nothing further so as to avoid causing any suspicion at her enquiries. Besides, Miss Murray had revealed enough to give Dido sufficient reason to confirm her suspicions from her talk with her uncle yesterday. So Captain Davinier was indeed to be her prospective suitor! Dido would see to it that their plans would not succeed, where it was in her power to do so. She could not be a willing victim of their scheme. That it was her uncle, and not Ann Murray, who was responsible for choosing Captain Davinier as her prospective suitor, did not sit well with her. In fact, this revelation caused her great pain, as she had always trusted her uncle explicitly. But so much had changed in the last year. Everything she had known and cherished was being slowly taken away from her. She was merely a helpless spectator observing in dismay the scene before her. Mr Arden and Captain Davinier returned to the drawing room accompanied by Ann Murray to take their leave of the ladies. Dido eyed Captain Davinier's manner carefully for any hint or sign of partiality but saw nothing to suspect him of being an ardent suitor of any kind! His manners were so indifferent that Dido began to wonder at her earlier assumptions. But yet they would not leave her, as she lay in bed incapable of sleep. The morning provided her with little relief. Dido kept her anxiety to herself, attempting to take great pains to remove any thoughts of the visit from her mind. Though she had ample opportunities to question Lord Mansfield, Dido forced herself to remain silent on the subject of her uncle's mysterious meeting with Mr Arden and Captain Davinier.

# CHAPTER 27

The weeks passed and there was no talk of Captain Davinier, and Dido was glad of it. She decided to think no more on the subject but it proved a difficult undertaking as it seemed impossible for her thoughts to keep from dwelling back to their first encounter. Dido lived in dread at the mention of his name but neither Lord Mansfield nor Ann Murray said anything of the gentleman, so as to make Dido think that she had imagined their matchmaking scheme. Lord Mansfield's condition was much the same. He remained confined to his dressing room, with regular visits to the Orangery or to the terrace. Dido cherished the moments spent alone with her uncle, away from the interference of his nieces. He would often ask her to write letters or simply read to him whenever he became too tired to read himself. Dr Robertson, who visited regularly to check on the patient's progress, continued to be astounded at Lord Mansfield's constitution. He had not expected Lord Mansfield to last out the year but two years had passed and he continued to improve. Leaving Dr Robertson more optimistic of Lord Mansfield surviving several additional years, providing he continued to rest and keep his activities to a minimum. He said as much to Ann Murray.

"Your uncle has a very strong constitution. He'll probably out live us all." He added with humour, which Ann Murray failed to appreciate, as the idea of a sick man surviving those healthier than himself was quite ridiculous to her.

"We have a guest for dinner tomorrow. Do you think that Lord Mansfield will be well enough to join us?" Ann Murray inquired.

"I don't see why not. If his lordship feels up to it." Dr Robertson replied

"Thank you doctor, I will speak to Lord Mansfield."

Later that afternoon at tea Ann Murray made a similar announcement to Miss Murray and Dido.

"Captain Davinier will be joining us for dinner tomorrow."

Dido looked up unexpectedly from her sewing on hearing the news.

"Captain Davinier coming here?" Miss Murray asked excitedly.

"Yes. He wrote to express his gratitude for our kind hospitality. I simply replied that we were glad of the acquaintance and that he was welcomed at Kenwood at any time." Ann Murray answered casually, ignoring Dido's startled look.

"I'm so glad that he enjoyed our society. He is such a pleasant young man." Miss Murray remarked.

"I personally think it is a *certain* society he enjoyed. I think it rather sly of him." Ann Murray said shrewdly pressing her lips together into a smile.

"But I can't think why he would want to renew an acquaintance with us. After all we are only two old ladies" Miss Murray replied in confusion completely missing her sister's hint, while Dido was left in no doubt of its meaning. She was horrified at the insinuation.   Ann Murray deliberately chose to ignore her sister's confusion and continued,

"Captain Davinier has no more interest in us than he has in Mrs Jenkins," Ann Murray began again, trying to make clear her meaning for the benefit of her sister.

"Really! Has Captain Davinier an interest in Mrs Jenkins?" Miss Murray asked incredulously.

"Really Marjory, how can you think such a thing!" her sister exclaimed exasperated by her sister's outrageous question.

"But you did say-" Miss Murray began

"Please do not interrupt dear," Ann Murray cut in and again attempted to correct her sister's misunderstanding, as Dido sought to digest what had just passed. Captain Davinier was coming again to Kenwood? By Ann Murray's insinuations he was coming with the intention of renewing an acquaintance with her.  How was she to act or behave? She must think quickly, a plan of action was needed!

 "As I was saying, Captain Davinier will be joining us for dinner. Dido, you will be expected to join us of course." Ann Murray made a point of saying.

Dido was unable to speak, so vexed was her feelings she did not trust herself to speak civilly.

 "Captain Davinier is such an amiable young man. I found him rather charming, especially as he was wearing he regimentals." Miss Murray said again giggling childishly.

"Dido we do expect you to conduct yourself with propriety and for heaven's sake do not be as outspoken as you was the last time you met." Ann Murray warned threateningly.

"Perhaps I should remain in my room." Dido answered with mock civility

"Do not be so impertinent girl!" Ann Murray cried angrily unable to hold her temper.

"Please excuse me, I feel my presence is no longer required." Dido whispered, unable to sit a moment longer to endure the insults and reproach of her relation, stood up from the table without waiting for a response and hastily left the room. Miss Murray and Ann Murray were left both astounded at Dido's sudden departure. The latter more so, as her temper sorely stretched to its limit. Her first thought was to call for Mrs Jenkins to bring the wretched girl immediately back to the table, but thought the better of it. Perhaps what the girl needed was time to consider her conduct.

Dido decided against joining Miss Murray and Ann Murray for dinner that evening, but instead asked Sarah to inform both the Misses Murray to excuse her, as she was too ill to attend.   Dido's thoughts were so troubled by the morning's event that she had developed a terrible headache brought on by her continuous weeping at the hopelessness of her situation.  How she despised her position!  She was a slave having neither rights or say in the decisions affecting her future.  Her whole existence depended on the will or whims of others, to be patronised by all who cared to do so! But then Dido remembered poor Elizabeth? Did she not suffer the same fate that was now forced upon herself?  How much of her present suffering was due to her sex rather than her colour?   How many women were entering into loveless marriages against their will for the sake of social status and family obligations?  In this respect her sufferings were no different and no less painful than any other young woman in her position.  But Dido could not reconcile herself to this universal truth.

Miss Murray received the news of Dido's illness with genuine concern while Ann Murray, certain that Dido's absence was due to spite, felt nothing but impatience at the girl's insolence. But she resisted the urge to insist upon Dido's presence at the dinner table, regretting her earlier mistake in revealing Captain Davinier's intentions as she did.  She had played her hand too early and had underestimated Dido's disposition. Clearly the girl was going to proof more difficult than she had anticipated.  But Ann Murray had no intention of letting Dido ruin what she considered to be a most favourable match.  A match approved by Lord Mansfield himself, who had gone to considerable trouble to transfer  Captain Davinier from India to join a local regiment in England. If they were ever going to secure its success, Ann Murray concluded that Lord Mansfield would have to be called upon to persuade the girl of the benefits of the union.  Ann Murray could see the need for urgency in this matter, as to delay would prove detrimental to her plans. She was determined to act and act swiftly.

"Captain Davinier is dining with us tonight." Ann Murray reminded her uncle the following morning.
"I rather concerned about Dido's behaviour. She may try to, how can I say, resist the acquaintance."
"I do not see why she should, after all nothing is settled as yet." Lord Mansfield replied.
"Yes, but if Captain Davinier shows an attachment and there is no inclination on the ladies part, then it is likely that he will look elsewhere." Ann Murray hinted.
Lord Mansfield sighed heavily
"And what if she does not feel so *inclined*?"
"What if? Uncle William you know as well as I do that Dido is unlikely to find a better suitor than Captain Davinier. It is up to us to ensure that Dido sees it in the same light. She must be left in no doubt that you favour Captain Davinier advances." Ann Murray persisted
Lord Mansfield looked gravely at his niece and nodded. He did not need to be reminded of Dido's position, as he knew all too well. Dido was dear to him and he had great respect for her fine character and accomplishments. But her chances of marrying into the finest families as was expected of a lady living in her position, was made virtually impossible by her illegitimacy and colour. It pained him that he could not protect her from future disappointments in life. But if he could ensure that she would be taken care of by one who would treat her well, this at least would alleviate his concerns. It was with this conviction that Lord Mansfield decided to give his niece his full support. He saw no reason to delay in talking to his ward, and asked his niece to send her directly to him.
"You wish to see me sir?" Dido asked as she entered the room
"Yes Dido come and sit down." Lord Mansfield answered.
"I'm not going to hide anything from you. I know you are too intelligent for that."
Dido was surprised by her uncle's frankness. Could he be referring to Captain Davinier? How opportune for Dido if her uncle were to bring up the subject.
"Captain Davinier has expressed an interest in forming an attachment with you."

Dido was momentarily lost for words. She had not expected such a declaration.

"This is why he will be dining here tonight." Lord Mansfield continued not failing to see the expression of astonishment on Dido's countenance

"Am I not to have a say in this, sir?" Dido asked earnestly, moving forward suddenly from the seat she had not long occupied.

"I want you to promise me that you will at least give Captain Davinier your attention." He said, disregarding her question.

Dido went to speak again eager to express her distress at his plans but her uncle held up his hand to stop her.

"Please let me finish child. Do not reject him for the sake of it. Captain Davinier is a very favourable catch."

Dido remained silent struggling to control her emotions.

"Promise me Dido." Lord Mansfield insisted before grasping her hand.

Dido gave her uncle a surprised look.

"Have I not always done what is best for you?" he pleaded

"Yes." Dido was forced to answer truthfully, but she could not look into her uncle's pleading eyes for fear of him knowing her true feelings.

"I am asking you to trust me now." He said, almost out of breath.

Dido faltered. She stood in doubt of his judgement. The one person she most trusted. But how could she refuse him, especially now that he was so ill? She squeezed his hand affectionately, not able to speak her consent. But this was enough to reassure her uncle. What choice did she have? She thought as she observed the look of relief on her uncle's face but his comfort was given at the expense of her own.

Left alone in her room Dido allowed her tears to flow freely surrendering to every sensation. She had not known how long she lay in a state of misery until coaxed, with much sympathy, by Sarah to dress for dinner.

"Miss Dido, come now, let me help you." Sarah said looking pitifully at her mistress. She had just heard the news in the kitchen. Nichols, the butler, in an excited but low voice had announced that Miss Dido was to be given into marriage to the first gentleman that would have her.

"It did not so much matter as long he was a decent sort." He had concluded mockingly. Oh how she had wanted to curse him for his thoughtless gossiping.

"You can't be seen like this. Let me wash your face, Miss Dido."

Dido forced herself to stand and allow Sarah to wash and dress her. As she looked in the mirror, she could not recognise the reflection that stared back at her. Who was this creature? Dido thought, her eyes filled with sorrow. How was she to keep such an unbearable suffering to herself? The knock at the door caused her to jump.

"Miss Dido, Miss Ann is awaiting your presence in the drawing room." Mrs Jenkins announced before closing the door.

Dido took a deep breath in an attempt to compose herself as she allowed Sarah to finish her toiletry without her usual playful fussing and complaints.


"Ah Dido, you remember Captain Davinier." Ann Murray asked as soon as Dido entered the drawing room. Dido thought the question to be totally unnecessary, as it had been no more than a few weeks since she last saw the gentleman. Captain Davinier stood and bowed gracefully.

"Miss Dido. I hope you are well?" Captain Davinier asked cordially

Ann Murray stood nervously watching Dido's countenance closely. She hoped her uncle's talk would make the girl's manner more agreeable.

Dido curtsied but did not respond to Captain Davinier's inquiry, as she could not be insincere. Captain Davinier glanced curiously at Ann Murray, who felt it necessary to say,

"Dido has not been well of late."

"I'm sorry to hear it. I hope you are much improved?" Captain Davinier said expressing his concern that Dido felt obliged to put him at his ease. She could not be uncivil at such an enquiry.

"I am much better. Thank you, sir." Dido replied politely to Ann Murray's satisfaction.

"I was just conveying Lord Mansfield's apologises to Captain Davinier as he is not well enough to sit for dinner with us this evening." Ann Murray was saying as she took Captain Davinier's arm as they walked into the dining room. Dido and Miss Murray followed on, Dido looking momentarily surprised at the possibility of the event.

"Yes, it is such a shame as I'm sure he would have enjoyed the company" Marjory Murray added.

"Please do convey my best wishes to Lord Mansfield for his speedy recovery" Captain Davinier replied earnestly, but Dido did him an injustice of believing his words to be half felt.

Ann Murray made every effort to keep the conversation at dinner alive, with the help of her sister. Captain Davinier obliged when called upon and Dido remained conspicuously silent throughout. The latter too preoccupied with her thoughts and with the occupation of discreetly observing Captain Davinier. She wondered to what extent Captain

Davinier was at liberty of making his own choice. Or did he fair no better than herself? Captain Davinier was out of his regimentals and dressed in eveningwear. Dido had to concede that his appearance was agreeable. She thought he did very well to appear interested in the conversation of the sisters. He seemed to do so with ease as if use to the practice. Perhaps he had two such aunts of his own, Dido mused. In her silent contemplation Dido had been totally unaware that Captain Davinier was also observing her closely. He did not fail to see her look of both amusement and pity in her expression. There was something about her proud and defiant spirit yet gentle disposition that intrigued him. He thought if he could draw her into a conversation, the evening could prove far more interesting. After all, he felt he had earned the right to some amusement after listening to the tedious discourse of her elderly relations.

"I had the opportunity recently of meeting an acquaintance of yours Miss Dido." Captain Davinier began mysteriously and received with satisfaction an inquisitive look from the lady.

"A Captain Alwyne." He continued and realised immediately that the mention of the gentlemen's name had provoke an unexpected reaction from the lady. Dido could not hide the embarrassment and confusion that overcame her countenance for several seconds. Captain Davinier had met Captain Alwyne purely by chance at a dinner party in London, several weeks before his visit to Kenwood. Captain Davinier thought him to be a very agreeable fellow, although a little boastful. But the acquaintance had proved rather beneficial.

"Ah, Captain Alwyne, such a charming young man." Ann Murray remarked enthusiastically, remembering the gentlemen as being well spoken of, though she had only met him briefly few years previously.

"Do you remember Captain Alwyne Marjory?" Ann Murray asked her sister before realising her mistake in making the enquiry as her sister had difficulty remembering her own relations much less a gentleman of whom they had a fleeting acquaintance with. Captain Davinier continued observing Dido with interest as she attempted to recover her composure.

"I cannot recall the name." Miss Murray was saying with great thoughtfulness.

"He spoke very highly of you Miss Dido." Captain Davinier continued watching the lady intently.

"But surely Dido could not have seen Captain Alwyne since Lady Elizabeth's coming out ball." Ann Murray remarked.

For once Dido was thankful for Ann Murray's interruption, as it gave her time to recover her composure. Why was Captain Davinier so keen to draw her into a conversation about Captain Alwyne? For what purpose Dido could not tell. But if Dido had known that the only reason for Captain Davinier's enquiry was to gain the opportunity of having a more lively conversation, she would not have felt the need for suspicion or to feel so ill at ease.

"I am not that well acquainted with the gentleman. I have only met Captain Alwyne on two occasions." Dido replied feeling compelled to do so in hope of putting an end to the unpleasant subject.

"You must have made quite an impression." Captain Davinier replied graciously.

Again Dido could hardly contain her composure, as his words, unbeknown to the gentleman, took on entirely different meaning. She knew she must be blushing and felt awkward for it. What must the gentleman think? Was it possible that Captain Alwyne could have divulged to Captain Davinier his proposal to her? The thought mortified her. Why else would he speak with such insinuation? Dido desired to run from the room but her legs refused to consent to such an act. She could not move her frame rigid with shame and discomfort. Captain Davinier confused by Dido's expression, could only conclude that there must have been much more to the acquaintance than he had previously thought. Perhaps Captain Alwyne had injured her in some way? His boast of her partiality towards him now seem reasonable in the light of the lady's reaction. Perhaps he had done Captain Alwyne an injustice in believing his boast to be an exaggeration.

"I think that Captain Alwyne was far too generous in his praise." Dido recovered herself sufficiently to force a reply.

"You may be a better authority than myself as I do not know the gentleman well enough to judge his character. I cannot say. I hope I did not cause any offence in my remark?"

"Of course not Captain Davinier. Please don't apologise." Ann Murray cried after an awkward silence had ensued. What was wrong with the girl? She thought crossly. Ann Murray could hardly contain her vexation at what she saw as a deliberate sabotage of an excellent opportunity of their catching Captain Davinier.

"My apology was to Miss Dido." Captain Davinier said gallantly to Ann Murray's displeasure and Dido's surprise. Could she have misjudged him?

"As Miss Ann said, your apology is not necessary Captain Davinier." Dido felt incline to add.

After dinner Dido was called upon to play by an enthusiastic Captain Davinier, who previously having the pleasure of hearing Dido play was eager to be entertained. Miss Murray and Ann Murray deliberately sat at the far end of the room in hope of giving the couple an opportunity to be more intimate under their keen supervision. Dido saw through their plan and was sure that it was just as glaringly obvious to Captain Davinier what their intentions were that she felt immediately awkward and embarrassed. Captain Davinier chose a seat near to the pianoforte and seemed quite content to listen.

"Dido why don't you sing for us. Captain Davinier, Dido has such a delightful voice." Miss Murray said pleasantly, forgetting that Captain Davinier had already received the pleasure, and that her request had caused Dido some distress. Feeling as she did Dido did not trust herself to sing a single note.

"I have had the pleasure but I would be delighted to hear you sing." Captain Davinier replied fervently in an attempt to persuade her, which made Dido feel rather foolish to refuse what was after all a simple request. But the uneasiness brought on by the intimacy of Captain Davinier's presence had caused Dido to be out of sorts. And yet she had no choice but to concede to his wishes. Thus Dido composed herself and began her performance with an air of nervousness that brought a slight tremor to her voice but she soon after exerted herself and all nerves were forgot and she could enjoy the pleasure of performing. Once again Captain Davinier was liberal with his praises, that Dido was not untouched by his compliments as she felt she ought to have been.

"You have an exquisite voice. I have not heard such fine singing in all my existence." He said warmly after she had finished.

Dido thanked him, while hiding her hilarity at his exaggeration of her performance. She could not believe his words, though there was sincerity in his commendation and manner. He stood up and came over to the pianoforte, while Ann Murray looked on with interest from the other side of the room.

"I am sure you are used to hearing such compliments, Miss Dido."

"It is sometimes difficult to know whether such praises are genuine or not." Dido replied, and then thought perhaps he had mistaken her comment to imply that there was insincerity of his praises. Dido felt duly ashamed at the thought and attempted to make her feelings clear.

"I did not mean to say that you were insincere." She said quickly, blushing as she spoke, unable to hide her awkwardness.

Captain Davinier laughed agreeably

"How subtle you are in not injuring my feelings." He said with mock affront.

"You are mistaken. I had no intention of offending you, sir." Dido replied, wanting to put an end to the conversation.

"But yet you do not like me."

Dido was shocked by the frankness of his words and in her agitation played the wrong key. It took her a few seconds to recover herself.

"I do not know you well enough to like or dislike you." Dido replied tactfully.

"Well said, but perhaps that could be rectified when we are better acquainted."

"Then you could be a better judge of my character. Or perhaps you would have me on the gallows?"

Dido found herself smiling at the thought.

"Miss Dido, I recommend that you smile more often. It is very becoming."

Dido desired to say that she had little to smile about but thought the better of it, as she felt uncomfortable by his compliment.

"Please continue." Captain Davinier urged as Dido came to the end of another recital. He moved to the front of the pianoforte beside her and reached for one of the music sheets.

"What about this one?" he asked

"This is one of my favourite pieces'" she replied, surprised by his choice.

"We have something in common then." Captain Davinier announced pleasantly.

Dido looked at him inquisitively.

"Our love of music."

"Everybody loves music."

"Ah, that's where you are wrong! Observe Miss Murray and Miss Ann." He said amusingly as he turned in their direction. Dido followed his gaze to find the sisters thus preoccupied, one reading a book and the other dosing quietly. Dido let out a laugh at Captain Davinier's jest, which caused Miss Murray to awaken suddenly with some alarm.

"What! Have I missed something?" she asked a little disorientated.

"Go back to sleep dear." Her sister replied looking at the young couple with great satisfaction. It appeared that they were getting along splendidly, far better than she herself could have wished.

Perhaps I am no longer on the gallows?" Captain Davinier teased.

"Perhaps." Dido responded in kind.

She had found Captain Davinier's manners surprisingly pleasing, far more than she had expected, which made it all the more difficult for her to be unpleasant. Not that she had any intention of being so, but she had desired, at least, to remain aloof and indifferent, which she had failed to do. Instead, to her horror Dido found that by the end of the evening she had enjoyed Captain Davinier's company more than she would have liked to admit.

# CHAPTER 28

"Well I think yesterday evening was a great success. I trust you did not find Captain Davinier so disagreeable?" Ann Murray said with a hint of irony as they sat at the breakfast table the next morning.

"I see no reason to be uncivil to him." Dido replied indifferently giving more attention to her food than was required.

"Captain Davinier is a charming young man, any woman would be happy to receive his addresses." Ann Murray remarked

"Yes, I am sure you are right Miss Ann." Dido agreed to the surprise of Ann Murray, who could not tell whether Dido was being sincere or not.

"I am glad you agree as Captain Davinier will be a regular visitor at Kenwood from now on." replied Ann Murray decidedly.

Dido did not reply, as she could not bring herself to take in the full meaning of Ann Murray's words.

"Well I think the captain is certainly taken with you Miss Dido." Miss Murray exclaimed decidedly. Dido was appalled by her comment and did not know how to look but Miss Murray was totally oblivious to Dido's alarm and continued,

"Don't you think so sister?"

"Don't be ridiculous. Captain Davinier is simply being cordial." Ann Murray insisted to the amazement of both Dido and Miss Murray. Having observed Dido's reaction, Ann Murray did not want to spoil the success that had been so satisfactorily achieved the night before. She did not intend on making the same mistake again.

"But you said last night..."

"That's enough dear. Uncle William is probably already up and will be calling for Dido. I told him you would go to him directly after breakfast." Ann Murray said, deliberately interrupting her sister in mid-sentence, fearing that she had already revealed too much to arouse Dido's suspicion. Getting Dido's attention away from talk of Captain Davinier was foremost on her mind. She had merely thought up the excuse of her uncle to get Dido from the room.

"May I be excused?" Dido asked cordially before leaving the table to attend to her uncle.

"So, I hear that Captain Davinier is more to your liking?" her uncle said teasingly. Dido in turn was mortified by his jest and adamantly declined to entertain his humour. No doubt Ann Murray had wasted little time in informing her uncle of yesterday's proceedings. She began to berate herself severely, as she had no one else but herself to blame for the general impression now presumed by all.

"I'm afraid you have been misinformed, sir." Dido vigorously attempted to dismiss her uncle's comment but in vain.

"Come now, it's no shame to find someone you had hoped to be disagreeable, not so after all." Lord Mansfield laughed heartily not caring for Dido's protestation. He continued to tease her for the duration of the visit, which left Dido entirely distracted that she decided that only a long walk would clear her head. But the exercise proved to do the opposite. Dido could not think of anything else but her uncle's teasing words and the knowing looks of both Miss Murray and Ann Murray. Her uncle's humour had been ill timed indeed! How she regretted her conduct last night, as she recalled every smile and pleasant gesture, which had merely given new hope to those who were planning her fate! Now she had only to scold herself again and again for letting her guard down so easily. She had not expected to be disarmed by Captain Davinier's charm and easy manner. If with such little effort he had caused her to change her opinion of him, what chance would she have if they were continually thrown together? She would be lost! This thought caused her great agitation, as she had no intention of being agreeable to anyone or worst still to find Captain Davinier so! The thought was intolerable! Dido had no desire to be married to anyone! Thus she resolved within herself that Captain Davinier would not find her so agreeable on their next meeting.

Ann Murray announced casually at dinner that she had received a correspondence from an old acquaintance. Dido almost raised her eyes to the heavens in dismay at hearing of yet another acquaintance, having no desire of society, thus feigned to show little interest in the news.

"Mrs Harris is coming for a visit next week with her son Mr Jeffrey Harris." she continued with satisfaction, as Dido continued to despair at the prospect of entertaining more guests.

"You'll have an opportunity of meeting them both, of course," said Ann Murray in Dido's direction. At which Dido thought to ask for what purpose would she be required to be present but already guessed the motive for her invitation, and decided it simply disgusting the candidness of her scheming!

"Mr Harris is a fine young gentleman." Ann Murray added, but in truth had no idea what kind of gentleman Mr Harris was, as she had not seen him since he was a young lad.

"Is my presence really necessary?" Dido asked, knowing that her desire of being excluded was in vain.

"Of course, there is no question of your not being there!" Ann Murray replied sharply, appalled at Dido's lack of interest. Having complained earlier to her sister of her impatience with Dido's indifference to all the efforts she had been making to secure her future, Ann Murray could hardly contain her temper. Dido, for her part, wished this were one occasion when her presence was not desired.

"The ungrateful girl! She is simply resisting every effort I am making on her behalf." Ann Murray cried as soon as Dido had left the room.

"You know she has no interest in beaus. In that respect she is a lot like myself" Miss Murray observed. Personally, she could never understand the excitement and hysterics of young ladies at the mere mention of a ball or a party. Miss Murray found balls overcrowded, noisy and tediously dull. The idea of dancing with a complete stranger seemed frightful to her. In this respect she was very much in the minority. She had always preferred the quiet comfort of home, where she could read or draw sketches or enjoy some such pastime. Thus after many years her sentiments had remained the same. But Ann Murray was in no mood to listen to her sisters' wise observations. While *they* could afford the fortunate position of choosing to remain single, as Ann Murray could never acknowledge that her single status had been forced upon her by circumstance and not by choice, such a situation could not be permitted in Dido's case. After all, Ann Murray decided, it was better to confess that one had chosen never to marry than to admit to the trifling detail of never being asked!

"The trouble we have gone to just to reacquaint ourselves with inferior families with suitable sons for her benefit is outrageous!" Ann Murray exclaimed with displeasure. In truth, she was expressing an outrage she did not actually feel, as she had set about the business of finding a suitable husband for Dido with more energy than she had been able to display in many years. Rather, her displeasure came from the absence of Captain Davinier's society at Kenwood. Ann Murray had hoped from his last visit that the gentleman would have returned almost immediately to continue his courtship with equal success. As it was there was not one word from the gentlemen for the past few weeks, which Ann Murray, taking the injury of the slight solely upon herself, thought his behaviour to be very discourteous indeed.

"She has been nothing but insolent," continued the lady sourly, venting her anger on Dido.

"Come now sister, you cannot blame her for being so. Some people do not like decisions to be made for them, you know." Miss Murray reasoned, at which Ann Murray looked at her sister in astonishment and was unable to speak for a moment. She wondered if there was something in the tea, and rolled her eyes impatiently, as now was not the time for her sister's sympathetic outpourings, especially when Dido's behaviour was continually jeopardising any chance of securing a suitable match, whether agreeable or not! Mrs Harris' letter had come at the most opportune time, as it had saved Ann Murray from being in a horrid temper for the rest of week. With no word from Captain Davinier, Ann Murray saw no reason to waste any more time in delaying her invitation to Mrs Harris. It would also give her an opportunity of observing Mr Harris, who, thankfully, being very much single despite approaching forty, to determine whether he would be a suitable husband for Dido.

"Please try to encourage Dido to think better of marriage. Perhaps she will listen to you. Yes. Perhaps I should leave you two alone after dinner that will give you the opportunity of raising the subject." Ann Murray stated warming to the idea.

"If you think it would do any good." Miss Murray answered hesitantly

"And it's best not to mention that I suggested this little talk." Ann Murray warned her sister at the risk of her not giving everything away.

That evening after dinner Ann Murray acting according to plan, made her excuse of feeling fatigue, and a need for an early night. Miss Murray, who, had forgotten about her *talk* with Dido, looked up with concern at the news.

"Dear Ann, you work far too hard. Is there anything I can get you?" she asked anxiously.

"No. I think I just retire." Ann Murray replied, giving her sister a queer look.

"Stay and have a talk with Dido." Ann Murray hinted to her sister, whose eyes widened suddenly as if she had just been awakened from sleep.

"Ah, yes, of course." She answered winking knowingly, at which Ann Murray despaired at the possibility of their little scheme being found out. Anne Murray retired, hoping that her sister would have some success with Dido for all their sakes.

Turning to Dido, Miss Murray smiled nervously,

"What good luck that we are alone."

Dido returned her smile, as the thought was not unpleasant to her.

"Well that's good." Miss Murray began, but was not sure of what to say next. There was a moment of silence at which Dido being use to her relation's absence of mind continued to preoccupy herself with her book.

"Ah yes, I remember now!" Miss Murray exclaimed with relief, which caused Dido to look up at her with amused curiosity.

"When I was your age I had no desire to be married either." she began

"Really?" Dido asked with interest putting aside her book.

"No. I found men absolutely dull and simply abhorred parties."

"But did you not fall in love?" Dido asked earnestly

"No dear, certainly not!" Miss Murray cried as if love was some kind of contagious disease. Dido smiled at her response.

"I chose to remain unmarried. But it is not a life suited for just anyone, dear. Just be sure that you make the right choice. There is no going back once the decision is made." She continued rather philosophical.

"Do you ever regret not marrying?" Dido enquired curiously

"No. I'm quite content with my situation. I certainly have no regrets"

"So you understand how I feel." Dido cried happily at finally finding an ally.

"Yes, but...oh dear" Miss Murray began, then became rather confused

"You must consider your position, whether you are able to live independently or not," she said in an attempt to rescue the situation.

"But if I can do so then I would have no need to marry." Dido replied simply with an air of decidedness. She felt at that moment a feeling of freedom and optimism. Miss Murray could do nothing more than shrug her shoulders resignedly. Though her talk did not go as planned, she had learnt from experience that it was best to act more ignorant than one actually was, and in doing so could avoid her sister's displeasure. Thus when questioned by her sister, Miss Murray omitted to say that she had failed to change Dido's mind but only divulged that the talk had went well, which, though not completely accurate, was not completely untrue.

The anticipated arrival of Mrs Harris and her son Mr Harris had come at last but instead of their guests, an overly apologetic note from Mrs

Harris was sent with the humble hope of rearranging the day of their visit as a matter of great urgency had arisen to detain them.

"How preposterous! What could be more important than an invitation to Kenwood?" Ann Murray cried in disbelief, as she forced herself to control her irritation as she wondered what *urgent* business could delay people of little consequence from honouring an important engagement. An invitation, Ann Murray might add, would not have usually been extended had it not been for the present necessity! A new date was fixed for the following week and instead of dinner the guests were to come for afternoon tea. Dido was curious to know what kind of gentleman Mr Harris was. Not that she was in the least bit interested in his regard, knowing precisely Ann Murray's motive for extending the invitation. It no longer concerned her, as she had decided to adopt a more optimistic view of her future. Her talk with Miss Murray had given her courage to hope. Surely being a well accomplished and educated lady she would be able to secure an occupation as a governess, if the worse came to the worst. For far too long, Dido had allowed the misery of her situation to weigh upon her until she had not known herself. She had begun to detest the anxious and fearful creature that she had become. All her sorrow had done nothing to alleviate her present position, instead it had plummeted her into the depths of despair, so as to make her uneasy at the slightest word or look, until she could think of nothing else but her pending gloom. Dido was ashamed to admit that even her uncle's illness had taken second place to her own feelings. But presently she felt able to throw off the cloak of doom and face her future prospects with a more determined attitude.

Armed with this newfound optimism Dido greeted Mrs Harris and Mr Jeffrey Harris with an air of detached civility. She thought Mr Harris to look much older than his nine and thirty years. She decided that his receding hair and the severe frown that sat permanently across his brow, was the probable cause. He looked about himself with an air of nervousness, but when he spoke it was with a sombre and pious manner. His mother was a very talkative woman who did not finish her sentences before she began another. She was a petite woman with rather a booming laugh that seemed overly boisterous for a woman of her size. It was no wonder her son spoke as little as she had energy enough to speak for the both of them! As the weather was so favourable Ann Murray had decided to have tea on the terrace. This was a particular pleasure for visitors to Kenwood as the view from the terrace was one of the best in London.

"How splendid the view is here. It is absolutely breath-taking –"

"Oh my, what delightful sight" the lady continued excitedly without taking breath.

"Indeed. Uncle William said that the King considered it a better prospect than his own at Kew." Miss Murray announced proudly

"It is certainly spectacular!" Mr Harris agreed

"Well Kenwood is a delightful estate with many beautiful prospects." Ann Murray remarked with a superior air.

"How fortunate Miss Dido for you to have the pleasure of calling Kenwood your home." Mr Harris said

"Yes sir. I am very fortunate indeed." Dido replied civilly. Ann Murray appeared pleased at Dido's response. She noticed that Dido looked rather fetching in her pale pink dress, even her manner appeared serene. Perhaps now, she hoped that the girl was coming to terms with the inevitability of marriage.

"Perhaps you will do me and my mother the honour of showing us around the garden?" Mr Harris enquired with much humility.

"Yes, certainly." Dido forced herself to reply with all civility, though she could think of nothing more unpleasant than to accompany Mr Harris on a tour of the gardens.

"What an excellent idea. It is such a pleasant day for a walk." Ann Murray declared.

"I hope you don't mind if my sister and I accompany you?"

Dido was pleased to have Miss Murray and Miss Ann along. The thought of having to listen to Mrs Harris for the entirety of the walk proved a rather challenging prospect. But within less than half an hour Dido realised the motive behind Miss Ann's request to accompany them. The ladies had already fallen behind, walking in a rather laboured stroll that Dido was sure a tortoise could out run. She was left to walk beside Mr Harris who continued to ask questions of the various trees, plants and flowerings that they passed. Dido did not dislike their conversation as she saw that Mr Harris was genuinely interested in nature and confessed to having a small garden of his own which he spent many an hour in.

"You have a great variety of plants here." Mr Harris observed keenly.

"Yes. The gardener is very efficient at his work." Dido replied, as she could not take any credit for its beauty.

"It will be a pity to leave such a place." Mr Harris said suddenly. Dido was astonished for a moment that it robbed her of her power of speech. It took her a few seconds to recover. Perhaps she had mistaken Mr Harris meaning entirely. He could not have possibly been referring to her presence, as she was sure he was most likely speaking of his own. This thought gave Dido the assurance she needed to regain her hospitable manner, as they walked on in silence.

"I am indebted to your hospitality Miss Dido." Mr Harris said with much alacrity. His praises was so overly bestowed that Dido could not help but think him far too ostentatious.

Dido was forced to reply civilly rather than truthfully, that she was happy to oblige.

On the walk back to the house, Mr Harris expressed a keen interest of seeing the Orangery, which contained several orange trees and a variety of exotic plants that was carefully supervised by Lord Mansfield. Dido had no objection in showing Mr Harris the Orangery as it was one of her favourite places in which to spend time with her uncle and listen to him speak of the many different varieties of plant species. Her only displeasure was that the visit would demand her to remain in Mr Harris society for much longer than she would have liked. She had not the inclination to tolerate another *possible* suitor, in her present state. The business of showing Mr Harris the Orangery was done with much forbearance and with a desire for the hasty return of Miss Murray, Ann Murray and Mrs Harris. The visit finally came to an end, and the carriage summoned, as Mrs Harris said her goodbyes to Miss Murray and Ann Murray, Dido noticed that Mr Harris observed her openly until she hardly knew where to look. The gentleman made no effort to start a conversation, which would have eased her feeling of awkwardness, as she could not think of what to say but became impatient for Mrs Harris to conclude her salutations. So relieved was she when Mrs Harris finally ceased from her chatter and made a step towards the awaiting carriage, that she could have kissed her. But then the lady turned again to repeat her salutations before climbing into the carriage, which lasted a further few minutes. Mr Harris followed his mother into the carriage but not before thanking Miss Murray and Ann Murray for their hospitality. He glanced at Dido but only nodded in her direction.

Mr Harris left Kenwood feeling decidedly satisfied with the visit, more than he had ever hoped to be before coming hither. On first seeing Dido, he thought her to be fairly attractive but what struck him most was her modesty and mildness of manner. She appeared rather regal that one could forget that she was of inferior birth. There was no denying the aristocratic blood and her accomplishment on the pianoforte was exquisite. Mr Harris was rather pleasantly surprised by his good fortune of having such an opportunity of obtaining a suitable wife.   His mother's insistence of his considering Miss Dido as a prospective match had at first insulted his pious nature. Mr Harris had considered himself a good enough catch for any young lady of his circle. Though he was still in the process of taking his orders, he felt it only a matter of time before a good position could be obtained and then his felicity could be pursued. Now that he had received his ordination and the hope of a possible parish position had been assured he was ready to make his marital choice. The Harris' acquaintance with the Murrays was purely through the late Rev. Jeffrey Harris, who was the curator at the parish on the Murray estate.   Miss Murray and Ann Murray had condescended to permit the Harris' the occasional visits to the house, with a philanthropic air of doing a good deed for their inferior neighbours.  This marked inequality went unnoticed by a grateful Mrs Harris but was received with much resentment by the son, who being of a more conceited nature, felt the injury of his inferiority.  Now that he found himself in an advantageous position, Mr Harris was willing to abandon his earlier apprehension and now considered Dido as beneficial to his domestic felicity.  Her colour could be easily overlooked when compared with the nobility of her family connections. Yes, Mr Harris agreed that his visit to Kenwood had gone exceptionally well.

"What a pleasant afternoon." Miss Murray remarked with delight as they walked back into the house.
"Yes and Mr Harris is such a pleasant young man." Ann Murray agreed. Dido was wont to disagree with Miss Ann in her referring to Mr Harris as young. It could not have been more possible for a young man to look so ancient!
"And to think him still single. His mother seems sure that he will find himself a wife. With his modest earning any woman will do well to consider him a good catch." Ann Murray continued pleased at the how well the afternoon events had gone.
Were there no end to her hints and insinuations? Dido thought with vexation. But she forced herself to respond.
"I'm sure you are right."

"I'm glad you agree as we shall be seeing a lot more of the gentleman."
Ann Murray said with much satisfaction, as she determined that this
one would not get away.

# CHAPTER 29

Ann Murray was true to her word. Mr Harris returned to Kenwood the following week to stay for the weekend. Dido was no longer shocked by the means by which the art of matchmaking was devised. She knew that his visit at Kenwood was purely for the purpose of courting her. Though she could not prevent them from being thrown together at every opportunity, she could attempt to dissuade Mr Harris from his choice by using arts of her own. Dido remembered as a young child how she had sworn a vow of silence against Lady Mansfield, which had backfired. In the case of Mr Harris's society, it would do better to be saying the wrong things than to remain silent, as Dido was sure this would do much to shock Mr Harris' pious airs. That evening at the dinner table Mr Harris began talking of his charitable work with the poor. Dido could not have hoped for a better opportunity to put her plan into action.

"How excellent to be so attentive to the needs of others." Miss Murray praised warmly.

"It is my Christian duty." Mr Harris replied modestly. His character was such that he naturally craved acknowledgement for his accomplishments but knowing this to be a weakness he would invariably feel self-conscious of this failing when praises were given. Determined to resist this evil, Mr Harris would assuage his guilt by becoming more pious in an attempt to outdo the pleasure of the praise. In talking of his charitable work Mr Harris motive was to show how hard working he was and not as a reason to boast, as he hoped to illustrate the type of temperament his wife would need to have in order to assist him in his work. Mr Harris had succeeded with those with whom he had no intention towards, as both Miss Murray and Ann Murray were vastly impressed by his oration, while Dido, who was determined to find him unpleasant, did him a disservice of viewing his words as false modesty.

"Yes it is a worthy cause indeed." Ann Murray remarked encouragingly. Mr Harris again had to restrain himself from being overcome by her praise.

"What of your Christian duty to the slave, sir? Dido asked, knowing that her question would displease her relations.

"Dido I implore you not to speak on such a subject." Ann Murray intervened, trying to conceal the annoyance from her voice.

"I am only trying to ascertain whether Mr Harris feels if one can be a Christian and a slave owner at the same time."

"Dido!"

"Oh…" Miss Murray muttered looking rather flustered and agitated at the prospect of a scene.

Ann Murray's countenance had become cold and austere. She knew exactly what the girl was up to. She had deliberately set out to make herself an unsuitable match for Mr Harris. Ann Murray needed all her powers of restraint to stop herself from rebuking Dido in front of their guest. Instead she smiled maliciously in Dido's direction.

"Pray forgive us Mr Harris. Dido is of such an inquisitive nature she sometimes becomes carried away." Ann Murray cried with such gaiety as she could muster.

"It is quite all right, Miss Ann. Please do not apologise. One cannot deny the curiosity of the inquisitive." He replied civilly, hesitating in whether to answer the question. He looked to Ann Murray for direction but on seeing none he proceeded.

"In answer to your question Miss Dido, I think one may be so. As long as he treats his slave fairly." Mr Harris answered humbly.

"Well said Mr Harris." Ann Murray added in agreement.

"I cannot agree with you no matter how well your argument is. The trade of slaves is an evil system that only serves to line the pockets of slave owners. A Christian could not treat a fellow human being as a possession." Dido stated defiantly

"I think that is enough talk of slaves." Ann Murray said with such finality that Dido was forced to keep quiet on the subject.

"May I suggest we sit on the terrace as it is such a pleasant evening?" Ann Murray added at the conclusion of dinner.

Everyone was in agreement, with the exception of Dido who sat silently. As they proceeded to the terrace Ann Murray held Dido back with the pretence of needing her assistance. As soon as they were alone and out of earshot of Mr Harris and Miss Murray, she turned on Dido in such a violent manner that Dido was astonished at the ferocity of it.

"How dare you conduct yourself in such an appalling manner!" she whispered menacingly

"Do you think by behaving so that you will discourage Mr Harris of his intentions towards you? If it were up to me, I would give you leave to do as you please and see how well you can fend for yourself. Then perhaps you would not be so proud when you are without the privileges that you take so much for granted." She finished with malice, taking a deep breath to calm herself.

"Now, you will go out on the terrace and conduct yourself in a suitable manner. Do you understand?" Ann Murray commanded fiercely.

Dido had stood impassive and emotionless throughout the attack, as she found that she was neither intimidated nor touched by Ann Murray's threats. Ann Murray could not abuse her any more than she already had. Dido had nothing to lose and absolutely nothing to gain by giving in to her threats. Her mind had already been fixed. She had no intention of marrying anyone against her will, and the very thought of meekly accepting the advances of Mr Harris was repulsive to her. At that moment, with indignation beating violently in her breast, Dido was willing even to choose destitution over marriage.

"Yes, perfectly. But I cannot promise that I will conduct myself in the manner in which *you* choose." Dido replied calmly, before moving away and leaving a startled Ann Murray with no time to respond.

"Uncle William you simply must do something about that girl! She is totally out of control and will not see reason!" Ann Murray exclaimed impatiently, after giving Lord Mansfield a lengthy account of Dido's behaviour towards Mr Harris, which was expressed with far greater embellishment of the actual truth. By the end of it, Ann Murray was satisfied that she had succeeded in convincing her uncle of the severity of their situation and of his duty to intervene, before Dido jeopardised another opportunity of securing a husband. Lord Mansfield did not speak but looked more grave at each expression of his niece.

"Believe me sir, she has already chased Captain Davinier away with her antics and by her behaviour to Mr Harris last night I should think she has succeeded with him as well!" she added forebodingly.

"I have done everything in my power to help the girl but she has been nothing but ungrateful." Ann Murray continued to complain until her uncle wearily lifted his hand having heard enough.

"Call Dido to me at once; I shall speak to her directly, she will know my feelings on this matter." Lord Mansfield answered brusquely. His niece's revelation had troubled him deeply. If this was true, he could not allow Dido to continue her present conduct without feeling the full force of his displeasure. If only for her own sake, he could not show any partiality to her feelings in this matter. Though he had known for some time that Dido was not partial to the idea of marriage, yet he had always believed that she would eventually come around to it. There was no question that marriage was the best and only solution to securing Dido's future after his death. As her guardian, his primary concern was that she was well cared for. Any attempts, on her part, to deliberately sabotage their efforts could not be tolerated.

"Is it true?" he asked sternly as soon as Dido had entered the room. The severity of his tone stunned her into silence. She had not prepared herself to meet her uncle's wrath.

"Do not play with me child!" he growled angrily, before catching himself, attempting to control his temper.

Dido was fully aware of the reason for his anger. She had not failed to notice Ann Murray's smug look as she informed her that she had been summoned to see her uncle. But she had thought that her uncle being a reasonable man would be willing to listen to her feelings that she was guiltless of any wrongdoing.

"In what way have I displeased you sir?" Dido asked calmly as she could, though she willed herself not to cry. Her response received an impatient intake of breath from Lord Mansfield.

"Miss Ann has informed me of your behaviour towards Mr Harris. If by conducting yourself with so little propriety you think to remove your chances of marriage, I caution you now." He said soberly

"It is well within my power to forbid you any of the privileges you now have. Do you not know that your behaviour only brings shame to me?" he added with much dissatisfaction.

Dido remained silent. She could not bring herself to look in his eyes for fear of seeing his displeasure. The severity of her uncle's words shocked her. He left her with no doubt that he intended to force her to marry against her wishes. How foolish were her actions yesterday, which she had believed to be perfectly decent and certain of not incurring the censure of anyone, except Ann Murray. How wrong she had been! Though it pained her dearly to know that she had displeased him, but if she had acted differently she was sure of feeling dissatisfaction of having so easily succumbed to the wishes of others. Yet her uncle's words had made her feel unworthy of all the love and kindness that he had shown her. She felt ashamed of her conduct only where it affected him, though she could not feel any remorse where Ann Murray was concerned. No she could never feel repentant! Ann Murray, who had done nothing but belittle her since she arrived at Kenwood and had continued to make her to feel like a servant in her own home. She would not be made to marry like Elizabeth! Had she a desire to marry, her situation would have been much easier to bear. As it was her heart reviled at the very prospect.

"I do not want to hear any more talk of your improprieties! I will expect you to conduct yourself in a proper manner befitting your position. Do you understand?" her uncle continued, expecting no resistance to his authority.

His words stung at her heart. The greatest wound of all was the sudden realisation that his protection was lost to her. All her life she had known no other protector; No other advocate and friend. Now he sat before her as an adversary. Dido shuddered at the vulnerability of her position. She was entirely alone. How could she possibly resist his wishes?

"Yes sir." Dido whispered submissively, as she struggled to contain her tears that threatened to overcome her.

Dido wept bitterly at the recollection of their painful meeting and the severity of her uncle's words, until she thought her heart would burst. It pained her to realise that her uncle intended to use all of his influence to force her to accept the hand of anyone who would have her! While her uncle had remained partial, Dido had hoped to influence him against any such decision. But without her uncle's support her fate had been decided without appeal or thought to her feelings. Such a revelation now threatened her present optimism and beckoned the return of her old gloom. Perhaps she had been foolish to think that her conduct towards Mr Harris would not have resulted in some form of repercussion. But while Dido had expected censure from Miss Ann, she was not prepared for her uncle's displeasure. How could she hope to win his support again? He had been her defender and champion since an infant, and having been so accustomed to enjoying his favour, Dido could not bring herself to think of the possibility of being without it. Surely it was better to obey the commands of a loving guardian than to be left defenceless and miserable? Dido reasoned within herself the sensibility of such a decision. But before she could surrender herself to its will a feeling of resentment burst upon her heart and led her sentiments in an entirely different direction. How could she succumb to such a situation? To be used as a piece of property to be given to anyone who wish to possess it! Was she not worthy of making a choice, if a choice had to be forced upon her? How she despised being treated so patronisingly and to be considered a person of little consequence not worthy of being consulted on the decisions that affected her alone! Then, at lengths, Dido was left to feel immensely ashamed for having felt such a growing resentment towards her uncle. She had no such regret concerning her feelings towards Ann Murray, as in this instance her judgment was just and sincere. But her feelings of resentment towards her uncle were so wholly new to her that Dido struggled against any renewal of them, and wondered how such sufferings were to be borne! For many days her sentiments altered between wounded indignation and humble contrition depending on the words of her relations. When sitting at the dinner table with Miss Murray and Ann Murray, Dido was determined to conduct herself accordingly until Ann Murray's words would threaten to rekindle her feelings of resentment.

"I hope that Lord Mansfield's talk has made you come to your senses, Dido. One cannot behave childishly merely to prove a point. If we all behaved in such a way what would become of civilised society?" Ann Murray asked sardonically.

Dido could hardly contain her vexation at the lady's cynicism. If she had behaved childishly it was only because she had been treated thus, particularly by the lady in question.

"If Mr Harris will not have you I do not know who will." Ann Murray added mockingly, desirous of injuring Dido's feelings. Her motive was not lost on Dido, who having felt the intended slight, had no intention of giving Miss Ann the satisfaction of knowing that her remark had indeed wounded her. Instead she sat expressionless showing an outward calm while inwardly struggling to stifle her misery. Ann Murray had to be content with just a minor victory as her words had not had the affect she had hoped. Had she known the state of Dido's inward agitation she would have enjoyed the full satisfaction of her triumph but as it was she remained in ignorance of her success. Dido was only saved from her present misery by the thoughts of her plans for escape from Kenwood. It was no longer her beloved Kenwood, her safe haven from the cruelties of the world outside instead it had become a place of torment and shame.

Then on speaking with her uncle her sentiments were changed once again.

"It displeases me to speak to you in such a way Dido." Lord Mansfield said softly reflecting on the memory of their last meeting. His appeared breathless and his words laboured. Dido looked alarmed, her thoughts were only for his health.

"Are you not well, sir?" Dido asked with concern, looking at her uncle intently. But he waved his hand dismissively

"I am just a little tired." He replied and continued,

"You know that everything that I have done is for your benefit?"

"I know." Dido answered meekly, feeling once again the remorse of having caused him much displeasure.

"Elizabeth is settled. You are my only concern."

Dido thought to discourage him from his concerns for her but reconsidered and instead kept silent.

"As your guardian I have a duty to your welfare. Have you not been like a daughter to me?"

Dido was unable to speak so affected was her feelings. How she had longed to hear him say those words. She rejoiced in the knowledge that he should consider her as such. He had been the only father that she had known. There was no other opinion that she cherished above her own. It made her feel wretched that she had caused him such pain in going against his wishes. At that moment Dido's joy was so great that she would have willingly obeyed him and marry even Mr Harris.

"I am honoured sir." Dido said tearfully

"Make a dying man happy and consent to my wishes."

Dido only nodded her response; she had no other desire but to please him. How could she have known that it would be the last time she would speak to her uncle and that within a week she would be mourning his death and the end of a sheltered and privileged life?

# CHAPTER 30

The death of Lord Mansfield brought both sobriety and immense grief to Kenwood. Dido could hardly feel for being overcome by her sorrow. She walked and talked but hardly knew what she said or did. Lord Mansfield's funeral was a stately affair presided over by royalty, dignitaries and distinguished aristocratic families. There were countless faces many of whom Dido did not recognise. She was thankful to be in the background and not having to be called upon to say the right things or to receive the endless condolences from well-wishers that must be said and in turn accepted. Ann Murray viewed the guests with great satisfaction knowing that the presence of such important personage showed a mark of respect for her uncle and the superior social standing of their family. David Murray's feelings were much the same. Miss Murray and Lady Finch-Hatton found the occasion more difficult both being of an emotional disposition were tearful throughout. For Dido, only Elizabeth's presence gave her comfort. But she was glad for every opportunity of being alone as it was at those moments that she could give way to her grief and for all that she had lost. Her unimaginable pain was only surpassed by her uncertainty of her future. Seeing Mr Harris at the funeral did little to relieve her anxiety as she had hoped, in her naivety, never to see him again. His greeting to her although civil, was rather cold. Dido hoped that this was a sign of his intentions not to pursue her and was at least grateful for that. For days it seemed that the library had become a fairway of a famous London park, as visitors passed through to pay their respects. Dido sat without comprehension of what was said. She could not decide whether she preferred the awkward pauses or the repetitive condolences and commendations of their guests. How much more of this could she bear? In the afternoon, Dido pleaded to Miss Ann to excuse her, as she felt unable to sit any longer in company. Her request, to Dido's surprise was granted with such ease as to make her regret that she hadn't asked earlier.

"You do look quite unwell." Ann Murray conceded, she had noticed for some time that Dido had looked rather distracted, even absent-minded to the point of being discourteous. On one occasion Miss Haversham had attempted several times before she could gain Dido's attention.

"Poor dear. Is she well?" Mrs Haversham whispered to aside to Ann Murray with a look of concern.

"Lord Mansfield's death has been very trying on all of us." She replied

"She looks rather lost." Miss Haversham remarked sympathetically

"We all feel our uncle's lost dearly." Ann Murray added pointedly and with much feeling.

"Ah, but you must own that she must feel it all the more. After all she has been under Lord Mansfield care since a small infant." Miss Haversham stated at which Ann Murray reluctantly agreed.

"Poor child." Miss Haversham continued to say intermittently throughout her visit.

Instead of returning to her room Dido walked towards the garden feeling the need for some fresh air to clear her head. She had not proceeded far along the path before she heard the sound of another carriage approaching the house. Her first instinct was to walk quickly along the path so as to avoid being seen. But before she could make her escape she found herself rooted to the spot unable to move either back or forward, at the sight of Captain Alwyne stepping out of the carriage followed by Captain Davinier. She let out a gasp of astonishment, as the unexpected appearance of both gentlemen could not have created in Dido a more heightened sense of agitation. If the gentlemen were to turn in the direction of the garden, Dido would have been seen by both. But as it was they went directly into the house, without detecting Dido's presence, giving her a feeling of great relief at having gained a fortuitous escape. She could not dare breathe easily until she had reached the safety of her room and only then did Dido allow herself to feel grateful for her timely decision of taking a breath of fresh air. Fate had saved her from an evil that Dido could not contemplate without blushing with shame at what she might have endured had she remained in the library. The thought of facing Captain Alwyne's addresses while being observed by Captain Davinier filled Dido once again with a heightened sense of agitation. She was only able to calm herself with the knowledge that she was quite safe from the possibility of any such incident occurring.

"Captain Alwyne and Captain Davinier were both sorry to hear of your illness Dido." Miss Murray informed Dido the following morning at the breakfast table.

"Captain Alwyne in particular seemed rather concerned for your welfare." Miss Murray continued, unaware that this news only bought displeasure to the hearer. Dido chose to ignore Miss Murray's hint.

"I'm sure Captain Alwyne's concern was no more than usual." Dido replied indifferently.

"I disagree, He seemed quite distracted by your absence." Lady Finch-Hatton added then remembering the incident at Eastwell Park, coloured and said no more.

"Captain Alwyne has no more interest in me than in Miss Murray." Dido replied adamantly, unable to hold her tongue.

"Good heavens!" Miss Murray exclaimed giggling childishly at the thought.

"I do not know where you get such an idea!"

"Perhaps Captain Davinier is not entirely lost." said Lady Finch-Hatton with a desire to see Dido settled. The idea of her being unprotected and alone in the world gave her great concern. But Dido, unaware of her cousin's concerns, could not decide whether she was more horrified at Elizabeth's insinuation or by the very thought of such a suggestion being made. Dido found the conversation too provoking to wish for any further continuance of it. Ann Murray, who had sat in complete silence throughout, now chose her moment to speak.

"It matters little whether Captain Davinier is interested or not. Mr Harris has already received our blessing in asking for Dido's hand in marriage." She announced coolly, expecting the obvious outburst from her announcement. Instead it produced a stunned silence as all eyes turned to her. She smiled pleased with herself as she took the folded letter from the table, a correspondence that she had only received this morning, which contained the expressed joy of Mr Harris in having their consent in asking for Miss Dido's hand in marriage.

"Is it true?" Lady Finch-Hatton asked breaking the silence, as she looked to her aunt and to the letter that she now held in her hands.

"Well this is good news!" Miss Murray said but stopped short on seeing Dido's countenance. Dido in stunned silence could hardly contain her emotions and could not be prevailed upon to stay seated any longer but jumped up hurriedly from the table without excusing herself.

"Dido, come back here at once!" Ann Murray called but her command went unheard. The shock of the news left Dido with no power of sensible thought for several minutes. How dare she speak so openly of a matter that concerned herself alone! She had borne meanness and cruelty of Miss Ann for far too long and cared little of what became of her future, as it mattered not in her present distress.

"I cannot live here another day!" Dido cried unaware that Sarah had entered the room, looking anxiously at her mistress with a message from Miss Ann to bid her back to the breakfast table.

"How much more can I bear?" Dido sobbed openly unable to contain her suffering any longer. Her outburst startled Sarah, who moved quickly to her side.

"Please miss, let me help you." Sarah pleaded, attempting to assist her mistress to the bed.

"Can you help me?" Dido asked fervently as she grasped Sarah's hand, completely misunderstanding her meaning.

"I need to leave Kenwood...!"

"Leave Kenwood?" Sarah asked in astonishment, "Where would you go miss?" Sarah asked in bewilderment, though she could see that her mistress was distraught and not thinking clearly. She knew all too well the reason for her mistress' distress. The butler had burst into the kitchen not moments ago with the news of Dido's marriage to Mr Harris, causing a stir of animated gossip among the staff.

"Rest now, miss and I'll see what I can do." Sarah encouraged, with the sole purpose of calming her mistress.

"I'll tell Miss Ann that you are too ill to come down." she continued, as she undressed her mistress and helped her into bed, and then went directly to inform Ann Murray. All received the news of Dido's illness with alarm and anxious concerns, with the exception of Ann Murray, who felt the others to be too easily duped by Dido's tantrum.

"Perhaps we should call for a doctor?" Miss Murray suggested apprehensively.

"I don't think it will be necessary. But I shall go and attend to her personally." Ann Murray replied and left the room directly before any further discussion could follow.

"Good idea." Miss Murray was heard saying to Lady Finch-Hatton, who was left to feel that perhaps she should have been the one to check on Dido instead of her aunt.

"Your insincerity does little to commend you." Ann Murray said coldly, as she stood beside Dido's bed, un-swayed by her tears.

"Mr Harris will be here the day after tomorrow and you shall be here to receive him. I hope I have made myself clear?" she added austerely before leaving the room. Dido remained tearful throughout unable to defend herself. Ann Murray's words had made her decision to leave Kenwood all the more urgent. To stay and receive Mr Harris's proposal was unthinkable. There was no other option but to leave. But how would she find suitable accommodations within one day? Surely any accommodation would be better than this? Dido felt she could live modestly with the help of her small inheritance bequeathed by her father and Lord Mansfield, now that she was a free woman, as her uncle had granted her freedom in his will. Though Dido had never consider herself a slave, the law had condemned her to this cruel status. Thus as she heard the word spoken during the reading of her uncle's will, her heart burnt at the abhorrence of it. Surely now she was under no obligation or duty to marry where she did not wish? What did it matter to her relations whether she married at all? Dido remembered the promise she had made to her uncle, and felt momentarily ashamed of her betrayal to him. But she could not allow her feelings to sway her actions. Besides, she had promised her uncle only to consider the possibility of marriage to Captain Davinier. Now that Captain Davinier was out of the way, in principle, she was no longer obliged to keep her promise. At least Dido told herself so, though her conscious would give her little peace.

"Forgive me." Dido whispered, somehow hoping to relieve her guilt.

Could she truly be happy with a man whose life was led by the dictates of his mother? Dido wondered what benefits Mr Harris had hoped to gain through their marriage. It could not be for her income, as that was far too modest. Perhaps it was the connection to an aristocratic family that had enticed him? Marriage to the ward of Lord Mansfield was not to be snubbed at regardless of her colour and background. Could Mr Harris be persuaded to receive payment for the privilege of taking her off their hands? As horrifying as the thought may have been it was not uncommon. Dido knew this to be true, but it left her sentiments in such a troubled state of vexation that she became impatient for Sarah's return. Instead, she got up and began pacing the room in hope of relieving her anxieties but received no relief from the exercise. Dido thought to call for Sarah and proceeded to ring the bell but then thought the better of it, as she did not want to arouse any suspicion. Her patience was rewarded as Sarah entered the room with much excitement to inform her mistress that she had made arrangements for Dido to leave Kenwood at dark. But she would have to hurry, as the horse and cart, which was used to fetch food from the market would be waiting outside the gates to take her into London. Sarah could not believe her luck when she bumped into Tom the young lad that drove the cart to and from the market, just as he was leaving the kitchen and took the opportunity of asking for his help. He always had a friendly manner and had often tried to draw her into conversation when they were alone. He agreed readily to Sarah's request without any questions asked. Sarah knew he was soft on her but she could not think of his motives now. Her mistress was desperately in need of her help and she could not let her down. Sarah was sure her mistress would be pleased with the news but instead Dido received it with silent trepidation, rather than the expected relief. It seemed so sudden, that the finality of it made Dido grow cold with fear. Was she doing the right thing in leaving Kenwood and all that she knew? Dido stood hesitant, struggling against her feeling of momentary weakness.

"You still want to leave, don't you miss?" Sarah asked, seeing her mistress look of uncertainty.

"Yes, of course." Dido replied, attempting to pull herself together, and again reassured Sarah to prepare her belongings.

Ann Murray having returned to the breakfast table, unperturbed by Dido's outrageous display of defiance, felt confident that her words had produced enough force to put an end to all her protests. The unpleasant incident had merely caused Ann Murray a moment's impatience but had done nothing to diminish any of her previous satisfaction at Mr Harris' proposal.

"May I see the letter?" Lady Finch-Hatton asked, curious to read Mr Harris' proposal.

"Will Dido agree to it?" Miss Murray asked doubtful of there being any success as Dido was so against the idea.

"Dear Marjory, it is not a case of whether Dido will agree or not. It has already been arranged. " Ann Murray said decidedly

"Do you think that Mr Harris is suitable?" Lady Finch-Hatton asked with concern, after having read the letter.

"There is no question of it my dear. We all want what's best for Dido. Marriage to Mr Harris will give Dido security and moral decency." Ann Murray assured her niece. Though Lady Finch-Hatton knew her aunt to be correct in her statement, she did not feel assured, as she ought.

"I hope you are right." Miss Murray replied thoughtfully, surprised by her sister's confidence.

"Where is Dido?" Ann Murray asked the following morning after breakfast had concluded and there was no sign of the girl.

"Perhaps she is sleeping late. She was rather upset last night."

"Please inform Miss Dido that she is wanted in the drawing room." Ann Murray said to Mrs Jenkins.

"What if she is ill?"

"It will not do Marjory. The girl is too spoilt, the sooner she gets accustomed to the idea of her marriage the better." Ann Murray stated adamantly ignoring her sister's look of concern. When Mrs Jenkins returned to inform Miss Ann that Miss Dido was not in her room, the news was met with considerable surprise.

"Not in her room? Are you sure?" Miss Murray cried anxiously

"Marjory please! Have one of the servants search the gardens. Perhaps she has gone for a walk." Ann Murray said attempting to hide her own surprise at the impudence of the girl. Her suspicion was immediately aroused that the girl was up to no good. Probably sulking somewhere in the garden, no doubt, Ann Murray concluded. The footman was summoned to begin the search for Dido.

"Just one moment. Where is Dido's maid? Send her to me at once."

A few moments later Mrs Jenkins re-entered the room with the news that Sarah was absent as it was her morning off and that she was expected back in the afternoon.

"Send her to me as soon as she arrives." Ann Murray commanded before curtly dismissing Mrs Jenkins. Both Miss Murray and Ann Murray were left to wait for almost an hour while the grounds were searched for Dido but without success. At which the house was in a commotion all morning at the news of Dido's sudden disappearance.

"Foolish selfish girl!" Ann Murray exclaimed at the realisation that Dido had run away.

"How dreadful! Where will she go? How will she survive?" Miss Murray asked scarcely unable to think of it without disturbance for Dido's welfare. Ann Murray had no such concern as she could only think of Mr Harris pending visit and proposal. If he should come and not find Dido at home then an excuse would have to be made. If the worst came to the worst Mr Harris visit could be put off with an apology for Dido's illness or perhaps some excuse of an emergency visit to Eastwell Park. Ann Murray could only think of their present predicament with vexation at Dido's deliberate sabotage of their plans. Though she knew that some sort of effort should be made to locate the girl yet she did not want to cause any unnecessary alarm to the rest of the family until she had spoken to Dido's maid, as she was sure the wretched girl had a hand in Dido's disappearance and would no doubt know of Dido's whereabouts.

## CHATPER 31

Dido stepped down from the cart to meet the cold gloomy darkness of the London night air. The strong pungent smell of sewage struck her forcibly, causing Dido to catch her breath, searching her purse to retrieve a handkerchief to cover her nose. The sudden outbreak of showers provided Dido with some temporary relief from the unpleasant odour. All around her dark shadows scurried for protection from the rain. But Dido observed them impassively, struck by feelings of repulsion and apprehension, which produced within her an overwhelming desire to return to the cart. Dido turned back instinctively, only to see the cart already moving speedily away. She watched its departure with a feeling of immense regret at having missed the opportunity of returning to its safety. But knowing this reflection to be a useless one Dido turned dejectedly to the dark stone house, now her place of refuge. The miserable frame, neglected and long forgotten for hundreds of years stood observing the unfamiliar face of this forlorn figure. The appearance of the house caused Dido a moment of alarm; as it seemed to her unimaginable that anyone could live in such a wretched place. Forcing this feeling of uneasiness aside, she roused herself to knock the heavy door. The silence went undisturbed at her first attempt. It took another more forceful knock before a faint stirring could be heard from inside. The door was finally forced open, reluctantly giving way to a woman who stood behind it. Dido observed that her face was contorted with irritation at the late disturbance, as the light of the candle added a more unattractive glow to her aging features. Her curly brown hair flecked with grey was shoved untidily into a nightcap and her shoulder was covered with a dark shawl hiding a coarse nightdress.

"What do ya want?" she growled, before looking hastily behind herself as if fearful of disturbing someone inside.

Well?" she glared at Dido when there was no response.

Dido stood stunned unable to take in the sight that was before her. This vulgar woman was so unladylike. Her face was frightful her words even more so. She now doubted whether she had come to the right address.

"My name is Dido Belle. Sarah sent me." She forced herself to answer, scarcely able to speak above a whisper. Sarah had assured her that this would be enough to gain her access to a safe place. Dido trusted Sarah completely. Being of a cheerful and lively disposition, Sarah's nature was well suited to her mistress that it was inevitable that an immediate friendship should develop between them. Though Dido ensured that the proper positions were maintained, the years had only added to their mutual affection and Sarah's devotion to her mistress. But looking on this hostile creature Dido felt doubtful of any success.

"Who?" the woman screeched, her face wrinkled unpleasantly and for a moment Dido supposed herself to be speaking in a foreign language. She proceeded to repeat herself, and the woman's face suddenly softened with the recognition of the name.

"Oh, Sarah. Right, ya betta come in then." She muttered moving back reluctantly as if letting Dido in was going against her better judgement. She stood aside, holding the candle up as she let the door fall open.

"Gawd blimey yor black!" She cried looking shocked as if seeing some ghastly apparition. Dido hesitated expecting the woman's exclamation to follow with a refusal to let her enter. She attempted to hide her irritation, as well as to contain her contempt at the outburst of this ill-bred woman. How horrid, to be looked down upon by such an inferior creature as this! How was such a humiliation to be endured? Dido felt the full injustice of her race, as she observed the creature's expression, which would have been rather amusing, had it not wounded her pride. Perhaps this awkward scene could have been avoided had Sarah informed this woman of her colour. Dido started to say as much,

"She told me but I didn't 'no what to expect," the woman replied brazenly, still holding the light to Dido's face. Dido thought it useless even to attempt to imagine what the creature was expecting, just as it would have been foolish to suppose that she could apply herself to observing polite etiquette. There was nothing else to be done but to ignore the impropriety. Holding her head proudly aloof, Dido was determined not to be intimidated by the creature's bold gaze. The light was suddenly removed from her countenance and began dancing along the dark walls. Dido heard the creature mutter to herself as she preceded her into what Dido could only describe as a hovel. The woman continued to lead Dido to the back of the house until she came to an abrupt stop before a narrow door.

"You can sleep in 'ere." She muttered roughly, before stepping back for Dido to proceed.

"Thank you very much for your kindness," Dido began, but the creature had moved away before she had even finished her salutation, taking with her the light. To Dido's alarm she was left alone in the cold dark hall, and for a moment she stood bewildered by the hostility of her surroundings. With a feeling of trepidation, Dido pushed open the door, which gave way, but not without some resistance. She was struck by her sudden blindness, and it took several seconds for her eyes to adjust and yet she could scarcely see anything but dark shadows before her. Dido looked behind her hoping even to see the miserable creature return with the lamp. But silence and darkness remained her only companions. Reprimanding herself severely, Dido decided it foolish to remain standing in the doorway. Forcing herself to take courage, she stepped tentatively inside. As she did so she could hardly see her feet in front of her, and her tentative action was such that anyone observing her could not be blamed for thinking that she was about to jump off a precipice. Dido had not proceeded far into the room before she felt a soft object beneath her feet and kneeling down, she picked up what was a coarse sheet or blanket, before dropping it in disgust after felling a damp substance through her glove. How dreadful, Dido thought fearing her gloves to be in a filthy state. This will not do! She would have to find the wretched creature and demand a lamp. But what good would it do? Dido reasoned to herself. She could barely see to find her way around this dark room. It would be foolish to attempt finding her way back through a darkened hall. No, she was far too tired and desirous of rest. Dido decided it was easier to search for a bed. Holding the wall for support, Dido moved more quickly, but soon discovered that her way was barred by what felt like enormous clay like jars, which stood along the length of the adjacent wall. As she proceeded to walk gingerly towards the opposite wall, Dido soon discovered that the room was not much larger than a storing cupboard!

"Where am I to sleep?" Dido exclaimed, turning around anxiously while fighting back tears of vexation.

"How can I be treated in such a manner? How dare she!" Dido cried indignantly, her anger lasting only as long as the words sounded, before they were overwhelmed by weariness and despair at the misery of her situation. Remembering the coarse blanket that she had earlier discarded, Dido moved reluctantly towards it. This was no time for snobbery, she told herself, hoping that the wretched item might serve as a buffer to soften the hardness of the cold floor. But to Dido's frustration, the blanket did little to serve its purpose. She sat wearily against the wall thankful, at least, for the cloak she was wearing, though its warmth was lessened by the dampness of the rain. Pulling the hood over her head she drew her knees up towards her body, wrapping her cloak securely around herself, in the hope of keeping away the chill.

Closing her eyes tightly to stop fresh tears from falling proved to be a fruitless exercise as all efforts to prevent them failed miserably. Her sorrow had nothing to do with the severity of the condition in which she found herself, though she had sufficient cause to grieve. Even the hostile welcome and the cold dark room could not have produced such suffering that filled her heart at the painful recollections of the past few months. Her pain came not only from such contemplation, but also from the knowledge that her uncle and her beloved childhood home would be lost to her forever. This thought caused much anguish of spirit, so as to provide Dido with ample excuse to lament for weeks, even months, if self-pity was given liberty to flow freely and all restraint removed. It was with a heavy heart that Dido surrendered herself to the torment of her feelings and wept bitterly.

# CHAPTER 32

Dido was awakened by the sound of muffled voices behind the door, and the coldness of the wall against her back. On seeing the ugliness of the room, Dido realised that last night had not been a frightful dream. The room was not much lighter in the day than it had been at night, the only light coming from the crack under the door. She could hardly move her body for stiffness brought on by the discomfort of her position. The voices became more distinguishable and Dido could just comprehend what was being said.

"You put her in 'ere? Ma why?" Dido heard Sarah's voice rise in astonishment

"Where else I'm supposed to put 'err?" the creature replied unrepentant.

"Oh, ma. You were supposed to put her in my room." Sarah cried with distress at knowing her mistress had been left to sleep in a cupboard!

"Are you crazy? The likes of 'err?"

The door opened suddenly. Dido found herself in the awkward position of attempting to stand up, while the stiffness of her body in protest did not yield quick enough to the demands made upon it.

"Oh Miss Dido, I'm sorry miss. I didn't kno' she would let you sleep 'ere." Sarah cried, shocked at the sight of her mistress. Sarah's horrified expression caused Dido some alarm. She now imagined her appearance to be in a worst state than even she could imagine. Sarah moved quickly to help Dido to her feet. The mother stood in the doorway with her arms crossed surveying the scene with increasing exasperation.

"What ya grovelin' to 'err for?" she snorted shaking her head.

"Oh ma, out of the way." Sarah replied with irritation as she supported Dido's arm with her shoulder and moving towards the door forcing her mother to step back to let them pass. Sarah led Dido to a chair near to an open fire and sat her down, still apologising profusely as she knelt beside her. Dido could feel the sun as it rested on the table taking away the gloom of the room, which contained a large worn wooden table with four matching chairs, behind them stood a stone stove. In one corner a tall cupboard leaned holding itself up against a wall. At least it could be said that the room was warmer, Dido thought, observing the unpleasantness of the room with much distaste.

"Oh Miss Dido please speak to me" Sarah pleaded, her voice full of concern.

Dido heard a sharp exclamation from behind her. That sound could have only come from the insufferable woman.

"Ya think she was the queen or something'" she muttered turning away in disgust.

"I'm ok Sarah." Dido said, finally finding her voice to reassure and alleviate her friend's anxiety.

"Miss Dido, I'll get you something to drink to warm you up." Sarah encouraged as she moved towards the stove to take the boiling pot from the fire. Dido did not refuse Sarah's offering. She was willing to drink anything to take away the chill she felt that neither the inviting sun rays nor the heat from the stove could improve. Dido held her hands around the hot cup welcoming the heat it gave to her hands and face as she put the cup to her lips to drink. The beverage tasted slightly sweet and repulsive to Dido and for a moment the desire she had was to spit it out but instead forced the liquid down in several gulps. Dido had no idea what this concoction was but it did well to alleviate her chill.

"Thank you Sarah." Dido said cordially, forcing herself to smile in an effort to relieve the poor girl rather than any feelings of her own.

"No trouble miss. We just need to get you cleaned up. I've got your trunk in my room." Sarah said looking pleased. The news of her trunk gave Dido such a relief at the prospect of having something clean to wear that she could even try to forget the abhorrence of the miserable night spent here. It also allowed her to remember the gratitude owed her helper of whom she was indebted to. Sarah could not be blamed for her mother's vulgar manners or the squalid-ness of their home. Perhaps if she herself was wont to live in such conditions she too may have reasons to act in a similar fashion. Sarah had done so much already but Dido knew that she had to impose upon her kindness for a little while at least.

Dido felt almost herself again after having washed and changed into clean attire. She felt at least now she could think about her predicament with some sense of calm to plan her cause of action. Her new state of independence felt less favourable now that she was struck by her sudden change of position of comfort and security to a near state of destitution. It weighed gravely on her mind that she was now totally alone in the world. This thought would have given her much discomfort if she had not remembered her cousin Elizabeth. There was also her inheritance from her father as well as a modest annuity from her uncle.

It was by no means large but if she could find a suitable position as a governess she could at least hope to have a modest yet comfortable living. Dido pondered her future in this manner until interrupted by Sarah's voice.

"Is there anything else I can do for you miss?" Sarah asked cheerfully. Dido marvelled at her cheerful disposition, as it seemed so out of place in this dull house and even more so in contrast with her own uncertain future. How could anyone manage to smile in this squalid place? It had not occurred to Dido that whenever Sarah went home on her odd days off that she lived in such an abode.

"Yes. I need you to keep my things just until I find somewhere decent to stay." Dido said insensitive to any offence her words may have on Sarah's feelings.

"Where will you go miss?" she asked, her face looking troubled.

"I do not know. But one thing is for sure, I cannot stay here." Dido replied decidedly but on seeing Sarah's face becoming downcast put out her hand to touch her arm affectionately.

"Oh Sarah, please do not fret for me. I have no doubts that I will be able to get a position more suitable. You do understand?" Dido asked in her effort to console her.

"Of course miss." She replied meekly.

"You could help me find somewhere suitable to stay." Dido said as an afterthought. The poor creature was beside herself Dido thought. But if Dido had known that Sarah's anxiety was out of pity for her mistress' predicament she would have been mortified.

Yes, of course miss I'll try." She answered brightening up.

"Good." Dido replied pleasantly, and then turning once again about the small room that only had space for a small bed and a drawer, was unable to stifle her disdain. Not even a looking glass was to be seen! No, she could not stay here!

"Sarah!" her mother voice screeched from below.

"Excuse me miss." Sarah said before running hurriedly from the room.

"I not 'ave the likes of 'err 'ere to bow and scrape to while there's work to be done!" the disagreeable creature could be heard shouting from outside. No doubt it was said intentionally for her to hear, Dido thought, pleased by the prospect of leaving this place as soon as possible. There was no question of imposing any longer on the woman's hospitality. She had put poor Sarah in enough trouble just by her presence in the house, if she could dare to call it such. Now as she contemplated the prospect of finding herself new accommodations, she was left with the dissatisfaction of not knowing how or where to start! How wretched to feel so completely helpless, Dido thought to herself. Where would she apply for rooms to rent? She was a stranger to London with the exception of knowing two squares, one being Bloomsbury square the former home of her great uncle, until it was destroyed when she was still a child, the other Maple square the home of Miss Haversham.

"I'm sorry miss I 'ave to do some chores for ma before I get back to Kenwood." Sarah said coming into the room suddenly.

"Yes, of course, when do you need to return?" Dido asked, at which Sarah answered that she was expected back in the afternoon. So preoccupied with her escape that Dido had completely forgotten that Sarah would have to return to work or risk the chance of being missed. She spared a thought to the reaction of her relations at her absence but then dismissed it immediately as it was too unpleasant to contemplate. No doubt she would not be missed, certainly not by Ann Murray. She would have incurred the lady's wrath for having spoiled her plans. How she would love to see Mr Harris' expression on receiving the news that any plans of marriage to her were infinitely removed! But she could not dwell on the pleasure for long as her present needs were far more pressing. Dido had hoped to have Sarah's aid in looking for suitable rooms. Oh, what a nuisance it was to be entirely dependent on others! And yet Dido supposed that she had always lived in a state of dependency since she could remember. Her life had been one of privilege and sheltered indulgence. Why else did she find herself so incapable of dealing with her dreadful position? She felt totally at lost as to what to do. Dido chided herself. How difficult can it be to find accommodations? She would just have to apply herself more dexterously. And felt a momentary surge of courage. Sarah reappeared smiling gaily.

"Don't worry miss. I know someone who might be able to help you. Here's the address. He'll sort you out." Sarah said confidently handing Dido a slip of paper with a scrawled hand that was almost illegible. Dido smiled without saying a word, she could have kissed Sarah, as she took the paper, folded it and placed it in her purse. So much for independence, Dido thought pushing the feeling of ineptness aside. She was none the less relieved for the help, reminding herself that she was more than capable of helping herself but Dido decided it would be imprudent to decline Sarah's help.

"Sarah, there is one last thing you could do for me. Would you be able to obtain a carriage?"

"Yes of course miss." She replied kindly before quitting the room. Dido moved towards the small window that faced directly onto the street in hope of glimpsing Sarah's efforts in hailing a carriage. Dido grew more impatient with every second that went by, as there was not a carriage to be seen. She could not help but sigh aloud as her disposition gave way to increasing apprehension at her future prospects. If she had to wait much longer she would be left with no confidence at all! Just as Dido attempted to admonish herself for her weakness, she heard the sound of horses approaching. Hastening to take her position by the window, Dido was pleased to see Sarah conversing with the coachman. Sarah turned to look in the direction of the house before turning again to address the coachman, whose face could not be seen under the tall hat that sat low upon his head. Presently she turned to walk back into the house as the carriage waited. Dido moved away from the window and slowly took up her purse and cloak. Taking a deep breath she walked towards the door, feeling no more prepared than if she was walking to the gallows.

"You fool. Still scurrying around that girl?" The creature's voice could be heard saying.

"Oh ma please!" Sarah pleaded looking ashamed as she saw Dido exiting the room.

"Ah, where the queen going now?" she asked, her voice filled with sarcasm as she stood directly before the open door. Dido chose to ignore her abuse and instead walking to Sarah held out her hand to her to take her leave.

"Thank you Sarah. I'm truly grateful for your kindness." Dido said earnestly, as a grunt came from the miserable woman. Dido turned to her smiling graciously, determined to show this creature that she was a lady of superior breeding and manners.

"Thank you for your kind hospitality. I will be back to collect my belongings. I hope you do not mind my imposing on you for a few more hours." Dido said with all the politeness she could muster.

The creature muttered something under her breath that Dido thought to be her attempt at mimicking her in her guttural English. Bustling pass her the creature continued to mumble as she went back to the stove.

"Take no notice of 'err." Sarah said directing Dido outside and to the awaiting carriage. Dido thanked her again before stepping into the carriage.

"Where to miss?" the driver asked nonchalantly.

Dido hesitated for a few seconds. She held the piece of paper that Sarah had given her but denied the inclination of giving the driver the address. Instead she heard herself instructing the driver to take her to Maple square, the home of Miss Haversham. As the carriage moved away Dido spent the first few seconds berating herself for doing so. But with the reprimand came a feeling of relief, so as to make Dido to wonder why she had not thought of it before. Of course her friend would be more than willing to aid her in her quest to obtain a profession. For the first time Dido felt optimistic about her future.

# CHAPTER 33

Dido could give no thought for where she was going as the carriage bumped, hobbled, twisted and turned its way around noisy and sometime crowded London streets. The cold greyness of the day did nothing to impede sellers from sounding their wares. The carriage stopped briefly while a trail of cattle was manoeuvred with little haste along the road. Dido paid little attention to the scenes before her. Her thoughts were more preoccupied with the explanation she would give to Miss Haversham for her unexpected visit. Ever since Dido could remember Miss Haversham had been an intimate friend of the family and had always shown her great kindness.

"Oh you must come and visit me when I'm in London, especially you Dido. I'm sure you'll be an absolute delight to everyone." Miss Haversham said enthusiastically on more than one occasion. Her large frame always seemed to move surprisingly graceful whenever she was animated or excited by some event or gossip. Miss Haversham had an extremely rounded face that always seem to wear a knowing smile as if holding all knowledge of the heart. She often giggled girlishly although she herself was twice that age if not a few years over forty. Miss Haversham had never married. It was said not only by others but more often repeated by Miss Haversham herself that she had fallen in love with a certain gentleman named James Russell, who had entered into business with her father in the Caribbean. After a brief courtship the couple were intended to marry. But before the wedding arrangements had even been finalised the gentleman was exposed as a scoundrel who had for some time been involved in a scandalous relationship. Miss Haversham was removed to the country and the young man was never again seen in good society. Miss Haversham was left with the pleasure of nursing a broken heart. A few years later her father William Haversham died leaving Miss Haversham, as his only surviving daughter, a large fortune. The lady having never married therefore thought it her duty as a wounded survivor of an unhappy love affair, to be the guardian of all her friends' daughters and nieces. Because of her wealth and position she was often indulged and in some cases even encouraged.

"Oh, why don't you let me take Dido to stay with me for a little while? Surely you won't miss her." Said the lady again as if it were the first time she had spoken on the subject.

"You know she will be missed. She is needed here. Who will look after my correspondence?" Lord Mansfield replied giving Dido a wink.

Dido smiled at him but the thought of spending time with Miss Haversham in London was not unfavourable to her. It would be more of a welcome diversion than what she was use to at present. Lord Mansfield had continually refused Miss Haversham's repeated offer until one day, much to Dido's surprise, and no doubt Miss Haversham's, Lord Mansfield had agreed to let her go. The memory of that visit came back to her as she observed the familiar streets and recalled the face of the young black boy.

"We are here miss –." the coachman said, before stopping suddenly on catching a glimpse of Dido's face. Dido being so preoccupied with her thoughts had not realised that the carriage had stopped and the driver had opened the door. She did not fail to notice the surprised look the driver gave her, which did little to calm her nerves, as the driver continued to stare in such a foolish manner. Suddenly she felt momentary weariness at the prospect of having to experience the same reaction wherever she went but she knew that it was inevitable if she were to make her own way in the world.

"Thank you." Dido said politely ignoring his stare as he helped her out of the carriage. Dido looked toward the house with rising uneasiness before turning to pay the driver.

"Could you please wait?" Dido asked, not sure of what to expect from her visit. At least if she did not need him she could pay him for his time and send him away. He nodded without saying a word.

Dido walked to the house and presently knocked on the large door. It seemed to be opened immediately by the doorman, who looked at Dido quizzically.

"Good day. I'm here to see Miss Haversham." Dido said trying to sound as confident as she could.

"I'm afraid Miss Haversham has just left a few days ago for the country." He announced noticing the effect his words were having on the young lady.

"Oh no, are you sure?" Dido asked foolishly, knowing as soon as she spoke that the doorman must think her a complete simpleton.

"Yes miss. We are just preparing to close the house up until the spring. I doubt if Miss Haversham will be back until then." He answered looking at her with concern.

"Are you ok Miss?"

Dido did not know how to answer. Miss Haversham had been her last hope. Again she was left with a feeling of helplessness and despair. Now where was she going to find dwellings? Why had she not thought to write to Miss Haversham but she knew that this idea could not have entered her head with the haste of her sudden departure from Kenwood.

"Miss?"

"I'm sorry, yes I am fine thank you." Dido murmured distractedly, before turning to walk back to the carriage her thoughts disturbed.

"Where to miss?" the coachman asked awaiting Dido instructions. Dido was appalled at herself when nothing but tears came. The coachman looked away awkwardly as Dido attempted to retrieve a handkerchief from my purse and dabbed her eyes. After she was able to compose herself she spoke,

"Please, do you know of any respectable rooms available for rent?" Dido asked, hoping that perhaps the coachman would be able to direct her to suitable dwellings. She took no thought as to what he might think of her forwardness. Who better to ask than a coachman so familiar with London? His brow creased as if the effort to think was too much for him. Dido stood waiting for his response barely breathing in the hope that her humility may have given her some reward. The thought of returning to Sarah's house filled her with dread. Poor Sarah. She had tried so hard to help but how could a woman in her position be expected to live in conditions fit for an animal.

"Well, there are a few places..."

"Oh, excellent. Could you take me to one of them?" she asked eagerly before he could finish. He gave Dido a hesitant look, scratching his head as if wanting to say something but thought the better of it.

"These are respectable dwellings?" Dido asked afraid that he may have misunderstood her meaning.

"Yes, miss, of course."

"I will pay for your time." Dido said as a way of encouragement. The coachman delayed in answering as if in two minds to accept. But the possibility of earning a little extra did much to sway his decision. He helped Dido into the carriage and walked around to the front still frowning as he went.

Dido settled herself back into the carriage a little perturbed by the coachman's behaviour. But she did not dwell on it for long as she felt more relief now that she would at least find somewhere to stay. Once she was settled she could write to her cousin Elizabeth or Miss Haversham for aid in finding a suitable employment. This thought gave her some immediate relief. She was determined that even the gloominess of the skies would not take away her feeling of optimism of finally finding a place to reside. They had not driven more than half a mile before the carriage suddenly halted so abruptly that Dido was jolted forward and almost out of her seat. She had no time to recover before she was thrown back again. Dido could hear the horses neighing as they reared their front legs trying to avoid the obstruction before them. Dido steadied herself still stunned by the suddenness of their stop. She recovered herself enough to look out to try and alert the driver to find out the reason for the delay.

"Easy now, girl." The driver was saying softly.

"Is there anything wrong?" Dido asked but her words went unnoticed. The driver jumped down quickly moving to stand in front of the horses as he tried to calm them.

"Whose carriage is this?" The voice demanded rather angrily. Dido could hear the voice but the person was obscured from her view.

"Is this not Sir Milton's carriage?" the voice could be heard to say again with an air of accusation.

Dido could not catch the response of the driver, which made her feel a little apprehensive. Her impatience to know what was happening did not allow her to stay in her seat for a moment longer. Getting down from the carriage Dido walked toward the front to where the driver was standing with his back towards her. Directly facing him was a young gentleman, wearing a tall hat, coat and breeches. He eyed the driver with an angry scowl.

"I am just running an errand sir." the driver replied uneasily, his voice sounding rather subservient.

"And is this your errand?" the gentleman asked mockingly looking toward Dido with a familiar look as Dido was struck unexpectedly on recognising Captain Alwyne.

The driver turned around suddenly and on seeing Dido, looked away embarrassed, his face reddening. Dido found herself rooted to the spot unable to move, utterly overwhelmed by the encounter.

"I think the lady will need to find alternative transport. Permit me to take you wherever you wish to go, Miss Dido." Captain Alwyne said gallantly.

Dido was irked by Captain Alwyne's boldness but she was too overcome with embarrassment to respond to his offer.

"I'm sorry miss, I have another errand to run." He said abruptly before moving quickly to mount his carriage.

"Wait! You promised…" Dido started to move towards the departing driver and carriage. She had momentarily forgotten Captain Alwyne who stood looking on with some amusement at the scene before him. Dido was beside herself as the coachman was not only driving away with her hope of a new situation but leaving her stranded in an unfamiliar street of London. Dido stood transfixed staring dumbly at the disappearing carriage.

"My offer is still available if wish to be taken anywhere Miss Dido?" Captain Alwyne asked again.

Dido turned and looked at him with disdain and could barely response civilly.

"Captain Alwyne at your service." He stated gallantly and smiled with pleasure despite the look of aversion that Dido gave him. Dido was dumbfounded at the audacity of the rogue. He was mocking her! How she cursed the inopportune work of providence that had brought her into Captain Alwyne's path. He was the last person she wished to see. It horrified her that *he* should be the one present to witness her humiliation. Dido could not contain her shame and discomfort as she recollected their last meeting. She did not know how to look, her distress was too acute. Captain Alwyne felt no such awkwardness at their opportune meeting. He continued to grin openly, thinking to himself that since Lord Mansfield funeral he had been waiting for just an occasion to visit Kenwood in hope of seeing her again. Now here she was unaccompanied in London and Captain Alwyne was curious as to know why.

"Are you with Miss Murray or Miss Ann?" he asked, knowing instinctively that she was alone. Her countenance coloured and she avoided his eyes. He could see that she was uncomfortable in his presence and for a moment he became annoyed at her distrustful manner.

"I am" Dido started but broke off too ashamed to reveal her secret. What would he think of her?

"I will obtain a carriage for you." He said, noticing her distress, felt a momentary pang of compassion and presently went away without waiting her response. Dido wondered at how Captain Alwyne could dare to address her without a hint of embarrassment or shame. Why was it that he who should be embarrassed should have so much boldness, while she who had done nothing to be ashamed of was overcome with it! He came back directly and stood before her, smiling amicably as if she could ever be fooled again by his civility.

"Your carriage awaits Miss Dido." Captain Alwyne announced with humour, and Dido wished that she could have the pleasure of refusing him but her predicament was so dismal that she had no other option but to accept his offer. Anyway, there was no other means of escaping his presence so expediently.

"Thank you." Dido forced herself to reply with much civility as she could muster, willing herself not to recoil as he helped her into the carriage. Captain Alwyne held fast to her hand then bent his head to kiss it but Dido quickly pulled her hand out of his grasp before he had the opportunity to do so. Captain Alwyne laughs.

"Good day Miss Dido, please send my regards to Miss Murray and Miss Ann. I am sure to visit soon. Until then." he said still smiling as he removed his hat, certain now that he would visit Kenwood before too long. Dido was spared the trouble of responding as the carriage moved off. Though she was sure she could not have responded sufficiently as her feelings were in such a turmoil despite every attempt she made to compose them. It took her several minutes to recover from the shock of her encounter with Captain Alwyne until she realised that she had no idea where the carriage was taking her. In a panic Dido leaned out the window and attempted to attract the attention of the driver but her efforts proved futile. Again she tried to knock on the roof of the carriage but to no avail. She decided it was foolish to continue and sat back resignedly in her seat, there was nothing to be done but to wait until the carriage stopped.

# CHAPTER 34

Dido's heart sank on seeing the familiar environs of Kenwood as she realised too late her intended destination. What duplicity could be in the mind of Captain Alwyne in sending her back here? "No! Surely he could not know?" She cried, feeling even more wretched at the thought that Captain Alwyne could be laughing at her failed attempt at leaving home. No, Dido reasoned with herself. He could not possibly have known of her secret departure from Kenwood just the night before and therefore his actions in instructing the driver to take her to Kenwood would have been a perfectly natural one. Dido reassured herself with this supposition, which provided an opportunity of calming her anxieties. But it did not solve the immediate problem. Soon she would be arriving at Kenwood and risk the possibility of alerting the attention of both Miss Murray and Ann Murray. Dido despaired at the prospect, as she had no desire to see her relatives again, at least, not so soon. She thought perhaps if she could alert the driver of her change of destination as soon as the carriage stopped, she could even leave Kenwood without being noticed by the servants. But no sooner had the carriage stopped the door was hurriedly opened by the footman, dashing all Dido's hopes of a swift escape. Standing directly behind the footman was Ann Murray and Miss Murray and Captain Alwyne, not long alighted from his horse, grinning shamelessly. The first lady wore a look of severity, and the latter a look of concern.

"Perhaps it will not be too much trouble Dido to ask where you have been." Ann Murray inquired with cold sarcasm. Dido gave no response as she reluctantly stepped down from the carriage, wholly surprised at seeing Captain Alwyne again. No doubt she had him to thank for her relations knowledge of her unexpected arrival.

"Unfeeling girl!" Ann Murray cried, unable to hold her temper as she followed Dido into the house, completely forgetting Captain Alwyne's presence.

"Dear Ann, please do not upset yourself. I'm sure Dido can explain herself." Miss Murray said, wishing that this matter could be conducted in a civilised manner. Ann Murray recollecting herself turned and forced herself to smile for Captain Alwyne's benefit.

"Perhaps Marjory dear, you could take Captain Alwyne into the drawing room for some refreshments. I'm sure we will join you presently." Ann Murray said with all the civility she could muster. Captain Alwyne looked bemused and enthralled at the scene before him but nodded politely and followed Miss Murray into the drawing room. As soon as Captain Alwyne and Miss Murray was out of earshot, Ann Murray turned on Dido.

"Just one moment. Do not think you can escape so easily!" Ann Murray called, forcing Dido to delay her flight to her room.

"I do not believe I need to explain myself to you." Dido said boldly, ignoring the gasp that came from Miss Ann, who looked as if she would have gone into an attack of fits.

"How dare you be so insolent to me? Do you have any concern for what your actions could have caused this family? Have you no sense of duty?" Ann Murray exclaimed angrily, her face becoming red with vexation. Dido could find little compassion for her relation's feelings. What had she done that she had not been driven to by their actions? Did she think her a simpleton? What harm could her departure from Kenwood possibly do to the family's reputation?

"There could be little difference in my leaving Kenwood a married woman or as that of a single woman looking for respectable employment." Dido remarked firmly, desiring to end the conversation, again turned as if to leave.

"Do not think that I am unaware of your little accomplice." Ann Murray said with great satisfaction, her words caused Dido to stop suddenly. Ann Murray on seeing the change in Dido's countenance gained much pleasure in the effect of her words.

"Yes. I've always thought the girl to be quite useless but now I have a perfectly good reason to dismiss her," said Ann Murray tersely, and then smiled maliciously.

"She has nothing to do with this." Dido replied but she could scarcely speak for the reality of Ann Murray's threat.

"I think that is where you are wrong." She said coldly, knowing now that she had gained the upper hand.

"Please. Surely this is not necessary." Dido pleaded, unable to hide the wretchedness of her sentiments at the thought of being responsible for Sarah losing her livelihood. Until that moment she had not considered the possibility, so concerned was she with her own needs.

"It's a pity that you did not think of this prior to your little scheme. It seems to be a habit of yours in helping servants lose their livelihood. Of course it is of a great help to me." Ann Murray declared wryly, seeming to take pleasure in Dido's misery. She listened to Dido's pleading without sympathy, feeling that the girl had bought this all upon herself, running away in such a dreadful manner, just when they had settled the arrangement of her marriage so agreeably.

"It is not necessary to dismiss Sarah. I am here and I do not intend to leave again." Dido said resignedly, feeling numb at the cold reality of her situation.

"I am glad that you have come to your senses. I will forget that this little incident ever happened. After all, you were hardly missed if it were not for the fact that I could not find Marjory's reading glasses I'm sure *no one* would have noticed you were gone." Ann Murray added maliciously. A sinister smile crossed her features, which added to the cruelty of her words. Dido duly felt the pain that they were intended to inflict and could do nothing else but flee in tears to her room. How could she bear such misery as this? Dido wept openly, her pain was too acute, the humiliation so final, that there seemed to be no escape from its power. When Dido remembered the look of triumph on Ann Murray's face, she felt a fire of indignation rise up within her but its sudden flame soon gave way to resignation. Her fate was now sealed. Marriage to Mr Harris seemed inevitable. What choice was left to her? Her future held nothing but unhappiness and despair. Her only hope was her cousin Elizabeth. Yes, she would write to her dear cousin for aid! Surely she will support her in her hour of need! Dido wasted little time in finding pen and paper, hardly knowing how she wrote, her pen ship made increasingly illegible by the agitation of her spirit. Dido's petition to her cousin was filled with desperate urgency for intervention and little sense of coherence. The letter was despatched the following morning with the aid of Sarah, and with much relief and expectancy on Dido's part. All was left to do was to wait for her cousin's response, which proved moderately difficult a task for Dido's impatience.

Lady Finch-Hatton arrived at Kenwood a few days later, with Dido's letter, and in a state of anxious concern for her cousin's welfare. Her unexpected arrival caused much surprise to both Ann Murray and Miss Murray, who having expected there to be something terribly wrong, found instead that their niece had come to see Dido.

"Dido? I know that your intimacy with Dido should bring you to Kenwood but why with so sudden urgency and so unexpected? If we knew you were coming we would have at least prepared tea. " Ann Murray asked suspiciously staring at her niece intently for any clues. Lady Finch-Hatton looked surprised at her aunt's response.

"You were not expecting me? But I received a letter from Dido only a few days ago telling me to come to see her on a matter of urgency. I had no idea that you were not aware of it." Lady Finch-Hatton replied, with little notion of what her words had revealed.

"Is there anything wrong?" Lady Finch-Hatton asked on seeing her aunt's countenance change to one of irritation.

"You have no idea what that girl have put us through during the last week. I simply do not know what to do with her. If it was not for Captain Alwyne's intervention, I do not know where she would be." Ann Murray continued to the surprise of Lady Finch-Hatton, who pleaded to know what was happening and why Dido had written to her in such desperation. Ann Murray proceeded to tell of Dido's disappearance to London and her refusal to consider marriage to Mr Harris, though Mr Harris was more than willing to marry her. Her words were said with such feelings of outrage, and of one being unappreciated in her efforts to secure Dido's future.

"She has been nothing but ungrateful and has attempted to ruin all her possible chances of happiness!"

"I'm sure that Dido can be made to see reason." Lady Finch-Hatton asserted, wondering why her aunts had not informed her of this earlier. The situation was far worse than she had expected.

"Since Lord Mansfield's death she has become positively uncontrollable and has done everything in her power to go against my every word."

"Surely not." Lady Finch-Hatton said adamantly, unable to believe her aunt's description of Dido's disposition.

"Well, I think she is rather unhappy." Miss Murray added, and received a sharp glare from her sister.

"Perhaps I should speak to Dido." Lady Finch-Hatton stated feeling rather more concerned than when she first arrived.

"Yes, by all means see if you can talk some sense to the girl." Ann Murray replied and then proceeded to call for the maid to find out Dido's whereabouts. Dido had ventured to go for a walk, though the weather was quite cold and the wind rather blustery, but as it was dry the prospect seemed far favourable than staying indoors. On her return, she was met by one of the servants, who announced that she was wanted in the drawing room. Dido felt an instant feeling of displeasure at hearing the request. Since her return to Kenwood she had received only the reserved manner of Ann Murray, which had made Dido to feel like an un-welcomed guest in her own home. She was no longer called upon to sit with the sisters while they were at leisure, this she was grateful for, though she was required to dine with them. Miss Murray, in her kindness, had attempted to treat her as she always did, but Dido knew that she would never go against her sister's wishes. Thus Miss Murray was often refrained from conversing with Dido by a steely glare from her sister. She could not blame Miss Murray for her conduct, but rather pitied her for being under the constraint of such a domineering sister.

It was with surprise that Dido entered the drawing room to find Elizabeth seated with Miss Murray and Ann Murray. She observed from Elizabeth's countenance and Ann Murray's look of satisfaction that she had been told everything.

"Lady Finch-Hatton is here to see you. I'm sure you've been expecting her." Ann Murray said slyly.

"I hope you won't think me dreadfully rude if I request to speak to Dido alone." Lady Finch-Hatton said to the displeasure of her Aunt, who had wanted to be present during their exchange, but seeing that her niece to be quite adamant, decided to consent. Once Dido and Lady Finch-Hatton were alone, Dido fell at her cousin's feet overtaken by tears of despair. Her cousin in stunned concern attempted to encourage her to refrain from her tears. It took Dido several minutes to control her emotions and be able to speak.

"I am in a state of wretchedness, I have no-one but you to turn to!"

"Come now it cannot be all bad. In time you will see that your marriage is all for the best -"

"No! How can I find favourable something which is abhorrent to me?" Dido cried fervently as she held tightly to Lady Finch-Hatton's hand. Lady Finch-Hatton becoming alarmed at Dido hysteria attempted to calm her but in vain.

"Good heavens, you must see that marriage is the only option for you? Listen to me, Aunt Ann -"

"Do not speak to me of that creature!" Dido said so violently that Lady Finch-Hatton began to think that perhaps her aunt had not been exaggerating about her conduct.

"You are being unjust and unkind in your opinion. It would do no good to make an enemy of Miss Ann, Dido. It is not only Miss Ann's wishes that you are going against it was also the wishes of Lord Mansfield."

Dido hesitated feeling uneasy at the truth of Elizabeth's words. Ought she to succumb to such a fate?

"And if it is not my wish?" Dido replied in her own defence, at which Lady Finch-Hatton sighed deeply.

"Oh Dido, you are far too naïve. I did warn you of this many months since. It is not a matter of our wishes, in many a case."

"But you could help me to live independently and to find a suitable employment -"

"Stop this foolishness at once!" Lady Finch-Hatton shouted unable to hold her temper. Dido fell silent, stunned by her cousin's refusal to help. Lady Finch-Hatton regretted the harshness of her words but knew that there could be no thought of Dido attempting to live independently or of her supporting such a decision. Both her father and husband had made it clear that Dido only future security was in her marriage, which was after all the wish of the late Lord Mansfield.

"Dido, you simply must get use to the idea of marriage. After all it is not so dreadful as you think and I've been assured that this Mr Harris is of a good character and as a clergy's wife, you will be well looked after. Do not despise such an opportunity dear cousin." Lady Finch-Hatton attempted to persuade her cousin, though it pained her to see her tearful disposition, which reminded her of her own despair on hearing of her own engagement to Mr Finch-Hatton. How long ago that all seemed now, Lady Finch-Hatton sighed. But being successfully married, if success was measured by social standing, security and children, then she could be satisfied that at least this was true in her case, she could at least speak confidently to her cousin. Love was merely a bonus that few marriages could hope to enjoy. It was best for Dido to come to the realisation of her duty to her family in accepting Mr Harris.

"You have a duty to the memory of our dear uncle and to your family."

"How can I be sensible to such a duty if it goes against the duty to my own wishes?" Dido cried.

"Family duty comes before self. Your privilege standing comes at a price dear Dido. It is the way of things and you must accept it."

"Think of marriage as an occupation, a dreary one perhaps but there are far worst evils." Lady Finch-Hatton laughed, trying to make light of the subject. Dido could not find the humour in such a disagreeable prospect. Her only hope had been dashed by her cousin's refusal to go against the wishes of their relations. Dido felt her miserable fate sealed with grave finality. With such opposition against her how could she not consent to Mr Harris' proposal?

# CHAPTER 35

During the subsequent days, Dido was forced to reflect on the full humiliation of her failed attempt at independence. In just two days she had surrendered to the vulnerability of her position, having found herself ill prepared to cope with the insecurities that she had faced. Though the urgency of her flight had given her little preparation for what would befall her, Dido's pampered lifestyle did little to assist her cause. What must her relations think of her? Ann Murray had accused her of being spoilt. At the time she had thought the accusation to be ridiculous! But now she confessed that there was some truth in it. Though she was no more spoilt than her cousin Elizabeth or any other young lady who had been accustomed to living in high society, her indulgent lifestyle had left her ill prepared for life's realities. She had always been cared for and protected by her uncle, and had known no other way of living. Had she always to suffer the injury of being born of a self-indulgent parent. Her father lived to please himself and had suffered little consequence for his actions. What of her mother? How had she fared without knowing the child that she had born? Dido supposed them to be both victims of her father's debauchery and impropriety; immoral sexual behaviours that was openly disapproved of, but where male infidelities were concerned, was rarely ostracised within refined society. Dido could not think of her father without some feeling of bitterness, and yet she had little to complain of until now. Yes, she had to tolerate the snobbery and prejudice of those who considered her race to be beneath their society. But she was sure that her uncle's protection had shielded her from the worst kind of discrimination. Now that his protection was removed the absence of his influence could already be felt. Ann Murray's behaviour towards her was bordering on incivility. Dido felt that it could not be long before all pretence of civility would be completely removed. Her time at Kenwood was at an end, there could be no doubt of this, she concluded with a heavy heart. Perhaps her relations were right. An independent situation without the support and protection of her family would prove most unfavourable, if not highly improbable, if Dido be true to herself. Perhaps marriage to Mr Harris would prove more beneficial than an independent situation? Though she reviled the prospect of marriage, at least with Mr Harris she would be treated well. Dido could not question Mr Harris' integrity, though she thought there to be some weakness of character. Mr Harris had a propensity to be overly pious and pompous but Dido could think of far worse evils. Poor Sarah. Her selfless efforts had been all in vain and had almost threatened her livelihood. How could Dido repay her kindness with so little resistance? And yet she had gone against every principle of family honour and duty in her attempts to resist an arranged marriage. Nevertheless Dido felt an overwhelming feeling of shame at the ease in which she had surrendered to her fate.

After breakfast Dido was informed by Ann Murray to prepare herself to receive a visitor. She assumed from Ann Murray's excited manner, that her expected visitor was Mr Harris and therefore cared too little to ask for the identity of the caller. Dido wondered at her need for secrecy of a matter that was known to all the servants!

"I expect your behaviour towards Mr Harris to be cordial." Ann Murray warned, disliking the show of indifference in Dido's manner.

"Yes, of course." Dido replied resignedly, her response causing Ann Murray to hesitate for a moment having expected some resistance.

"I'm glad to see that we understand each other." She said, though rather cautiously as if suspecting some kind of deception on Dido's part. But Dido felt nothing but bewilderment at the ease of her own feelings. Ann Murray's words had done nothing to affect her manner. She felt completely indifferent. Even the prospect of meeting Mr Harris and receiving his proposal did not cause her any feeling of anxiety. In fact she wondered whether her presence was needed at all, as her answer must inevitably be yes. Perhaps Miss Ann could save her the trouble and accept on her behalf. Or better still perhaps a note would suffice! This thought gave Dido some amusement as she sat with Miss Murray and Miss Ann in the library awaiting Mr Harris' arrival. The footman entered to announce the arrival of Captain Davinier, to the surprise of all the occupants seated. Captain Davinier was not expected and for a few seconds the news was met with stunned silence. Dido did not know what to think. For what purpose was Captain Davinier here?

"Captain Davinier, what a pleasant surprise!" Ann Murray exclaimed recovering swiftly from her initial surprise.

"I apologise for intruding upon your kindness. I was in the vicinity and I thought that I could not leave without first paying my respects." Captain Davinier said eloquently but with some awkwardness of manner. He then turned and bowed in the direction of Miss Murray and Dido.

"Captain Davinier, your presence is always welcomed at Kenwood." Miss Murray said graciously. Captain Davinier seated himself and then proceeded to ask after the welfare of all the ladies. Miss Murray answered for all to Dido's relief.

"Yes, we are all well but I am just in a state of flurry as we have been so busy lately preparing to move our possessions." Miss Murray remarked with a hint of melancholy, as she had always been fond of Kenwood.

"Are you leaving Kenwood?" Captain Davinier asked in surprise.

"Yes, our brother Viscount Stormont will take up residence here with his family in the next few months as the next Lord Mansfield." Ann Murray explained

"Of course" Captain Davinier replied and then fell silent.

"You shall be sad to leave Kenwood Miss Dido?" he asked, his words seeming to hold much more meaning than was meant.

"Naturally, I am sad to leave my childhood home but it is to be expected." Dido replied, attempting to show as little emotion as possible.

"Where will you live?" he asked without thought of the impropriety of his question. An awkward silence followed. Dido was not sure how to answer and felt immediately ashamed at the thought of her future domesticity. Again she was grateful for Miss Ann's intervention.

"Dido will stay here until arrangements can be made for her." Ann Murray replied civilly but her answer was deliberately vague.

Captain Davinier gave a quick glance in Dido's direction, whose eyes were downcast. He could see that they had no intention of revealing the news he had come to hear for himself. Captain Davinier had no qualms about exposing their secret.

"Miss Dido, may I wish you all happiness on your forthcoming marriage." Captain Davinier stated graciously, knowing the affects his words would have on the ladies present.

"Oh!" was all that could be heard from Miss Murray. Ann Murray remained composed but felt quite irritated by Captain Davinier's inopportune visit. Dido gasped, her eyes flew up to meet his in astonishment before blushing with embarrassment.

"Where did you hear such news Captain Davinier?" Ann Murray enquired with an air of cordiality that she did not feel.

"I believe it is common knowledge, madam. Captain Alwyne heard it from Mrs Harris herself, who has been announcing the engagement openly." He declared, taking in the expressions of the ladies. Dido could not hide the humiliation she felt at the idea of everyone speaking of her engagement to Mr Harris. That she should suffer this humiliation in Captain Davinier's presence, knowing that he knew her marriage was arranged against her will, caused her to feel it more acutely. Dido felt completely exposed that she could hardly keep herself from running from the room. It took all her power of fortitude to remain in her seat.

"Then it is true?" he persisted to the displeasure of everyone except Miss Murray who thought nothing of the strangeness of his question. Dido was pained. How she wished he would stop talking! Why was he here! She bemoaned wretchedly.

"Well, it is not completely settled but Mr Harris is expected at any moment." Ann Murray conceded, seeing no reason to keep Captain Davinier in the dark. Dido could not stay to listen any longer. The enormity of her anxiety and shame soon overcame her fear of displeasing.

"Please excuse me." Dido said hastily hurrying from the room before she could be detained. Her escape had been timely as she could hardly control her breathing and found herself panting frantically for air. Captain Davinier's knowledge of her intended marriage had caused Dido great distress. The thought of people talking of her engagement filled her with indignation. How humiliating, that such gossip had reached the ears of Captain Davinier. He who was previously one of her intended suitors! There was no doubt in Dido's mind that he had come with the very intention of laughing at her after having turned down the opportunity of marrying Lord Mansfield's black ward! Dido could hardly contain her emotions. She needed fresh air. She needed to walk, to think, to be alone in order to regain her composure.

"Permit me?"

Dido turned in frightened astonishment at the sound of Captain Davinier's voice. He was standing directly before her. If her manner was perturbed it was more so now that the object of her thoughts was before her. She hardly knew where to look. Captain Davinier stood calmly reaching out to open the patio door to the terrace, which Dido in her state of agitation had struggled to open. Dido could not find the voice to thank him but stepped out hoping to be left alone but instead found the gentleman following behind. She wanted to ask him to leave but did not have the courage to speak.

"Do you want to know why I am here?" Captain Davinier asked to her surprise. Dido found herself blushing though she did not know why she should. Somehow his question brought back the humiliation of her position.

"Well I shall tell you." He continued with ease that caused Dido to feel a sudden pang of resentment. How could he stand there so calmly before her, enjoying her humiliation? Dido thought.

"Can I be permitted to speak plainly?" He asked awaiting her reply. Dido remained silent though she longed to ask him to leave her in peace. There was a momentary pause as if the gentleman was considering his words.

"You must know that Miss Ann Murray with the consent of Lord Mansfield approached me in hope of obtaining my – interest in considering you as a possible match."

As he spoke Dido felt even more distraught at hearing his words that she could not look at him. She had only turned slightly so as not to allow him to see her face but the gentleman thinking that she had intended to return to the house stopped her.

"Please allow me to finish." He requested earnestly so that Dido was forced to turn in his direction. When she remained silent Captain Davinier continued.

"On meeting you I found myself pleasantly surprised and before departing from Kenwood assured Miss Ann that I was willing to pursue the courtship."

Dido gasped at his frankness of speech. It was the unexpectedness of it that made her to speak without thinking.

"Why are you telling me this?" she whispered with much feeling.

"Please do me the curtsey of sitting with me for a moment. Please I will explain everything." Captain Davinier insisted and for once his manner was not so calm. Dido did not know what to say or do. Her hesitation gave the gentleman some uneasiness. Dido looked to the house as if expecting Miss Ann and Mr Harris to appear at any moment. There was so little time until Mr Harris expected arrival. But she could not refuse him such was the urgency of his request. Also, Dido confessed that there was a curiosity to know what Captain Davinier would say. Turning back to Captain Davinier, she nodded and taking a seat, she sat rather rigidly unable to appear comfortable. Captain Davinier was too preoccupied by his own thoughts to notice her discomfort.

"Do you remember me mentioning my meeting with an acquaintance of yours, a Captain Alwyne?"

Dido felt again the need to blush at the mention of that name. She could only nod, as she did not trust herself to speak.

"I met the gentleman a few days after leaving Kenwood. He seemed eager to renew our acquaintance and invited me to dinner. I consented, of course, not thinking anything untoward. For the whole evening he spoke of you-"

Dido looked up at him unable to hide her surprise.

"- he talked rather intimately and led me to believe that there was some – kind of attachment between you."

"It is a falsehood!" Dido cried in horror not wanting to imagine what Captain Alwyne could have said of her. Could it be that Captain Alwyne could have revealed his repulsive proposition to Captain Davinier? The thought made her weak with apprehension. How scandalous and ruinous such a rumour could bring to her reputation. Now she was no longer ignorant of the reason for Captain Davinier not pursuing her. Not that his advances had meant anything to her. If anything, she had rejoiced in its absence.

"I saw no reason to continue my previous plans regarding yourself. To be true I considered myself to be rather duped by you and Miss Ann." He paused for a moment as if contemplating what to say next. Dido struggled to take in all that she had heard and its implication to herself and her family. She was astounded beyond words. How shocking! If Captain Alwyne could put into question her reputation where Captain Davinier was concerned, what of other gentlemen? Dido could not think of it without abhorrence, but forced herself to ask what she least wanted to know.

"Have you heard of this attachment spoken of elsewhere?"

"No, I have not." He replied. His answer gave her some relief though it did not conclude that Captain Alwyne had not spoken of it in some other society.

"It was not until recently that I heard that you were intended to a Mr Harris."

"I could only pity the fellow." He continued with regret knowing by the lady's expression that his words were causing her pain but he felt that he had to be candid.

"But a few days ago I had the pleasure of meeting a Miss Thorpe another acquaintance of yours I believe?" he enquired, knowing it already to be the case but insisting on seeing an affirmation to his question so as to assure himself that he had her full attention.

"I have only met Miss Thorpe once at Eastwell Park." Dido was forced to reply.

"She talked very highly of you and considered you to be a very amiable creature."

"It was Miss Thorpe who informed me that there was no such attachment between yourself and Captain Alwyne. She even laughed at the thought." He revealed but said no more, as Miss Thorpe had been far more candid with him in her revelation, disregarding all modesty. It was clear to see that the lady's relationship with Captain Alwyne was of a far more intimate nature. Miss Thorpe spoke freely of the gentleman's corruptible manners and infidelity. She also spoke of Captain Alwyne's dishonourable intentions towards Miss Dido and laughed openly at Miss Dido's refusal at his advances. Captain Davinier kept all this to himself knowing that his words had already produced a grievous affect upon the lady. But what Miss Thorpe failed to reveal, and what Captain Davinier guessed from Miss Thorpe's manner, that she was jealous of Captain Alwyne's attention to Dido. By revealing Captain Alwyne's character Miss Thorpe had hoped to put an end to his advances. On hearing this news Dido regretted her previous opinion of Miss Thorpe, whose praises she felt were far too condescending in their magnitude that she was convinced that there could not be any sincerity in them. But now she felt that perhaps she had been unjust in her estimation and was left to feel regret at her earlier criticism of Miss Thorpe.

"It appears that Captain Alwyne had set out deliberately to deceive me of your character." He concluded feeling only regret at having believed in a falsehood without attempting to gain evidence of the facts.

"I am sorry to pain you but I thought it better that you should know the truth."

"Yes of course. I thank you for your candour Captain Davinier." Dido replied politely.

Captain Davinier hesitated for a moment and then started as if to speak again but stopped himself. He gave a sharp intake of breath.

"It appears that I owe you an apology." He began at last.

"You are mistaken" Dido said weakly.

"No, I allowed myself to be deceived without giving you the opportunity of defending yourself." He continued as if not hearing Dido's protestation. He would have said more if the maid had not interrupted them.

"Excuse me sir, Miss Dido you are wanted in the library." She announced, trying to hide her surprise at the presence of the gentleman. Dido nodded and stood up unable to hide her awkwardness at the interruption. She was sure from the maid's expression that she had misinterpret what she had just witnessed.

"Please tell Miss Ann that I will be there directly." She instructed and waiting for the maid to leave she turned to the gentleman.

"Please excuse me, I must leave now."

"Yes of course, I too must take my leave." Captain Davinier stated quickly.

"Permit me to call again?" he requested.

Dido was surprised by his request that for a moment she did not know what to say.

"I am not at liberty to say, sir." She answered truthfully. She thought he would have fared better addressing his request to Miss Ann rather than to herself. Did he not know that she had no more control over her fate than a servant?

"Nevertheless I will call again. Good day. " He stated adamantly, leaving Dido astonished at what had just passed between them.

## CHAPTER 36

Dido desired to go directly to her room to reflect on everything that had occurred with her meeting with Captain Davinier but her presence was required in the library. How was she to appear normal when her sentiments were in such a disturbance! Dido was almost tempted to plead her excuses but she knew that her request would be looked upon with great displeasure. No, it was better to get the matter over with, so that she could be left alone with her thoughts. She entered the library to find Miss Murray, Ann Murray and Mr Harris seated together.

"Ah, Dido we wondered where you had gotten to." Ann Murray remarked impatiently. Now that everything was finally working according to plan, she did not want anything to go wrong at the last minute. She eyed Dido closely as she came into the room, noticing that her manner seemed distracted.

"Miss Dido." Mr Harris stood up immediately and bowed cordially.

"Mr Harris." Dido replied curtseying accordingly.

"I was telling both Miss Murray and Miss Ann for the purpose of my visit. Perhaps you will allow me to speak to you in private." He said emphatically turning to Miss Murray and Ann Murray with a knowing look and a vulgar wink, which caused Dido a moment of unpleasantness. Oh that she could simply say yes I accept and then immediately beg to be excused and put an end to the pretence. But she stood in silence, willing herself to stay calm.

"Certainly." Ann Murray answered for Dido.

"Come along dear, Mr Harris would like to speak with Dido *alone*." She said with some emphasis on the word alone for the benefit of her sister. Miss Murray took the hint, and smiling broadly, followed her sister out of the room. Dido watched with disdain as she thought the whole matter rather degrading. Once alone Mr Harris wasted little time in reaching the purpose of his intentions. Dido could have spared him the trouble of asking what she already knew she had no desire to hear. He spoke eloquently but with little feeling that Dido supposed him to be dictating a letter. She felt nothing and expected to feel nothing. She would be more surprised if she did! As it was she stood passively and received his address with forbearance. He spoke proudly of his intended ordination and his position of clergy and what was expected of a clergyman's wife. He felt that she could with her qualities, assist him in his work. Mr Harris thought that in time she would be beneficial to his ministry. It was over after several minutes, at which Dido was required to respond in kind. She hesitated for a moment, though she knew that she had no choice but to accept his hand. It was simply the finality of it that proved rather shocking. But Dido forced herself to make the necessary response, at which Mr Harris expressed his delight at her acceptance, with much confidence, happy in the foreknowledge that his address would not be refused. Miss Murray and Ann Murray were called in to congratulate the couple and did so with much excitement. Dido said and did what was expected of her but she felt as one in a trance. She scarcely knew how she managed to contain her composure throughout the evening for the smiles, praises and salutations sounded strange to her and so much in contrast with her own feelings. Though Dido was required to respond on occasion and to join in the merriment, she could not consent to such false expressions of elation. She would have sooner be at a funeral!

"Surrey is a beautiful county." Mr Harris was saying proudly of the county of which his parish resided.

"I am sure you'll both be comfortable there." Ann Murray declared enthusiastically.

"I am sure that in time Miss Dido will think it as beautiful as Kenwood." Mr Harris said humbly, which compelled Dido to answer in kind.

"I am sure there are places just as beautiful as Kenwood."

Mr Harris appeared pleased with her response and continued his glowing praise of his situation in Surrey. He spoke with self-satisfaction that could easily have been mistaken for conceit by those who were not intimate with his character. Dido in her efforts not to think ill of him gave him the benefit of the doubt. After all it was not his fault that she was feeling somewhat ill tempered by his increasing gaiety. Dido only wished that he would not smile at her as often as he did. She found his smile ghastly, as it was more like a grimace that made his features to appear all the more frightful. She could not bring herself to think of how many additional oddities she would have to tolerate in her future husband. The evening continued in the same vain, as Dido struggled to concentrate on the conversation before her but was often distracted by thoughts of Captain Davinier. She could not hide her relief when Mr Harris finally took his leave.

At last she could be alone in the solace of her room to reflect on all that had occurred! Mr Harris's proposal could not be thought of without uneasiness for her future. How could there be anything else but unhappiness? Perhaps she was doing Mr Harris a disservice but what else could become of a marriage without mutual love. Dido was absolutely certain that Mr Harris did not love her, no more so than her feeling for him. His was a marriage of convenience. There was nothing to consider here, as it was better, in any case, not to think of it at all! It was her conversation with Captain Davinier, which had preoccupied most of her thoughts even while sitting with Mr Harris. She could not forget the way in which Captain Davinier had addressed her without blushing. Dido wondered at his intentions for speaking to her so openly. Though he had revealed that in doing so he had wanted her to know the truth, yet Dido felt that there was much more to it than this. How in contrast was Captain Davinier's expressive and forceful manner to that of Mr Harris's insipid proposal! When she remembered Captain Davinier's words and his conduct she blushed again and again. His manner was so violent that she had not known him. Though his address did not in any way disgrace him. But why was he so insistent of seeing her again? Knowing that she was engaged to Mr Harris, what purpose would it serve? In a few months she would be leaving Kenwood. Dido had no reason to believe that she would ever return again. Neither was there little likelihood of her seeing Captain Davinier again. Somehow this made her meeting with him all the more peculiar. The more she thought on the matter, the more she became increasingly bewildered. Could it be that Captain Davinier was now reconsidering his position and wishing to renew his advances towards her? Surely not! Dido admonished herself. Was she having feelings for Captain Davinier? She could not say. His manners were not displeasing and certainly she was susceptible to his charms. He was far more agreeable than Mr Harris but this did not conclude that he would be a more suitable husband. What good would it do to confuse the matter further? No, she simply had to learn to accept a future life with Mr Harris. Dido thought it best to think positively of her present engagement. After all Mr Harris was not a disagreeable man, though he could never be considered her choice. She could not fault his character and was certain he would not mistreat her. But this commendation was based entirely on what she had observed from his visits to Kenwood. Dido had little time to really know his character. That would come later. His manners appeared sometimes severe and lacking in tolerance. But on reflection, Dido could see no real reason for alarm. It was best to reconcile herself to the prospect of marriage to Mr Harris and forget Captain Davinier. And yet

Captain Davinier's words continued to haunt her thoughts until she fell into a fitful sleep.

Dido awoke the following morning with a determination to appear more optimistic regarding her future. She also decided to say farewell to her beloved Kenwood before the new occupants arrived to signal her final departure. Until then Dido vowed to visit every part of the house and estate for the last time, though the thought gave her much pain and threatened to destroy her newly found optimism. But Dido reasoned within herself that it would do no good to be of a sorrowful disposition, as her departure from Kenwood must be faced with all fortitude. Thus by the time of Sarah's arrival to attend to her dress, Dido had already fixed upon a walk around the lake directly after breakfast.

"What a commotion it is and on such a fine morning as this!" Sarah said shaking her head as she placed Dido's dress on the bed. Dido was scarcely listening as Sarah was often complaining of something and nothing about what Mrs Jenkins had either said or done.

"Fancy Captain Davinier coming here at this..."

"Captain Davinier here?" Dido asked abruptly, stunned by the mention of the gentleman's name.

"Yes Miss. He is with Miss Ann." Sarah answered calmly, before noticing the anxious countenance of her mistress, who was at that moment struggling to make sense of Captain Davinier's presence at Kenwood. Dido was filled with wild curiosity to know the reason for his visit that she could hardly contain her impatience for Sarah to finish. When she entered the breakfast room she had prepared herself to see both Miss Ann and Captain Davinier seated but instead found only Miss Ann present. Her disappointment was so great that she felt instantly ashamed of herself. Ann Murray appeared rather thoughtful but her manner did little to give Dido any clue of what had previously passed. If she had not heard the news from Sarah she would have been totally in ignorance of the fact that Captain Davinier had visited at all!

"Ah, Dido" Ann Murray said absently.

"Miss Murray is not feeling well this morning. She slept rather poorly last night." She continued between mouthfuls of fruit. Although Dido was concerned at hearing this news, it was not what she wanted to hear, thus she received it with less care than she ought to have. When Ann Murray said nothing else, Dido waited patiently in hope that she would make mention of Captain Davinier's visit. She watched Ann Murray intently but nothing could be perceived from her manner or countenance. Could it be that she had no intention of telling her of Captain Davinier's visit? Her motive for her secrecy was plainly obvious to Dido. She could not keep silent, as Ann Murray's discretion forced her to be indiscreet.

"I heard that Captain Davinier was here-" Dido began casually.

"Who told you-?" Ann Murray asked sharply.

"Why did Captain Davinier call?" Dido enquired, ignoring both Ann Murray's question and look of displeasure.

"It is of no consequence now." She said after a moment pause.

"If you must know Captain Davinier came here to request to speak to you." Ann Murray announced inconsequentially, seeing no need to conceal this news from Dido. Dido could not hide her astonishment at the news. She did not know how to feel, as she had not dared to consider her own feeling where the gentleman was concerned.

"I told him of course that you were officially engaged to Mr Harris and that all the arrangements have been made_."

"You did what?" Dido whispered in astonishment.

"Come now, even you cannot marry two men at once." Ann Murray answered sarcastically.

"As you know, I had no say in accepting Mr Harris' proposal, and no opportunity of rejecting it!" Dido replied with such fervency that Ann Murray was stunned by her response.

"May I remind you that you are engaged to Mr Harris and that everything is settled?" Ann Murray stated curtly

"Am I not to be given a choice?" Dido asked

"Are you saying that you would prefer Captain Davinier to Mr Harris?" Ann Murray asked exasperated. Dido hesitated at the enormity of the question. She knew no more of her feelings towards Captain Davinier than she did of her lack of feelings towards Mr Harris. How could she? She had been forced into a situation against her own will.

"I do not know." She replied honestly

"But I would have at least liked to be given time and the opportunity to choose accordingly." Dido said attempting to explain herself.

"Don't be ridiculous girl. What of Mr Harris? Are you to reject a gentleman of good standing on a whim?" Ann Murray said dismissively, her anger increasing at the impudence of the girl.

"Really! It is far too late for second thoughts. Captain Davinier is gone and Mr Harris will be here presently." Ann Murray added with finality that would tolerate any further arguments from Dido, before calling for the butler. Dido gasped with astonishment at the coldness of Ann

Murray's manner. How easy it was for her to be so dismissive of a matter that did not affect her! It was with this feeling of disturbance that Dido took her walk on the conclusion of breakfast. For the first time Dido failed to admire the beauty of the sun as it peeped behind the tall trees and the birds nesting in the security of the branches. Neither the tranquil stillness of the woods could ease the turmoil of her thoughts. The walk to the dairy usually provided Dido with much pleasure but today her heart was too filled with indignation, her senses too disturbed to enjoy the satisfaction of the walk. So preoccupied was she with her conversation with Ann Murray that no other thought could prevail. So overwhelmed was her sentiments at Ann Murray's unfeeling manner that it produced in her a spirit of bitterness that Dido had fought so hard to resist. "Malicious and unfeeling woman!" Dido cried in vexation. Did not her feelings count for anything? It was apparent that it made no difference to her relations whom she married! As long she was married! They were no longer under any obligation to care for her, now that her marriage would place her conveniently out of the way.

"Miss Dido."

Dido could not conceal her astonishment at finding herself face to face with Captain Davinier. Nor could she conceal her embarrassment at meeting the gentleman who, for the past two days, had taken up the preoccupation of her thoughts.

"I am sorry for startling you." He began feeling for the first time the awkwardness of someone preparing a speech.

All this went unnoticed by the lady, who herself was too concerned with her own feelings to even consider his. Dido could hardly find her voice such was the turmoil of her senses. She avoided his eyes, looking about herself as if attempting to discover from where he had come from.

"I waited in the house to speak to you but one of the servants informed me that you had gone for a walk." Captain Davinier said answering her unspoken question.

"I thought you had gone. I mean" Dido said with agitation and then blushed shyly and was unable to continue.

"I am not so easily got rid of." he replied with a smile.

"If I am to be rejected I would prefer to hear it from the person whom I am proposing." He said wryly

"What did Miss Ann say?" Dido asked, amazed that he could be so frank.

"I hope by that you are not implying that I was proposing to Miss Ann?" Captain Davinier feigned shock at which Dido could not help but smile at the very idea of such a proposition.

"I am asking you Miss Dido. Would you consider my proposal of marriage?" Captain Davinier enquired becoming more serious. His proposal, though expected, still caught Dido by surprise that she could not answer for the confusion of her thoughts. How was she to answer him?

"At least give me the courtesy of replying." Captain Davinier said impatiently, taking her silence for rejection.

"Please do not be so severe on me, sir." Dido forced herself to speak, "It is not for dishonour that I do not answer but more from uncertainty." She confessed. How could she make him understand how she felt?

"I am not at liberty to say no to anyone. I have been forced into marriage against my will." Dido spoke plainly wishing to repay his honesty with her own.

"And yet I must choose." She said to herself, pausing for a moment in contemplation.

"Does your mother still live?" Dido enquired and this time it was Captain Davinier's turn to look surprised.

"No. She passed away two years ago, hence my return to England. I have a sister but she is not dead merely married." He replied curious to know as to where her question was leading.

"Where do you live, sir?" Dido asked, knowing that her questions were rather impertinent but they could not be avoided.

"I live in London."

"You live in London?" Dido replied pleasantly surprised at this news.

"Yes. We are soon to have company." He said looking behind her towards the house. Dido turned in the direction of his gaze to see the familiar figures of her relations gathering on the terrace.

"Captain Davinier, I'd be pleased to accept your proposal." Dido said suddenly while she had the courage to speak.

"You do me a great honour, Miss Dido. What was it that swayed your decision? I hope it was not my residing in London."

Dido smiled timidly. He was not so far from the truth. At least here in London she could still be close to her beloved Kenwood.

"You do not expect me to owe to such an accusation."

"In time I hope you'll find that I have a great deal more qualities to commend me to you than my address." Captain Davinier teased.

"I do not doubt, sir." Dido replied sincerely as she was sure that he had many qualities that she could come to admire, perhaps even love. But that was afar off to even contemplate. For now Captain Davinier was content with her response.

"I see no reason to delay in telling your relations the good news." Captain Davinier declared as they walked back towards the house. Dido knew his decision to be correct but felt rather uncertain by the suddenness of his declaration.

"Could we not wait..." she began to say hesitantly feeling suddenly fearful of facing Ann Murray.

"I do not see the advantage in doing so. There is also Mr Harris to consider."

"Yes, of course." She conceded, ashamed for her weakness.

When Captain Davinier requested to speak to Ann Murray in private to announce the engagement, the news was received with such violent opposition that the house was in an uproar for several hours afterwards. Captain Davinier left the house almost immediately, only stopping briefly to inform Dido of the outcome and that he would speak to Mr Murray, the 2nd Lord Mansfield regarding the matter. Dido could see from his angry expression, which he was unable to control, that he did not intend to take Ann Murray's rejection without redress. A few minutes later, Ann Murray appeared onto the terrace.

"How dare you accept Captain Davinier's hand when you are already engaged?" she cried scathingly, she could hardly contain her temper at the insolence of the girl. Dido had no time to respond before Ann Murray continued her attack.

"Your behaviour has been disgraceful! Have you no thought for Mr Harris and what your actions will do to his reputation? You will tell Captain Davinier that you have changed your mind."

"I will not." Dido said quietly

"How impertinent! Do you wish to bring shame on this family?"

"May I remind you that Captain Davinier was one of your own choices and not mine?"

Ann Murray was caught off guard by the truth in Dido's statement that she could not answer for several seconds.

"Is it not better if Dido makes the choice for herself? If she prefers Captain Davinier to Mr Harris what of it?" Miss Murray declared attempting to put a stop to the ugly scene before her. She simply hated confrontation but her words instead of appeasing invariably made matters worse.

"Don't be so ridiculous!" her sister exclaimed angrily.

"It has already been settled. Dido shall marry Mr Harris and that is the end to it!" Ann Murray announced forcefully expecting no resistance from Dido.

"I shall not marry where I do not choose." Dido answered unafraid of the furious look she received from Ann Murray.

"You mean to disobey me you insolent girl?"

Dido remained silent. She had no intention of rising to Ann Murray's bait. Miss Murray looked on in distress, as she had never before seen her sister in this state of rage. It was so unbecoming. How she wished that this matter could be resolved.

"Perhaps our dear brother can settle the matter?" Miss Murray said as the thought came to her.

"An excellent idea sister." Ann Murray replied with satisfaction that she wondered why she had not thought of it herself.

"Let us see if you will remain so proud in your refusal." She snapped in Dido's direction. Ann Murray was sure that her brother would take her side in this matter. Miss Murray was relieved that for once that she was able to make a useful suggestion and was pleased at the outcome. At least her sister had returned to civility and her calm demeanour was once again restored. Though Dido refused to be intimidated by the threat, she could not help but question whether Captain Davinier would be any more successful in appealing to the 2nd Lord Mansfield for her hand. Should he be refused, would he abandon her to Mr Harris? This thought troubled her and she was left once again to feel the vulnerability of her situation. How she despised being at the will of her relations, who cared little for her welfare!

Mr Murray, the 2nd Lord Mansfield arrived at Kenwood not many days hence and went immediately into private consultation with his sister. Dido waited anxiously to receive news of their decision. So impatient was she that she could find no diversion in reading or sewing, and began pacing her room in a hope of relieving her agitation. What could they be talking of for so long? Perhaps Mr Murray was informing his sister of his meeting with Captain Davinier? Could it be possible that Mr Murray had given his consent? But if so, why had Captain Davinier not come to inform her of this? Dido waited in this state of disturbance until she was finally summoned to the library. Mr Murray scarcely greeted her before he began his enquiries.

"Is it true that you have agreed to marry both Mr Harris and Captain Davinier? He enquired in astonished condescension. Dido could hardly contain her irritation at his manner, for had it not been for the meddling of his sister she would not been forced into such a predicament.

"The decision to marry was not of my own choosing but has been forced upon me, sir. What choice did I have but to consent to Mr Harris' proposal? In doing so I did not know that there was any other choice. But since I must marry I would at least like to be given the opportunity to make my own choice. I don't feel that I am being unfair in stating that I *alone* am the best judge of who is the most suitable match for me." Dido replied with frankness and as much fortitude as she could command. Her response shocked her relations.

"Did I not tell you how impertinent her conduct has become?" Ann Murray cried angrily unable to control her temper at the girl's insolence. "Do you think that we are incapable of judging what is in your best interest in such a matter?" He asked incredulously.

"In regards to the wishes of my guardian, the late Lord Mansfield, I do not believe that I have disgraced him. I have consented to marry and to someone that he himself had considered a suitable match. All I ask is that my choice be respected." Dido answered earnestly.

There was a moment of silence at her words before Mr Murray spoke,

"Captain Davinier came to see me to ask for my consent to the marriage. Ann has told me that he has disregarded her wishes in this matter but I have had time to consider both sides and I see no reason why I should not consent to your marriage to Captain Davinier if he is your choice. I shall make the necessary apologies to Mr Harris on your behalf and that will settle the matter." He said with such finality that Dido was reminded of her uncle.

"We shall arrange for the marriage to take place in the next few months. I see no reason for any further delay."

Ann Murray sat in silent resignation, outraged at the ill judgement of her brother's decision, yet having little choice but to consent. However, once the decision had been made she found she had no further interest in the matter and put up no further resistance, as she decided that the sooner Dido was out of their society the better. Dido felt she ought to be content with the outcome of the meeting. Hers was a hollow victory of having the sensation of being proposed to and having that proposal accepted but feeling none of the happiness that it should bring.

In the months that followed up until the day of their wedding, Dido had the opportunity of becoming further acquainted with Captain Davinier. To say he was her ideal would be an exaggeration of the true romantic. Dido knew little of romance and less about love. She found his character and manners admirable. He was honest and in time she knew that she would learn to trust him. Dido felt at liberty to speak openly with Captain Davinier, and this was the freedom that she valued above all. For so long her heart had belonged to her home and to her uncle, the one man that gave joy to her life. But now she was forced to concede that she must learn to give her heart to her future husband, if she was to have any hope of happiness.

Dido and Captain Davinier were married in a London church, in the presence of Lady Finch-Hatton, Miss Murray and Ann Murray, Mr Murray, the 2nd Lord Mansfield and his wife Louisa Schaw Cathcart, Countess Mansfield. It was a quiet ceremony, with little fanfare. When it was over, to the relief of Ann Murray who looked sober throughout, there were muted congratulations, with the exception of Lady Finch-Hatton and Miss Murray whose salutations appeared overly in contrast to the indifferent gestures of the other guests. If Dido expected her married life to bring the restraints and duties of a wife that could be considered burdensome and even grievous to some, it was not so with her. For she found with marriage came the security that she had craved, though they lived far modestly than what she was used to, this was compensated by her feeling of belonging and having a home that was finally hers to govern. With Captain Davinier, Dido was content in knowing that she had made the right choice. His manner and character was well suited with her own and his humour, which endeared her to him, in some ways reminded her of her uncle, whom she missed dearly. Captain Davinier would often tease her that he had not forgotten her motive for marrying him, simply on the basis of his residing in London. In those instances Dido would insist that it was always so, though they both knew that she had long grown in regard for him and had fallen in love with his goodness of character and his liberal manner. When their first child was born Dido knew the joy of motherhood of which Elizabeth had talked of. How different things now appeared! Dido could wish for nothing more except to see her dear cousin more often than she did, as she was her only family connection and her link to the cherished childhood memories of Kenwood. Dido received an annual invitation from Elizabeth to visit Eastwell Park, of which Dido prevailed upon her husband to accompany her when he could. She never saw Ann Murray again after her marriage of which she was glad. Of Miss Murray she heard of her death with sadness as she always considered her with warm affection. Dido never returned to her beloved Kenwood again though she always thought of it with both fondness and bittersweet regret.

The End

## Author's Note

This historical novel is based on a true story of Dido Elizabeth Belle, who was born into slavery (by colonial law) in 1761. Her mother, Maria Belle, was an African who was captured and sold into slavery and shipped to the Caribbean. Dido's father was an aristocrat, Captain John Lindsay, nephew of Lord Mansfield. Captain Lindsay found Maria Belle aboard a Spanish ship which he captured while captain of HMS Trent. Dido was born in the Caribbean and was taken to London by her father probably after the death of her mother. Captain Lindsay returned to England around 1765 with Dido, who was given into the care of her great-uncle Lord Mansfield and lived in Kenwood in Hampstead for most of her life. By all accounts Dido was treated like a member of the family by Lord and Lady Mansfield, and was particularly spoilt by Lord Mansfield. She was said to have influenced Lord Mansfield with his rulings on slave related cases like the Somerset case* and the Zong Massacre*. One account by an American businessman and politician who lived in London and was a friend of Lord Mansfield, stated that Dido "was called upon by my Lord every minute for this thing and that, and shewed the greatest attention to everything he said". After the death of Lord Mansfield in 1793, Dido was officially granted her freedom in his will and was given a modest annuity to live on. Later that same year, Dido was married to a Frenchman John Davinier, a gentleman's steward at St George's church in Hanover Square. Dido had three sons, twins born Charles and John in 1795 and William Thomas in 1802. Dido died two years later in 1804 at the age of 43.

*Somerset Case
http://www.nationalarchives.gov.uk/pathways/blackhistory/rights/slave_free.htm

*James Walvin, The Zong A Massacre, the Law and the End of Slavery (New Haven: Yale University Press, 2011); See more at:
http://www.blackpast.org/gah/zong-massacre-781#sthash.IPmFYAbh.dpuf

Dido Belle

Printed in Great Britain
by Amazon

17657968R00139